Christine,

LOST DREAMS

STORMS OF NEW ENGLAND, BOOK 5

KARI LEMOR

Never lose your Dreams!

Kari Lemor

RYCON PRESS

BOOKS BY KARI LEMOR

Love on the Line – light romantic suspense

Wild Card Undercover

Running Target

Fatal Evidence

Hidden Betrayal

Death Race

Tactical Revenge

Storms of New England – small town contemporary

Elusive Dreams – Erik & Tessa

True Dreams – Sara & TJ

Stolen Dreams – Alex & Gina

Broken Dreams – Nathaniel & Darcy

Lost Dreams – Greg & Alandra

Forgotten Dreams (Christmas novella)

Coming soon 2021

Faded Dreams – Luke & Ellie

Sweet Dreams (Christmas novella)

Last Chance Beach World

Secrets Under the Sun (Nov 2021)

ACKNOWLEDGMENTS

I have many people to thank on this journey. My husband and children who give me all their love and support. Kris and Meredith for so much support and encouragement, even when you are short on time yourself. Especially to Em, who has been the best editor I've ever had, giving me suggestions, guidance, and so much assistance making my books super shiny. To Donna for the honest feedback. To all the Gems authors who encourage and share my books with others. To all the amazing readers who have left reviews letting me know I have a purpose in writing. And especially to the fabulous Storm family. So many have asked to be adopted by you because you are so warm, loving, and accepting of everyone.

This book is dedicated to all the brave firefighters who risk their lives every day to keep us safe. And to MK, I'm thrilled you finally found your Greg Storm.

CHAPTER ONE

"*The Crisis Team Meeting will begin in three minutes in the office conference room.*"

Alandra Cabrera glanced up at the speaker in her classroom and frowned. Why couldn't she ever be on time for these things? It would take her that long to hit the bathroom in the staff room, then walk all the way to the end of the hall and down two flights of stairs. If she didn't use the bathroom, she could make it with a minute to spare. But the meeting would run long. It always did. She wouldn't have time to go again before the kids started arriving in her classroom, and it was two hours before they went to Art, which was the first break she had. Her bladder wouldn't last that long.

Grabbing a pad of paper and a pencil, she tore off down the hall. Good thing the kids weren't here. She usually reminded *them* not to run inside. Luckily, she didn't see any of the typically gabby teachers in the staff room and managed to get in and out fast.

She slid into the conference room just as Reggie Thorpe, the principal, started passing out agendas. A quick scan

1

showed her the only seat vacant was...oh. *Madre de Dios.* Right next to Greg Storm, Captain of the Squamscott Falls Fire Department.

It wasn't that she didn't like Captain Storm. Quite the opposite. The man was gorgeous and incredibly nice, but he turned her into a giddy schoolgirl. No one had inspired that sort of reaction in a long time. Way before Jeff had screwed her over and deserted her and Jillian.

Ali threw Captain Storm a pleasant smile and took the handout he passed her. *Keep your eyes on the paper. Play it cool. Pay attention to the meeting, and don't stare at the handsome fireman.*

While Reggie droned on, as principals tended to do, Ali kept her hands busy taking notes. Fire drills. Lock downs. Fire Safety Week. New video monitors being installed near all the entrances to the building. Still, she couldn't stop taking peeks at Greg Storm, all in the guise of listening to the other members of the committee as they spoke. Which was ridiculous because they'd both been on the Crisis Team for three years now. She also had his son, Ryan, in her class this year. She should be comfortable in his presence.

Yeah, it had been a fun parent conference last fall. Her stomach had twisted into knots, and she'd been practically punch drunk after it was over. Good thing she'd had all her information in front of her and had gone through the same spiel almost twenty times before. Ryan's conference had been the last of the day, and they'd taken a bit longer than she'd allowed other parents. Not that Ryan had needed extra discussion. He was a great kid and excellent student. His father had been concerned, however, because he didn't have a mom at home and wanted to make sure his emotional skills were on par as well as his academics.

Of course, she hadn't minded. The man was dreamy in so many ways. His soft, light brown waves were cut short, yet long enough to have a touch of curl to them. His bright blue eyes, like his son's, shone with intelligence and humor. And those shoulders. *Dios*, those shoulders. Broad and strong, they bracketed his defined pectorals currently showcased in his navy SFFD t-shirt. She wouldn't even think about how his blue chinos fit over his firm ass and thighs. No, best not think about those.

Is it hot in here? Pushing her hair off her neck, she took a deep breath and focused on Reggie. He was going over the fire drill routine for a third time. Like they'd never done a fire drill before. The tall, stick-like principal looked over his glasses at his paper, then smoothed his hand over his bald head.

"Alandra, have you talked to the rest of your team about scheduling your classes to go in the smoke house?" Every year the fourth-grade students got to go in the trailer simulator, learn what to do in case of a fire, and then practice going out through a window on a rope ladder.

Ali flipped her notebook to the correct page. "I have their schedules here. We can plug them into whatever time frame the firefighters have set up."

Reggie pointed to Captain Storm. "Greg, why don't you and Alandra go over that schedule and make sure Maggie gets a copy in the office?"

Ali turned to the man next to her, but before she could say anything, the bell rang. Reggie, of course, was still talking. Why couldn't he ever let them out of a meeting a few minutes before the bell, so they'd have time to get to their classrooms before the kids did?

The specialists who didn't have students waiting for them sat listening to the principal, but Ali and the other classroom teacher on the committee stood and pointed to the door. The sound of kids in the hallway stomping their way to their classes finally made Reggie dismiss the meeting.

"I'm sorry, Captain Storm, I need to get to class," she said as she picked up her notepad and pencil.

"I'll walk with you, and we can figure out a time to go over that schedule."

They left the room, and awareness zinged through Ali's bloodstream. Was everyone staring at her? Her face must be crimson by now and sweat trickled down her back. Why did this man send her nerves into a tizzy?

He stepped closer to avoid a group of eager first graders and leaned down. "Please, call me Greg. We've known each other a while now. No need to be so formal. I'm still getting used to the Captain title. I've only had it for a few months."

"Greg. And congrats on the promotion. Ryan was so excited when he came in after Christmas break and announced it to the class."

They started up the two flights of stairs, weaving between scurrying little people.

"Hey, Mrs. C."

"Good morning, Aiden. If you get to the classroom before me, make sure everyone's following the routine, okay?"

The boy's eyes shot up, and he grinned. "Will do." He took off walking even faster.

Greg chuckled. "Apparently, he wants to follow your directions."

Shaking her head, Ali said, "He just likes to tell people what to do."

Greg laughed again and ducked around the kids barreling past. "Boy, they sure are in a hurry to get to class."

"Yeah, get to class, dump their bags, then go meet their friends in the bathroom. Or visit last year's teacher and get something out of the candy jar."

The smile on Greg's face showcased his dimples. Man, those were dangerous.

"You don't have a candy jar?"

"Oh, I do. But they have to work to get a piece from mine. If they had Mr. Lavallee last year, they know he'll let them have one every day simply because they show up to say hi."

"It means more if you have to work for it." That grin grew bigger.

As they approached her classroom, the din inside spilled into the hallway. She took a step inside, flicked the light off and on, and called out, "Morning routine. Even if I'm not here, it's the same every day."

The noise level lowered as sheepish kids put backpacks and coats away, took out homework, and got started on their morning work set out on their desks. Stephanie Long, another teacher on her team, peeked through the connecting door to her room and waved.

"I figured you had a meeting this morning. Let me guess. Reggie was running it and it went over?"

"Yep. Thanks for keeping an eye out." Stephanie closed her door, and Ali swiveled back to Greg, who still stood in the hallway.

"Sorry. It's always crazy first thing." Several students gave her hugs as they slipped past to get inside the room.

"Don't apologize. Makes me have more respect for what you do. When's a good time to get the schedule figured out?"

"I have a prep period from ten to ten-forty and lunch at twelve-thirty for a half hour. If those don't work, school is out and the kids are usually gone by three fifteen-ish."

Greg pursed his lips and glanced at his watch. "I've got paperwork that has to be done this morning as long as we don't get a call. But I'd hate to take up any of your short lunch break, and I don't want to keep you from heading home. I know you've got your daughter to take care of."

"I don't pick her up until four or four-thirty, since I need to get work done here. Once I'm home, it's almost impossible to do anything. Plus, I want to give Jillian all my attention."

Greg nodded. "I can be here at three-fifteen sharp, and we can whiz right through it."

"Sounds like a plan. I'll see you then." Two more students walked through the hallway and wrapped her in a hug before heading into the room.

"Dad! What are you doing here?" Ryan Storm sauntered down the hallway, his sandy blond hair curling out from under his baseball cap.

Greg scooped the hat from his son's head and held it out. "I had a meeting here this morning, then needed to arrange some stuff with Mrs. Cabrera about the smoke house."

Mrs. Should she remind him it was only Ms. now, since her ex walked out leaving her with a small child?

"The kids are all stoked about that, but I've seen it a bunch of times." Ryan shrugged.

Ali chuckled at the boy's bragging. It must be cool having your dad as the fire captain.

Greg ruffled his son's hair, then swatted him playfully on the back. "Go do your morning routine. I'll see you later."

"And I'll see you right after school, Greg." It felt weird calling him that, even though they'd seen each other outside of school during town events often enough.

"I look forward to it, Mrs—"

"Ali is fine."

"Ali. See you after school."

As she pivoted to work with the students who'd all taken their seats, she knew she was looking forward to seeing Captain Greg Storm again, too.

Greg checked his watch and finished tapping in the report he'd been working on. It only took about five minutes to get to Lincoln Elementary School, but he'd promised Ali he'd be right on time.

Ali. Alandra. Such a pretty name. Such a pretty woman. The thick walnut-colored hair that hung down past her shoulders framed an adorable face covered with a smattering of freckles. Her eyes were such a dark brown, he could almost get lost in them. Not a thought he should be having about his son's teacher.

Closing his computer down, he stood and stretched. So much paperwork came with being promoted to captain. Fortunately, there was also a raise included. With a growing son, he needed the extra pay, especially since he'd bought his parents' house last year when they'd moved across town to an adult community. Which left him with a huge mortgage and no consistent childcare. But he liked being on his own, just him and Ryan. Living with your parents after turning thirty was a bit embarrassing.

"BB, I'm heading out a few minutes early."

Bobby Bishop, BB to anyone who knew him, grinned. He threw the rag he'd been using to shine up the engine over his shoulder. "Going to see that cute little teacher you've got the hots for over at the elementary school?"

"What are you talking about? She's Ryan's teacher, and she's in charge of scheduling the smoke house. You didn't forget we have that next Wednesday, did you?"

BB raised one eyebrow. "I didn't forget. Maybe you did. With the rotation, you'd normally have next Wednesday off."

The full-time firefighters in Squamscott Falls did a three-days-on and two-days-off rotation, so their schedule changed every week, which made it tough finding someone consistent to take care of Ryan on weekends and after school. At least with the Captain's position, he was almost always guaranteed the day shift.

"I am off that day, but I'll still be doing the smoke house

and fire safety lessons. That way if there's a call, I can stay and the kids won't be disappointed."

BB smirked. "Yes, we wouldn't want to disappoint those kids...or their teacher."

Shaking his head, Greg grabbed the keys to his truck. "There's more than one fourth grade teacher, and the one you're referring to is my son's. I'm betting there's some rule about teachers not dating a parent of a student."

"Only three more months until summer vacation," BB called out as Greg trotted out to his vehicle.

As he drove, he thought back to BB's words. Ali. And dating. She was definitely the type of woman he'd be interested in. If he dated. Which he didn't. Being a single parent didn't give him much time for a social life, and after what had happened with Wendy, only months after Ryan was born, he didn't know if he could attempt another relationship.

He pulled into the parking lot of Lincoln Elementary just as the last bus was pulling out. Perfect timing. Hopefully. Maybe Ali had expected him to be waiting outside her door at this time.

As he walked down the now quiet halls to her classroom, he thought back to the parent/teacher conference a few months ago. She had a great personality, and it was obvious how much she loved her job and was dedicated to her students. When he'd found out he was her last conference for the day, he'd started asking more questions. All things he wanted to know about his son, but maybe stuff he could have accomplished in an e-mail.

Then, he'd felt guilty that he'd kept her from her daughter and apologized, but she said Jillian was staying the night at her father's house. Her lovely face had hardened at the thought of the man who'd walked out on her and her daughter when the child had only been a year old. Squamscott Falls wasn't so big that details of this kind could stay hidden. What kind of schmuck walked out on his kid? Same kind of person as a mom who could abandon her new baby.

A few teachers still wandered their classrooms, writing on boards or wiping down desks. He'd seen a number of them exiting the school, large bags in hand. Even when the day was done, their work wasn't finished.

He gave a small tap on her door frame as he peeked inside. Ali walked around depositing papers on desks. She glanced up, and her mouth turned into a genuine smile. Good. He'd felt bad about taking her time after school, but she didn't seem too upset.

"Hi, Cap...uh, Greg. Come on in. Let me finish putting out tomorrow's morning work and then we can do the schedule."

Greg gazed around the room, taking in all the little details that showed what a great teacher she was. Fun, colorful cartoon characters graced the walls, reminding students of good manners, grammar rules, and a variety of other lessons. Neatly stacked books all sorted and labeled. Comfortable areas on the floor with pillows or bean bag chairs for students to use instead of cramped desks.

Ryan had mentioned what a great teacher she was and had begged him for weeks to see if he would talk to the principal and get him in her class. In the end, Greg had given in and chatted with Reggie. He was almost ashamed to admit he'd played the dead-mom-card, saying that Mrs. C. already knew Ryan and had a lovely maternal way about her. Something Ryan sorely lacked and seriously needed. It had worked like a charm.

"Sorry," Ali said as she maneuvered between desks to where he stood. "If I don't get their morning work on their desks the night before, guaranteed I'll have something slow me down the next day so it doesn't get done."

"No problem at all. Where do you want me?"

Her eyes shot up, and her face grew pink. Okay, weird reaction. Could she be having similar thoughts to his? No, he'd merely surprised her.

She waved at a half circle table in the back of the room. "I've got the schedules in my plan book over there."

As she walked over, he couldn't help but watch her. The dress slacks she wore hugged her curvaceous backside and tapered down her long legs to slim ankles encased in strappy shoes with a wedge heel. She slipped behind the table where there was a small half circle cut-out and a rolling chair. Obviously, where she taught small groups. His sister, Leah, was a teacher here and her classroom had a similar set up.

"Have a seat."

Settling into the chair, he pulled out the notebook he'd stuck in his pocket. "I guess once you get to fourth grade, you graduate to the big chairs. I barely fit in the student seats the last few years."

She laughed, her voice melodic and her eyes shining. "The kids sometimes start shooting up in height in fourth. I had one student a few years back that was almost as tall as me."

She couldn't be much more than five foot two or three, so that wasn't a stretch. Ryan hadn't had any growth spurts lately and was average for his age.

Looking at the schedule and rearranging the different classes with the times didn't take more than ten minutes. He almost wished it had been more complicated, but he had to get back to Ryan, and she had things to do and a child of her own.

"Well, I'll let you get back to work. I've got to get home and figure out what to feed a ten-year-old boy who's always starving." He stood, and she followed him to the door.

"Is he home by himself?"

Was that merely curiosity or was there concern for Ryan?

"I'm not quite ready to leave him by himself yet. Luckily, my cousin Alex lives across the street. He works from home, so if I'm running late, Ryan can go over there. Or Alex's fiancée, Gina, sometimes hangs out with him at our house. She's a computer whiz and is teaching Ryan all sorts of interesting stuff to do with technology."

"It's nice to have family to help out. My mom takes Jillian a few days a week, so I don't have to pay the exorbitant daycare bills for full time. But since she's almost four now, she needs interaction with other children so she can learn all those important social skills."

He nodded his agreement. "I'll see you next Wednesday."

Her eyes lit up. "Oh, are you working the smoke house?"

"Yeah. It's not my scheduled shift, but I'd hate for the kids to be disappointed if we get a call."

Her face softened. "That's so sweet and considerate. I know the students are looking forward to it. Ryan's been telling them how cool it is."

"You can tone down his bragging any time you'd like. You have my permission."

"No, he's got a right to be proud of what his dad does. Thank you again for coming in."

With that dismissal, he did an about face and headed down the hall. Once on the first floor, he passed by Leah's Kindergarten classroom. The light was still on, so he peeked his head in.

"Hey," he called out to where his sister sat on the floor organizing blocks. "The kids all left a half hour ago. Shouldn't you be out of here?"

Twisting around, she stuck her tongue out at him. "What are you doing here?"

"I had a meeting with Ali Cabrera."

Leah's brows knit together. "Is everything all right?"

"Yes, worrywart. We're doing Fire Safety in the school.

The fourth graders do the smoke house. We were coordinating schedules."

Rising to her feet, Leah flipped her long braid over her shoulder and glanced slyly at him. "You know, Ali's a super nice lady, and she's single."

What was up with the matchmaking? "And she's Ryan's teacher. Isn't there a rule against that? Unprofessionalism or something?"

Leah tipped her head and scrunched her face. "Not sure there's an official written rule, but yeah, maybe...I see your point. Although, there are only a few months left of school." Her eyebrows went up and down comically. "Give it some thought."

He gave his sister a hug and said he'd see her later. But as he left the building and drove home, he thought about what could happen this summer after Alandra Cabrera was no longer Ryan's teacher. Was he ready to put his trust in someone again?

CHAPTER TWO

$\mathcal{A}$li walked into the staff room and dug around in the fridge for her lunch bag. She wasn't looking forward to a bologna sandwich yet again, but she hadn't had time to go grocery shopping this week. And Jillian had been especially whiny over the weekend. She hoped the little girl wasn't coming down with something. Even a spring cold could be miserable when you were three.

"Hey, Ali," Phyllis Sherwood called out as Ali grabbed a paper towel from the holder over the sink and sat down. Phyllis had been teaching at Lincoln for close to thirty years. She could teach fourth grade in her sleep. "You've got the smoke house this afternoon, right?"

"Yes, I've got the last slot. Jamilla's class is right after lunch."

"My kids were such brats all morning," Jamilla Fremont said. "I had to threaten them with not going if they didn't quiet down and do their assignments." Her classroom was across the hall from Ali, and she'd been given a difficult group of students this year. Luckily, Jamilla knew exactly how to handle rowdy kids.

"I'm guessing you were successful," Phyllis said. "For a while there, I thought you'd taken your class somewhere. I peeked through the window in our connecting door and was surprised that bunch you have were all focused on their work."

Stephanie flounced into the staff room in her typical extravagant way, fanning her face. "That is one mouth-watering dish."

Ali gazed at her bologna sandwich. "Whose lunch are you talking about?"

Jamilla laughed. "I think she's talking about the attractive firemen."

"Yeah, the other one was okay. But that Greg Storm? I could definitely eat him up."

"Down, girl." Jamilla pushed a chair out for Steph. "I will admit he's a tasty morsel, and if I didn't have such a fine man myself at home, I might be tempted to take a nibble."

Steph shook her blonde mane so it floated around her head and sighed. "And he's so damn nice and good with those kids. It's a shame he's only got the one. Poor guy must be lonely. I mean, his wife died how many years ago?"

Ali didn't like spreading gossip, but she knew Steph, and the woman was likely to start asking everyone in the entire room. Best to cut her off at the pass.

"His wife died in a car accident a few months after Ryan was born. Ryan was ten in January."

"That's got to be tough." Phyllis frowned, spooning some yogurt into her mouth.

Steph started peeling her avocado and grinned. "I wonder if he's still grieving. Maybe I could offer him a little support and comfort. Like rub his back...that nicely muscled back. God, have you seen him in a t-shirt?"

Ali couldn't deny that Greg Storm in a t-shirt was one of

the natural wonders of the world. Well, her world anyway. She didn't get out much obviously.

"Steph, you might want to tone it down a bit. Captain Storm is also a parent in this school," Phyllis stated, forking salad into her mouth.

"Yeah, but his kid isn't in my class." Steph glanced at Ali. "There's no rule against dating a guy from town. Now, if you were interested in him, that would be another issue."

"Like Phyllis said, he's a parent of one of my students. Nothing more."

"Oh, he's definitely more, girl," Jamilla added. "I've seen the way you smile at him, all coy and innocent. But you're a professional and would never put your job in danger by dating your student's dad."

"Who said I wanted to date him?" Okay, she might had fantasized about him a time or two. Or twelve. But there had been no thoughts about dating him. She was still trying to get past what Jeff had done to her.

"Have you been out with anyone since that bastard left you?" Jamilla never called her ex by his name. Sometimes she used more creative monikers for him.

Shaking her head, Ali took another bite of her sandwich. Boy, bologna sure got boring after a while. "Between my job, taking care of Jillian, and the piano lessons I do on weekends, there isn't a whole lot of time for anything else."

Steph waved her hand in the air. "You have got to make time, Ali. Otherwise, your fancy bits will shrivel up and atrophy from disuse."

That may have already happened. Jeff hadn't touched her often after Jillian was born. She could still hear him saying he'd find her more attractive if she wore something other than sweatpants and could lose all that fat on her stomach and hips. Well, all that fat on her stomach and hips was why she could only fit in sweatpants, and he was so tight with money she couldn't afford to buy new clothes that fit her post-pregnancy.

Phyllis rolled her eyes. "Don't listen to her, Ali. You'll meet a guy when you're ready to. You've got time. You're young still."

True. She was only twenty-eight, but she wanted to have a few more children at some point. It might take her years to find a guy who didn't mind that she already had a child and a few extra pounds on the hips and thighs. Then, assuming he decided he was willing to take on a readymade family, how long would it take to have another baby? And all that depended on finding a guy who wasn't a turd like Jeff.

When her ex had walked out the week before Christmas, saying he needed time to think, about what she didn't know, she'd felt all her dreams slip away. Lost. Could she find them again?

"Oh, crap. It's time to get back for the rug rats." Steph tossed her avocado skin in the trash as the rest of the staff scurried about cleaning up the remnants of their lunches. Ali took a second to refill her water bottle with ice from the fridge and then more water.

As the fourth-grade team walked down the hall to their wing, Steph elbowed Jamilla. "Be nice to the firemen, Mrs. Fremont."

"I'm always nice to everybody, Ms. Long, so of course, I'll be nice to them. Just not as nice as you were."

Ali laughed, then turned into her classroom. After stashing her lunch bag under her desk, she glanced at her plan book and perused what she was doing this afternoon. Shortened lessons due to the smoke house. Who knew if she could even keep the kids on task?

Moving to the doorway, she waited as the stamping of eighty pair of fourth-grade feet echoed up the stairway. Jamilla stood across the hall, a smile pasted on her face. Kids after lunch and recess always took a while to get back into work mode.

Jamilla told her kids to dump their lunch boxes, keep their coats on, then get back in line. Ali simply let hers come in, reminding them the afternoon schedule and list of assignments were on the board.

The students weren't too bad for the first forty-five minutes, but then Aiden got distracted.

"What time is it? Aren't we supposed to do the smoke house right now?"

"We've got fifteen minutes." That didn't help since the reminder set everyone off, and it was impossible to get them back on task. She finally gave in and suggested bathroom runs for anyone who needed one.

Of course, practically the entire class needed to go and by the time they'd all returned, they were almost late for the trip outside. It was still the end of March in New Hampshire, so with coats on, they marched outside to the trailer the fire department had hauled to the edge of the playground.

"Please, make sure to be courteous and listen to the firefighters. If you have a question, you need to raise your hand and wait to be called on." She shouldn't need to tell fourth graders this, but with a special event, they needed reminders.

Bobby Bishop stood outside and greeted the children as they filed in. Where was Greg? Had he been called away? No, that wasn't disappointment running through her veins. Just curiosity, since he'd mentioned last week about being here on his day off, and obviously he'd been here this morning or Steph wouldn't have been mooning all over him.

"Hey, Ms. Cabrera. Thanks for getting this all set up for us." Bobby greeted her.

"Happy to do it. The kids love being able to climb out the window. They think it's so fun."

She climbed up the step into the trailer, and the tingles

started again. Greg stood on the other side of the room, twisting knobs on a built-in screen on the wall. Those muscles Steph had wanted to rub pulled his t-shirt taut across his back.

Yeah, those fancy bits definitely hadn't dried up. Right now, they were quivering with excitement, hoping to do the horizontal mambo.

∼

GREG PUT the DVD into the player, selected the menu option he needed, then paused it until all the students were inside and ready. Teasing voices from some of the boys floated around the room.

"Hey, Ryan, isn't that your dad?"

"Do you get to hang out in here whenever you want?"

A throat clearing got the noise to stop. Ali.

"Pretty impressive," he said as he faced the students and teacher. "You'll have to teach me that trick."

Her gorgeous smile lit up her face. "You have to major in education to learn all the super secret behavior management tricks. They should be great listeners for you." Her eyes bore into her students, the meaning apparent.

"Good afternoon, boy and girls. How are you all doing today?"

Lots of words were hurled across the room. He held up his hand. "I'm going to take that as you're all great. For those of you who don't know me, I'm Captain Storm and this is Lieutenant Bishop. We've got a few things to teach you today, then we'll be showing you a video, and once you've learned all about fire safety, you'll get a chance to practice what to do if your house is ever on fire. It's a choice, and if you don't feel comfortable climbing out the window, you don't have to."

He'd given this spiel so many times he could say it in his sleep. He showed them the cooktop and stove and how to stay safe while cooking. They discussed candles and matches and other items that could start fires. A few children had questions, so he answered those as they pertained to fire safety. Not all of the questions did. How did teachers deal with all the off-topic remarks and stories of a kid's life?

BB took over about halfway through and directed the kids to the screen on the wall. As he turned the video on, Greg crept to the back near the door. Next to Ali. She'd kept herself off to the side and allowed him and BB to lead the group. It was nice to be trusted. One of the teachers this morning had attempted to repeat everything they'd said and quiz the kids throughout, making the presentation last longer than planned.

"Thanks again for arranging the schedule. I appreciate it," he whispered. Luckily, the video was loud enough and the students were closer to the screen, so they didn't hear the conversation in the back.

"Happy to help. The kids get such a kick out of this. Or maybe they simply like getting out of classwork."

Greg shrugged. "I think I was the same when I was in fourth grade."

"What?" A grin popped out. "You didn't want to be in school every second, gathering in all the knowledge of the world?"

"Well, not *every* second."

"I'm guessing you did well enough. You've made it to Captain. That's an accomplishment."

Not exactly the accomplishment he'd been aiming for. He'd been pre-med, looking to become a doctor. However, an unplanned pregnancy with a girl he'd only been seeing a few months had derailed that train pretty quickly.

"I think I got the captain job because I've been in the

station the longest and no one else applied for the job when the previous captain retired."

"Don't sell yourself short. I've lived in this town most of my life, and I know they'll look at outside candidates if they aren't happy with the ones applying from inside. Look at our new assistant principal. There were a number of teachers who applied but weren't considered."

"Did you apply?" He'd hate to see her in administration when she was so wonderful with the students.

Her eyes flew up and her lips twisted. "Me? No. I like being in the classroom. I have no desire to tell anyone over the age of twelve what to do."

He gave a soft chuckle, then checked that the students were all listening. Ali had her eyes on them, too, and with a simple lifted finger caused two chatty girls in the back to face the screen and pay attention.

"Very impressive. Does your daughter react like that when you crook your finger?"

"I wish. She's three going on thirty. She's hinting she wants a cell phone for her birthday."

"Is it soon?"

Ali shook her head. "Not until September, but she's making big plans already."

"I hear ya. Ryan turned double digits this year and wanted a dirt bike. With the number of calls we get every year for kids having accidents, breaking limbs, dying, I wasn't keen on buying one for him."

"Oh, *Dios*, yeah. The thought of Jilly riding a dirt bike hurts my heart. I'd rather her play hockey or football."

"Sure. The gentle, safe sports."

She bit her lip to stop from laughing. That slight tug of her teeth on the pink skin did something to him, and he had to look away. *This is Ryan's teacher. Forbidden. For now.*

Yeah, he shouldn't have thrown in those last words. Ali

Cabrera had her own family issues. She didn't need to get involved with a guy who had a hard time trusting anyone except his family.

They chatted softly about some homework Ryan had found challenging and the upcoming Inventor's Fair his son wanted to enter but hadn't decided on what he wanted to invent yet. Greg should be paying attention to the presentation and the kids, but he'd seen this video a hundred times. And with a tilt of her head, Ali had those kids under control.

When the movie was finished, he and BB took turns asking questions to make sure they retained the tips they'd learned.

"Now, who wants to learn how to escape using a window ladder?"

The roar and waving hands made him smile. "Okay, Lieutenant Bishop will help you from this side and I'll be waiting for you outside. Ryan, want to show them how it's done?"

His son strutted over to the window and said, "Sure. I've done it a million times." So humble.

After a few instructions where Ryan demonstrated how to do it, he left the trailer and strode to the open window at the end of the unit. Ali stood in the doorway, checking in and out, but once three children had climbed down the ladder, she moved outside and addressed the students.

"When you're done, you can sit in the grass right there and talk to your friends. Talk, not roll around or play. Understand? Enjoy this time outside now, since once we're done here, we'll be back inside doing work."

The four boys now there shook their heads, but grins popped out on their faces as soon as she turned away. Oh, to be ten again.

When a few more students came through, she stepped nearer to observe.

"Did you want to try Mrs. C?" Greg lowered a small girl to the ground, then waited for the next one.

Ali laughed, looking at her slim skirt and heels. "I'm sure that's exactly what the principal would like to see me doing. I might even make the local newspaper."

"You'd be famous. Kids love that."

"Infamous is more like it." Her head twisted, and she put a hand up toward the kids on the grass. Three of whom were rolling around on top of each other. They quickly stopped. He loved how she didn't even need to say anything to get her message across.

"You should think about bringing the class to the fire station someday. We love giving tours and showing them what we do all day and all our equipment. We don't get a chance to do that with the smoke house."

"I'm sure they'd love it, except doesn't first grade do a tour? I don't know if I'd get permission to bring them again."

"I could mention something to Reggie. I may have a little pull with him." He winked at her, then reached up to help the next child.

What was he doing winking at her? Or pulling strings to get her to come see where he worked? He wasn't a randy teenager anymore trying to impress a girl. Last time he'd done that he'd ended up married with a baby on the way. Not that he regretted having Ryan. Not even for one second. But the situation was far from ideal and had left a bitter taste in his mouth he'd had a hard time getting rid of.

"I'd love to have the class visit the fire station. I'll put in a request for a field trip and see what happens. Thank you."

"Happy to help."

As the rest of the students climbed through the window and down the ladder, he realized talking to Ali Cabrera was something else that made him happy.

CHAPTER THREE

"*D*ad, they're here! Are you ready to go?" Ryan yelled up the stairs, urgency in his tone.

Greg grabbed his denim jacket and trotted down the stairs. Shaving would have to wait until later. Or the next day he worked. It was Sunday and grooming wasn't essential today.

"Right here, sport. I don't think they'll leave without us."

His cousin, Erik, waited outside with his wife, Tessa, and their kids, ready to walk to the town green for the big Easter Egg Hunt. Ryan had scoffed at going this year, claiming he was too old. But when Erik's son, Matty, who looked at him like he was a superhero, asked if he'd go, Ryan had relented. Greg had a feeling he wanted to attend but needed a reason.

Tessa pushed a double stroller, two-year-old Kiki in the back with the baby, Joey, in front. Erik, cane in one hand, held Matty's hand with his other. Until Ryan jogged out to the street. Then, Matty detached and grabbed hold of Ryan. Ever since Erik had brought the two children back from Kandahar, where he'd been seriously injured, Matty had followed Ryan around like a puppy anytime they visited from Maine.

"Glad you could make it down." He shook hands with his cousin and nodded at Tessa. "How's this little guy doing?"

"Finally starting to sleep through the night." Smiling, Tessa eyed the children in the carriage.

They started walking, the boys a few steps ahead, chattering away like magpies.

"Did you stay at Alex's house last night or drive up this morning?"

Erik pointed back at his brother's Victorian, which was across the street from Greg's. The only other house on the street sat at the end in between. Alex's fiancée, Gina, had inherited the house from her grandmother. It was finally looking in better shape after a fire destroyed the top two floors last year.

"We drove up last night. Trying to get all three kids ready and in the car early enough to get here for this egg hunt wasn't in the cards. Luckily, there's enough room in the house."

Erik and his three siblings had grown up in the house with their parents, his Uncle Pete and Aunt Molly. Greg had loved living across the street when they were kids. It was great that both he and Alex had been able to buy the houses and keep them in the family.

The walk to town was less than a mile, and they took their time. Tessa pushed the stroller slowly, and he wondered if it was a way to allow Erik to keep pace without being embarrassed. Ryan was cautious with his little cousin once they got to the main road and held his hand tight.

"Alex told me they have a new bunny maze this year that he designed for the town." Greg's cousin was an architect and loved giving to the community.

Erik nodded. "Yeah, he and Gina are already down there. His buddy, John, helped him build it."

Greg nodded. "Sofie decorated it." His sister was a trained interior designer who was still trying to build her own business. Until she got more clients, she worked setting up functions at The Inn at the Falls.

As they got closer, the buzz of excited children drifted toward them. Colorful rope cordoned off the town green, and crowds of parents with their kids milled around. A huge, white wooden rabbit stood at one end of the green with a massive basket in from of him.

"Is that the maze Alex built? Wow, impressive."

"The basket is the maze," Erik explained. "The kids can go and explore through it before or after the egg hunt. We got a peek at it last night when we first got here."

A speaker crackled, and the head of the town council, Shirley Erskine, cleared her throat. "Good morning and Happy Easter."

The crowd settled down and listened as the councilwoman spoke. Looking around, Greg noted the neighbors and friends who were here with their children. A familiar dark head above a shapely figure stood about fifteen feet to his left. Ali Cabrera and her daughter.

His feet started moving closer of their own volition. Okay, maybe Greg also wanted to be cordial and say hi.

"Happy Easter, Mrs. Cabrera. Ali," he corrected, wanting the informality.

She twisted at his greeting, and a smile crossed her face. "Hi, Greg. Happy Easter. Is Ryan still doing the hunt? Lots of the kids in class were acting like they were too old for this now."

"Yeah, he had that attitude for a while, too, but my cousin's kids came down from Maine and specifically asked Ryan to come. I think it helped him save face, because he seems excited. They're all over by the bench." He pointed to where his cousin and family stood. His other cousin, Nathaniel, and his brood had joined them.

"So many cousins. Jillian only has one, and he's too cool to escort her here."

Greg knelt down and held his hand out to the little girl. "Hi, Jillian. I'm Greg. My son, Ryan, is in your mom's class."

Jillian's dark eyes, so like her mother's, gazed up at him. She smiled hopefully. "Can Ryan play with me?'

When Ali started to object, Greg interrupted. "You're welcome to join our party and hang out with the kids. If your mom says it's okay."

Ali looked torn. "That's very sweet."

"Then, say yes. We've got kids of all ages who'll be hunting eggs. The more the merrier."

She shrugged and nodded. Greg placed his hand on her back to guide her and her daughter back to his family.

"Hey, everyone, this is Ali Cabrera and her daughter, Jillian. She's Ryan's teacher this year."

They all nodded, and he introduced them. "My cousin Erik, his wife, Tessa and their brood, Matty, Kiki, and Joey. And this is my cousin, Nathaniel, his wife, Darcy, her brother, Zane, and their kids, Hope and Tanner. And I think you know Ryan."

"There'll be a test later, Mrs. C.," Ryan teased.

"I may need you to help me study, Ryan." She winked at him, and his son actually blushed.

Shirley Irskine finally finished up her speech. "And I want to give a special thanks to Alex Storm for designing and helping to build this marvelous Easter Bunny and basket maze. Thanks also to John Michaels for the construction supplies and assistance, and Sofia Storm for decorating the common and the basket. It looks wonderful. I now open the Easter Egg Hunt. Enjoy."

Hope, who was six, glanced up and smiled. "Can Jillian come with me and Tanner to hunt eggs?" The little dark-haired girl held her hand out.

Jillian bounced up and down and looked at her mom. "Can I, Mama?"

Ali sucked in her bottom lip but nodded. "Okay, but stay inside the ropes and with the others."

Jillian took Hope's hand and wandered off into the fray. Nathaniel and Darcy hovered on the edge of the group, eyes intent on their children.

Ali watched the children run around, picking up colorful eggs. "Talk about children taking after their parents. Hope looks just like her mom and Tanner like his dad."

Greg spotted Ryan running after Kiki and helping her pick up her spoils. "That's because Hope is Darcy's daughter, and Tanner is Nathaniel's son. They only got married a few months ago."

A faraway expression grew in Ali's eyes. "That's nice that they found love again. Gives me hope."

It wasn't exactly the situation with Nathaniel and Darcy, but Greg wasn't about to air his cousin's dirty laundry to the public. His own laundry certainly didn't have any past love in it either. Only deceit. Better to stick with small talk.

"Are you and Jillian doing anything special today other than the egg hunt?"

Jillian waved an egg in the air so her mother saw it. Ali lifted her hand in acknowledgment. "We'll be joining my family at church after this, then going to my sister's house for dinner."

"Is your sister here in town?"

"No, she and her husband live in Portsmouth. My mom has a small condo not too far from them. Valeria, my sister, and her husband, Max, have a huge house and like to entertain. Mine isn't big enough to do a suitable dinner."

Ali's face hardened at her words, and he wondered what had soured her thoughts.

"I hope you and Jillian have a great day. I've got Easter dinner cooking back at my place right now."

Her eyes sparkled. "Are you a good cook?"

He chuckled. "Oh, I'm not making it. My mom is an excellent cook. Best in the family. She works as a pastry chef at that little bakery downtown, Sweet Dreams. I recently bought the house I grew up in when my parents wanted to downsize, so it's kind of the family homestead. My sisters prefer having holidays there. It's familiar. Mom's home right now getting everything ready."

"And you get along with all your family? I mean, you're here with your cousins, and Leah is always talking about you and Ryan."

"Well, yeah, he's the only nephew so far. I keep telling her and Sofie to get a move on and get Ryan some first cousins. Luckily, *my* cousins have kids and we're all close."

Ryan came running over to them with Jillian trailing behind. "We found so many eggs. Jillian wanted to show you, Mrs. C."

"Thank you for helping her, Ryan. That was so sweet of you. I appreciate it."

Ryan's face turned red, and he beamed. Yeah, definitely worth coming today for him to get brownie points with his favorite teacher.

Ali glanced at her watch and frowned. "We should get going, sweetie." She took Jillian's basket from her and held out her hand for the girl to grasp. "We need to meet your grandmother at church. Say thank you to Ryan."

"Thank you, Ryan. I wanna play with you again, okay?" Jillian bobbed up and down, excited.

Ryan laughed and said, "Sure. That'd be fun."

As the two walked away, Greg said, "Great to see you again. Hope you have a wonderful day."

"Isn't she cute, Dad?"

Greg whipped toward his son and tilted his head. "Who?"

"Jillian. She's a sweet kid."

Ah, okay. As long as Ryan wasn't talking about Ali. Though she was awfully cute, with her adorable smile and freckles.

"You know, Dad, when I was helping the kids do the egg hunt, I kind of felt like a big brother to them. But I'm not. It would be sort of nice to have a little sister like Jillian. Or a mom like Mrs. C. Don't you think so?"

A heaviness settled in Greg's chest. Ryan had never talked about having siblings before or the fact he didn't have a mother. Which had suited Greg fine, since he had no plans to get married again. It would take a special person to get him to trust someone that deeply again.

But as he gazed at Ali and her daughter strolling hand in hand down the street, he wondered if maybe that person did indeed exist.

ALI RAN a comb through Jillian's unruly hair and straightened the bow on her dress for the eighth time. After grabbing the bakery box, she took Jillian's hand and led her up the walk to Valeria's house.

"Remember, sweetie, we need to have good behavior at Auntie's house. She doesn't like lots of running or yelling."

Ali hated giving her daughter this reminder. She was three years old. She *should* be running and yelling. It's what three-year-olds did. Valeria's son, Manny, certainly did plenty of it, yet somehow he was considered a cute little bugger while Jillian was called wild.

Gritting her teeth and adjusting the bakery box in her hand, she gave a swift knock on her sister's door, then let herself in.

Martina Cabrera appeared in the hallway and opened her arms. "There's my beautiful granddaughter. Come give Abuelita a hug."

Ali laughed. "You saw her ten minutes ago at church, Mama."

"I know, but we had to be proper in church. Now, she can give me a beautiful kiss."

Jilly ran to her grandmother and jumped into her outstretched arms. "Love you, 'Lita." The little girl planted a wet kiss on Mama's cheek. Good thing her mother didn't mind Jilly running.

Ali pressed her own kiss to her mother's cheek. "Happy Easter. I brought lemon pound cake. I know it's your favorite."

"Oh, you're too good to me. Your sister never has anything sweet in the house."

Yeah, because Valeria thought sugar was sinful and fattening. Heaven forbid anything have flavor in it.

"Did you make it?"

She shook her head. She loved to bake but rarely had the time. "I got it at Sweet Dreams."

Mama's eyes gleamed. "That means Luci Storm probably made it. That woman's baking could make God himself come down from Heaven to taste it."

Ali followed her mother into the large kitchen at the back of the house. Valeria bustled about stirring pots and checking temperatures.

"Happy Easter. Can I help with anything?"

Valeria pushed her lips in Ali's direction in an imitation of a kiss, then rolled her eyes. "I've got it all under control.

What's in the box? I told you there was no need to bring anything."

"Lemon pound cake. For Mama. But I'll bet she'd share if you asked nicely."

"I'll ask real nicely," Manny shouted from the family room doorway.

Valeria narrowed her eyes at Ali, then pursed her lips at her son. "You know you aren't allowed sweets. I've got some wonderful zucchini bread for dessert."

The downtrodden expression on Manny's face almost made Ali feel bad for him. Of course, the kid was spoiled in so many ways it was often difficult.

Valeria's husband, Maximo Delgado, owned one of the big arcades and indoor mini golf places on Hampton Beach. He worked hard for nine months of the year and made enough to afford this big house in a fancy section of Portsmouth.

The few times Ali had offered to host any holiday, Valeria waved it away, saying her tiny kitchen was too cramped for decent eating. It might be small, but there were only six people to feed and two of them were kids. Of course, then Val would complain how she was required to host all the holidays.

Shaking her head, Ali brushed off the negative feelings she always got when she was with her sister. It was like walking on eggshells when they were together. Ali was always on alert, so she wouldn't say anything stupid. Not that Valeria needed any excuse to cut her down. In the nicest way, of course. All meaningful, well-intentioned comments. Didn't mean they didn't hurt.

Max wandered into the kitchen, snitched a tiny slice of ham as it sat on the counter cooling, then greeted her.

"Alandra, how've you been? Have you got a good class this year?"

He'd asked the same question the last time she'd seen him a few weeks ago at Mama's birthday, but at least he asked.

"It's a great class this year. Thanks. I'll miss them when they move up in a few months."

Ali wished her sister would let her do something, so she wasn't simply standing here twiddling her thumbs. She peeked into the dining room, but the table looked like Martha Stewart herself had been here. Mama had both kids in the family room, and she was singing them a little song. It was one Mama had sung to her and Valeria when they were little. She loved listening to her mother sing, but if she stood here her sister would start making faces even after she'd said she had everything under control.

"Can I start bringing food to the dining room, Val? Are we ready for that yet?"

Her sister's brows smashed into each other as she perused the kitchen. Ali could see her checking things off on an imaginary list.

Valeria sighed and waved at the basket of rolls and the butter dish. "I guess. Yes. Take that and that." She pointed at a few items, and Ali immediately started back and forth to and from the dining room.

Once space had been made for everything, they called the kids and Mama into the room. Bowls and platters were passed around, and Ali got Jilly's plate ready as well as her own. She made sure to keep her portions small. For all the money Valeria and Max had, her sister only ever made enough for each person to have one measured portion. No one dared say anything, yet she noticed Max always made sure there was plenty of the main dish. Today was ham, and the large, spiral-cut meat glistened with a juicy glaze.

Mama said the blessing over the food, then they dug in. Ali kept her attention on Jillian and how much of a mess she was making. Mama had tucked a dish towel into the little girl's collar, so it draped over the front of her dress, then anchored it under her plate. If anything fell, it was caught in the towel. Her Mama always had good ideas when it came to children.

"Max has been working round the clock to get the arcade up and ready for the season. So, of course I've had to do everything around here. And now with this dinner...I haven't had a spare minute for myself." Val pushed a stray strand of hair back into her updo.

No time for herself, yet her nails were perfectly manicured and her hair recently cut, highlighted, and styled. Valeria didn't work, so Ali wasn't sure what she spent all day doing.

"I'm happy to help with the holidays. I've offered before."

Valeria's eyes rose and her mouth sported a tight smile. "Your place is too small. Plus, then I'd just have to cook everything here and bring it over."

The words were on the tip of her tongue to tell Val she could do far better than the overcooked meal she constantly made. It wasn't worth the animosity she'd get in return. Biting her lip, she kept all the frustration inside, stewing as she always did.

Max threw her a grateful look once Val had gone back to chewing. "Thanks for offering, Alandra. We don't mind having it here."

Mama chatted about a few of her friends who were taking a bus trip to Foxwoods in a few weeks. "I've been thinking about going. It might be fun."

"It's a gambling place, Mama." Valeria frowned. "You'll lose a ton of money. Why would you want to go there?"

Mama cocked her head. "Because I'm an old lady, and I'd like to have some fun before I die."

"You're not old, Mama, you're only fifty-eight." Ali scolded, laughing. "You've got plenty of life left in you."

"Unless you keep putting all that salt and butter in your body." Valeria pointed at the pile of mashed potatoes on Mama's plate. Her mother took in a deep breath and glanced away. *Dios*, her sister was such a jerk at times.

Max took a bite of his potatoes, then smiled at Mama. "Foxwoods sounds great, Martina. Are there any good celebrities performing that weekend?"

Interrupting the conversation, Valeria began a discussion on the newest release from her favorite singer and how Max had gotten them front row tickets to the concert. Ali was lucky if she could afford to fill her gas tank every week. Good thing she only lived a short distance from the school. If she had to, she could walk.

Jilly had been well-behaved all through dinner, and Ali gave thanks that her sister couldn't put her parenting skills down today. Most likely, she'd find something else Ali was lacking in. She always did.

"Thank you for being so well-behaved at dinner, Jilly. You can go play in the family room if you want."

"Be careful you don't break anything, Jillian," Val called out after her.

If it weren't for her mama, Ali would end the visit right now. Mama followed Jilly and Manny into the family room and laughter ensued. She was so good with those kids. Ali wasn't sure how she'd gotten so lucky, especially since her mama watched Jilly a few days every week to allow her to save money.

As Ali helped clean the table—there were no leftovers—and load the dishwasher, she turned to her sister. "Jilly and I are going to visit Tito once we leave here. Did you want to come with us?"

"I have too much to clean up here." Even with Ali helping her do it all now. "Plus, I saw him a few weeks ago. He doesn't know who we are, you know."

Sebastien Cabrera, their father's father, had Dementia. There were still times he thought his son was alive or that she was his wife, but some days were better than others.

"He does at times. He has good days and bad days. But I know who he is, so I'll keep visiting. He loves seeing Jillian." All the residents of the nursing home loved seeing the little girl. Often, she sang some of the songs Mama had taught her and those who were able would applaud. Jillian ate it up. Hopefully, today, she wouldn't be too tired or cranky once they left here.

"Well, give him our love and say Happy Easter. I'm sure we'll go see him soon."

"I wish we could bring him here for the holidays. I'm sure he'd love getting away from the nursing home for a bit."

Valeria peered over her shoulder from where she was rinsing pans in the sink. "He still thinks Mama was the reason Papa had a heart attack. Mama hasn't forgotten that yet."

"Papa worked too hard, and that's why he had a heart attack."

"And he ate all that fattening food," Val reminded her. "His arteries were all clogged with crap. You won't find me that way. Healthy eating and daily exercise. It's the only way to go."

Yeah, Val had the time to spend all day cooking healthy meals and going to the gym or spa. And she could afford all those things, too.

"You know, Ali, maybe if you started working out and eating better, Jeff might wander back into your life."

The thought almost choked her. "Why would I want him back in my life? He doesn't even care about his own child. He barely sees Jillian unless I bug him."

"I'm simply saying, Ali, you have such a pretty face. If you slim down, you might be able to get a man easier."

Just what she wanted. Another man who wouldn't love her if she wasn't in perfect shape.

"I'll get right on that."

Val didn't seem to notice the sarcasm in her voice. "Maybe a little more makeup—really accentuate those eyes. I can help you. My esthetician has some great products to get your skin clear and glowing. The products she carries are animal cruelty free and have the finest ingredients."

"I'm not sure I could afford most of that, Val."

"But you need to invest in yourself if you want to find a man. Put some time and effort in now, and you can snag yourself someone to help you pay all those bills." Her sister's eyes rose suggestively.

"Do I honestly want someone who can be snagged?"

Again, Val wasn't listening. "You know, if you did something with your hair, some product for adding volume and scrunch it a bit, you could have that tousled, just-got-out-of-bed look."

Ali sighed. "Yeah, 'cause that goes so well in a classroom full of nine and ten-year-olds."

Valeria slung a dish towel over her shoulder. "You never know. Maybe you'll have a nice single dad some year."

When Val moved off to wipe down the table, Ali thought about Greg Storm. You couldn't find much nicer than him.

CHAPTER FOUR

"A re we done, Dad?" Ryan asked, slipping some scraps of his dinner to Guinness under the table. The eight-month-old black and tan Springer Spaniel puppy was in his glory.

Greg shook his head and glared at his son. "What happened to 'May I be excused?' and the word *please?*"

Ryan craned his neck to peek out the dining room window. "I was gonna say that, but I needed to know if we were done first."

"What are you in such a rush to go and do? What's more important than visiting with Nonna and Poppi and your aunts?"

Sofia made a face and waved her hands in the air. "Yeah, nothing's more important than your Auntie Sofie, right? I'm the cool auntie."

Leah chuckled as she rolled her eyes. "But he visits me in school almost every day. Right, Ry?"

Greg laughed as his son nodded his head, not quite sure what to do about the feuding aunties. His sisters actually got along well and shared an apartment a few streets over across from the school. Excellent for Leah, since she didn't need to use her car to get there.

"Oh, hey, look. Matty, Kiki, Hope, and Tanner are outside," his mom announced in a fake surprised voice. "Ryan, you should go play with your cousins next door."

His son couldn't bob his head in acknowledgment fast enough. He started to get up, then froze. "May I be excused from the table, Dad? Please?"

Greg pointed to his plate, the one he'd cleaned quite nicely of every scrap of food. He had a feeling his grocery bill would be going up soon. "Rinse your plate and put it in the dishwasher first. Then, you can go."

The boy disappeared faster than a magician, then reappeared in the doorway. "Nonna, you are bringing dessert next door, right?"

Greg's dad let out a huge laugh. "Oh, I don't think anyone would ever forgive us if they didn't get some of your Nonna's desserts. We'll be over soon enough."

The adults sat back and took their time finishing their meals.

"Did Ryan have a good time at the Easter Egg Hunt this morning?" his mom asked as she buttered one more biscuit to sop up any leftovers on her plate.

"Yeah, he wasn't too sure about going at first. Apparently, some of the kids at school think they're too old for it now. But having Erik and Nathaniel's kids going kind of gave him the push to go. He feels like a big brother to all of them."

Sofie tipped her head. "Ryan would be a great big brother. He's so good with the younger cousins. You have any plans to help him with that any time soon?"

Greg sighed. He'd heard this question before. "Sure. As soon as you can find me a woman who doesn't mind a guy with a kid. One who doesn't care about my odd work hours. A woman who doesn't play games. I don't have the time or energy for any of that crap. And she'd have to put up with this crazy, nosy family I have."

Sofie snorted at his last words. Yup, the crazy family part was absolutely true, but he wouldn't trade them for the world. His parents, sisters, aunts, uncles, cousins, and now his cousins' spouses and kids. Seemed every time they turned around, they'd added a new family member or two.

"What about Ali Cabrera?" Leah suggested, not for the first time.

"She's Ryan's teacher. We had this conversation, dear sister."

"Give it a few months, dear brother. Start making plans and being extra friendly, so you're in a good place once school lets out."

He narrowed his eyes at his sister. "Yeah, 'cause that's not too stalkerish."

His mom hummed in thought. "It's got to be hard dealing with that little girl all on her own. You should know that with having to raise Ryan by yourself. Your son could certainly use a mother figure."

"You're a mother figure for him," he pointed out.

"I'm his grandmother. It's not the same thing."

"So you want me to get together with her just so we can co-parent each other's kids?"

His mother put on her scary mom face. "That isn't what I'm saying, Gregory Ryan Storm, and you know it."

Both his sisters held their hands up to their mouths like they were in shock. It wasn't often his mom pulled out the middle name. Especially for him. He'd been the quintessential poster child for good behavior. Until he'd gotten—

"You haven't dated anyone since Wendy passed away," his dad filled in. Yup, getting Wendy pregnant had been one of his first big screw ups. In so many ways. His family didn't even know the half of it.

Didn't know that Wendy had been leaving him when she'd gotten in that car crash. Her bags had been packed and sitting in the trunk. The embarrassment and shame he'd felt, for getting her pregnant to begin with but also to have fallen for her lies, was bad enough. He'd never revealed what her letter had said or even that she'd left him one.

"I'm sure Ali gets help from Jillian's father, which gives her free time for herself. Better than my situation. Except I do have all of you."

"Actually." Leah rested on her forearms on the table. "Ali's ex is a total jerk. He basically left her because she wasn't being his slave girl anymore. When she had the baby, she stopped waiting on him hand and foot to take care of Jillian, and he didn't like that. Poor Ali has to fight just to get him to keep up with his child support. He rarely takes Jillian, which suits Ali perfectly, but it doesn't give her any time for herself."

He didn't realize how crappy her situation was. Regardless, he didn't plan to date her only to provide a father for her kid. He'd never dated specifically to find Ryan a mother either. He hadn't dated anyone since Wendy died. There had been an occasional hookup at a bachelor party, but he could count those on the fingers of one hand. Ryan was ten years old. How sad was that statistic?

Greg stood and started bringing dishes to the kitchen. The rest of his family followed suit. His sisters put the leftovers into containers and stacked the ones they'd be taking in a corner of the fridge. He filled the dishwasher, and his father started doing the pots and pans.

It didn't take long before the place looked as clean as it had been before the cooking had started. With the exception of the platters filled with his mother's desserts taking up most of the island.

"Are we ready to head next door?" His mother picked up

the platter filled with cookies. Dad took the one with the cupcakes, and Greg and his sisters each grabbed the others. His mom was an excellent baker and never minded providing dessert for the whole extended family.

Aunt Molly was the first to greet them, holding the door open as they marched inside.

"Oh, you made those strawberry cookies again, Luci. You're spoiling us as usual."

The dessert had no sooner touched the dining room table than swarms of Storms descended on them. Gram and Gramps got to go first. No one ever argued that fact. His mom always made enough for everyone to have plenty.

His dad, Uncle Pete, and Uncle Kris followed Gramps to the kitchen where they'd talk sports or about Storm Electric, the business all three brothers owned. Gram, Aunt Molly, Aunt Anna, and his mom went into the living room. Greg, his cousins, and their spouses huddled around the dining room table for a bit, checking in for anything new going on.

Joey, Erik and Tessa's eight-month-old started to fuss. Gina, Alex's fiancée, pointed her toward the sitting room. "I'll make him a bottle if you want to change his butt."

Tessa nodded at Erik. "Can you take some of the cookies out to the kids while I feed Joey?"

Erik hobbled to the table and started putting a variety of desserts into a pan. "Better bring a few extra for Nathaniel, since he volunteered to watch the kids outside."

Greg grabbed a few napkins and tossed them into the container. "I've seen my son eat brownies. The resulting chocolate face is frightening."

His cousins, Kevin, Alex, and Luke, along with Sara's husband, TJ, and Alex's friend John, all trooped out to the backyard where Nathaniel stood with his arm around his wife, Darcy, as they monitored the kids playing.

"Zane seems to be having fun," Greg said. Zane was

Darcy's older brother, but with his developmental delays, he had the innocence and fun nature of the kids.

Darcy's dark eyes sparkled. Figuratively and literally. The woman wore the most outlandish eye makeup, along with black or dark red lipstick. It still surprised the entire family how well she and Nathaniel, the staid corporate attorney, fit together.

"Zane loves coming here. He pretends to be all responsible like he's keeping an eye on them, but then he has a blast playing."

Greg put two fingers in his mouth and let out a long whistle. The kids froze and pivoted toward him. He pointed to the container Erik held. In seconds, they were inundated with salivating children.

Greg, Erik, and Nathaniel made sure everyone got something and made the youngest of them sit while they ate. It seemed strange to Greg that his two cousins, with whom he'd gone to school, now had more children than him. Greg had become a father ten years ago. Within the last year, Erik had adopted two children from overseas and had another with his new wife. Nathaniel only recently found out that Tanner was his child. And now they had Darcy's daughter, Hope, with them as well.

God sure did work in mysterious ways.

"Anyone want to shoot some hoops?" Luke asked, heading to the driveway.

Erik looked torn, more because his children were out here playing than his injury. He might still need his cane, but he didn't let it stop him from having fun.

Nathaniel patted Darcy on the arm. "If you want to go in and gossip with the ladies, we can keep an eye on the kids."

"Yep, that's me. Love to gossip." She threw Nathaniel the evil eye. "At least I know Zane will watch them." She gave Nathaniel a kiss, then sauntered into the house.

Luke bounced the ball to Nathaniel and laughed. "How's that ol' ball and chain feeling now?"

"It feels damn good actually." Nathaniel dribbled the ball, then shot it in the air. It swished right through the net.

Erik picked up the rebound and let it fly. "I have to agree with Nathaniel. I wouldn't change a thing."

Luke snorted as he ran to catch the ball. "You men have disappointed me. You might as well go in and gossip with the women."

Greg positioned himself to block Luke's shot. Erik and Nathaniel's comments settled deep inside him with a twist of envy. He'd been married for less than a year, and it had been the worst time of his life. Wendy was always moody and distant, something he'd attributed to her pregnancy at the time. She hadn't wanted to hang out with any of his family. She'd refused to let him touch her. He'd kept hoping they could grow closer once the baby was born, but that dream had been lost like so many others.

Maybe his sisters and mom were right that he should consider getting married again. But the memories of his disaster of a marriage wouldn't go away.

Ryan ran over to them. "Hey, Uncle Luke." Luke was Greg's cousin, but all the kids called the adults either *aunt* or *uncle* as a sign of respect.

"What's up, kid?" Luke stepped into the grass to avoid the ball being thrown around.

"I've got this Inventor's Fair coming up at my school next month. I was wondering, since you're an engineer, if you'd help me invent something."

Greg planted his hands on his hips. "You know you're supposed to do that by yourself, right, pal?"

Ryan's lip popped out full force.

Luke clapped the boy on the shoulder. "I'd be happy to sit and chat with you. We can throw around some ideas and brainstorm the best way to make your idea a reality. But your dad's right. You have to do all the work yourself. That doesn't mean you can't bounce thoughts off me and ask my advice."

Greg let out a sigh. "Thanks, Luke. I appreciate the offer and your understanding Ryan's part in this. You'll make a great dad someday."

The horror on his cousin's face was priceless. "Don't even joke like that." Luke ruffled Ryan's hair. "We'll figure out a time to meet soon."

Ryan thanked him, then darted back to play with his younger cousins.

"I think we need some teams," Kevin called out. "I'm taking TJ."

TJ gave a tiny smirk but didn't say much else as was typical for him.

Without hesitation, Alex pointed at all of them. "Fine. Kevin, TJ, Erik, and Luke on one team. I've got Nathaniel, Greg, and John on this team."

As they ran around the makeshift court, they gave Alex, the ever-ready organizer, some crap. He probably had his wedding to Gina mapped out before the ring was even on her finger.

Eventually, Greg passed the ball to Alex. "What are you doing with Gina's grandmother's house? The renovations are coming along."

Luke jumped and batted the ball as Alex threw it toward the hoop. "I might live there for a bit to give the newlyweds some privacy. But it's awfully big for one person, so not sure how long that'll last."

"You don't want to hold onto it for when you get married and have kids?" John questioned Luke.

The cousins all doubled over laughing. Luke most of all. "I don't plan on getting married or having kids for a long time...if ever. I like my life exactly as it is, thanks."

John's face darkened. Greg didn't know his story, but he seemed like a loner at times. "Anyone else here like the idea of marriage?"

Erik and Nathaniel peered at Greg, who shook it off. "Not me. I've already done it once. That was plenty."

Kevin and Luke made noises of agreement. "Don't look at us."

Nathaniel pulled the ball out of Luke's hands since he hadn't been paying attention. "I thought I felt the same way, but everything changed once I met Darcy." He looked around, a small smile on his face. "We haven't told anyone yet except my parents, but since it's past the three-month mark…"

He took a deep breath in.

"Three months?" Erik tipped his head. "Is Darcy expecting?"

Nathaniel's face almost glowed with excitement. "Yeah. In October."

Luke held up his hand and ticked off his fingers.

Greg swatted Luke's arm. "How did you pass engineering school?"

"Someone didn't wait for the wedding night." Alex dribbled around a grinning Nathaniel.

Greg rolled his eyes and noticed Luke and Erik also shook their heads. "Gina's living with you, and you aren't getting married until July."

Alex clenched his jaw. "How do you know we're sleeping together? I have five bedrooms in the house."

Luke slapped the ball from Alex's hands. "I sleep right down the hallway. Gina is not quiet when she orgasms. We won't even talk about the creative ways you guys screw. Which is ridiculous, since at first you wouldn't even hold hands if I was anywhere nearby. Now…"

Alex turned red all the way from his neck to his ears.

Kevin chuckled. "It's always the quiet ones."

Nathaniel glared at his brother. "If it hadn't been for the bad condoms you gave me, Kev, Darcy wouldn't be pregnant."

Kevin looked thunderstruck. "Dude, I gave them to you like three or four years ago." He faced Greg. "Cuz, when you do get back in the game, make sure to buy some new condoms."

Greg wondered if he'd ever get to the point of needing them again. He hoped so and not just for a one-night stand. "Duly noted."

CHAPTER FIVE

A li counted heads one last time, hoping the parent chaperones on this trip were reliable. She still had nightmares from the time one of the parents forgot a child was in the bathroom and left the area of the museum they'd been visiting. Fortunately, one of the staff had found the child and swiftly returned her to the group.

Today, they were walking to the fire station two streets over from the school, and a child lost on the streets of Squamscott Falls would not be a good thing. Granted, the town was small and most people who lived here were lovely, but you never knew when a visitor could drive in with evil intent.

Man, she had to stop binge watching crime shows.

Mrs. Ferrera clicked along behind her on her three-inch heels, chatting with Mr. Lebowitz. Ali took note of where their assigned kids were, then turned around and continued down the road. At least Mrs. Farmer was at the end of the line and that woman could handle almost anything. She certainly did with her four children.

The brick building came into sight as they turned the corner, and Ali sighed with relief. The field trip had been approved easily, especially since it didn't cost the parents anything, and Reggie loved having the community involved with each other. A word from Greg Storm had helped, she was sure.

Ali adjusted the lightweight peach sweater she wore and tugged it over her belly. Her dress slacks had a good built-in tummy control panel, and she loved how they smoothed out her baby pouch. The one she should have gotten rid of within months of having Jillian, according to her sister.

Unfortunately, she'd had to wear a pair of sensible walking shoes for the trip. How Mrs. Ferrera managed without tipping over, she wasn't sure.

Ali's heart skipped a beat as the bay doors opened and Greg Storm strode out, waiting for them. His crooked smile and adorable dimples made her breath hitch.

"Good morning, Mrs. Cabrera. And class."

"What do we say to Captain Storm?" Ali prompted her students.

They all shouted, "Good morning." It was hardly polished or together, but at least they were enthusiastic. Most likely because they got out of schoolwork.

Greg waved them all closer, then welcomed them. "It's great having you at the fire station today. Before we start, we do have a few rules we need to go over first. Has anybody been here before and know what they are?"

A few students raised their hands, while Austin Lebowitz jumped up and down. Like that would get him called on first.

Greg pointed to AJ Farmer in the back. AJ shuffled his feet, then said, "We can't touch anything unless you tell us it's okay."

"Absolutely correct. There're lots of tools inside the fire house. We need them to fight fires and help people if they've been in an accident. Some are heavy or dangerous, and we wouldn't want anyone to get hurt today."

"Because then you'd have to call an ambulance," Cheslyn Ferrera called out. The little girl pointed to the ambulance parked behind Greg and laughed. Seemed the girl didn't care that her mother was standing a few feet away. The way her mother stared at Greg Storm, Ali wasn't sure she cared what her kid was doing. Not that she blamed her. Greg was something to look at. He was in his blue SFFD t-shirt again, and it was difficult to look away from how it molded to his chest.

Ali threw her a patented teacher look, and Cheslyn clamped her lips together.

Greg's only response to the joke was a quick smile, and Ali was grateful. The last thing some children needed was encouragement to misbehave.

"The other thing you need to know is what to do if the alarm rings."

Ali could see Aiden with a funny snap on the tip of his tongue, so she sauntered nearby and gently laid her hand on his shoulder. He got the message.

"The firefighters and paramedics have to get to the equipment, so you'll need to get out of their way. Let's take a walk inside, and I'll show you where to go if the alarm rings."

The children all followed Greg inside the building, their heads zipping this way and that at the array of equipment and supplies. He guided them to a large open area and encouraged them to sit.

Three other firefighters in similar uniforms joined their group. Greg turned and introduced them.

"Most of you probably remember Bobby Bishop. He helped with the smokehouse a few weeks back. This is Seamus Lowell, another firefighter who drives the engine. And this is our paramedic, Fallon Ambrose."

Bonnie's hand went up and Greg pointed to her. "Yes?"

"What's a paramedic?"

"I'm going to let Fallon answer that question. Then, maybe Bobby and Seamus can tell you what they do. When they're done, we'll take you on a tour of the firehouse and the engine. Maybe even let a few of you try on the gear. How's that sound?"

The kids all cheered, and Fallon stepped forward to begin telling the children about her job. Bobby and Seamus dragged some coats, the fireproof pants, and boots over behind Fallon and waited until she was done.

Ali stood in the background, her eyes open for any students who needed a simple nudge, but they were all listening intently for the moment. The four parents who had come along on the trip sat or stood near the children, also focused on the speaker.

"I'm glad you were able to arrange this trip," Greg murmured near her ear.

Dios, he smelled good. She wanted to lean in closer and take another whiff. That wouldn't be too creepy. Clasping her hands tightly in front of her, she gave him a nod.

"The kids were thrilled, and the weather is perfect for walking over here."

"Yup, perfect day." His gaze flicked to the kids for a second, then back to her.

Seriously? She was discussing the weather with the hottest guy she'd ever known. *Find something better to talk about.*

"Thank you for including Jillian in the Easter Egg Hunt with your family. She hasn't stopped talking about Ryan and the other children. Hope was especially nice to her." It had been two weeks since she'd seen him at the town green, and she hadn't had anything interesting to say then either.

"I'll have to invite you and Jillian over sometime when the

kids are all visiting next door. My cousin, Alex, and his fiancée live there. His house is a lot like mine. Been in the family their whole lives, so it gets used for all the holidays and celebrations. The rest of the cousins have a tendency to find our way there at some point in the day."

"Your parents honestly lived next door to each other? Willingly?"

"Yep," Greg replied with a smile.

Ali held her breath but knew he was only being kind with the invitation. "It's so nice how big your family is and how you all get along. Not everyone has that."

Greg's brows drew together. "You said you were visiting your sister on Easter, right?"

He remembered. "Yeah, but it's only my mom, my sister, her husband, and their son. Not quite as large as your extended family." And she and her sister didn't get along as well as it seemed the Storms did. She'd heard Leah talk about how much fun the cousins were. Fun was not a word she'd use to describe Valeria.

Greg nodded, touched her arm for a second, then headed to where the other firefighters were answering questions. He'd been paying a lot more attention to the presentation than she had, thankfully.

"Last few questions, then you get a tour of the firehouse. Yes." He pointed to Jack who had his hand up.

Ali maneuvered to where she could best keep a few of the students from jumping out of their seats. They'd only been sitting maybe fifteen minutes, but for some of them that was too long.

Greg finished up listening to a long, drawn out story from Cheyenne that had nothing to do with firefighting. He had lots of patience. When the little girl stopped for a breath, Ali dove in.

"And that's a great place to move into the next part of our trip. If you have any other questions, I'll bet we could make that into a writing assignment and mail letters to Captain Storm and the others."

A few groans drifted her way. Yeah, she didn't think anyone wanted an added writing assignment.

As Greg led the group through a set of doors, Ali gave the eye to Mrs. Farmer who nodded and took up the caboose. Thank God for that woman. Ali wanted to stay up front to reel in any kids who tried to start long-winded conversations with the firefighters. Okay, and maybe she wanted to stay close to Greg Storm.

Winding her way past the kids in the middle, she sidled up next to Ryan Storm. It showed how good a father Greg was that his child was happy to be seen with his dad and didn't feel the need to hide in the back of the line. Cheslyn kept on the opposite side of the group from her mom. Or maybe Mrs. Ferrera was the one maneuvering to stay closer to Greg.

The students got to see the kitchen where the fire staff cooked and ate their meals, the area where they watched TV or played cards, and where they slept if they were on a night shift.

"Captain Storm?" Mrs. Ferrera purred. Ali couldn't call the tone of her voice anything else. "Do you stay in these sleeping quarters, also?"

Greg's face flushed as he pointed to a small room next to the office. "I have my own room, here. One of the perks of being captain. Let's head back to the engine bay and check out the vehicles."

The kids gave a little cheer and followed along to where Seamus had the doors of the engine, ladder truck, and the back of the ambulance open.

"We thought we'd have the students rotate through the vehicles as well as trying on the turnout gear." Greg said to her. "Maybe we can station a parent at each location."

At her nod, Greg directed Mr. Lebowitz to help lift the children into the engine with Seamus. Mrs. Farmer and Mrs. Baker got to file the children through the ladder truck with Bobby. He pointed to Mrs. Ferrera and said, "You can help the students in and out of the back of the ambulance while Fallon shows them what's inside."

Ali opened her eyes wide as he pointed to her. "Why don't you help me with the turn out gear, Mrs. C?"

"Happy to." And she was.

She split the children into four groups and sent them to one of the stations explaining where they'd go after their turn. Checking with each of the parents, she made sure they knew where to send the students after they were done.

At the large empty space they'd sat in before, Greg helped a little girl slide her feet into the boots and pull up the turnout pants. He then settled the large coat on her and placed the helmet on her head. There were two sets of gear, and Ali helped the children try them on, then take them off.

As she and Greg worked together, Ali made sure the rest of the class was following the route. The kids all seemed to be having fun.

When they'd all rotated around, Greg had them sit back where they'd been before.

"You know what? Mrs. Cabrera didn't get a chance to try on the turnout gear. Do you think she should?"

Her class all cheered as she shook her head in horror. "I'm fine."

"Nope, it's not fair that everyone had a turn but you. Come here."

Throwing him a death glare, she stepped forward and

whispered, "I'll pay you back for this." She peeked over her shoulder and smiled for the students.

Greg held her waist as she toed her shoes off, stepped through the pants and into the boots. As he pulled up the pants and settled the straps on her shoulders, his hands touched her in a few spots. She wouldn't admit how nice it was having a man touch her again, romantic intentions or not.

"Now for the coat." He helped her into the coat, and she marveled at how heavy it was. The helmet was next. It nearly sent her over.

"How do you walk in this stuff?"

"Not only do we walk with the gear, we usually wear a breathing apparatus." He pointed to a huge air tank and mask Bobby held up. "But we won't make you put that on today. We should show you what it's like to get in and out of the engine with the gear."

Ali whipped her head around and frowned. Greg was grinning, his dimples flashing at her, taunting her. Holding out his hand, he escorted her to the engine and helped her step up into it. His hand pushed at her butt, and she almost lost it. When she glanced at him, he was biting his lip to keep from laughing. Oh, yeah, she'd have to think of some way to get him back.

Up in the seat, she waved to the kids like she was a queen, and they clapped. Now to get down. Greg was right there, holding his hands out ready to assist her. When she got on the last step, her foot slipped in the overlarge boot, and she stumbled. Greg caught her and slung her over his shoulder.

"And this is how we carry someone out of a burning building." Slowly, he lowered her to the floor. Ali's face had to be crimson with the amount of heat swirling within her cheeks and neck.

Bobby, Fallon, and Seamus passed out plastic fireman hats and stickers as Greg assisted her in removing the gear.

"Thanks for totally embarrassing me in front of the class." She made sure to sound playful, so he'd know she wasn't too upset. "I will have to think of something to get back at you."

"I have two younger sisters. I've heard that threat before. I can handle it." He winked at her.

As she stepped out of the pants and boot combination, Greg held her waist again. Little shivers ran down her back. Between his touch and the wink, she was coming unglued. *Get it together, girl. You've got a class to take care of.*

When she attempted to tug on her shoe, she almost lost her balance and grabbed onto the closet object. It so happened to be Greg's bicep. Wow, that was one nice muscle. No wonder he'd been able to pick her up and throw her over his shoulder so easily.

"Thank you. I've got it now." With her shoe finally on, she faced the kids and instructed them to line up.

"We hope you had a good time today," Greg called out to the kids who chattered like magpies.

Ali shushed them all. "Let's say thank you to the firefighters."

The children practically screamed their thanks, and Ali cringed. She held out her hand to Greg. "Thank you for helping me arrange this. They obviously enjoyed themselves and hopefully learned something in the process."

Greg's hand lingered in hers, and he held her gaze for a fraction longer than she thought necessary. Who was she to complain? She enjoyed the touch, then pulled her hand out of his grip and said goodbye.

She instructed Mrs. Farmer to lead the way back to the school and Ali took caboose this time. Once they'd gotten to the cross street, she took a minute to glance back at the firehouse. Greg still stood near the bay doors, his hands on his slim hips watching them.

What would it be like to have a man like that waiting for her when she got home at night? Or for her to wait for each night? She'd never heard of him dating anyone from town, so she had to wonder if he was still mourning his wife. It had happened ten years ago, but some loves lasted forever. Too bad she hadn't been lucky enough to find one of those.

CHAPTER SIX

Greg clipped the visitor's badge to his shirt and bounded up the stairs. Nodding at the few children who lingered in the halls, he headed to Mrs. Cabrera's classroom. Alandra. Ali.

He bit his lip to keep from smirking as he remembered the field trip to the station last week and how he'd carried her over his shoulder. It had only been a few seconds and mostly because she'd slipped on the step down, but he shouldn't have liked it as much as he did. That and giving her a slight boost up into the engine. Right on her shapely backside. It had been naughty of him, but he didn't regret it. When he'd helped her down, he'd held her hands and noticed how soft her skin was.

He'd felt guilty enough with what he'd done that when she had called out for a parent to help set up the Inventor's Fair, he'd signed up right away. Today was his day off, after all, and he had the time free. Not that he couldn't have used it to clean up the mess Ryan had made from his invention. Or paint the trim and the shutters on the house. Or a million other chores required of someone who owned an old Victorian house.

When he got close to the door of the classroom, he slowed down and peeked in. He was a few minutes early and didn't want to interrupt if she was in the middle of teaching a lesson.

Ali sat on the back kidney-shaped table, her legs dangling over the edge, an open binder next to her. She tapped her index finger on the page and said, "Number eight. Avoid. I like to avoid driving through town when there is too much traffic. Avoid."

Keeping her finger where it was, she peered around the class as the students all scribbled furiously on a long strip of paper on their desks. Some of the kids huddled over their work, their other hand hiding what they'd written. Others leaned back, not seeming to care if someone looked at their test. He assumed it was a spelling test.

Leaning in a bit closer, he focused on Ryan to see what his son was doing. Ali glanced up and he ducked back, not wanting to disturb her.

"Whole. I can't believe I ate the whole pizza. W-H-O-L-E. Whole."

Had she just...?

Some of the kids started chuckling, and Ali shook her head and let out a hearty laugh. Her entire body slumped on the table as her shoulders shook. Interesting. She'd made a huge mistake and spelled the word for the class, but she was laughing as hard as they were. Had she made the slip because she'd seen him in the hallway? Had he flustered her that much? He'd like to think he had that kind of effect on women but couldn't be sure.

Ali finally pushed herself to sitting and wiped her eyes. "Okay, so everyone should get at least that word correct. Last word. Number ten. Furious. I was furious when my friend embarrassed me in front of the class. Furious."

Was she talking about him? Oops. Greg watched Ryan as he listened, then confidently wrote the word. When Ali did a quick read of the entire list, he checked his spelling then smiled. Ryan never had any problems with reading and spelling. They were his best subjects.

Ali stayed sitting, swinging her feet back and forth under the table. As the kids started to get up, she called out, "Don't forget your name on the paper. Hand it to me with the word side up and name at the top, please."

The students lined up to hand her their tests, and she smiled and thanked each and every one. If someone had their paper the wrong way, she merely shook her head. One student handed her the page, and she held it back out. The kid looked confused.

"I don't know whose paper this is."

The child's face scrunched up, then he grabbed the paper saying, "Oh, my name." He scrambled back to his seat to write it.

Greg loved watching how cute she was and the easy rapport she had with her class. He was glad he'd gone the extra mile to have Ryan put in here. He peeked his head in further and waved.

"Captain Storm. Thanks for coming in to help. I have four students who signed up for the Invention Fair. I believe Mr. Thorpe is in the gym directing the inventors where to set up."

She stood up and tucked her hair behind her ear. "AJ, Ryan, Cheyenne, and Bonnie. Get your posters and supplies and go with Captain Storm to the gym. I think a few of your parents dropped your projects in the gym this morning if they were too big to bring up here."

She swiveled her head to face him. "Once they're finished,

you can send them back up here. They'll need to get their homework and bags. Thank you again."

It was almost the end of the day, and the Invention Fair was right after school. Ryan had invited his grandparents and his aunts to come see his invention.

The four children got their supplies and lined up. Greg gave a wave to Ali and led the kids down the hallway. He would have liked to spend a little more time with her. When he signed up, he hadn't realized today's job hadn't been with her. Oh, well.

They entered the gym, and he steered the kids to the right where half of the large room was taken up with long tables. Reggie Thorpe stood with a clipboard, peering around the room.

Greg told the kids to wait and headed over to the principal.

"Hey, Reggie, I've got the students from Mrs. Cabrera's class. Where do you want them?"

Reggie scanned his diagram and pointed. "The fourth graders are in the back row. There should be nameplates on the tables."

"Gotcha. Thanks." Back with the students, Greg showed them where they were to set up, then helped the ones who needed it carrying their invention to the table.

Ryan, Bonnie, and AJ finished setting up quickly, but Cheyenne's invention had a lot of little parts that had come undone in the move. Greg didn't know exactly what it was supposed to look like, so he let her work at it. He had a feeling she was simply stalling so she didn't have to go back to the class until the last minute.

A group of tiny munchkins marched in a line across the gym floor, and Greg smiled at his sister, Leah, leading the parade. Keeping his eye on Cheyenne, he took a few steps to intercept Leah.

"Hey, how's it going?"

"What are you doing here?"

"Helping Ryan and some of the other kids in his class set up for the Invention Fair."

"Miss Storm?" a little one yelled, hopping up and down with her hand raised. "Who's that?"

Leah grinned. "This is Captain Storm of the Fire Department. Remember we had some firefighters visit during fire safety month?"

"You have the same last name. Is he married to you?"

Leah laughed. "No, he's my brother. That's why we have the same last name."

The child seemed appeased. Leah waved for a child across the room to hurry up from helping the gym teacher put hula hoops away, then glanced at him.

"How'd you get roped into helping with the fair?"

Greg shrugged. "Ryan made an invention. And I kind of embarrassed Ali at a field trip to the fire station last week, so when she asked, I could hardly refuse."

Leah squinted at him. "What did you do? She hasn't said anything about it that I know of, but then I don't have the same lunch period as her."

His lips twisted to the side. "I made her dress up in the turnout gear, then climb into the truck." He wouldn't mention how he threw her over his shoulder. Or the fact he'd had dreams of doing that exact thing again only with a lot fewer clothes on.

"That's par for the course being a teacher. I'm sure she was fine with it. Gotta go. The bell's going to ring in a few minutes, and I've got to get these cherubs ready for dismissal. I'll come down to see Ryan's invention once they're all gone."

For the next twenty minutes, Greg puttered around the gym, strolling past the inventions and seeing if Ryan had a chance of winning. Luke had been true to his word and guided Ryan in figuring out what he wanted to create and then helped him brainstorm ways he could make it. The end result was...interesting.

At dismissal time, the intercom went off announcing which buses were here. Over the next ten minutes, more buses were called, and the sound of running feet and squealing children filled the halls outside the gym. He had sent in a note this morning stating he'd be here after school to pick up Ryan. Hopefully, that meant his son would come down once everyone was dismissed.

The halls quieted down, and an announcement was made for all Invention Fair students to report to the gym.

It was another seven or eight minutes before Ryan showed up with Ali.

"There you are."

Ali smiled and ruffled Ryan's hair. "Ryan was helping me with a few things in the class, and we decided to walk down here together."

The other three children walked in behind her and immediately went over to check on their projects. More students wandered in, and suddenly the room was filled with chattering voices, excited and nervous. Ali meandered around the four children from her class, stopping at each one for an explanation.

Greg stood next to Ryan's invention, a sand toy sorter and cleaner, as Ryan read over his poster explaining the device. He put sandy cars, action figures, and other small toys in the top part and shook it until all the sand fell off and sifted into the bottom section. Then, he could dump the sand out in the trash or on the beach and it wouldn't get all over everything else.

After Ryan had given his demonstration, Greg grinned and stepped closer to her. "Do you always throw the kids a freebie on the spelling test?"

One dark eyebrow went up.

"W-H-O-L-E."

When she laughed, it brightened her whole face. W-H-O-L-E.

"Yeah, I don't know what that was. I like to point out when I make a mistake to show them it's okay and that everyone does, but I'll bet there are still a few who get it wrong."

Greg loved that she could make fun of herself, like when she'd sat in the engine and waved like a queen at a parade. He could tell she hadn't wanted to put the turnout gear on, but she'd been a trooper with her students watching. He had a feeling there could be a lot about Ali Cabrera that he'd like.

ALI TOOK in the noise and excitement of the students and the few parents that had started to trickle in. The Invention Fair was a favorite of hers. It wasn't required for anyone, which meant every student who participated wanted to be here. That always made it better.

Standing next to Greg Storm as he grinned at her wasn't too bad either. Alas, she had work to do. Judging work.

"Good luck to Ryan. I've been tagged as a judge for the first graders, so I need to go and chat with them about their inventions. Thanks again for helping today."

Greg shrugged. "No worries. The least I could do after the field trip."

"Don't even worry about that. The kids loved seeing me all dressed in fireman gear."

She wouldn't mention being thrown over his shoulder or the pat on the butt he'd given her to help her up into the engine.

As she headed toward the judges' table, Stephanie Long

sidled up next to her. "Whoo, that man gives me chills. How do you talk to him without melting into a puddle on the floor?"

"I assume you mean Captain Storm, Steph. It's called professionalism. You should try it some time."

Steph rolled her eyes and laughed. She knew Ali was only kidding. For the most part. Steph was a great teacher, but her man crazy ways sometimes got the better of her.

At the table, Mrs. Poulin, the assistant principal, handed them official badges and a clipboard with score sheets. Steph was judging the kindergarten inventions. Leah Storm came up behind her and took her clipboard.

"What are you judging, Leah?" Ali asked. "Your nephew has an invention in the fair."

Leah nodded. "Yeah, I know. That's why I'm doing third grade. I think we need to give the parents a few more minutes to check everything out."

The gym got more crowded as more parents and guests arrived. Ali kept her eyes on her students to see who showed up for them. Edele and Jay Farmer were here with their three other children. That was a nice family. Always supportive of the others.

Bonnie's mom and grandmother stood by her side as she demonstrated how her invention worked. Good to know her mom had gotten the time from work to show up here.

Poor Cheyenne stood by herself in front of her creation. If history repeated itself, her mom would show up a few minutes before the fair ended, just in time to take her home.

Ryan had his grandparents, his dad, his aunts, Leah and Sofie, and another guy who definitely had a Storm look about him. It wasn't one of the cousins she'd met at the Easter Egg Hunt.

It was almost time for her to judge the first graders, but Ali's heart broke for Cheyenne. As she watched, Greg Storm inched his way toward her and began asking questions. Then, little by little, the rest of Ryan's visitors moved back and forth between Ryan and Cheyenne, giving her as much attention as they gave Ryan.

Ali's heart almost burst. Greg Storm wasn't the only one in his family who was super nice. It obviously was hereditary.

Mrs. Poulin had been making her rounds, talking to all the children, but now waved at them. It was time for the judging. Ali headed to the first graders while Steph took the younger ones. The other judges moved toward their inventors.

As Ali asked questions, she seriously considered moving to first grade to teach. They were so innocent and sweet and filled with awe of everything. But then she remembered the interesting conversations and jokes she was able to share with her slightly older students and realized she was in a good spot.

When Ali finished up her last score sheet and began filling out the comments, she noticed Cheyenne's mom had shown up. Phew. Better late than never.

Back at the judges' table, she figured out all the awards for each child. Even though they were choosing a first, second, and third place for each grade, every child would get some sort of award. The funniest invention. The sturdiest invention. The springiest invention. Now to figure out what title she could give to each of them.

She stood around with the other teachers helping each other with the silly award names and filling out the certificates. They had only a few more minutes to figure them out.

"Mine are done," Steph said, sighing. Then, she practically hummed. "Who is that delicious man hanging out with Ryan Storm?"

"You mean his father?" Ali laughed.

KARI LEMOR

Steph threw her a look. "He's delicious, too, but no, the other one."

Leah cocked her head and groaned. "First, stop calling my brother delicious. It's disgusting. Second, the other guy is my cousin, Luke. Believe me, you don't want him."

Steph's eyes narrowed. "I might disagree. What's wrong with him? Is he a jerk?"

Leah shook her head. "He's a nice person, but he's a love 'em and leave 'em kind of guy. He doesn't stay with a woman long enough to finish zipping up his pants, if you know what I mean."

"Oh, I get your message. Could be interesting." Steph started to saunter away.

Leah called after her, "Don't say I didn't warn you."

Ali laughed at the sexy pout Steph threw over her shoulder.

"Are all your cousins so gorgeous?"

Leah grinned and nodded. "Yep. You didn't want me to introduce you to Luke, did you?"

Ali gasped. "Love 'em and leave 'em? No thanks. I had one of those and have no desire to repeat the process."

A mischievous gleam twinkled in Leah's eyes. "How about a super nice family guy who loves kids? Great job, kind of cute. I know where I can dig one up."

Ali crossed her arms over her chest as she rolled her eyes. Leah and her matchmaking. Too bad she'd been having similar thoughts herself.

CHAPTER SEVEN

*T*he news reporters prattled on as Ali attempted to scrub her casserole dish. Caked-on pasta had stuck to the bottom. She wouldn't be winning any Betty Crocker awards this week.

"The fire seems to have started in the kitchen of the small restaurant, but the fire department isn't ruling out arson. This makes the fourth unexplained fire..."

"Mama, I done my sandwich. I have a cookie now?" Jillian held up her empty plate and grinned. That smile alone could make Ali give her everything in the world.

"Of course, you can, sweetie. Great job eating your lunch. Do you want more milk with the cookie?" The small cup she'd given her with the sandwich was empty.

Jillian licked her lips. "Yes, please, Mama. I love milk."

Ali deposited a chocolate chip cookie onto a napkin and placed it in front of Jillian with a kiss to her head. "And I love that you love milk. I'll get you a little bit more."

As she filled the cup, Ali glanced at the flames shooting out of the building on the television. Those poor people. Luckily, no one had been at work, but thinking of all they'd lost must be heartbreaking. Of course, the only thing of real importance that Ali had was her precious little girl.

"Here you go, sweetie. Don't drink it too fast."

"Firefighters from area towns have been called in to help fight the blaze. Portsmouth, Squamscott Falls, and Stratham Fire Departments have all sent units."

Squamscott Falls? Was Greg Storm working today? It was Sunday. Had he said he only worked during the week now that he was captain? Or was it only day shift? Biting her lip, she wondered how she could find out. She could call Leah. Most likely, she'd know if her brother was involved in fighting this fire. But what excuse could she give her?

Your brother is so adorable and nice I wanted to make sure he's not getting burned alive? Yeah, that was a good one. Or she could use the kid angle. *With Ryan in my class, I wanted to make sure he's okay and being looked after.* Yup. Still stupid, because if Greg was working, someone would be watching Ryan. His father had stated he didn't leave him home alone yet. He was only ten.

Glancing at the clock, Ali added a second cookie to Jilly's napkin. The little girl pressed a chocolate kiss to Ali's arm. Jeff should have been here by now to pick her up. It wasn't the first time he'd stood up his daughter. It had gotten to the point where she didn't even tell Jillian that her father was supposed to take her. No use disappointing her.

"The police and fire departments are investigating and have reason to believe the fires are being set. Unfortunately, they have not been able to find any traces of the chemicals used to start them."

Maybe they needed to call in a chemical specialist. Jeff would probably know what kind of chemicals could be used to set fires. He was a chemical engineer, although he worked at the shipyard creating paints and other stuff to keep the boats from rusting. Doubtful he even watched the news. He was more into game shows and trying to win big on lottery tickets. When she'd send him out for milk or bread, he'd come back with a few dozen scratch tickets. None of which ever resulted in more than ten dollars. And half the time he forgot one of the items she'd sent him to get.

Grabbing a face cloth, she ran it under the water, then wiped Jilly's hands and face. "Why don't you play with your dolls for a while, sweetie?"

Jillian bobbed her head. Typically, she went down for a nap after lunch, but if Jeff showed up, Ali didn't want to have to wake her up. The little girl was always cranky if her nap was cut short. Of course, if Jeff didn't show up, Jillian would be out of sorts later in the afternoon because she hadn't rested.

Damn her ex. If he wasn't going to pick up his daughter like he'd promised, the least he could do was call or text. It wasn't fair to Jillian, and it wasn't fair to her.

After drying her hands on a dish towel, she scooped up her cell phone and sent him a text. She worded it politely, even though she wanted to say, *"Where the hell are you, you loser deadbeat?"* Jeff had said he'd pick her up at ten and it was almost one now.

Jillian was quiet, so Ali peeked into the living room. Her daughter had her head resting on a stuffed lion, her thumb in her mouth. Her eyes were open but fluttering. Yep, she still needed to nap.

"Sweetie, how about you and lion lay on the couch, and I'll put a show on?"

She didn't let Jilly watch tons of TV, but it was the perfect way to get her to fall asleep for a nap if she was tired.

"We watch Paw Patrol?"

Ali scooped Jilly and lion up and deposited them on the couch, then clicked on the TV and queued up the show. Within seconds, her daughter's eyes were closed tight.

Well, too bad if Jeff showed up now. Jillian was asleep and doubtful she'd be happy to be woken up for at least an hour.

Standing in the doorway of the kitchen, she gazed at her sweet, sleeping child. Her time with Jeff had been anything but fun, however she couldn't ever regret having this beautiful little girl. Too bad her father didn't have the same feelings.

After Ali had delivered Jillian, she'd stayed home for six months. Jeff had complained the entire time. The house was too messy. Dinner wasn't ready when he got home. Or it wasn't good enough. His laundry wasn't washed, or if it was, she hadn't dried, folded, or ironed it correctly. Ali had been lucky to get a shower a few times a week. Jillian had been a fussy baby with colic and hadn't slept as well as other babies. Naturally, Valeria had all sorts of cures and ideas that would turn Jillian into a perfect infant. None of them had worked for Ali. Val said she must not be doing them correctly.

Her phone vibrated. She grabbed it and swiped across the screen. An email reminder to pay her credit card bill. Next to that email was one from Greg Storm. It was simply a polite reply to when she'd asked for help with the Invention Fair saying he'd be happy to come in anytime if she needed him. For some reason, she'd kept the email even after the Invention Fair was over.

Anytime she needed him.

She didn't want to admit she liked the thought of that.

With Jillian asleep, Ali switched the channel and cruised past the news. A recap of today's fire played with shots of the previous ones. No casualties. Firefighters were working round the clock to contain it. Her mind zoomed right back to Greg Storm, wondering if he was all right.

~

GREG WAITED outside the art room with several other parents while the kids finished their pictures. Ryan had wanted to take an after-school class given by the art teacher, Mrs. Dumond. This one focused on pencil sketches. Ryan had loved drawing from the time he was small, and his skill had grown as he'd gotten older. Alex thought he had talent, and being an architect, he would know.

The kids started gathering their bags and filing into the hallway. Ryan was one of the last ones out.

"Ready to go, pal?"

His son glanced down the hallway, then bent over to tie his shoe. The one that was already tied. Greg scanned the area Ryan had checked out and saw Ali Cabrera exiting her classroom, tote bag in hand.

When his teacher got closer, Ryan stood up and leaned in to whisper, "Piano lessons, Dad."

Greg chuckled at his son's no-so-subtle hint.

"Hi, Mrs. C." Ryan hefted his bag over his shoulder and smiled at his teacher.

"Hi, Ryan. Greg. Is your art class just getting out?"

"Got out a few minutes ago, but Ryan's a little slow moving at the moment."

Ryan's eyes widened hopefully. "Are you walking out to the parking lot?"

"I am. What about you?" Her lips twitched, like she knew what his son was up to. Most likely, Ryan wasn't the first student to crush on the pretty brunette.

"Yeah." He paused and looked at Greg. "You're parked in the parking lot, aren't you, Dad?"

"I am. We'd be happy to escort you down there. Seems my son wants to make sure his favorite teacher gets home safely."

Ryan rolled his eyes and ducked his head, color sprouting on his cheeks.

Ali bit her lip, but he could see humor in her eyes. "I'd be honored to have two such handsome men escort me to my car. Thank you."

As they started down the stairs, Ryan sent a look Greg's way, tipping his head toward his teacher. Greg tipped his head back.

Sighing, Ryan said, "So my piano teacher is retiring."

"Oh? Who's your teacher?"

"Mrs. Gullo. She was my dad's piano teacher, too. And all my aunts and my dad's cousins. She's been teaching for a long time."

"I've heard of Mrs. Gullo. Seems she has been teaching for a while if your Dad also had her." She cocked her head at Greg. "Do you still play?"

"Um, not as much as I should. My grandparents paid for all the grandkids to have lessons. Now, my parents are paying for Ryan to have them. A family tradition, I guess."

Ali gazed at Ryan as the boy held the door open for her. "Do you like taking lessons?"

Ryan skipped ahead of them in the parking lot then circled back. "Yeah, but now I can't take them, with Mrs. Gullo not doing them anymore."

Greg picked up the reins that his son had dropped. "Leah mentioned you had some musical background and might be able to recommend someone else we could use."

"So happens I teach piano lessons. I do one student after school and the rest on Saturday mornings. But Ryan might think that's a little overexposure to me. I can probably—"

"No, no, it wouldn't be too much, Mrs. C." Ryan rushed back next to them. "I mean, I'll only be in your class for another six weeks. But if I take piano lessons, then I get to see you this summer and next year, too."

"You don't happen to have any availability, do you? I can't imagine you want to take too much time away from Jillian."

"I recently had a slot open at ten-thirty on Saturday mornings. Is that time okay?"

Greg glanced down at his son who stiffened, his expression anxious.

"Oh, that won't work. Ryan often has baseball games on Saturday mornings. He's only got another month, but for now that doesn't fit in our schedule. Is it possible to do afternoons? I don't want to take up your entire day."

Ali stopped by a dark blue Ford and lowered her bag. "What time do the games typically end?"

"Noon at the latest."

"How long were his lessons? I give my beginners only thirty minutes but then slowly increase to an hour."

"Ryan's been taking lessons since he was seven. Last year he got moved up to an hour."

"Hmm, I like to have a little time in between lessons in case one runs long. If you started at one o'clock it would bring us to two."

Greg could see her struggling. She wanted to accommodate them but also needed to take care of her daughter. "It's okay if you can't. We understand."

Ryan's face grew solemn.

Ali closed one eye and cocked her head. "Well, my eleven-thirty student had originally wanted an earlier timeslot. I can check with them and see if they'd move to ten-thirty. I'm right around the corner from the ball field. If you could come as soon as Ryan was done, but no earlier than eleven-forty-five, it would be doable. I could get Jillian's lunch ready after my ten-thirty left."

"Ryan might be a little sweaty and dirty, but we could make it work."

"I'll have to contact my student's parent first and check about the time change. I'll get back to you."

"And payment? Do you prefer a check or cash? Either is

fine." He rambled off the amount his parents had paid Mrs. Gullo, and Ali's eyes opened wide.

"Uh, yeah, that's a bit more than I charge, but I don't have forty plus years of piano teaching experience."

"Well, you should take it since we're muscling in on your time with your daughter. Besides, Ryan is my parents' only grandchild, so they're happy to pay it. Once my sisters have kids, they might be singing another tune."

Ryan started bouncing up and down. "Can we start this weekend?"

Greg looked at him with a Dad look. "Today's Thursday. Saturday's only two days away. We might not hear back from Mrs. C.'s other student by then."

"I'll send them a message right now and let you know when I hear." She pulled out her phone, and her thumbs flew across the screen. "Do you want me to email you when I hear back?"

Maybe it was underhanded of him, but he'd love to have her phone number. Even if he didn't use it. The more he talked to her, the more he wanted to use it.

"Why don't I give you my number and you can call or text?"

Ali scrolled a bit, then tapped a few things. "Here, you can put it in."

Greg took her phone and punched in his number. When she took it back, she tapped again for a few seconds. His phone pinged.

She laughed, her voice tinkling like a wind chime. "That's me. Now you've got my number, too. I've got to go get Jillian. My mother is amazing, but after a while she gets tired."

Greg put his hand out. "Thanks for offering to rearrange things for us. If this doesn't work out, we can talk about another option or wait until baseball season is over."

Her handshake was firm while her skin was soft. Too quickly, it was over, and she was getting into her car.

"Thanks, Mrs. C. I can't wait for my first piano lesson with you." Ryan practically twirled in a circle.

"I'm looking forward to it, too, Ryan. We'll see you tomorrow in class."

As she drove away, Greg realized he was looking forward to yet another opportunity to see Ali.

CHAPTER EIGHT

Greg tucked the cash into the envelope and handed it to Ryan. "Here you go. Don't forget to thank her."

The two of them trotted up the front walk of Ali's house. Ryan gripped his dad's hand. "Are you gonna stay with me?"

Greg tilted his head. "This is your teacher. Remember you begged to get put in her class. And begged me again to ask her about piano lessons. You aren't afraid, are you?"

His son's eyes darted around. "No, but this is the first time I'm here. Maybe you can stay a little while. Please, Dad."

"No worries, pal. I wasn't planning on going far, anyway." It wasn't often Ryan needed him anymore. At least not emotionally. His little boy was growing up.

Greg gave a sharp rap on the door. Little footsteps pounded inside, then the door opened. Jillian peeked through the small crack she'd made.

"Hi, Ryan. My mama said you were coming here now."

Ali hustled up behind her daughter and sighed. "Jillian, sweetie, you know you aren't supposed to open the door if we don't know who it is."

"But it's Ryan and his daddy." Jillian jumped up and down and pointed.

Shaking her head, Ali opened the door the rest of the way. "Come on in. Sorry about that. Most of my students come in through the side door into the kitchen. I forgot to tell you."

"Um, I brought some of my sheet music, 'cause you said you wanted to see what I could do already."

"Excellent. How was your game today?" She led Ryan over to the large upright in her living room.

Ryan pulled the baseball hat off his head and grinned. "We won. I took my cleats off in the truck and changed into sneakers. Dad said you probably wouldn't want them on in the house."

Greg folded his arms over his chest. "I don't want them in our house, so I'm sure Mrs. C. doesn't want them getting dirt all over hers."

Ali laughed. "Okay, ready to begin?" She waved at the piano indicating Ryan should sit. He did but looked over his shoulder.

"Can my dad stay today?" Why in the world was Ryan nervous? It wasn't like him. Greg hoped it would be okay with him here.

"Of course, he can." Ali swiveled to look at him. "Some of the parents stay and watch. Others leave and come back. I usually have some coffee and pastries in the kitchen if you'd prefer to sit in there. Jillian's in there playing with her little kitchen set."

Greg examined Ryan's expression and tipped his head. His son nodded. "A cup of coffee sounds great. Thanks."

Greg stepped behind the half wall into Ali's kitchen. Her house was cute and homey. It was a simple ranch with a front living room that opened into an eat-in kitchen, and there was a small hallway to the right. Bedrooms and a bath, he'd guess.

Jillian occupied a little table and chair set in the corner next to a child-sized kitchenette. "Hi, Jillian. Do you mind if I get a cup of coffee?"

"I have coffee. I get you some." She rummaged around in the cabinet of her kitchen set and pulled out two teacups and plates to put them on. "You want milk and sugar? Mama like milk and sugar in her coffee."

"I'd love some. Thank you." He didn't actually need a real cup of coffee.

"You sit here." She pointed to the small plastic chair next to the matching table. He wasn't sure he'd fit.

"Okay. Appreciate it." Crouching down, he settled his backside on the chair but placed one knee on the floor to keep most of his weight off the tiny piece of furniture.

Jillian dug out a teapot and service set and placed them all on a tray, then carried them to the table. At a guess, she'd done this before.

Setting a cup and saucer in front of him, she asked, "One lump or two?"

He couldn't hold back the smile that crossed his face. It was like seeing his sisters again when they were little. Leah was four years younger than him and Sofie was six. He'd had to sit for many tea parties in his day.

"I think I'd like two, please."

Her little fingers pretended to lift two sugar cubes from the sugar bowl and plop them in his cup. Then, she plopped some in her own cup, making an appropriate clinking noise.

"Milk?" She lifted the creamer.

"Oh, just a splash, please."

As Jillian dumped what would have been a few pints of milk into his cup, sound came from the piano. Up to now, he'd only heard Ryan and Ali chatting softly. It had sounded like they were skimming through his music books, finding something for him to play.

One of Beethoven's easier preludes drifted through the air, perfectly played. No way he'd tell Ali that Ryan had practiced quite a few of the songs he knew last night. He'd obviously wanted to impress his new piano teacher.

"That sounds wonderful, Ryan. I like your hand placement, and your posture is good. Of course, I've heard Mrs. Gullo was one of the best piano teachers around, so I'd expect nothing less."

Greg stood and peeked over the half wall. Ryan was beaming with pride. Ali sat next to him on the bench but had her back to the kitchen. Turning around, he picked up one of the small apple strudels sitting on the table.

"Would you like one of these, Miss Jillian?"

The little girl's eyes got big. She sucked her lips in, then nodded. Maybe she wasn't supposed to have one or had already had a few today.

He brought two over on a small paper plate and set it next to his teacup. Jillian positioned a few stuffed animals on the table around the teapot and started chatting to them. She was adorable, and he couldn't believe how well behaved she was while her mom taught lessons. He wondered if she was always this calm. Ryan had been hell on wheels until he was about five. It had taken Greg that long to figure out how to keep him under control.

Or maybe it had taken that long to get over what Wendy had done to him, and in turn, Ryan. Not that he'd ever regret his son. Greg loved him to distraction, but he wished he'd had more common sense back when he was younger and had made better decisions. Maybe Ryan wouldn't have been raised in a father-only household with no mother figure. He'd turned out okay, but Greg still worried. Jillian seemed to be doing okay without her father here. Leah had hinted the guy wasn't around much and had basically walked out on Ali and Jillian. Like Wendy had walked away from him and Ryan. But Jillian's dad hadn't died in a fiery crash.

Greg spent the rest of the lesson chatting with Jillian, checking his phone for emails or texts, and listening in on the conversation between Ali and Ryan. She was so good with her students. So much patience. Guess that's why she'd chosen teaching. She was a natural with kids.

When the lesson was over, Ali peered into the kitchen and laughed. "Have you been sitting in that little chair the whole time? You poor man. Jillian, Captain Storm is too big for your kitchen set."

"No, he not, Mama. See? He have tea with me, and he shared his apple tart."

"That was nice of him. Greg, please feel free to sit in one of the big chairs next time."

Would there be a next time? Ryan didn't look in any way nervous currently.

"My dad has been playing the piano lately, too, Mrs. C. He's pretty good."

Greg chuckled. "I was seeing if I still remember any of the songs I learned when I was younger. It wasn't pretty."

Ryan smirked and crossed his arms over his chest. "Maybe you need piano lessons from Mrs. C., huh, Dad?"

"Nah, pal. You'll have to get real good and then you can give me lessons. Time to go. I'm sure Mrs. C. has things to do that don't include us."

Ali nodded. "Yup. Jillian, sweetie, I need you to get your shoes on. Remember we're going to have lunch with Tito Sebastien today."

Jillian popped out of her seat and ran down the hall. Two seconds later, she was back, sneakers in hand. She held them up to Greg. "You help me put them on, please."

Greg knelt down as Ali scolded, "Jillian, they need to go."

"I don't mind helping, especially after Miss Jillian served me such great coffee today."

He slipped the shoes on the little girl's feet and tied them for her. "Thank you for the fabulous tea party. We should do it again soon."

Jillian nodded and jumped into his arms for a hug. He wrapped his hands around her quickly, then settled back and stood up.

Ali rolled her eyes. "Thank you for humoring her. So, we'll see you next week. This time worked out okay, then?"

"It was great. Appreciate your shifting things around for us." Greg tapped Ryan on the arm, and the boy echoed his thanks.

As they left, he could hear Ali praising Jillian on how good she was during the morning's lessons. Sounded like there might have been some bribery with ice cream involved. Yup, that usually worked.

They got in his truck, and he drove down the street. For some reason, he couldn't wait to come back and have another tea party with sweet Jillian. Or maybe it was her sweeter mom that he really wanted to see.

"Make sure to hold my hand, sweetie, while we cross the street, okay?" Ali knew very few cars came down this road, but when there was a game on the ball field, it could get crowded.

"Okay, Mama. We watch the kids play ball?"

"Yep, we'll watch for a little while. But you need to make sure you stay right near me, understand?"

The first game had already started, and Ali paused to check out the players. Often, she and Jillian would take a walk to the ball field after supper. It gave them something to do and allowed them to get fresh air.

Standing over to the side, she scoured the field looking for any of her students out there. Past or present. She spied a few, then smiled when she saw Ryan Storm on third base. Did that mean his dad was somewhere around? The boy didn't have a mom to bring him, but he'd said his grandparents or aunts sometimes took him places if his dad had to work.

Ali picked Jillian up and used her as a shield while she scanned the bleachers. She didn't want anyone catching her searching for a specific handsome firefighter. Even if she was. *Dios*, she needed to stop. He was a parent of one of her students. She shouldn't be so giddy around him.

That's when she spotted him, on the far left, up a few rows. Mrs. Ferrera was sitting next to him, practically in his lap. Okay, meow. Maybe not in his lap, but they certainly looked cozy. And as she stared at him, she knew why she got giddy. Those dimples when he laughed were adorable. She wouldn't even get into his trim but firm physique. It was his combination of extremely nice guy and fabulous looks. Lethal. Ali wasn't the only one glancing his way.

Ali took an empty seat on the bottom row. This way Jillian could prance around in front of her and not fall off or get hurt. It also gave her a clear view of Greg.

Her mind wandered back to last week when Ryan had begun lessons with her. Greg had been so sweet with Jillian. She'd been paying attention to how Ryan was playing but had kept her ears tuned in to what was going on in the kitchen. Greg spoke to Jillian in a gentle manner but never treated her like a baby. He humored her by participating in the tea party, over and over again. Ali usually ended up having about ten cups of tea whenever she played with her daughter. Good thing it wasn't real liquid or she'd spend all day in the bathroom.

The teams switched on the field, and one of her former students came up to bat. She gave a loud yell to cheer her on. She never rooted for teams; she rooted for players.

When it was Ryan's turn at bat, she gave a whistle and yelled, "You can do it, Ryan. Home run."

Tilting her head, she checked to see if Greg was paying attention. She'd noticed Mrs. Ferrera had been gabbing away next to him this whole time, even when Cheslyn had been on the field. His gaze met hers, and heat rushed across her face and down her neck. Damn, he'd caught her gawking. She threw him a smile and a nod, then started casually talking to Jillian.

Ryan got a hit and ran all the way to second. Greg's deep voice echoed through the air. "That's the way to do it, Ryan. Great job!"

The next two children struck out, then AJ Farmer got to bat. She'd heard him in class talking about how much he loved baseball, and that he usually did baseball camp over the summer. The first two pitches were out of bounds, but the next one was dead center. The bat connected with the ball. It soared past center field and continued on.

"Yes! Home, Ryan, run home. You've got this." Greg's voice echoed again, cheering on his son.

Ali couldn't keep her eyes away from the handsome man bellowing with pride. Mrs. Ferrera clung to his arm, her face openly excited. Were these two dating? Cheslyn's parents were divorced, but she'd met them both. Her father was a nice man and showed how much he cared about his daughter. As she looked around the stands, she found him a few rows behind her. What did he think of his ex and her new boyfriend? If indeed that's what it was. Ryan hadn't said anything about his dad having a girlfriend. So many kids shared all sorts of information their parents probably didn't want public. Drinking, sleepovers, skipping work for a beach day. Adult fun. Ali was never one to gossip about news she'd gotten in class.

"Jillian, did you see? Ryan got all the way home."

The little girl jumped up and down and clapped as she spun in a circle. "Yay for Ryan."

AJ's hit had gotten their team two runs, but the next batter struck out. The teams switched again, and Ryan came out to man third base.

Jillian spotted Ryan on the field and yelled his name. The boy whipped his head in their direction, gave a shy wave, then focused back on the person coming up to bat.

"Thanks, Jillian, for cheering for Ryan." The deep voice behind Ali startled her, and she almost slipped off the metal bench. Greg must have walked to this side along the back bench and come down the stairs next to her.

She hadn't even noticed. See? She wasn't spying on him the whole time.

"Greg, hi. Ryan's doing a great job tonight."

"He is. Thanks." Slipping into the space next to her, he focused on the game for a moment.

Ali tried to see where Mrs. Ferrera was, but a few of the parents in that area had stood and were cheering their kids on.

"I wanted to let you know Ryan really enjoyed his piano lesson last week."

Was that the real reason he came down to see her? Of course, it was. She was merely his kid's teacher, now piano teacher. Ali could hardly compare to Mindi Ferrera with her platinum waves and spiked heels. She wouldn't even mention the skinny jeans or snug top that showcased the woman's attributes.

"I'm glad. I know I don't quite have the experience of Mrs. Gullo, but I enjoy seeing new skills take place."

Greg leaned in closer and grinned. *Madre de Dios*, what was he doing? Sweat beaded on her neck and trickled down her back. "Don't tell anyone, but Ryan said he liked the lessons with you more than with Mrs. Gullo. According to him, you're prettier and you smell better."

Ali laughed and faced toward the game so he wouldn't see her cheeks turning pink. Did Greg have the same opinion as his son?

"I also wanted to ask you about the book report Ryan has due next week."

Ah, so that was the true reason for him to come over to her. Ali explained the assignment, and Greg asked for clarification on a few points. The teacher in her took over and banished the nervousness she often got in his presence.

"Mama, I hungry. I get something to eat?" Jillian dropped her head on Ali's lap.

"You ate dinner only an hour ago, sweetie. But I suppose I could get you something from the snack shack." Ali hated to spend the money, but Jillian often got tired at this time of the day, and when she was tired, she could be a little monster. The last thing she wanted was someone talking about how the schoolteacher couldn't control her own child.

Greg stood and held out his hand. "Can I take Miss Jillian over and treat her? She's been such a good cheerleader today."

Jilly bounced up and down. "Yes, mama. Yes, please."

Once Jilly's hand was in Greg's, he glanced her way. "Why don't you come with us, so you can let me know what's okay and what isn't? There are some things I won't let Ryan have after a certain time of night."

"I appreciate that, but you don't have to pay."

They ambled over to the snack shack where Mrs. Farmer was taking orders.

"AJ's got a great swing there, Edele," Greg said as he gazed at the limited menu on a chalkboard above the window. "Is he teaching the rest of these rug rats how to play?"

Mrs. Farmer peeked at the other three children behind her inside the small building. "The boys, yes. Aeryn still prefers her dolls and tea parties."

"I like tea parties," Jillian called out. "Mama, can Aeryn play tea party with me? I know her from school."

"Probably not right now, sweetie." Ali checked out the bored kids in the shack. "Would they like to play on the playground with Jillian for a short while? We plan to be here for another half hour, and I'd be happy to watch them for you."

Edele's face beamed. "Would you mind? They hate being stuck in here, but I don't want them running around unattended while I work the window."

"Happy to. Come on Nick, Asher, and Aeryn. Let's go." Ali breathed a sigh of relief when she wasn't corrected about the names. All the students in her class had a picture taped to the front of their desk listing who was in their family. Apparently, she'd remembered correctly.

As she pivoted to go, Greg touched her elbow. "How about French Fries for Jillian? Will that do?"

Ali was about to say no, but if it meant he'd spend a few more minutes with her, she'd allow it. "Thank you. I can come—"

"I'll bring them over when they're done." Jillian and the three Farmer children sprinted to the playground next to the ballfield. It was mostly for children to use while their siblings played ball, so it wasn't huge. You could still see most of the playing field.

Aeryn looked a similar age to Jillian and the other boys, Nick and Asher, a few years older. Her daughter was in her glory. She loved playing with other children, and Ali felt like she was lacking by not having siblings for her daughter. Blame that on Jeff.

She could arrange playdates, but between school, piano lessons, shopping, cleaning the house, making dinner, and the million other things that came up when you owned a house, the last thing she wanted was lots more kids in the house when she was exhausted.

With the kids all occupied, running around and climbing on the equipment, Ali allowed herself the luxury of watching the handsome fireman as he chatted with Edele, then stood to the side as the woman waited on another customer.

Movement from the left caught her eye. Mindi Ferrera slinked her way in her heels toward where Greg stood. He hadn't seen her yet, and Ali wanted to see his reaction. The woman touched Greg's bicep and actually preened. Greg's face stiffened, then he smiled and said something to Mindi. Ali wasn't sure what to make of that. And why did she have to make anything of it? Greg Storm was not hers nor would he be. Men like him had their choice of women, and it wouldn't be a mousy schoolteacher who already had a kid and a past bad relationship.

Yes, he had a kid, too, but his wife had died. She didn't desert her child and spouse like Jeff had. Obviously, Ali wasn't good wife material and couldn't hang on to a man and satisfy him the way he needed and wanted. The words Jeff had thrown at her when he'd walked out had stuck in her head like glue. She'd tried to wash them away, but they remained strong and bright.

Edele handed Greg a small box. He said something to Mindi and headed their way. Would Mindi follow? Or would she wait there for Greg once he delivered the food?

"I bought two orders of fries since we've got more kids now," he said as he approached them.

*We've got more kids…*Was he planning to hang around with them? "Thank you. Hey, gang!"

The children scurried over and quickly devoured the food once Greg set it on a bench. He leaned against the chain link fence and positioned himself so he could see her and the ball field.

Mindi eyed them for a minute, then flounced away back to the bleachers.

"I didn't mean to take you way from Mrs. Ferrera. Did you come together?" Whoa. That was ballsy. Where had that courage come from? Or was it stupidity?

Greg twisted his mouth to the side and stared at her strangely. "No, we didn't. We're both on a committee for the rec center, and she had stuff she wanted to share with me."

"Oh, okay. That's great that you're helping out the rec center."

What Ali really meant was, "That's great that you aren't dating Mindi Ferrera." Why it mattered to Ali, she hadn't figured out yet.

CHAPTER NINE

"Good morning, good morning," Ali cried out as her students ducked past her into the classroom. She loved this time, first thing at the beginning of the day where everything was new and everyone got a brand new start.

Several students sidled up for a hug or to tell her some exciting news that had happened since they'd seen her yesterday. Some of last year's students wandered by, chatting for a few minutes or giving her a hug. That was another thing she cherished about this time of day. Revisiting old friends and seeing what they were up to now.

Glancing over her shoulder, she called out reminders. "Notes in the bin. Planners on your desk to be checked. Homework checkers are coming around. Make sure your name is on your homework. I can't give you credit if I don't know who you are. Bathroom now and not when we start work."

Kids bustled about, in and out of the room, fiddling in their cubbies and backpacks, sharpening pencils, finishing up their morning work. Ali peeked at the check-in board to see who hadn't gotten here yet. Bus four kids for sure. That bus was never on time. She noticed a few kids who'd forgotten to turn their name tags over to show they were here.

"Oh, it's too bad Austin and Cheyenne aren't here today. I think they've earned enough stickers for a trip to the candy jar."

Austin and Cheyenne zipped across the room to flip their tags, then grab their behavior chart. Ali checked off their chart and waved toward the candy jar on her desk.

Skimming the hallway again, she noticed Ryan taking his time getting to the room. Normally, she'd wave him on or call out to hustle, but there was something off about him this morning. There was no zip in his step and no mischief lurking behind his blue eyes.

"Hey, Ryan. You okay?"

His eyes misted over, but before a tear fell, he blinked a few times and cleared his throat. "I guess."

Resting her hands on his shoulders, she bent to his level. "What's wrong, sweetie?"

His lips tightened, and his eyes ping ponged around the area. Ali stepped fully into the hall, so the kids in the room weren't part of whatever discussion he wanted to have.

"My dad was working last night, and there was a really bad fire he had to go to."

Her heart pounded so loudly she wondered if anyone could hear. "Is he okay?"

Ryan shrugged. "I don't know. My Aunt Sofie stayed with me last night, but Dad still wasn't back this morning. On the news, it said the fire was still going on."

"You're worried. I understand. If you need to take a few minutes at any time today and go for a walk, maybe get a hug from your Auntie Leah downstairs, let me know."

Ryan sniffed and walked into her arms. Patting his head, she held him tight and allowed him a few minutes to get himself together. When the bell rang, he startled and looked up.

"Thanks, Mrs. C. I'm so glad you're my teacher."

Ali smiled at him and ruffled his hair. "I'm glad you're in my class, too. Now get your stuff out of your bag. Were you able to do your homework last night?"

She'd cut him some slack if he'd been too worried about his dad to do it.

"Auntie Sofie made me do it. She said it would get my mind off the fire."

Ali walked into the class and started her morning routine. She kept her eye on Ryan as she went about with lessons, making sure he was okay. Her own stomach did a little dance of its own with worry. Hopefully, Greg would be fine and come home soon without any problem.

After taking the kids to music, Ali returned to her desk and searched the Internet for any news of the fire. Reports of all the fires over the past few months came up, but she couldn't find anything on this newest one. Clicking on a few other links, she finally found a local news report that showed video of the flames erupting from the building. The sight of them made her shiver, imagining anyone inside with those.

Firefighters trotted in and out, dragging hoses and other tools like those Greg had shown them at the fire station. Ali pressed her face as close as she could to the screen to see if she could get a glimpse of Ryan's dad. Impossible to tell with the turnout gear on.

When the students got back from their music class, they settled in for a quick snack and Ali prepped the math lesson. Ryan was quieter than usual and didn't have his hand up at all when she asked questions.

Throughout the rest of the morning, Ali passed by Ryan's chair often and rested her hand on his shoulder, squeezing to let him know she was there if he needed her. His sweet smile let her know he appreciated it.

Once the kids went down to the lunchroom, Ali grabbed her phone before heading to the staff room. She wanted to see if there was any more information on the fire.

She stuck her leftovers in the microwave for several minutes, then swiped her hand across her screen. There was a text message from not that long ago.

—*Hey, just checking in. My sister said Ryan was nervous because I wasn't home this morning. Can you let him know I'm okay and back at the station?*—

After removing her dish from the microwave and placing it on the table, she sat and sent a text back.

—*Glad to hear it. He wasn't quite himself, but he confided in me why, so I gave him a little extra TLC. I'll let him know. He'll be relieved.*—

She placed her phone face side down on the table and began to eat. Steph gave her a side eye and grinned.

"Texting at lunch, Ali? Someone special we should know about?"

She needed to keep this casual, so Steph didn't blow it out of proportion. "Ryan's dad was at that bad fire last night and this morning. He wanted me to let Ryan know he's okay."

"That's sweet," Phyllis said in between bites of salad. "It's refreshing to see a parent care about their kid's feelings."

Jamilla cocked her head. "What's the story behind that comment?"

Ali didn't listen as Phyllis launched into a detailed account of one of her students and the parent. She was more concerned with letting Ryan know his dad was fine. Taking another few bites, she hurried to finish her meal.

As she was taking the last bite, her phone vibrated again. She never had the ring tone on while in school. If someone needed to tell her there was something wrong with Jillian, they knew to contact the school office.

—*I'm sorry to bother you again, but I was wondering if I could stop in and see Ryan and give him a hug? I want him to see that I'm okay. Would that be all right?*—

Ali's fingers flew on the screen. —*Of course. He's at lunch and recess now. He'll be back in the room in twenty minutes.*—

—*Thanks for the schedule. I need to take a shower first. I smell like a campfire. See you in a few.*—

Steph glanced over and smirked. "Is that still the hunky dad checking in? An awful lot of chatting just to say he's okay."

"He wants to stop in to see his son. I told him that was fine."

"Because he is so fine." Steph laughed. The other teachers moaned at the bad joke.

After consuming the last few bites of her meal, she wandered through the playground to see if she could find Ryan. Easy enough. He sat on the bench by the monkey bars, staring at the trees behind the school.

"Hey, Ryan." Ali lowered herself to the bench and patted his knee. "I got a text from your dad. He's okay. Your Aunt Sofie told him you were worried this morning."

Ryan's face brightened, and tears filled his eyes again. This time they were happy ones. He did a nosedive into her, hugging her tight. Ali wrapped her arms around him and stroked her hand down his back. Like any mother would do. But this poor boy had never had a mom to console him. It broke her heart.

A few sniffs later, Ali handed him one of the tissues she always carried in her pocket. Hazards of being an elementary school teacher. Ryan eased back and wiped his face.

"I know it's silly that I was so worried. My dad's been a firefighter my whole life."

"Is there a reason this time made you more anxious?"

Ryan shrugged and stared across the playground at the kids zooming by. "Ricky and I watched this movie last week. It had a huge fire in it and a couple of the firefighters got killed. I guess I was thinking about the movie last night when my dad didn't come home."

"I'm sure it got worse when he wasn't there this morning either."

Ryan nodded and heaved a big sigh as Ali glanced at her watch.

"Your dad said he planned to stop by a little later to see you. He knows how worried you were. Recess will be over in about seven minutes. Why don't you go enjoy the last few minutes before you have to come in?"

His head bobbed up and down, his eyes free of the anxiety she'd seen all morning. "Thanks, Mrs. C."

After he dashed around the yard, Ali went back inside and started prepping for the afternoon lessons. Okay, so she combed her hair and added a touch of lipstick to her mouth also, but that was only because the wind had blown her hair all over the place when she'd gone outside.

The stomping of feet echoed through the hallway warning Ali her class was on their way in. She gave them five minutes to use the bathroom, get a drink, splash some water on their sweaty faces, and get settled in their seats. The first twenty minutes after recess she always reserved for silent independent reading.

Today, Jamilla was at the bathroom doors limiting the kids to a five-second drink. Otherwise, they'd spend all day at the bubbler. Ali waved the kids in the hallway into their classes, attempting to get them into afternoon work.

Most of her students had their heads buried in a book, some in their chairs, others draped over beanbag chairs or sitting on the floor, leaning against the wall. Ryan sat in his desk which faced the doorway. He might have been relieved when she'd told him about his dad, but there was still a small part of him that worried.

Ali puttered around, putting her supplies on the back table, ready for her first reading group. A shuffle at the door had her peering up. Greg stood in the doorway, his hair slightly damp, a serious expression on his face. Ryan glanced up and darted out of his seat, then froze and looked at her. She nodded, and he finished the dash right into his father's arms.

Ali's heart almost melted right there. Greg obviously loved his son immensely. The fact Jeff rarely wanted to see Jillian always hurt and made the Storm's bond so much stronger in her eyes.

Greg pulled Ryan into the hallway, and Ali didn't bother checking to make sure they weren't going far. The corner of Greg's strong shoulders could be seen, letting her know he was crouched down talking to his son. Ryan's smaller hand crept on his father's arm holding tight.

A minute later, Ryan reappeared and trudged to his seat. Greg stood in the doorway and lifted his chin when she glanced at him. He wanted to talk to her? Okay, get the jitters out and gone before you reach him.

"Everything okay?" she asked quietly as she approached the door.

"Yeah, I wanted to thank you for letting him know and allowing me to interrupt your class to see him. I'm not sure why this time was any different from any other day I go to work. I know typically we deal in smaller kitchen fires or car accidents, but—"

Ali placed her hand on Greg's arm and steered him into the hall. She had to pull her focus away from the hair on his arm and onto what she was saying.

"I talked to him a little bit earlier. He told me he and a

friend had seen a movie recently where some firefighters were caught in a huge blaze and died. I'm sure that didn't help. And these fires that have happened nearby recently seem to be a bit more dangerous."

Greg took hold of her elbow and nodded. "Thanks for letting me know. And again for allowing me to come in and see him."

"You're a good father, Greg Storm. That's something to be proud of. Not all of them are."

He squeezed her elbow and gave her a smile. "Thanks. See you later."

She'd love to see him later. For many reasons. And none of them had to do with his being a good father.

GREG OPENED the menu and pushed it toward Ryan. "What do you want on your pizza, champ?"

Ryan ran his finger down the list of toppings, his eyes growing bigger with each one he stopped at. They'd had a big math test this week covering much of what they'd learned all year. Math had never been Ryan's best subject, but he'd studied hard and pulled off a solid A on the test. Greg figured that deserved a treat. It was Friday night, and Bruscetti's was packed. They'd been fortunate to get here as the Farmers were leaving, and Jay and Edele had waved them over to offer the table.

"How many toppings can we get?" Ryan lifted his gaze, eyes hopeful. Then, his head shifted and leaned across the table. "Dad, Mrs. C. and Jillian just walked in."

Greg peeked over his shoulder to where Ali stood with her hand in her daughter's. Her head swiveled back and forth as she searched for somewhere to sit. With the crowd tonight, she might not find a place for a while.

"Dad," Ryan whispered, not really being quiet. "They won't be able to get a table. It's too busy here. Can they sit with us? Please?"

He'd had the same thought but hadn't wanted to infringe on his son's special treat. You'd think after being in her class all year and now taking piano lessons from her each weekend, Ryan would have had enough of Ali Cabrera. Apparently not, and he could see why.

"You can certainly go ask her." He'd put the ball in Ryan's court. He didn't want her to feel uncomfortable if he asked.

Ryan skipped over to her, and her face brightened when she saw him. Jillian immediately took Ryan's hand and jumped up and down. Ali's eyebrows knit together as she gazed at Ryan and then toward their table. Greg lifted his hand to wave and nod, so she'd know it wasn't just Ryan inviting them. After searching the restaurant once again, she nodded and followed Ryan back to the seat.

It wasn't until they got back and Ryan slid into his seat, Jillian climbing up right behind him, that Greg noticed the problem. Not that it was a huge problem to have this attractive, nice woman next to him, but for some reason he always felt a little unnerved around her. In a good way, but still he was super aware of her presence.

"Hey, there. Come on in." Greg scooted over to make room, and Ali settled on the bench.

"Thank you so much for inviting us to sit with you. The place is hopping tonight. Have you eaten yet?"

Ryan tapped on his menu. "We were just deciding on toppings." He bent over Jillian. "What do you like on your pizza?"

"Cheese." Jillian smiled back at Ryan.

"I'm afraid Jillian is still a purist when it comes to pizza. Personally, I like a few toppings, but typically we get at least half of the pizza plain."

Greg tapped the menu. "Why don't we get a few pizzas? Ryan is getting to the point where he'll eat half of it in one sitting. Did you decide what you wanted, Ry?"

"I like bacon and pepperoni."

Jillian stood up on the bench and said, "I like bacon. Mama, we get that on pizza?"

"We can, sweetie. But if we order it, you need to eat it. Will you?"

Jillian bobbed her head. "I like bacon."

Greg slid the menu over to Ali. "What does your dream pizza have on it? Please, don't say pineapple, because we'd have to kick you out of the booth."

Her eyes glowed as she peered down at the menu. "I do love veggies on my pizza. Onions, peppers, mushrooms. Or even one of those. But Jillian would never eat a pizza with anything like that on it."

Greg closed up the menu. "I happen to like mushrooms and peppers myself but have the same problem, because—" He pointed to his son who sat with his tongue hanging out of his mouth and his eyes crossed.

"So, Dad, you and Mrs. C. can share a pizza with all that gross stuff on it, and me and Jillian can have a bacon pizza."

Greg glanced at Ali. "Does that work for you?"

Ali nodded as their waitress came over.

"I'm so sorry for the wait. It's a madhouse in here tonight."

"Don't worry about it, Sabrina. We're in no rush." Ali peeked at him to make sure he agreed.

"What can I get you?"

Ryan sat up straighter. He liked to order when they went anywhere. It made him feel grown up. "Jillian and I will have a bacon pizza. And I'd like a lemonade to drink, please."

Jillian bounced on her knees. "Mama, I have lemonade, please?"

Ali sighed and responded, "Sure, sweetie. I guess it's a special night all around. I'd like an iced tea, please. And we'll also have a pizza with mushrooms and peppers." Again, she gave him a look like she was checking that it was all right.

Greg usually ordered a beer when he was here, but he felt a little strange doing it in front of Ryan's teacher. "Iced tea is fine for me, too. Thanks."

Sabrina left and returned shortly with a few kid placemats and crayons. She eyed Ryan. "Did you want one of these?"

Ryan chirped, "Sure, Jillian and I can do them together."

As the kids chatted and Ryan helped Jillian color, Greg adjusted so he faced Ali.

"Are you and Jillian celebrating something special tonight, too? We're here because of Ryan's fantastic math test."

A proud smile crossed her face. "I was so pleased to see how he did. He's worked hard this year to get those multiplication and division facts memorized. And the fractions are especially difficult once we begin mixed fractions."

Ryan pretended he wasn't listening, but he almost glowed when she mentioned how well he did and then grimaced at the talk of mixed fractions.

"I needed to brush up on mixed fractions myself when he was learning about them. I'm not sure what I'll do when he gets much beyond that."

"He can always come back and ask me for help. I was a wiz at math in school."

Greg played with the napkin. "I did okay but really loved science. I wanted to be a doctor."

Whatever Ali was about to say was paused when the waitress came back with their drinks. The kids took a sip, then Ryan asked if he could take Jillian to play some of the video games.

"I'm not sure how good she'll be. We don't have anything like that at home, and she's only three."

"I watch Ryan play, Mama. Okay?"

Laughing, Ali said, "Sure, sweetie. Be good."

Sabrina returned to the table and waved toward Ali. "I forgot to ask. Did you want those gift cards again this year for your students? The owner will give you the fifteen percent discount if you buy at least ten."

"Yes, Sabrina, thank you. I've been meaning to come in to arrange that. I'll take those tonight if it's not too much trouble to make them up."

"Sure thing."

"Gift cards for the students? That's nice."

Her face flushed, and she glanced down at the table. "I usually have a few students each year who come from families that don't have lots of extra income. I have a raffle at the end of the year and pick names from a hat to give the gift cards to. It's totally fixed, and the kids who need them get them. When the school has the book fair or other giveaways, the school will have winners for certain prizes. It's always the children who need a little help. It's our way of doing this without the kids or parents thinking they're getting charity."

"Wow, I had no idea the school did that. Makes me proud to live in this town. But it sounded like you're the one paying for these gift cards. You also mentioned a candy jar, and Ryan goes on and on about the prize box he gets to choose from every now and then."

"The prize box has really great things," Ryan said, from beside the table. Greg hadn't noticed the kids return, but obviously his son had noticed Sabrina delivering their food. It was set on the table along with plates and extra napkins.

Ali pulled a cheesy bacon-filled slice onto a plate for Jillian and set it aside. "It's still a little hot. You need to wait."

Greg waited until Ali took a piece from their pizza before selecting his own. "Candy jar. Prize box."

"And she has a snack closet, too. With really great snacks if a kid forgets his."

Greg pulled his lips to the side. "Has Ryan ever forgotten his snack?"

Ali narrowed her eyes and stared at his son. "Maybe a time or two."

Ryan groaned. "Only when Nonna makes my snacks. The ones Mrs. C. has are so much better."

"Hmm. Looks like I may need to refill your snack closet. Does the school pay for any of this stuff? I've heard Leah complain about how much money she spends on supplies for her classroom."

The laughter from Ali was like music. "Hardly. Teachers spend tons of their own money for school. I have to budget carefully if Jeff hasn't sent—" Her eyes opened wide as she pressed her lips together.

Greg could fill in the blanks. Her ex had a habit of not paying child support. What kind of scumbag didn't provide for his child?

"I guess that's one of the reasons I give piano lessons on the side." She picked up her pizza and took a large bite. Attempting not to spill any more secrets perhaps?

Greg was even more glad now that he'd been sending Ryan to piano lessons with her. His parents paid for it, so it didn't hurt his budget, but still he liked providing her with a little more financial stability.

They ate in silence for a bit with the occasional question from Jillian to Ryan. The little girl sure did seem to have a monster crush on the boy. Almost as big as Ryan had on his teacher. When the kids finished eating, Ryan asked if he could take Jillian to the video games again. He was so good with her, allowing her to hold the stick with him and move it.

"I wanted to thank you again for helping Ryan keep it together last week when I was at that fire overnight. Generally, small town firefighting isn't too dangerous. Car accidents, kitchen fires, and the occasional trash can fire. These bigger ones recently have gotten out of hand, and Ryan is old enough now to understand the dangers. I'm sure that movie he saw didn't help."

Ali wiped her hands on a napkin, then took a sip of her drink. "Do they have any idea what's causing them? I heard they weren't ruling out arson."

"I can't comment on an ongoing case, but let's say things have gone missing in some of the homes or businesses that have been affected. Luckily, no one has been inside when the fires started. But the speed at which they combust indicates an accelerant is being used. We haven't been able to figure out what yet."

"I hope they figure it out soon and stop it. I have to say it's a scary thing."

Greg had to agree. But as he watched Ali's face go through so many emotions, he knew he was beginning to have serious thoughts about her. And after what had happened with Wendy, that scared him, too.

CHAPTER TEN

*G*reg climbed the front steps of his Victorian house, and the smells coming from inside had his stomach doing a happy dance. They'd been busy at work, and he'd only managed a few bites of his sandwich at lunch. Chatter and dishes clinking could be heard as he walked through the door.

"Honey, I'm home," he called out as he zeroed in on the dining room. Their puppy, Guinness, whined from behind the baby gate holding him in the kitchen.

Sofie shot him a typical little sister look, but his mother popped up from her chair and rushed to give him a hug.

"Gregory, you're here on time. That's so nice. I hate having Sunday dinner at your house when you're not here."

"Mom, this house was yours for over thirty years. I hope you don't ever feel like it's not still yours. Luckily, our last run was a few hours ago, so I got out right at three."

Nick Storm cleared his throat and indicated the seat at the other end of the table. "We're about ready for a blessing if you want to sit."

His dad was serious about his food, especially a Sunday

dinner that his mom made. They still attempted dinner every week if they could, and had it here since his house was the largest and most familiar to everyone. When he was working, someone would be here anyway to watch Ryan. They might as well use it for dinner.

His dad said a prayer of thanks for the meal and the family, and they passed the food around. His mom, Luciana —Luci to everyone who knew her—was from a very Italian family, and she'd been born with cooking in her blood. All of their stomachs were forever thankful.

"Hey, Ryan," Greg said after getting a few bites in. "Did you tell everyone about that fabulous math test grade you got?"

Ryan bobbed his head. "Yup, but I didn't tell them that we got to go get pizza and that Mrs. C. and Jillian sat with us."

Leah pursed her lips. "You went out with Ali Cabrera and her daughter for pizza?"

Greg sighed. "No, we were at Bruschetti's, and the place was mobbed. We managed to get a table, but they walked in shortly after us, and Ryan invited them to sit with us because there weren't any tables left."

"Jillian and I shared a bacon pizza, and Daddy and Mrs. C. had yucky mushrooms and peppers on theirs."

"You and Mrs. C. shared a pizza?" Sofie wiggled her eyebrows up and down.

"She paid for one of the pizzas and I paid for one. Just so happens she and I like the same things on ours, so we split one. The kids split the other one. It wasn't a date. We only sat together because the place was packed." Did his sister not get that from the first time he'd said it?

His mom reached for a roll and buttered it. "I'd ask you, Ryan, if you were going to miss your teacher when school ends in a few weeks, but she's your new piano teacher now, isn't she? How's that going?" She peeked at Greg, and he simply smiled.

As Ryan rattled on about Ali and her piano skills, he focused on his meal. His family didn't need to know he was absorbing every word. The other night with Ali and Jillian had been fun. Not that he didn't have fun with just him and Ryan, but it was nice for Ryan to have someone younger to hang with. Adult conversation with an intelligent, interesting woman hadn't been unpleasant either. Once they'd started chatting, that off balance feeling he'd always had started to fade, and he'd gotten more comfortable with her.

"And on Field Day lots of the parents volunteer to run the games and get to be with us."

Greg tuned back into what Ryan was talking about. He'd somehow segued from piano lessons to the coming fun day, where the whole school had races and games.

Ryan leaned into the table, his eyes wide. "But only one parent gets to come around to all the stations with us. Guess who was chosen for my class." He waited like no one would get it right.

Leave it to his mother to humor Ryan. "Hmm. Now, who is in your class? You've got that boy, AJ Farmer, right? His mother would be a good one to have help out. Or maybe Austin's dad. I know you said he's gone on field trips with you this year."

"It's Dad. He got chosen to be the parent helper with us that day, and he can do it because he has the day off. Right, Dad?"

"I'm sure Mrs. C. simply put the name of parents who were interested in a hat and pulled one out randomly."

His sisters couldn't hide their smirks. He wondered who'd make the first comment.

Sofie snorted. "Sounds like Mrs. C. may be showing a little favoritism in choosing parent volunteers. You, big brother, appear to be at the top of her list. What did you have to do to get chosen for this job?"

"It must be the pizza that tipped him over the top. Who doesn't love a man who buys you pizza? Especially mushroom pizza." Leah's grin was bigger than Sofie's.

"It had peppers on it, too." Greg lowered his head into his hands realizing what a stupid response that was. When Sofie and Leah double-teamed him, it often threw him off balance. Kind of how Ali made him feel at times. Which got him thinking…Had she chosen him purposely or had it been random? Doubtful she'd ever tell him.

"I'm done eating, Dad. Can I be excused? Guinness needs to go out and run around."

Greg pointed at his son's plate. "Why don't you give him those scraps of roast on your plate before he goes out?" As Ryan trotted over to the gate, Greg revised, "But not from your plate. Put it in his dog dish, please."

Ryan did as asked, and soon dog and boy had darted out the kitchen door to play in the yard. When he pivoted back to the table, his sisters and parents were grinning at him.

"What?"

His dad closed one eye and cocked his head. "Do you have a thing for Ryan's teacher?"

"Oh, he can't have a thing for her yet," Sofie said. "She's still Ryan's teacher, and big brother would never be unprofessional like that. Right, Greg?"

"But if you like her, dear, you should ask her out. Maybe after school ends." His mother had been harping on him for years to find someone new. Of course, she thought he was still grieving over Wendy.

"Will it be a problem if she's still Ryan's piano teacher?" his dad asked.

Leah straightened in her chair. "There is no written rule that teachers can't date a parent of one of their students.

There is a conflict of interest if you're giving grades to the child of someone you're romantically involved with, but once Ryan isn't in Ali's class anymore, there's no conflict. Piano lessons aren't through the school, and there are no grades."

Greg drummed his fingers on the table. "Did anyone ever think that Mrs. Cabrera might not want to go out with me? I mean...if I did happen to ask her."

"Look at you, sweetheart," his mother said. "You're handsome, intelligent, nice, successful, own your own home, and are a wonderful father. What woman in her right mind wouldn't want to go out with you?"

"Don't forget," Leah added with a grin. "He's got this incredible family."

Greg burst out laughing. "That's a reason for her to run for the hills."

He didn't mean it. His family was incredible in every way imaginable. They'd stood by his side when he broke the news he'd been stupid and gotten Wendy pregnant. They'd helped him out after Ryan was born and Wendy was too "sick" to take care of him. And when she'd been killed in the car accident, they'd all rallied—his cousins included—to take turns being with the new baby and helping him cope. He'd never had the heart to tell them he wasn't grieving for the loss of his wife. He was grieving that his beautiful son would grow up without a mother. One who hadn't even wanted him. And that was something he would never tell his son. Greg had enough love for two parents.

Excited barking sounded through the open window, and Greg peered out. Guinness was running around with his sister, Honeysuckle, who lived next door with Alex and Gina.

"You head on out and visit with your cousin for a bit. I'll get the dishes." Mom started clearing the table.

"No, mom, you cooked. I can clean up."

"Actually, I made Sofie and Leah cook. I just supervised."

Greg made a face at his sisters. "Is that why it tasted funny? I didn't want to say anything."

"Haha," Leah deadpanned and smacked him in the arm. "You weren't complaining when you were shoveling in your third helping."

"I didn't want to hurt Mom's feelings." He grabbed his stomach, hunched over, and slapped his hand over his mouth.

Sofie rolled her eyes and shook her head. "You haven't learned any new jokes, have you? You keep using the same old stupid ones again and again."

His mother laughed. "All of you, outside. I feel like you're little children again."

Greg pulled Sofie into a head lock and trudged out the door. Leah jumped on his back like she'd done when they were kids. Yeah, he loved his family.

Alex and Gina didn't even blink when they descended the stairs in the strange formation. Greg finally released his youngest sister, who followed up with a swat in the butt.

"Was Honeysuckle missing her brother?" Greg asked, kneeling down to scratch the little tan spaniel.

"I don't know why," Alex said. "They see each other every day."

Gina flopped to the grass, and both dogs frolicked around her. "I take them for walks every morning together. But they're just like the rest of the Storms...they love each other."

Greg chuckled as Gina fell to her back and allowed the dogs to lick every inch of her. Alex gazed at her with such love and longing on his face. These two were deliriously happy together, and Greg couldn't be more thrilled.

"So, Greg's got a secret crush on Ryan's teacher," Sofie whispered, like she was telling a secret. Luckily, Ryan had run off to find his baseball mitt and wasn't here to witness his father's humiliation.

"I don't have a crush." Well, he technically did, but it was stupid for a man his age to be smitten by a woman.

"Sure, you don't." Leah said. "Are you going to ask her out once school is over?"

Greg searched skyward for answers. "I'll think about it."

He hadn't planned to get married again after his ordeal with Wendy, but seeing Alex and Gina so happy together, not to mention his cousins, Nathaniel, Erik, and Sara, it got him thinking. Add in the great time he'd had with her at Bruscetti's, and all the other times he'd been with her, maybe he had to give it a second thought.

ALI GLANCED AROUND THE CLASSROOM, taking note of who'd gotten a pirate bandanna and who hadn't yet.

She held up the black, red, and white fabric with the skull and crossbones on it and called out, "Who still needs one?"

The school had planned a pirate theme for Field Day this year, and Ali wanted her class to be in the spirit. She'd bought the bandannas and cheap eye patches for the kids to wear. The patches would need to come off when the more extreme games began.

A few students scrambled over to her, reaching for the fabric. Several more appeared by her side asking for help tying them around their head or neck. Austin wanted his tied around his thigh, and AJ decided to tie his around his upper arm.

Ali had wrapped hers around her ponytail, knowing she'd be too hot with it on her head. Today was in the eighties with clear, blue skies. Perfect for time outside, but after running around all day in it, she knew she'd be wishing for a few clouds to drift by and cover the sun.

The sea of red shirts swarmed like ladybugs throughout the room. Each of the fourth-grade classes had chosen a t-shirt color to wear for class spirit but also so the teachers could easily identify their students. Her class had chosen red.

Footsteps sounded in the doorway, and Ryan Storm walked in followed by his father. Both wore red shirts sporting the Storm Electric logo, a lightning bolt striking a letter S and making it glow. Many of the children had logos or sayings on their shirts. Ali had worn a plain, red, fitted t-shirt that flattered her figure. Not for any particular reason.

"Just in time." Ali held out two bandannas toward the Storms, then picked up an eye patch and gazed at Greg. "Did you want one of these, too?"

The dimples appeared again, sending flutters through her. Lord, the man was electrifying. Like his shirt stated.

"I'll hold off for now. I hear these games can get challenging. I might need one later if it gets too rough."

"Dad, where are you going to put your pirate bandanna? I want mine around my neck."

Greg examined the room, his lips twisting to the side.

"Don't feel you need to wear it if you don't want to. The kids love having something to show their spirit."

"Well, if I'm part of this class today, then I need to have class spirit, too. I might follow my son's lead and tie it around my neck. I can't very well tie it around a ponytail."

Ali pivoted so he couldn't see the color rising on her face. "Boys and girls. Eyes on me." All of them immediately stopped what they were doing and swiveled to listen. It had only taken six months to get them to where they'd all do this. Now, in about a week, they'd be moving up to fifth grade and she'd get a whole new class to break in.

"Thank you. Please make sure all your lunches are in the

cooler. All water bottles should be filled and have your name on it. There'll be hundreds of children lugging water bottles over the fields today. You are responsible for remembering to bring it from station to station. Right now, I want everyone to use the bathroom, and then we'll head outside."

There was a rush to put the forgotten lunch bags in the cooler. Ali moved aside the large gallons of frozen water she'd placed in there earlier. It would keep the lunches cold and by this afternoon would be melted enough to refill the kids' water bottles.

"Did you bring a lunch?" She addressed Greg as children scurried past to get to the bathroom. Luckily, it was next to the classroom, so the students didn't need to go far. Unfortunately, the other fourth graders were also doing the same thing. Steph's parent volunteer was manning the hallway outside the bathroom, so Ali had a few minutes to make sure everything was all set.

Greg held up a plastic grocery bag. "My lunch is in with Ryan's. What exactly do you need me to do?"

Ali bit her lip. "Um, yeah, I was hoping you could carry the cooler down to the field when we go. And maybe refill the gallon jug if the kids need more water. That sun can get hot when you're standing in it all day."

"Sure, I can lug the cooler around. Is that why you chose me for today? I'm the hired muscle?" He flexed one arm and grinned. Ali nearly swooned.

She laughed but didn't give up her secret that, yes, she had cheated and picked Greg because she'd wanted him along for the day.

"Well, I couldn't see Mrs. Ferrera doing it in her three-inch heels."

Greg's loud chuckle made Ali's insides quiver. What a great laugh.

Glancing at her watch, she waved to the kids still milling

around the hall and shooed them into the room. When they were sitting on the carpet with their attention on her, she began her little reminder speech.

"This is going to be a fun day, but there are things we need to remember. First, you must stay with your class. No wandering off. If you need to use the bathroom, you have to clear it with Captain Storm or myself. The doors to the cafeteria will be open, so you can use the bathrooms there. You go and come right back. No fooling around. There will be adults all around, and we'll know if you do."

She pointed her first two fingers at her eyes, then flipped them to point at the students in an "I see you" gesture. They all laughed, but they'd gotten the message.

"Okay, the next thing is the most important one. It's good to win and challenge yourself, but what does Mrs. Flanners always say in Gym class?"

The class exploded. "If you had fun, you won!"

"Right, so let's go have fun."

The students lined up amid a few reminders to get their water bottles and to stop fooling around. Ali led them down the stairs and outside to the large field behind the school. Many of the classes were already there.

"You can put the cooler right over there against the wall," Ali directed Greg. Lordy, his arm and back muscles flexed fantastically when he hefted the blue plastic container.

The speakers screeched as Reggie turned the microphone on, then announced, "Good morning and welcome to our Pirate Field Day. Aaarrggghh!"

The students all responded, "Aaarrgghh," and lifted one fist into the air. Ali paced up and down the line, making sure her students had enough room for the opening dance. First, the national anthem played, and everyone placed their hand on their heart and sang along. Then, the music quickly changed, and a modern beat echoed through the speakers.

Ali scooted to the end of the row and got into position. Typically, she had a lot of fun with the dance the gym teacher taught the kids each year. This year, she had Greg Storm watching her. Or well, watching the students. Ryan was at least ten students away from her, so maybe he'd concentrate on his son.

The dance moves were so simple even the youngest or least coordinated among them could still participate. But there was a hip swish here and there, a few shoulder shakes, and lots of jumping. Ignoring the handsome man a few yards away, Ali got into it and encouraged her students to have fun.

By the end, she was out of breath and laughing. Some of the students closest to her wrapped her in a hug. Field Day was always so bittersweet, because they'd gotten to the point where the class really meshed together. But they only had a week or so left of it and then they'd be gone.

Hugging them back, she enjoyed the last contact she might have with them. She pulled the Field Day map out of the back pocket of her capris and checked where they started.

"We're at the relay races first," she announced and led the way. Steph's class met them there as they were partnered up together for the day.

Mr. Lebowitz, Austin's dad, and the art teacher, Mrs. Dumond, were in charge of this station. They began an explanation of the event and divided the students into four teams.

"So mostly it's keeping an eye on them while they play the games and rounding them up to go to the next?" Greg came up behind her, and she shivered at his breath on her cheek.

"For the most part, though often the adults get involved, too."

Sure enough, after the first two races, Mrs. Dumond waved Ali, Steph, Greg, and Katrina, Steph's parent helper, over to the line. She placed them each with a group. Greg got put on the team that kept coming in last.

Her team had won one of the races but came in third for the other one. "Okay, team, let's do this. We are gonna blast them out of the sky. Yes, yes, yes!" She got the kids all revved up and ready to go.

As the race began and the front of the line took off, she peeked over at Greg who was cheering his team on. Suddenly, he glanced over and made some sort of sign like "it's on" and grinned. He wanted a race, did he?

Turning back to her team, she yelled and encouraged those who were currently running. When it got close to her turn, she checked out Greg's team. Their second to last teammate had only just started her run. Greg still had them calling out with support.

Jack darted toward her, holding out his hand, ready to tag her. Ali bounced on her sneakers and got ready.

Tag. She took off running, noticing Steph was moving slow in her fancy rhinestone decorated flip flop sandals. As Ali rounded the cone marker, Greg finally got tagged. He zipped toward her, and she stumbled a bit at his intense gaze. Her students cheered her on, and she picked up the pace. Just as she was crossing the line to win, Greg appeared next to her and crossed at the same time.

Both teams converged on them, jumping up and down, yelling about winning. Steph and Katrina had only rounded the marker.

Mrs. Dumond came over and held up Ali and Greg's hands. "Looks like we've got a tie. Congratulations."

As the kids ran to grab a sip from their water bottles, Greg sidled up beside her. "She can run and she can dance and play piano and teach kids. What can't she do?"

"Oh, lots of things." Like keep a man's interest. According to her ex at least. And her sister.

Mrs. Dumond called out to the children and gathered them close. "The next race is the three-legged race. Each of you needs a partner, and you'll have your legs tied together. Remember we practiced in gym class."

Ali went around pairing kids up. Lots of groans drifted by, but she gave them her patented teacher look. The day wouldn't be fun for all if the kids who excelled physically paired up with each other. She'd already explained it to them earlier this week.

She and Greg went around tying the fabric around the team's legs.

"Mrs. C. should have to race, too," Ryan said.

"That's a great idea, Ryan. She and your dad did a fabulous job running. Shall we see how they do in this?" Mrs. Dumond held her hands out to the side.

The kids all laughed, and Ali knew her face had to be bright red. Holding up one of the extra ties, she cocked her head at Greg. "Are you ready to be tied to me?"

"Happy to be tied to you." He winked, then took the fabric and handed it to his son. "Can you do the honors, Ryan?"

The grin on Ryan's face showed his delight, and the rest of the class joined in the fun. They tried to share tips on how to keep from falling.

"You have to make sure to walk at the same pace."

"Count *one, two, one, two*, as you walk and put your tied feet out on the two."

"You should put your arms around each other's shoulder."

Mrs. Dumond blew her whistle and told everyone to line up. "You race down to the cone marker, go around it, then come back. Everybody ready?"

Greg's arm wrapped around her shoulder, but Ali wasn't tall enough for her arm to go over his. She had to slide it behind his waist. Oh, wow. It shouldn't feel this good. He shouldn't feel this good.

It was awkward getting to the starting line, and Ali said, "Sorry you got *roped* into this."

Greg chuckled. "I had nothing else *tying* me down today."

They both groaned at the bad puns and got in place. Mrs. Dumond settled everyone down, then blew her whistle. They were off.

Ali clung to Greg's waist as they attempted to run in sync with the other. But he was a good eight inches taller than her, and her legs didn't move as fast.

"I should pick you up and carry you. We might get there faster," he teased as they stumbled yet again.

"Not over your shoulder again."

The mischievous look in his eyes warmed her more than the sun overhead. They finally reached the cone and attempted to go around it. She tried to go left as he tried to go right. When they finally got going in the same direction, her foot snagged a hole in the ground, and she went down. Greg tried to adjust his speed and other foot, but her weight had pulled him off balance and they both went down. As they fell, he tugged her tighter and rolled. They landed with her sprawled all over every muscular inch of him.

CHAPTER ELEVEN

*G*reg wrapped his arms around Ali, trying to take the brunt of the fall. In any other instance, he might enjoy her touching him from head to toe, but they had over fifty kids and several adults nearby. Hopefully, they were all focused on the kids still running.

"Get up. Keep running, Mrs. C.," Bonnie encouraged as she and Cheyenne rounded their marker.

Grabbing her nicely curved hips, he assisted her to her feet and remembered his comment about being happy to be tied to her. What the heck had he been thinking?

"Are you okay?" He ducked his head to check.

"Only my pride hurt. Let's get moving. We can't let the kids think we've given up."

He placed his arm around her shoulder again and started counting. "One, two, one, two."

Ali let out a huge laugh and joined in. They made it back to the beginning just as the last pair of students did. The kids from her class who had already untied their bindings raced over and consumed both of them in a group hug.

"You did it, Mrs. C., you did it!"

"Great job, Captain Storm."

They were so enthusiastic, even with them basically coming in last. Obviously, this woman had taught her class how to be gracious winners and losers.

He collapsed onto the grass, which made Ali stumble and plop down next to him. As he untied their legs, he studied her face. Her cheeks were pink and flushed, but her eyes glowed with excitement.

When the fabric was off, he stood and held his hand down to help her up.

"Why, thank you, sir. Thanks for being my teammate." She shook his hand, and he noticed all the other students were thanking their partner as well.

Ali peeked at her watch and checked the map. "We've got a few minutes before the next station, class. Let's see if we can get a group photo."

She had the kids sit on the ground, some kneeling, some standing behind. Her phone was retrieved from the backpack she'd been toting around as she called out a few more directions for the students.

Greg touched her shoulder. "Go join them, and I'll take the picture. You'll want to be in with them."

Her eyes softened, and her lips pressed together. "Thank you."

She ran behind the last row and yelled, "Say pizza!"

The kids all yelled, "Pizza," and Greg snapped a few shots.

Ms. Long waved her hand. "You get in the picture, too, Captain Storm. You're part of this class today."

Greg started to shake his head, but the entire class called and motioned for him to join them. Ali nodded vigorously.

After handing the phone to Ms. Long, Greg trotted next to Ali and leaned close. Her smile grew even bigger.

Ali shouted, "Now, everyone make a silly face." The kids all tilted their heads or crossed their eyes or stuck their tongue out. Ali opened her mouth wide and threw her hands up in the air. Greg tossed his head back and laughed at this. So funny. This woman had so many facets to her, he wasn't sure which one was real. Or maybe they all were.

"Okay, next station, boys and girls. We're heading over to walk the plank."

The kids cheered and raced away to the next game, though Ali had to remind a few to grab their water bottles first. He'd have to try and remember to do that, as well, so it wasn't all on her.

"Walk the plank? For real?" he asked as he sidled up next to her.

Her laugh rang out, and he took a step closer with the desire to be near her. What was it about this woman that drew him in?

"It's a game. The person who runs it is the captain, and they call out orders. Swab the deck. Man overboard. Captain's coming. I always forget what to do, so I let the kids do it. It's fun to watch them."

When they caught up to the class, the students had all dumped their water bottles on the ground and stepped inside a roped-off area in the shape of a ship. Mrs. Poulin, the assistant principal, was leading this event. The woman wore a long pirate's coat and a pirate hat with a big feather in it.

"Avast ye maties. Are ya ready to be a real pirate?'

The kids all screamed, "Yes!"

Greg loved seeing the woman get into her role. She went over the rules one time, then started shouting orders.

"Hit the deck!" The kids all fell onto their stomachs on the grass.

"Crow's nest!" They stood on one foot, hands shading their eyes like they were searching in the distance.

"Man overboard!" Greg laughed as the students lowered to their backs and kicked their hands and feet in the air.

"Who comes up with these things?"

Ali shrugged, her grin infectious. "Who knows? I'm sure it's from some gym teacher manual. I only have the fourth-grade teacher manual."

"You must have memorized it, because you sure know how to make these kids have fun while still learning.

"Captain's coming!" Everyone saluted Mrs. Poulin.

"I do what I can. It gets easier every year."

"How long have you been teaching?"

"This is my sixth year, though I took half a year off when Jillian was born."

Greg did the math. If she'd started teaching right after college, she'd be about twenty-eight now. He was only three years older.

"Starboard!" The kids all ran to one side of the "boat".

"Port!" The kids all ran to the other side.

Greg watched the students, aware of Ali every second. "You've got these kids whipped into shape like a twenty-year veteran. I'm glad Ryan got you this year. He's enjoyed it." He wouldn't tell her he'd asked Reggie to assign Ryan to her.

"I try. It's mostly earning their respect. Then, they want to do everything to please you."

He could see why. He wanted to please her, too. Maybe if he asked her out once school was finished for the year, he could. Would she want to go out with him? On a date? More than one?

Mrs. Poulin blew her whistle and released the kids from their pirate duties. Ali's class scrambled over to where the two of them stood, while Ms. Long's class ran to her.

As they traveled to the next station, he noticed Ms. Long's blonde hair and slim shape in figure hugging shorts. She was pretty, and he'd bet most men would enjoy her company, but for some reason he was far happier walking beside Ali Cabrera, chatting with her.

For the next three hours, they kept an eye on the students as they played games, stopped for a quick lunch, and did activities. He and Ali joined in every now and again.

Water games, sack races, an obstacle course, balloon toss, and even a dance station. For that one, he most definitely stood to the side and watched. Ali's ears turned red, and she turned her back to him, yet she still danced with so much abandon and enthusiasm. She was having a ball and making sure to touch base with each of her students at some point in the event.

When Cotton Eye Joe started playing, she whispered something to Ryan and a few other children. They darted toward him and grabbed his arms, pulling him nearer to the circle of dancers. Ali waved them on.

"You grew up here in town, right? You can't tell me you don't know this. It's been part of the P. E. curriculum for over thirty years."

"Doubtful I remember it."

Her mouth twisted to the side, and her eyes gleamed. "You'll pick it up."

Her foot moved out to the front for two beats, then back for two beats. The students all joined in, some enthusiastically, others with a little less energy. Ali was incredible. Her whole body got involved. Arms, legs, hips, shoulders. The thing that drew him to her the most was how much fun she was having, and when her students saw how into it and how excited she was, they joined right in.

He stumbled over a few steps, especially when he had to grapevine and spin around. How he remembered what the step was called was beyond him. Somehow, he'd gotten as involved as the rest of the class. They all missed steps and laughed and carried on. No one cared. Ryan's face lit up like a Christmas tree as he watched his father embarrass himself. But the boy didn't seem embarrassed at all. More like elated.

The music ended, and all the kids clapped and collapsed on the ground. Ali bent over, hands on her knees. His posture was similar.

"Guess I won't need to go for that run today." Not that he'd planned to, but a little boasting was part of most guys' repertoire.

She snorted. "Why would anyone want to run unless you were being chased? My thought is I danced so much today I can have another brownie for dessert tonight." She patted her hips and scowled. "Or maybe not."

"Oh, the brownie definitely looks good on you." Shit, had he actually said that to her? The dancing must have jostled his brain.

Her eyes softened as she stared at him, then a ruckus behind her got her attention.

"Okay. Yup, we're heading to Tug of War. Grab a drink, boys and girls. We need you at your best if we're going to beat Ms. Long's class this year."

Ms. Long rolled her eyes and cocked her head. "In your dreams, Ms. Cabrera. In your dreams."

The two teachers made faces at each other and got their classes pumped up. Ali paced back and forth giving the kids instructions.

The kids scrambled to grab the rope, and Ali moved a few closer to the middle or farther away. When they seemed ready, she pointed at Greg, and he trotted over.

"This is where you come in. Another reason I picked you. I expect to beat the pants off Ms. Long's class. Got it."

He couldn't stop the laugh that burst from his lips. "You do have a competitive streak in you, huh? And here I thought you were so sweet."

Her face puckered up. "Not when it comes to Tug of War. We are gonna wipe the floor with them. Right?" She yelled, and her class cheered. She pointed him to the end of the rope. He wrapped the extra around his wrist for a better grip. He wouldn't disappoint her.

Mr. Pierce, the computer teacher, stood in the middle of the rope, keeping it hovered over the plastic cone. A ribbon dangled from the rope and two more cones stood about a foot away on each side.

"When I blow the whistle, you pull. The first team to get the ribbon over your cone wins. Ready, set…"

The whistle blew, and Ali jumped in the middle and grabbed the taut rope. Her chants of, "Go, go, go!" and "You can do this!" rang through the air, urging the students on. Greg pulled with all his might, and the rope inched toward him. He dug his feet in, and the rope inched back even more.

He knew he could pull even harder, but the kids needed a challenge, so he loosened his grip a tiny bit and the rope went in the opposite direction. But not too far. Soon enough, it was inching back toward their side again.

Greg took up the chants of encouragement and allowed the class to do this on their own. He held the line, so it didn't go back toward the other team, but was thrilled when the kids, and Ali, who kept yelling and cheering, were able to get the ribbon over their cone.

As soon as the whistle blew, the kids collapsed and started screaming with excitement. They hugged and high-fived each other, and Greg saw how unified this class was. Sure, not all of them were best of friends, but Ali had done something to these kids to make them become a real team. A group that worked together for the sake of the whole. W-H-O-L-E.

Since the tug-of-war didn't take as long as the other events, the school provided popsicles for after it was done. Parent volunteers handed out red, orange, and purple frozen snacks.

Ali walked over, two popsicles in her hands still wrapped in paper. "Purple or red?"

"Oh, I don't need—"

"Are you kidding? You kept us from losing horribly to Ms. Long's class. You need something cold. Purple or red?"

"Hmm. I guess red."

Ali sighed. "Phew, because I really like purple better."

He hadn't laughed this much in...forever. Taking the red treat, he sauntered away and found his son. He needed a short break from his teacher's magnetic pull.

"You were awesome, Dad. We pounded them into the ground."

Greg's brows crashed together, and Ryan looked sheepish. "I mean, it was a good match, but we won."

"Yeah, you did. I honestly didn't have to help all that much. Do you know what else we have left?"

Ryan glanced around and tilted his head. "Uh, I think just the pie throwing contest."

"You throw pies? Real pies?"

"Nah, they're plates filled with whipped cream. Could be shaving cream. I never had one thrown at me."

The hair on Greg's arms stood up. "Who do they throw them at?"

His son shrugged. "I don't know. Some of the people working Field Day. Usually Mr. Thorpe. Everyone loves to throw a pie at him."

Greg allowed his shoulders to relax. Reggie was a good sport.

"Are we ready to move on?" Allie called out to her class.

They all threw their wrappers away and took last bites of their melting treat. Then, they marched to the gym. Inside was taped off lines that ended in five chairs behind a table. The table was covered in plastic. The school principal sat in the chair in the middle. The guidance counselor. The crossing guard. And the head of the PTA. The last chair was empty.

As Ali came up beside him, he lifted his chin in the direction of the chairs. "Who's the poor sap that gets that seat?"

Her eyes gleamed, and her lips curled into a smirk as she stared at him. "Remember that fireman carry you did to me on our field trip?"

He couldn't stop the groan that escaped his mouth. "How could you do this to me? I ordered mushrooms and peppers on your pizza."

"You liked them, too." She gave a tiny shrug as she took his hand and escorted him to the empty chair, then wrapped a large garbage bag around his shoulders. Exactly like the ones the other poor saps were wearing.

As he sat and shifted in the seat, Ali leaned down and whispered, "I told you I'd get you back."

She stepped away just as the first pie was thrown and whipped cream splattered across his face.

CHAPTER TWELVE

*G*reg cracked open the truck windows a few inches, then patted Guinness on the head. Ryan's piano lesson was over in two minutes, and Greg had a plan. Now, if only he could get everything to fall into place.

School had gotten out a week ago, and Ali mentioned she'd finally finished cleaning up her classroom and putting everything away. He didn't realize how much work went into prepping the classroom for the summer, so the custodians could go in and do a deep clean.

Now, that Ryan was officially a fifth grader and no longer a student of Ali's, it should be okay for him to ask her out. He didn't want to do it in front of his son. Hopefully, Guinness could help out with that.

Walking up to the side door, Greg rehearsed in his head exactly what he wanted to say. It had been a while since he'd asked a woman out. Like before Ryan was born. The few hookups he'd been involved in were the result of bachelor parties, booze, and bad girls looking for fun.

The door stood open, and he gave a swift tap on the

screen door, then went in. Jillian sat in her kitchen set, stirring an empty bowl.

"What'cha making?" He crouched down next to the child.

After stirring one more round, she set her spoon down. "It's brownie mix. I love brownies."

"I like them, too." He leaned in and spoke softer. "But we don't want to give them to Ryan's puppy in the truck."

"A puppy? I wanna see the puppy."

First goal accomplished. Let's see if Ali cooperated with the rest. Greg stood and peeked into the living room. "Hey, there. Almost done? I've got Guinness in the truck."

Jillian skidded into the room. "Mama, I see the puppy? Please?"

"Oh, honey, I'm sure—"

"I'll bring her to see the puppy, Dad." Ryan twisted his head in a questioning way at Ali.

"We're not in a hurry if it's okay with you. The dog's pretty well behaved and doesn't bite."

Ali's lips pressed together. "I guess. But only for a minute. I'll—"

"Actually—" Greg interrupted, holding one finger up, "—I had something I needed to ask you. Ryan can take her out, if it's okay?"

"Sure." Ali nodded, and Ryan took Jillian's hand and led her outside. She scooped up the sheet music Ryan had left on the piano and stuck it in his bag.

Greg took the bag from her and glanced out the window. Okay, he could do this. His insides felt like the puppy scampering around on Ali's front lawn.

Ali came up next to him and chuckled as Jillian sat on the grass and the dog jumped all around her. "You had a question. About Ryan's piano lessons?"

Swallowing hard, he twisted until he faced her. "Not

piano, no. I was uh...wondering...if...man, I'm really bad at this." Suave, Storm. Real suave.

"Are you okay?" Her eyes softened, and she tipped her head.

"Oh, yeah, I think so. I mean...I wanted to ask you, um...if it's not too awkward being Ryan's teacher, but then you aren't anymore."

"No, not anymore." Her voice was tinged with humor.

"But you are his piano teacher. Though you work for yourself." Shit, he was rusty at this. Not that he'd ever been a smooth operator. He should have asked Luke or Kevin for pointers. Actually, no. They didn't have great staying power with women.

In high school and the first few years of college, he'd only had a few girlfriends. Then, Wendy had basically seduced him. Now, he could see it for what it was, but back then, all he could focus on was the hot chick rubbing her body all over his. He'd been thinking with his little head and had never noticed her ex-boyfriend across the room, making out with another girl.

For the moment, he needed to think like an adult. He cleared his throat and tried to man up.

"Ali, I was thinking...wondering, if you'd like to... maybe...go out to dinner with me. I mean, because you aren't Ryan's teacher anymore. So it's okay if I ask you, right?"

"Dinner?" She stood perfectly still, like she was holding her breath. Was that a no?

"Or lunch. Or we could go for an ice cream or a cup of coffee. It doesn't have to be anything big."

"Nothing big."

"Oh, okay. You don't want anything big." That was still okay, right? Starting small.

"I didn't say that." Her cheeks flushed a charming shade of pink. "Oh, well, maybe I did, but I was only repeating what you'd said. You want to take me to dinner? Like it would be a…"

Greg bobbed his head. "A date. Yeah, I'd like to go on a date with you."

Ali's eyes widened, but she didn't say anything. Shit.

"Oh, God, I'm sorry. I thought we'd been getting along pretty well, and I've been waiting for school to end. But if it's too early for this…or you just aren't interested, it's okay. No big deal." He really needed to stop talking. "I'll…uh…get Jillian and bring her in."

Before he could leave, Ali said his name. "Greg."

Pivoting, he faced her. She nodded.

"I'd love to go on a date with you. Dinner, lunch, ice cream, or coffee. Whichever you'd like."

He went boneless with her words. All this stress for nothing. She wanted to go out with him. Or was she simply being nice? No, he couldn't give himself something else to have an anxiety attack about.

"I'd love to take you to dinner, but I know you've got Jillian to think of."

"And you've got Ryan."

"I do, but my parents love watching him. They used to live with us until last year when I bought the house and they moved to an adult community. My aunt and uncle live there, too, and it's less yard work and maintenance. They were used to seeing Ryan every day and now they don't. And I'm babbling and probably scaring you off. I promise, I'll let you do all the talking when we go out. If—you still want to go out, right?"

Ali laughed, the tone like a wind chime in a soft breeze. "If I have a little advance notice, I can arrange for Jillian to sleep at my mom's house. Or there's a teenager down the street who I can sometimes get to babysit if I need to go out for a little while."

Greg had to stop and think. He hadn't been sure he'd get this far. "I'm off Thursday, Friday, and Saturday next week."

"School is out, and I'm finishing last little administrative stuff next week. Friday night would be good. What should I wear?"

His chest tightened. Why was she asking for wardrobe help? "I don't know what kind of clothes you have."

She threw her head back and laughed. "No, I mean should I dress casual or fancy or somewhere in between? I don't want to wear jeans if we're going to Roberto's, but I don't want to put on a nice dress with heels if we end up at The Granite Grill."

"I've seen women wear nice dresses to The Grill."

Rolling her eyes, she shook her head. "Yeah, women who want to pick up a guy. I assume you don't want me leaving with someone else."

"God, no. We'll go somewhere in Portsmouth. Dress nice, but not a ball gown. And bring a sweater. It gets chilly near the ocean."

Her eyes gleamed, and Greg got the impression she was excited about going out with him. Good. He was looking forward to it, as well.

"Is seven a good time?"

"Yeah, I'll be ready."

Greg stepped forward awkwardly and took her hand. "Thanks. I'll send Jillian in."

Should he kiss her? No, that was for the date. But maybe…he touched his lips to her cheek, then skedaddled as fast as he could, so he didn't make any more of a fool of himself than he already had.

~

ALI CALLED OUT THE DOOR, "Jilly, say goodbye to Ryan and the puppy. It's time for lunch."

Her daughter petted the dog on the head one last time, then waved as she ran to the house. Ali gave a wave also, and Greg tipped his head as he got in the truck.

He'd asked her out. On a date. To dinner. In Portsmouth. With nice clothes. And a sweater.

Did that mean they would go for a walk in the moonlight after dinner? Oh, wouldn't that be romantic. Was Greg the romantic type? His stuttered question about the date had been endearing if not a little awkward. She'd never have thought a man that gorgeous could be so tongue-tied when talking to a woman. It didn't make sense. He must date all the time.

But as she remembered back to some of what she'd over-heard from her students throughout the day, especially at snack time, she wondered if Greg didn't date much. A few students liked to share too much information about what went on in their household with single parents and their boyfriends or girlfriends. Ryan never shared anything of that kind. Ali had just assumed he kept to himself, but now that she thought of it, the boy had talked and talked plenty. About his grandparents and aunts and other extended family. Never a mention of any other woman.

No mention of his mom either. Ali wondered about Greg's wife. They hadn't been married long before she'd had Ryan, and then she'd been killed in a car accident only a few months after he'd been born. That must have been devastating, losing his wife after such a happy event.

But it was ten years ago and, apparently, he was ready to date again. And he'd chosen her. Wow. Never in a million years would she have called that one.

Jillian scampered into the house and jumped up and

down, yelling. "Mama, I want a puppy. Ryan's puppy is so cute. We get a puppy?"

Ali had to shake her head to clear the clouds from her mind. She'd been drifting on that ninth cloud thinking about Greg Storm. What had Jilly said?

"A puppy? No, I don't think we need a puppy."

"But he's so cute, Mama. I need him."

Ali could say the same thing about Greg Storm. Did she need him? She certainly wanted him. And gorgeous was more apt than cute in regard to his looks. What the heck was he doing asking her out?

Unless he was getting her back for the whipped cream pies in the face. He'd had to endure four of them from well-placed throws. But how was asking her out a bad thing? Would he cancel at the last second? Take her somewhere and embarrass her? Do something else to pay her back?

No. Greg wasn't that kind of guy. She'd bet money on it. He hadn't been thrilled about being volunteered for the pie throwing contest, yet he'd laughed it off and even rubbed some of it on her nose and cheeks after he was done. The students had eaten it up, and she'd taken it good naturedly.

"Maybe when you're a little older and can take care of a dog better, we can revisit the question. For now, you need some lunch."

They pulled out some bread, and she let Jillian help her spread peanut butter and jelly on it. Whatever Greg planned for their dinner date would be so much better than this. Would she be able to get anything she wanted? A steak? Lobster? Fried clams? Oh, she hadn't had those in forever.

What to wear popped up again in her mind, and she rifled through her closet in her head. Once Jilly had eaten her sandwich and been cleaned up, she grabbed the girl's comfort blanket and brought her into Ali's bedroom.

Placing her on the bed, she said, "Mama's got to look in

her closet for a pretty outfit. Do you want to take your nap in here today?"

Jilly's head almost bobbed off her shoulders. "Mama, where you go?"

"On Friday night, I'm going to have dinner with Captain Storm."

"Ryan go with you?"

"No, Ryan will be staying with his grandparents." Or his aunts. Greg hadn't said.

"I go with you?"

"No, sweetie. It will be after your bedtime. And we'll be doing boring grown up stuff like talking." Would they be doing anything else grown up? *Dios*, it had been forever since she'd done that. As much as Greg got her motor revving, she wasn't sure she was ready to take the car out of the garage quite yet. Not without a good tune up first.

"Where I go, Mama?"

"Maybe I'll get Destiny to come here. You like her."

Jilly stuck her thumb in her mouth and closed her eyes. She'd woken up early this morning and had to be tired.

Diving back into her closet, Ali searched for an outfit that would wow Greg. Did she even own anything like that? Something that fit her well, classy without being too extravagant.

Her sister had tons of clothes like that, but she'd never ask her to borrow anything. Doubtful her sister's clothes would fit her. She'd also have to sit and listen to a lecture about lifestyle versus diet and how changing the way you lived could be so much more beneficial to her health. Sure, maybe someday, when she wasn't working two jobs and taking care of a three-year-old, she might be able to find time to fit in workouts and specially cooked food. Right now, she needed an outfit for Friday.

Could she afford to buy a new outfit? Pulling her phone

from her pocket, she shot off a quick text, reminding Jeff his child support check for the month was overdue. Diplomatic in tone, cheerful even. She didn't mention all the other checks he'd never sent.

Jeff or no Jeff, she'd taken in extra money now that she had Ryan as a piano student. Greg had insisted he pay her the same amount he'd paid Mrs. Gullo, despite her objections and lesser experience. Greg had argued that Ryan liked his lessons with her more and it wasn't a hassle getting him ready to go. That was nice to hear.

She had gotten her last school paycheck, which was always larger since it covered most of the summer months. But it had to cover her bills until she went back in the fall. One new outfit wouldn't break the budget, would it?

Maybe she'd ask her mom to watch Jilly tomorrow, so she could go to the outlet stores. They were bound to have something that looked nice in her budget.

She had six days until her date. Six days to find something that would knock the socks off Greg Storm.

CHAPTER THIRTEEN

Ryan skidded as he entered Greg's bedroom, and his mouth dropped open. "Are you really going out with Mrs. C. tonight?"

Greg had dropped the bomb only a half hour ago as he skipped up the stairs to take a shower. Apparently, his son had been waiting for him to finish before he pounced.

"I am. Is that okay?" What would he do if it wasn't? No way he was calling Ali and backing out last minute. But he'd never dated anyone since he'd had Ryan. Would his son be jealous that some woman might take his father's attention away?

"It's very cool, Dad. Is she going to be my new mom?"

"Whoa, whoa, pal. This is our first date. I'm not ready to propose yet." Guess Ryan didn't have a problem with him dating.

"But you could, right? I mean you've known her for a while, and she's really pretty and nice. Plus, she already has a kid, so you know she's a great mom. I've seen her with Jillian, and she's perfect."

Greg chuckled, seeing that his son had gotten his gift of babbling.

"Why don't you let us go on the date first and then we can see where it goes?"

"Is that what you're wearing?"

Greg's chest tightened as he straightened his tie in the mirror. The navy dress slacks were in good shape, and he'd topped them with a forest green shirt. The tie was a lighter blue with some darker stripes.

"I thought I would. What's wrong with it?" And should he take style advice from a ten-year-old whose favorite article of clothing was sweatpants?

"Nothing. You look great. Mrs. C. hasn't seen you dressed up yet, right?"

"Hopefully, I won't be too disappointing."

Ryan waved his hand. "Nah, you'll be fine. She's so nice, she'd never say anything if she didn't like what you were wearing."

Tussling his son's hair, he said, "Good to know. Is your aunt here yet?"

When Leah had heard he'd finally asked Ali out, she'd volunteered to babysit. It had taken any worry he'd had out of the equation. He'd be in for the grand inquisition once he got back.

"Yeah, she's downstairs eating all the cookies Nonna left us."

With a last brush of his hair and peek in the mirror, Greg slung his arm over his son's shoulder and escorted him back downstairs.

Leah was ready for him. "Ooh, la la! C'est magnifique. You clean up nice for a hose jockey."

"Don't start or you're going in a headlock." He wouldn't do it. He didn't want to get messed up before he left, but he'd certainly done it in the past to both his sisters and she knew it.

Leah smirked. "Ali is in for a pleasant surprise. Where are you taking her?"

"I thought we'd do The Wharf in Portsmouth. Does she like seafood? I never thought to ask. Shoot. I think they have a few non-fish dinners there."

Pulling out his phone, he scrolled through to find the restaurant page. Leah placed her hand on his and stopped him.

"She likes all kids of fish. Stop worrying and enjoy yourself. Here are the keys to my car."

Greg took the key ring his sister held out and nodded. "Thanks for letting me borrow it. One of these days I suppose I should get something nicer than my truck."

"Your truck is fine and perfect for hauling your boat. But if she's wearing a tight skirt, it might be difficult to get in it."

Ali in a tight skirt. The image sent his blood pressure skyrocketing. He picked his denim jacket off the back of the chair and draped it over his arm. If they went for a walk near the ocean, and he was kind of hoping they would, he might need it. Or he could let Ali wear it, so she didn't get cold. Except that he'd told her to bring a sweater. That was stupid. He'd totally screwed up his chance to be a gentleman.

Well, he could be one in every other way.

"Be good for Auntie Leah and go to bed when she tells you to." He pointed at Ryan and shook his finger jokingly. It was summer vacation and a weekend to boot. With his aunt here to spoil him, Greg was sure it would be late by the time his son hit the sack.

"Be really nice to Mrs. C., please, Dad. I want her to like you." Ryan's anxious expression dug into Greg's heart. Had Ryan felt deprived of a mother's love because Greg hadn't dated? He'd never noticed before but now felt a little guilty.

Leah ruffled Ryan's hair. "Your father's always nice to everybody. Besides, I think Mrs. C. already likes him or I doubt she would have said yes to a date."

"Okay, yeah." Ryan bounced a little. "Have fun."

After giving Ryan and Leah a kiss on their cheeks, Greg started up the car and maneuvered onto the road. If he took his time, he'd be arriving at Ali's house right at seven. Leah had assured him no woman wanted a guy there more than five minutes early, because she would probably still be getting ready.

He took a deep breath as he pulled into the driveway and shut the car off. The curtain in the living room window fluttered, and he wondered if she was ready. Only one way to find out.

Picking up the small bouquet of supermarket flowers he'd gotten this afternoon, he strode up the walk and rang the bell. No piano lesson tonight. He was going in the front door.

The door opened seconds after it rang. That was a good sign. Ali's smiling face greeted him as she stepped back to allow him to enter.

"These are for you." He handed her the flowers.

Her face beamed as she took them. "They're beautiful. Thank you. Let me put them in water and then we can go."

As she entered the kitchen and reached in the cabinet for a vase, he checked out her outfit. Wow. The cranberry-colored dress was a light cotton but clung to her gorgeous curves lovingly. It had short sleeves and a round neck and stopped a few inches above her knees. She wore spiky heeled sandals that gave her an extra three inches. It made her face closer, so he wouldn't have to bend too much for a kiss.

When she turned around with the vase of flowers, he knew he'd like nothing better than a kiss. Her lips were a dark shade of something that almost matched her dress, and her eyes had some kind of smoky effect to them. And her hair. Man, her beautiful dark hair swirled around her shoulders in waves.

"You look incredible, Ali."

Her cheeks suffused with more color, and she bit her bottom lip, the white of her teeth so stark against the shade of her lipstick.

"Thanks. You look great, too." Her eyes lowered to the vase in her hand as she placed it on the counter.

"Where's Jillian tonight? Already in bed?" But then where was the sitter? In Jillian's room?

"She's at my mom's for the night. She usually stays over there at least once a month."

Greg's heart picked up the pace. Was she giving off hints about what she wanted to happen at the end of the date? Leah had certainly hinted that she'd be happy to stay overnight. Greg's spare bedroom was always ready for guests. Was he ready for Ryan to know he'd stayed over at his teacher's house for the night? Too many questions.

Ali picked up a black sweater and a small purse and preceded him out the door. After locking it, she took his elbow until he opened the car door for her.

"Your sister, Leah, has a car just like this. Did you get a two-for-one deal?"

He walked around the car and got in before answering her question. "No, this is her car. I have a high truck and wasn't sure it would be right for a date."

Ali canted her head and grinned. "Does she let you borrow her car for all your dates?"

Twisting the key, he started the car and backed out of the driveway. "Uh, this is actually my first date in a while." Would he sound completely pathetic if he admitted how long it had been?

She snuck a peek at him under her lashes. "Mine, too. Since Jillian's father left."

Jillian was three. She'd been a baby when the jerk deserted her, so that meant...a long time.

"Got you beat. It's been since before I got married."

Immediately, she took his hand and squeezed. "Are you okay?"

He took the corner onto the main street and flashed her a smile. "Yeah, I'm really looking forward to this. Ryan was excited, too, just so you know."

He wouldn't mention his son's other comments about getting married. She might like him, but that was pushing things.

As they drove to Portsmouth, they chatted about what she was planning to do over the summer and some of the activities he'd planned for Ryan.

"I actually have a boat that's moored in a boat club on the Piscataqua River, not too far from Portsmouth Harbor. We like to go out on it as often as we can. I usually alternate taking my parents or sisters or some of my cousins. It's a fun day out on the water."

"Do you go on the ocean or stay in the river?"

"Depends on who's with me and the conditions. If the sea's too rough, we'll stay on the river. But I've taken her up near to my cousin Erik's place in Maine. You met him and his kids at the Easter Egg hunt."

"Sounds like fun."

Should he ask if she and Jillian would want to go with him someday? Or perhaps wait until after their date to see how much of a disaster it was. He was sure he'd enjoy himself, but would Ali want to go out again?

They shared more stories of their respective families and where they all were now. When they reached the parking lot in downtown Portsmouth, Greg took her hand and held it while they walked to the restaurant. She'd stared at their entwined hands for a second, then smiled.

He'd called ahead for reservations. The last thing he wanted to do was get here and find that no place had a spot for them because it was Friday night at the end of June. The perfect time to be in downtown Portsmouth. They were shown to a small table on the deck overlooking the harbor, and he waited until Ali was seated before he sat. The hostess handed them each a menu and said their server would be right with them.

"Have you been here before, Greg? Do you know what's good?"

"It's been years since I came here last, but I remember the food being excellent. And some of the guys at work come here all the time. I've never heard them complain."

As she perused the menu, he picked up his and glanced at the appetizers. The waitress appeared, greeted them, and introduced herself.

"Can I start you off with a drink?"

Greg eyed Ali. "Would you like a glass of wine or some other drink?"

Ali flipped the menu and skimmed the wine list. "The white zinfandel, please."

"Two," Greg said. The waitress nodded and left. "Are you interested in an appetizer?"

"Oh, I hate to order too much. I'll be too full to eat the meal. Is there something you like? I'll take a few nibbles."

When their drinks were delivered, they put in an order for some bruschetta. Sipping the wine, he searched Ali's face for signs she was enjoying herself. Her lovely brown eyes were soft and focused when he spoke, and her lips curled up in a slight smile throughout their conversation.

The appetizer arrived, and Ali ordered a lobster and shrimp pasta dish while he got the fresh catch of the day. Swordfish.

Ali nibbled on the toasted bread smothered with chopped

tomatoes, then dabbed at her mouth with the cloth napkin. "You mentioned before something about wanting to be a doctor. How did you end up becoming a firefighter?"

The light feeling he'd been floating on all night scurried away. What would Ali say if he told her the truth? Or even part of it?

ALI'S NERVES began to shake as Greg's face darkened. Oh, no. She'd asked the wrong question. "I'm sorry. Forget I asked." She plucked her wine glass up and took a sip when she really wanted to down the whole thing.

"No, it's fine. Honestly." He took a deep breath and smiled. "You probably figured out I had Ryan fairly young. I'm only thirty and he's ten. That little accident happened in college. Needless to say, I required a job that paid enough to support a family. I already had a bunch of biology and anatomy and physiology classes under my belt, so I enrolled in the paramedic program and, shortly after, got a position at the firehouse. I've been there ever since."

Her mouth opened into a little bow. "Oh, you're a paramedic, too. I didn't realize."

Shrugging, he said, "Now that I'm captain, I don't actively do that job anymore. Unless there's a huge medical emergency where we need more help than we've got. I keep up my certification. You never know when you'll need the skills."

She took a small bite of the bruschetta, then wiped her hands on a napkin. She had such long, thin fingers. Perfect for playing the piano.

"Have you ever thought of going back to medical school?"

"Sure. Thought about it, but trying to raise an active ten-year-old who only has one parent already isn't conducive to long days in class and longer days doing rotations and being on-call. I get what I need from this job, and I think I do a lot of good."

"So the captain's job doesn't let you do the paramedic stuff?"

"Not really. Too much paperwork and administrative stuff. Luckily, it pays more and the hours are better. I got some insurance money for Wendy's accident. A good deal of it went into an account for Ryan when he gets older, and I used some of it to buy my parents' house."

"I'm so sorry about what happened to your wife. It must have been difficult, especially with Ryan being so young and having to raise him yourself."

Greg's lips pulled in tight. "Thanks. You're doing something similar with Jillian. Does she go with her father often?"

"Every now and then. Usually only for part of a day. He still doesn't feel comfortable having her overnight." That was an overstatement. He didn't feel comfortable ever with his own daughter.

The meal arrived, and they spent a few minutes digging into their food. Her seafood pasta dish was rich and creamy and had huge chunks of lobster and shrimp. Greg seemed to enjoy his swordfish, which smelled delicious.

"Who's watching Ryan tonight?" She made sure she'd chewed and swallowed every little thing in her mouth. Last thing she wanted was to drive him off with gross food stuck to her teeth.

"Leah volunteered once she heard I'd asked you out. I have to tell you she's been nagging at me to do that for a while."

What? Was that the only reason he'd asked her out? To appease his sister?

His eyes opened wide, and his face froze. "Wait. That didn't come out the way it should have. I didn't only ask you out because Leah told me to. I wanted to."

Ali tried to form a smile, but those niggling doubt crows that forever circled her head were swooping down to attack her. "Of course."

Greg closed his eyes and dropped his head. When he lifted it back up again, his eyes held remorse. That she'd found out why he'd asked for a date?

He reached across the table and took her hand. "Ali, listen. I'm sorry for that ridiculous comment. Yes, Leah had mentioned how she thought you'd be great to go out with. But I already had that on my radar. You being Ryan's teacher was a bit tricky, so I needed to wait. I guess. I don't really know the protocol for asking out your child's teacher. I've never done it before. I suppose I could have asked Reggie, but then if the answer was no, I couldn't do it, then he'd know I was thinking about it. And I'm totally babbling again."

The babbling was what made her laugh and get her back in a good mood. "So this isn't a pity date?"

"A pity date? Are you kidding me? Certainly not on my part. Is it on yours? You didn't have to say yes. I wouldn't have melted."

"Are you sure?" she teased, attempting to get the earlier humor back.

"My masculinity might have been dented a bit, but I would have survived." He narrowed his eyes at her. "You didn't say yes out of pity, did you?"

Was this gorgeous man seriously asking her if she'd only gone out with him to avoid hurting his feelings?

"I said yes, because I've enjoyed the other times we've been together. It's always been with the kids around, and I wondered what it would be like without them."

"How am I doing so far? Aside from the stupid babbling, which I promise I'll try not to do any longer. Just a nervous reaction."

He was nervous around her? Was that good or bad? "Is it my teacher vibe that makes you nervous?"

He squeezed the hand he was still holding. "No, it's just been a long time since I've been out with a beautiful woman. I wasn't sure if I'd remember how it's done. Apparently, I don't."

"You got dressed up, gave me flowers, took me to a great restaurant, bought me a fabulous meal. I think you're doing perfectly fine."

Greg took a deep breath and sat back in his chair. "Great. So we can forget all the stupid stuff I said and just keep going like it never happened."

"I like the fact you're a little nervous. It means I'm not the only one in that boat. I didn't expect someone like you to be nervous on a date."

His brows crashed together. "Someone like me?"

She waved her hand at him. "You know, intelligent, nice, successful, good looking. Mrs. Ferrera would be jumping at the chance to be me tonight."

His face tensed. "I would prefer not to think about Mrs. Ferrera if it's all the same to you. I'm sure she's a wonderful person, but I've found her to be...uh—"

"A little pushy," Ali filled in for him.

"I was going to say overzealous, but pushy isn't a bad description either."

They both laughed, then dug back into their meals. Ali wasn't sure she could finish the entire pasta dish and hoped she could take some home. She started to push the food to one side of the plate when she heard her phone go off. *Dios*, she hoped it wasn't something stupid.

"Excuse me. I just want to make sure it isn't my mother."

Greg waved his hand. "Of course."

Slipping the phone from her purse, her heart pounded louder. It was the nursing home her grandfather lived in.

"Hello." Please, let it be something minor.

As she listened to the nurse on her grandfather's floor, she clutched the phone in trembling hands as a weight settled in her chest.

She frowned at Greg. "I'm sorry. I've got to go."

CHAPTER FOURTEEN

*a*li's voice shook as she talked to the nursing home staff. Her heart beat double time. "Have you called the police to report this yet?"

Greg's mouth tightened as he signaled for the waitress. He'd never even asked her what was wrong, just started the process of leaving.

When she finally hung up the phone, he had the check and was placing some bills in the leather folder. After setting it on the table, he stood and held out his hand for her.

"Are you all right? Is it Jillian?"

He opened the door for her and guided her down the street, back to the parking lot.

"No, my grandfather. He lives in the nursing home up past the high school. Apparently, he's missing. They think he might have walked out behind a visitor as they were leaving. The person must not have realized he lived there and wasn't supposed to leave."

"When did this happen?"

"They aren't absolutely sure. It could have been any time

in the last hour. They had a sing-along in the main dining room downstairs and he had gone to that. One of the residents had a small seizure and things got hectic."

"What's his mental and physical status?" Was this the paramedic in him asking?

"He gets along okay with a cane, but he's got early stages of Dementia and can fade in and out of reality at times."

They approached the car, and he gripped her shoulders. "We'll get him back. Don't worry."

Once they were settled inside and he'd started the engine, she glanced at him. "This isn't your problem to worry about but thank you for cutting the night short. I need to get back as soon as possible."

"Let me help, Ali. I know a lot of people in town."

As they drove, her heart hurt thinking her grandfather was wandering somewhere alone and helpless.

Greg pressed a button on his phone and after a few moments said, "Alex, I need some help. I'm out with Ali Cabrera, and her grandfather has gone missing from his nursing home. Can you call out the troops? Kevin, especially, if he's not working. See if they can drive around town. I'll put you on with Ali, so she can give you a description of him."

He handed her the phone, and she was stunned by his behavior. Her own sister would have left it for the police to look into. She quickly gave Alex a description of Sebastien Cabrera and what the staff had said he'd been wearing tonight. Then, she thanked him for the assistance.

Greg said a few more things to his cousin before he hung up, but Ali couldn't do anything except try and keep the tears from falling.

"My cousin, Kevin, is a Portsmouth cop. He'll get his partner, and Alex will call in his brother Luke to help search. If I know my family, most of them will join in. The more people we have looking, the quicker we'll find him."

His hand snaked out and slid over hers. He stayed quiet after that but never let go of her hand except for a few turns. When they got closer to Squamscott Falls, Ali could barely breathe. What if they couldn't find him? What if he was injured or someone had hurt him?

They drove to the nursing home first, and Ali jumped out to talk to one of the staff members who was standing outside.

"I'm so sorry, Alandra. He shouldn't have been able to get past the front desk, but the clerk there had to scramble the nursing staff to handle the seizure."

"I understand. We'll find him. Who have you got looking?"

"The police have been notified and given a description. They've got every available person searching." That meant the three officers who were on duty in this small town tonight. That didn't instill confidence in her.

"Ali," Greg called out and waved his hand as he ran up to her.

Madre de Dios, what a mess. Her first date in forever and—

"My Uncle Pete and Aunt Molly found him. He's sitting in the gazebo in the town square."

Her legs turned to liquid, and Greg hauled her against him before she fell. Her head spun as tears coursed down her face.

"Come on, we'll go get him."

She couldn't do anything but nod as he tucked her back in the car and drove away.

"He's still there?"

"Yes, they're sitting with him until we can get there."

"Oh, *Dios*, thank you so much for getting the help. How did they find him so fast? It couldn't have been more than twenty-five minutes ago that I got the call."

"I have family all over the town, and Alex sent out a group

text. Molly and Pete happened to be out picking up some stuff at one of the stores on Main Street."

When Greg pulled to the side of the road near the town common, Ali flew from the car and dashed to the gazebo. There was her grandfather with a mature couple in their fifties.

"Hey, Tito Sebastien. What are you doing here?" She kept her voice soft and neutral. No sense getting him riled up.

His head swiveled in her direction, and he tipped his head for a second. Then, a huge smile broke out over his face. "Bonita, my darling. You are looking as lovely as ever tonight."

Bonita. That was her grandmother's name. They'd been married over fifty years. Ali had barely managed three.

"Who are your friends, Tito?"

"I'm Molly Storm," the blonde with the cute pixie cut said. "And this is my husband, Pete. We were taking a walk in the common and met Sebastien here. He was telling us about his wife, Bonita."

Ali threw them a grateful look. "I'm so glad you were here. Thank you so much. You don't know how much I appreciate it."

Molly patted her on the shoulder as she stood. "I think we do. I'm happy it worked out. We'll let Greg take over from here."

Greg stood behind her. She had completely forgotten about him. He said a few things to his family, then waved as they walked away. Slowly making his way toward them, he threw her a questioning look.

"Tito, I want you to meet my friend, Greg Storm."

Greg slid into the seat next to Ali and stuck his hand out. Tito shook it and gave Greg a once over.

"How do you know my Bonita?"

Greg stiffened and took in a deep breath. "Um, she gives piano lessons to my son. She's a great teacher."

"Oh, yes, my Bonita loved playing the piano. It was like listening to angels singing."

"Yes, Tito. She taught me, remember? I think I was only five the first time she had me sit on her lap and learn what each key was. I loved it so much."

Tito patted her hand. "Yes, you always did love making music."

Ali couldn't tell if he was still confusing her with her grandmother or not. It didn't matter. He was safe and she was with him.

They sat quietly for a few minutes and her grandfather looked around, his eyes filling with light. "This is where I proposed to her. Got down on one knee and asked her to be my wife for eternity."

Greg cleared his throat. "That's beautiful. It's the perfect spot to propose."

Tito stared at Greg, and his face grew confused. "Did you propose to your wife here?"

Oh, *Dios*. Wrong subject for the wrong person.

"No, I didn't. But I think next time I might have to. Can you tell me how you did it?"

As her grandfather rattled on about taking her grand-mother to dinner, then walking over here, she could have kissed Greg. Tito could tell you every single detail of a night fifty or sixty years ago, yet he didn't remember her name right now. That wasn't important. In his lost mind, he had found his true love and was reliving all those wonderful memories.

Greg continued to ask him questions about his wife and their children and things he'd done in town when he was a boy. Her grandfather was so lucid and descriptive in his answers. His face beamed, and he gushed on and on about his family and how he loved them all.

Finally, she could see the weariness on his face. "Maybe we should get back home, Tito. Okay? It's late, and I'm getting tired."

"Of course. How inconsiderate of me, Bonita." He looked past her to Greg. "We need to get the women home, so they can rest. It's been a long day."

"Why don't I give you a ride home, Mr. Cabrera? Both of you."

Her grandfather stood and peered around the common. "A ride. That might be nice. Thank you, young man. What was your name again?"

"Greg Storm."

"Greg Storm? I knew a Hans Storm a long time ago. Nice fellow."

"That's my grandfather. He is a nice guy."

She and Greg led Tito to the car and got him buckled into the back. When she slipped in beside Greg in the front, she grabbed his hand and whispered, "Thank you so much."

"It's not a problem. I loved hearing his stories."

The fact he downplayed the situation was so endearing. They drove through the mostly quiet streets of town until they got to the nursing home. Staff was waiting to help him inside.

"Why don't we bring him up?" Greg proposed. "Make sure he gets to his room and feels comfortable again."

She could have kissed him for the suggestion. He sure was making her fall for him tonight.

"Can I come visit you again, Mr. Cabrera? I'd love to hear more about what the town was like when you were younger. My grandparents have told me stories, but it's great getting a different perspective."

"Oh, yes, young man. Come by and visit any time. Bonita stops in every now and then. She brings that little girl with her. My granddaughter, Alandra. Named after my mother. She's such a cute thing."

"Yes, she is." Greg winked at her, and she was speechless.

One of the staff hustled in to help him change for the night, so she and Greg said goodbye.

"I love you, Tito. Have a good night." She gently kissed his forehead.

"Thanks for letting me go to the park today, Alandra. Bonita and I had a nice time."

Ali smiled. He'd gotten her name correct but still thought her grandmother was there, too. Who was she to say the woman hadn't been present somehow?

On the elevator ride down, Greg pulled her against his strong chest and held her. When was the last time she'd had this kind of comfort? Too long. Jeff had never been the type.

As they exited the building, he kept her at his shoulder. "Are you going to be all right?"

"I think so. I'm still shaking from the thought of Tito being lost."

He squeezed her hand and led her to the car. They were quiet on the short ride back to her house, and he walked her to the door.

"Is there anything I can do for you?"

What was he asking? If she wanted to sleep with him? Or something more innocent? She didn't know him well enough to read his body language. On the other hand, what she'd learned of him tonight had been so incredible.

"I'm just tired. You were great tonight. Getting my grandfather to talk about the old days and my grandmother. It was exactly what he needed. I'm not sure I would have had a clear enough mind to know that."

Greg shrugged. "In my job, we've had our share of dealing with elderly who are beginning to have a mental decline. We've actually had training on that very subject."

Ali sighed and bit her lip. "I'm sorry I ruined our first date."

He lifted his hand and flipped her hair off her shoulder, then left it there. "Nothing was ruined. We still got a nice meal, and I was able to spend time with a lovely lady. And then her grandfather."

"A spastic, lovely lady who cried all over you."

His laugh showcased his dimples. "It was unique. We'll have to plan another date and see if that one runs differently."

Hope fluttered inside. "You still want to go out with me after all that?"

His eyes focused on hers, and his hand brushed against her cheek. "Yeah, I kind of do."

He lowered his head, and Ali held her breath. But his lips only touched her cheek before he stepped back and nodded.

"I'll give you a call."

Please, let this be one of the times those words actually meant he'd call.

GREG PULLED into his driveway and shut off the engine. What a night. It hadn't ended like he'd hoped, but all in all, he didn't feel too bad about it. Not that he'd expected to be sharing sheets with Ali right now, but he'd been hoping he could at least give her a good long kiss. However, when he'd seen her face, lined with exhaustion and worry, he'd decided to go with a peck on the cheek.

As he trudged up the steps, his sister opened the door, her

face expectant. "Everything okay now?" She was on the group text.

"Ali's grandfather is all settled back in his bed at the nursing home. I just dropped her off at her house."

"How's she doing?"

Greg hung his denim jacket on the hook by the door and wandered into the living room where he plopped on the couch. Leah followed him in and sat opposite.

"Shaken up, but her grandfather seemed fine. No adverse effects. He wandered to the town common and was sitting in the gazebo. Apparently, it's where he'd proposed to his wife."

Leah's face softened. "Oh, that's so sweet. And sad. I know she passed away a few years ago. He must have been devastated."

"I'm not sure he was aware of that fact. Kept calling Ali by his wife's name. But he remembered every detail of his life back when they first got married. Guess he knew Gramps growing up."

"Oh, wow. I didn't realize. Did you and Ali get to enjoy any of your date before this happened?"

"Yeah, we did. Got through most of the meal before she got the call. I had hoped to go for a walk along the harbor or maybe stop at a nearby beach, but I'll have to save that for another day."

Leah leaned forward, her eyes gleaming with mischief. "So you're going to ask her out again?"

Greg shook his head at his sister's matchmaking interference. "Yeah, I think I will. Just to show her I'm not the babbling idiot I seemed a few times tonight. God, this dating thing is not easy. How do you do it?"

Leah eased back in her seat. "I don't all that much. You know me. I'd rather sit home reading a good book...or watching my nephew."

"How was he? Did he give you any problems?" Being a

teacher, Leah didn't put up with any shenanigans. She also knew exactly how to have fun with kids.

"He was typical Ryan. We played a few games and I let him watch a movie. When I got the text, I figured I'd better get him in bed so he was asleep if the phone started to blow up with messages. I was relieved when Aunt Molly found him so quickly. Ali must have been a mess."

Remembering her tears, he nodded. "I tried to comfort her best I could, but I'm a guy. What do I know?"

"Don't be hard on yourself, Greg. You do a damn fine job of comforting your son when he needs it. I'm sure Ali appreciated everything you did."

"I hope so. Now, I need to figure out the next date."

Leah tilted her head and pursed her lips as she gazed around the room. "I know! You should bring her to Dad's birthday party on Saturday."

Greg made a face at her. "Seriously? You want me to expose her to this crazy big family on our second date?"

"We're a very nice family as you well know. It'll be casual, so less pressure. She can bring Jillian and…Oh, invite her grandfather to come for a bit if he's able. I'll bet Gramps would be tickled to reconnect if he comes."

Invite her and her kid and grandfather. Brownie points would likely be awarded, but he doubted he'd get any time alone with her. And that was kind of the point of dating. But Leah's suggestion had merit. Ali knew some of the family already and might be more comfortable in a casual situation. Unless…

"Are we going to be bombarded with questions about our relationship? Because I hardly want to spend the day fielding snarky remarks from well-meaning relatives."

"Please. It doesn't matter whether you bring her or not. After tonight's SOS, you know everyone will want to know why you were playing white knight to Ali's damsel in distress. Might as well have her here. I'm sure Jillian will have a blast playing with the rest of the kids, and if the two of you don't hit it off romantically, you can always pull out the only-friends BS. She's a member of the community, and the Storms are all about helping the community."

True. His family was a good, supportive one, and they helped everyone who needed it. Like tonight when Ali's grandfather had gone missing. No one questioned the request; they just jumped right in. They would have done it for anyone in town.

"Maybe I will see if she wants to come. Thanks." After a brief pause, Greg eyed his sister. "Did you want to bunk here? The spare room's always ready."

Leah stood and stretched her back. "Nah, it's barely eleven. I think I can drive the three streets over to my house."

Greg pushed himself out of the chair and gave her a kiss on the cheek. Like the one he'd given to Ali. He hadn't been feeling at all brotherly with Ali. He'd have to do better next time.

After Leah took off, he moved around the house closing and locking everything up. He peeked in on Ryan to find him deeply asleep. He gave him a kiss on the forehead. Not something the boy wanted any time during the day in front of anyone else. Greg missed that younger age where his son would climb in his lap and want to snuggle.

In his room, he started tugging on his tie and thought about Ali again. He drew his phone from his pocket and sent a short text to her.

—*No need to answer. I hope you're getting some sleep. Just wanted to make sure you're okay. And to say again I enjoyed being with you tonight. See you soon.*—

He sent the message, then changed into a pair of pajama pants. When the phone vibrated on his dresser, his pulse jumped. Swiping across the screen, he saw it was from Ali.

—Aside from all the drama, I had a good time, too. Thanks for keeping me from freaking out.—

Greg grinned and tapped a short reply. *—Any time.—*

Thinking about all the times he'd been with Ali, he realized he really meant that.

CHAPTER FIFTEEN

"Jillian, sweetie, are you about ready?"

Ali peeked in on her daughter and stifled a groan. She'd placed a pair of shorts and a matching top on the child's bed. Which Jilly wore. Along with her pink princess dress over it. Did she have the energy, patience, or time to talk her out of it?

Probably not. Greg was arriving to pick them up any minute, and Ali still hadn't finished her makeup. Not that she wanted to look like she was ready to go clubbing, but she'd be seeing the entire Storm family today, and she at least wanted to look presentable.

When Greg had called at the beginning of the week to check how Tito was and make sure she had recovered from the ordeal, she'd thought it was super sweet. Then, he'd asked if she and Jillian would like to come to his father's birthday party. It was a big deal since Nick Storm was turning sixty. The party was at Greg's place due to the fact he had the largest yard and house. She'd waffled at first thinking it was only family, but he'd said many friends would be there, too.

That hadn't persuaded her either as she was hardly a family friend.

Then, when he'd invited her grandfather to come since he'd known his grandfather, she couldn't refuse. Tito didn't get out of the nursing home often. Since she had a three-year-old to look after, she sometimes worried she wouldn't be able to watch him as well if she took him someplace.

Greg had assured her his entire family would be there to make sure the man was safe and entertained. How could she refuse that? She couldn't and didn't.

Staring at her daughter in her flouncy dress, Ali sighed. Yep, not enough energy. And what did it matter? Who was going to judge a three-year-old for wearing a princess dress? None of the Storms she'd ever met.

"Put your sneakers on, please. I'll be right out of my room in a minute. You can watch for Captain Storm."

"Is he coming with Ryan, Mama?"

"I don't know, sweetie, but Ryan will definitely be at the party." That alone had made Jilly's behavior this week almost perfect.

Rushing into her bedroom, she stroked a brush through her hair and secured it in a large barrette in the back. Greg had stared at her hair on their date a few times, and she had a feeling he liked it down. But it was warm today and the last thing she needed was her waves turning into major frizz head or making her sweat more than she already would.

After tucking in some cute dangling earrings, she smoothed out any blemishes with concealer, dusted her face with powder so she wouldn't be all shiny, and added a few strokes of mascara. Luckily, her lashes were naturally dark. She skipped the lipstick, since she figured she'd chew it off in a matter of minutes. She always did.

The doorbell sounded, and Jillian squealed. "Mama, it's Ryan,"

Ali eyed herself in the mirror, hoping she looked okay. A pair of long, black walking shorts that helped hide her rounded butt and thighs were paired with a teal, sleeveless top that accentuated her smaller waist then flared to accommodate the bottom of her. After slipping into a pair of cute sandals, she scurried down the hall.

Greg and Ryan looked adorable in almost matching outfits. They both wore khaki shorts and navy polo shirts, except Ryan's had a red stripe across the chest.

"Hi. Sorry I'm running behind."

"We're a few minutes early," Greg lied. She could see the clock, but it was sweet of him to take the blame for her tardiness.

"I know you said I didn't need to bring anything, but I made brownies. I hope that's okay..." She shrugged, not knowing why she always made brownies to bring places.

"I love brownies, Mrs. C. Dad, she brought them to class before. They're the best."

Greg chuckled. "My family has a tendency to provide lots of food, but they won't go uneaten, believe me. The Storm appetite is famous for miles."

As they drove to the nursing home, Ryan and Jillian chatted in the back seat. Greg had borrowed an SUV from someone for the trip. Seems like the family played musical cars fairly often.

"Do you need me to go up and get him with you?" Greg offered as they pulled up to the nursing home.

"The staff said they'd have him ready to go. See? There he is."

Greg steered under the car port and right up to the door and got out with her.

"Good to see you again, Mr. Cabrera." Greg shook hands with her grandfather.

Tito's head popped up, and his brows knit together. "You're the young man with my Alandra last week."

Ali sighed at the lucidity he had today. For now, anyway. Hopefully, it was a good sign.

"Yes, Greg Storm. You know my grandfather, Hans. He'll be at the party today."

"Oh, it'll be good to see him again."

Tito muttered a few other things that Ali missed as Greg helped him into the back seat next to Jillian. Ryan had climbed into the third row.

"There's my little Jillian. How are you, sweetheart?"

"Hi, Tito. I wearing a princess dress today."

As the car rolled down the road, Ali heard her grandfather reply, "Well, of course you have a princess dress. That's what a princess wears, isn't it?"

Jillian giggled, and Ali felt as if all the weight of the world had flown away. She glanced at Greg and smiled. "Thanks so much for inviting him today."

"I'm sure he likes to get out when he can. Let me know if he's getting tired, and we can bring him back."

"There's no reason for you to leave your father's party. The nursing home has a shuttle they use for occasions like this. There're a few other residents visiting family in town today. They'll pick him up around four. Luckily, your house isn't far."

When they got to his place, Ali's eyes opened wide. The house was a huge Victorian on a street with only three houses. It was walking distance to the town center. She'd love living here.

"Your house is beautiful."

"Thanks." Greg leaped out and released the kids, then helped Tito get out. Ali came up to Tito's other side, and they made their way to where all the lawn chairs were set up.

"Across the street there is where my cousin, Alex lives," he continued, indicating each house as he spoke. "The house on the end belongs to Gina, his fiancée. She inherited it from her grandmother. It had a pretty bad fire that damaged the top floors last year, but renovations are almost done. I think she'll be putting it on the market soon if you're interested." His eyebrows went up and down comically.

"Oh, I wish I could afford something like that. I love Victorian houses."

Greg's mouth tightened for a second. "Some people think they're too old and outdated and prefer something more modern."

"Oh, never. They've got such character. Don't you think so, Tito?"

"Beautiful house. Who lives here?"

"I do," Greg answered, then waved as a dark-haired woman and lighter-haired man approached. "These are my parents, Luci and Nick Storm. Mom, Dad, this is Sebastien Cabrera and his granddaughter, Alandra."

"It's so wonderful you could come." Luci smiled graciously.

"Happy birthday," Ali said to Nick. "Thanks for having us."

"Her daughter, Jillian, is running around somewhere with Ryan. I'm sure you'll get to meet her soon."

Nick and Luci flanked her grandfather and walked with him over to a sturdy chair and helped him sit. An older gentleman and lady sat nearby, and the man stood and shook Tito's hand.

"That's my grandfather, Hans, the one your grandfather said he knew. Looks like he remembers. My grandmother might have known him, too."

Tears pricked her eyes, and Ali pressed her lips together to keep them from falling. What a sweet gesture bringing Tito here. So many people simply ignored the elderly once they got to a certain age or couldn't function as well physically or mentally. She'd been trying to visit her grandfather every week if she could. It wasn't always easy with two jobs and a three-year-old who got cranky at times.

Ali got bold and wrapped her hands around Greg's arm. "I know I've said it before, but thank you. This means a lot to me, and I can tell it means something to my grandfather."

Greg placed his hand on top of hers and lowered his head. "I like seeing you happy, Ali. And your grandfather's a great guy. I look forward to talking to him later. Looks like he's catching up with my grandparents for now."

Ali scouted out the yard and recognized many of the occupants. Some she'd met at the Easter Egg Hunt earlier in the year. A few she knew from community events. Leah she knew from school.

Greg slung his arm over her shoulder and guided her forward. "Come on, I'll introduce you to anyone you don't know."

"There's going to be a quiz later, right?"

Greg leaned down and whispered in her ear, "If you're real nice, I'll help you pass."

If he stayed this close and continue to touch her, she might pass out. His presence was overwhelming and made her as giddy as when they'd been on Crisis Team together.

For the next half hour, Ali was introduced to and chatted with Greg's family and some good friends. Sofie took her plate of brownies, saying, "I'm not making any promises that these will make it to the kitchen fully intact."

Ali's eyes wandered the yard often, searching out Jillian. The girl was in her glory. The cousins, Matty and Tanner, were only slightly older, and Kiki was about a year younger. Darcy's daughter, Hope, who'd helped her at Easter, was a few years older but had latched onto Jillian for some reason. Jillian danced and ran and jumped around like all the rest of the kids. The yard was good-sized, and the street was quiet with all the occupants of the three houses here at the party.

Greg took her elbow. "Do you want something to drink? I'm sorry. I should have asked you earlier. We've got lemonade, iced tea, bottled water, soda, and juice boxes. Or we have adult beverages, as well. Mostly beer, but you might be able to coerce Leah and Sofie to share some of their wine. I may have a bottle somewhere in the house, too."

"Do you drink much wine?" He'd had a glass at the restaurant last week.

"Not when I'm at home. I'm more a beer man, usually Sam Adams. The wine is probably left over from when Wendy lived here, but I don't think wine goes bad. It's supposed to age, right?"

Wendy? His wife. From what she'd pieced together, she and Greg didn't get married until after she'd gotten pregnant. He hadn't said it outright, but he'd hinted that was the reason. And she'd died shortly after Ryan was born. When would she have been drinking wine? Not when she was pregnant, hopefully. Maybe she hadn't nursed. Not all new mothers were successful with that.

Ali shook her head to clear it. It wasn't her place to make judgments on other people. She sure didn't want anyone doing that to her. She had plenty of faults, and she admitted to every one.

"I'd love some iced tea, but I can get it if you point me in the right direction."

He took her elbow and guided her toward the house. "I'd be happy to escort you there. I know this isn't exactly the ideal date, and we're hardly alone, but I was hoping to spend a little time with you today."

"You are spending time with me right now. You're right, though. We aren't alone."

The kids running around were loud and crazy enough,

but the aunts, uncles, and cousins made that number much higher. How did he keep track of all of them? But glancing around at the chatter and laughter and generally happy vibe, she knew she'd love to have this much family, especially when they all seemed to get along.

Greg took her into the house, opened the fridge, and pulled out a large pitcher with clear brown liquid in it.

"Iced tea." He dropped some ice in the glass first, then poured the tea over it.

"What a great kitchen. It's so big. Do you do lots of cooking?"

"My mom had it renovated years ago with all the fancy gadgets. She's a fabulous cook. It comes from being Italian, I guess. She works as a baker at Sweet Dreams downtown now. I use it, but I'm not sure I work the same kind of magic that she did."

Ali looked at the double oven and six-burner stove. "Oh, the meals I could make in here."

Greg's eyes gleamed with mirth. "Play your cards right and I might let you."

What did he mean by that? Her first thought was of her living here. But…no. No. He likely only meant she could come and cook for him. She'd love that. Jillian never ate much. Her sister didn't like most of the ingredients Ali put in food. Butter, cream, meat, eggs. All stuff that had too much cholesterol, calories, and fat. And cooking fancy meals for one person wasn't much fun.

"Um." Greg glanced around nervously. "Did you want a tour of the house?"

Was he only offering to be polite or was he nervous for another reason?

"I should probably keep an eye on Jillian." There. She'd given him an out if he wanted one.

After peeking out the kitchen window, he shook his head. "She's happy as a clam. Let me show you around."

The kitchen took up most of the back of the house, except for a small half bath, a pantry closet, and a mudroom filled with coats hanging on hooks and shoes underneath. Wouldn't that be nice to have a place for all the dirty shoes, so they didn't drag mud through the house? A stairway also curved up along the back wall.

"The dining room is through here." He led her to the middle of the house where a large room housed a huge table that could comfortably fit at least ten people. There were two built-in hutches in a gorgeous, light brown stained wood.

"Do you feed half the neighborhood?"

"There were times my mother used to feed the hockey team."

"You played hockey?"

"Yeah. I still do with some of my old teammates. We were undefeated my four years in high school. I coach Ryan's hockey team, as well. Over the summer, when we don't have regular practices, I run some hockey camps at the rink for kids who want to keep up their skills."

"Wow, your resume gets longer every time we talk."

Greg shrugged and brushed it off. She noticed he didn't dwell on his accomplishments often and made sure to point out good qualities in others.

"The living room is in here." He guided her through the doorway, and she almost fell over.

The room was gorgeous. Large, with windows that curved along the front of the house. She should have known it had to be like this from the shape of the wrap around porch, but she hadn't imagined this. The back of the room had a fieldstone wall with a massive fireplace in it. The tan and white stone lightened the room and gave it a rustic feel. Pictures littered the huge wooden beam over the hearth.

An upright piano sat against the inside wall, and several couches and chairs filled the rest of the room. It was open and airy but also had a homey feeling to it. More pictures lined the tables and walls, and Ali stole a quick peek at them. Mostly Ryan at various stages of life, from baby to now. A few pictures of Greg with his sisters and parents. No pictures of the wife that she could see.

Had Greg taken her death so hard that he couldn't even view a picture of her? The poor man, having to deal with a newborn when the love of your life wasn't there to share the joy.

"Come on. I'll rush you through the rest." Greg proceeded to the hall, and Ali followed.

A small room was nestled behind the curving stairway. "That's a family room and has the TV in it. My mom hated having it in the living room, and I guess I got used to it because I haven't changed it."

"There are five bedrooms upstairs," he continued as he climbed up in front of her.

"Five bedrooms? What do you do with all of them?"

He spun on the landing, and she nearly plowed into him. "When we were all growing up, we each had a room, and the extra was used as a sewing room for my mom."

"She sews and cooks? Is there anything she doesn't do?"

Greg chuckled. "She doesn't play the piano."

Greg showed her each of the rooms. Ryan's room was a typical little boy's space. Sports paraphernalia littered most surfaces, along with some team pictures and some of him with his dad. One picture sat back on the top of his dresser of a tall, slim woman with dark hair and a serious expression. Greg stood next to her and had his arm around her shoulder. His face was neutral, and she couldn't tell any emotions from this image. Was this their wedding? They both had on nice clothes but not what she'd call wedding attire. Unless it was a very informal wedding.

She wasn't about to ask. It wasn't any of her business. When Greg waved at his room, she ducked her head inside quickly. Warm and neat, it looked like a room that didn't have a woman's touch to it. There also were no pictures of his wife. Many of Ryan and his family, but Wendy hadn't made it anywhere in the room.

After seeing the guest room with a fancy bedspread Ali would bet money either his mother or sisters picked out, they stopped in the room at the back. He opened a door on the back wall. "This is the extra room, and there are stairs that lead to a large attic room up there. That's where my parents used to throw all of us cousins when we were together. Right now, it mostly has junk and old debris in it. Someday, I'd like to clean it out, but since it's only Ryan, he hasn't needed that much space to play."

"Wow. I can't imagine living in a house this size. You could fit my whole house on one floor here. I love all the little details like this." She pointed to the window seat and the built-in drawers underneath.

Greg stepped into the hallway, then the back landing where a washer, dryer, and large sink sat. One stop shopping with laundry on the same floor as the bedrooms. Even with a one-floor house, she didn't have that. Her washer and dryer were in the basement.

"There are some neat things in this house," Greg said. "Someday, I'll show you more. We should probably get back downstairs. Can't have anyone wondering where we are." He winked at her, then led her down the stairs.

As she made her way behind him, she allowed her imagination to wander. What would it be like to live in a house like this...with a man like Greg Storm?

CHAPTER SIXTEEN

*G*reg surveyed the yard from his back deck and smiled. His dad's birthday party was a huge success. Not that he figured it would be anything but. Technically, he was the host, yet every one of his relatives had brought food, chairs, and fabulous company. When the Storms got together, they always enjoyed themselves.

Zeroing in on where Ali stood with Sofie, his cousin Sara, and Nathaniel's wife, Darcy, he examined her face to make sure she was having a good time. She threw her head back and laughed at something Darcy said, and Greg's shoulders released from their hunched position.

"So you finally did it, huh?" Alex came up behind him and snickered. "Bit the bullet and asked her out?"

Greg sneered, aware he'd given Alex plenty of shit when Gina had first arrived back in town after inheriting the house from her grandmother. Living across the street, he'd seen how Alex practically panted after his now-fiancée, drooling and doing anything she asked. It had been amusing to see his uptight cousin lose all means of control. As opposite as Alex and Gina were, they complemented each other.

He'd heard Alex call her the missing piece to his puzzle. Corny but sweet.

"Our first date was the other night when her grandfather went missing."

Alex's mouth dropped open. "Shit. That was your first date? That's one for the books."

"Luckily, we'd managed to eat most of our dinner before she got the call. We just couldn't quite stick the landing." That was an understatement. The goodnight kiss had been laughable.

"I've met her a few times when she helped out with the community center. She seems nice. Hope it works out for the two of you. If that's what you want. I suppose you could be taking pointers from Luke."

Greg snorted. Alex's brother, Luke, was a renowned player. The guy had a new lady on his arm and in his bed every week. Although he was guessing he used someone else's bed. Doubtful Alex allowed that revolving door in his place.

"I'm not ready to propose, though Ryan would be thrilled if I did. I'd also like more than a one-night stand. This is my first foray into dating since Wendy, so I think I'll take it slow and make sure I don't completely screw up."

"I'd give you advice, but my dating life sucked. You're on your own."

Alex patted him on the shoulder, then cruised to where his future wife huddled with Tessa and baby Joey. Greg debated what he should do now. A few of his cousins were rumbling about getting a basketball game going in Alex's driveway. It was a tradition whenever a few of them got together. But Sebastien was leaving shortly, and he hadn't had a chance to say more than a few words to him. Fortunately, Gram and Gramps had been thrilled to see him.

Wandering over, he eased into the chair next to the

elderly man. "Have you been enjoying yourself, Mr. Cabrera?"

"Oh, yes, young man, it's been wonderful. Though I don't know where my Bonita got off to. Probably gossiping with all the other old biddies in her sewing circle. They sure do like to talk about the neighbors."

"I'm sure that's where she is. Can I get you anything else to eat or drink?"

"Oh, no. Hans and Ingrid have made sure to keep me fed and watered today. So nice to see you again. It must have been several months since we've run in the same circles." He directed that at Greg's grandparents, who smiled patiently. Their eyes held sadness that someone their age had such memory loss and confusion.

"You were telling me the other day about the job you had at the gas station as a boy. What was your first car again?"

Greg sat back and listened as Sebastien launched into specific details regarding the auto he'd bought and refinished once he'd been old enough to drive.

A touch on his shoulder had him glancing up. Ali stood behind him, smiling down at her grandfather. "You loved that old car so much, Tito. Wasn't that the one you had your first date with Abuela in?"

Greg reached for Ali's hand and tugged until she was leaning against the arm of his Adirondack chair. He'd seen his parents sit near each other like this, and he kind of liked the idea of Ali doing it with him.

"Tito, the shuttle is here to take you back home."

Sebastien blinked, then closed his eyes for a second. "I am getting tired. It's tough getting old." He peered at Greg and Ali. "Don't do it. Stay young for as long as you can."

The shuttle pulled into his driveway, so he and Ali helped Sebastien get up from his chair and went with him to say goodbye to those he had been chatting with. Ali called out to

Jillian to come say goodbye. The little girl's face fell, but Ali planted her fists on her hips and the child loped over.

"Bye, Tito. I see you soon."

Sebastien patted her on the head. "Thank you, Alandra. Now, go run and play."

Ali's body slumped, and she sighed. He'd been fairly lucid for most of the day. They escorted him to the van and helped get him buckled.

Ali thanked the driver and kissed her grandfather on the cheek. "I'll see you soon. Tito."

"Don't be too long, Bonita. I miss you when you aren't with me."

As the van pulled away, Ali stood stiffly, her back to him. A tiny sniff had him gripping her shoulders and rubbing up and down her arms. He wasn't sure what to say, but she leaned slightly back against him, so he figured maybe he didn't need to say anything.

"He had a good time."

Ali turned in his arms and rested her hands on his chest. "I haven't seen him this animated in a long time. I keep telling my sister and mom that we need to get him out with family more, but my sister can't be bothered, and my mom and he had a little falling out after my dad passed away. Tito said my dad worked too hard and that's what caused his heart attack. He suggested my mom was to blame."

"I'm sure he was upset from losing his son and said things he didn't mean. It happens to all of us."

Like all the things he'd said about Wendy after she'd died. Ranted and screamed at times when he was walking the floor with a fussy newborn. Fortunately, he'd never shared any of his feelings with anyone else. He'd simply allowed everyone to think he was mourning his wife. For the past ten years.

As he held Ali in his arms, he wondered why he hadn't

moved on long ago. But if he had, he wouldn't have been in a place to be with Ali now. He liked this place. A lot.

"My mom was planning to move the desserts outside for the kids. Want to help me carry some of the platters?"

Ali laughed as they hiked across the yard. "You honestly think those kids haven't been sneaking some of those brownies and cookies all afternoon? The plate I brought mine on is almost empty."

"Pretty sure Leah is to blame for that. Brownies are her weakness."

"Mmm. And there's nothing like a little chocolate frosting on top to help a woman appease certain cravings."

Greg was having some cravings himself, staring at her beautiful face and the sassy bounce of her ponytail.

Inside the house, they caught Sofie licking chocolate frosting off her fingers. She rounded on them, her eyes wide.

"Oh. My. God. These are the ones you made, Ali? Greg, you have to marry her, so she'll bring them to every party we have."

Ali threw back her head and laughed. Because that was a ridiculous suggestion or did she like the idea? *Too fast. Slow down, hose jockey.* This was essentially their second date, and he hadn't even kissed her. Not really. A peck on the cheek didn't count. Maybe when he dropped her off tonight, he could remedy that.

A few more relatives tromped into the house and helped haul the sweets out to the tables set up in the yard. In seconds, the kids, both young and old, swarmed like locusts, decimating the plates, leaving only bits of desserts here and there.

Greg steered Ali over to a group of chairs where Erik and Tessa sat with Nathaniel and Darcy. It was adorable how Nathaniel kept reaching over and stroking Darcy's baby bump. Leah joined them and soon they were deep in discussion about schools and education. Nathaniel and Darcy's son, Tanner, was on the spectrum so they tried to keep on top of his schooling and needs. Erik and Tessa had three children and had lots of questions about what they should know before starting in grade school.

Greg hung back and allowed Ali and Leah to share their experiences as teachers. Every now and then, he put in his two cents as a parent.

"I've been fortunate Ryan has gotten placed in classrooms with excellent teachers who've provided what he needs." He gave a side eye to Ali and winked. "Well, except for this year, but you can't win them all."

Ali's mouth dropped open. She glared at him, as her mouth quirked to the side. "Well, let me tell you about some of the parents we have to deal with."

Darcy laughed at their antics. "I bet it's the worst when the parent asks you out, huh? I had to deal with being the nanny where the kid's father had a thing for me."

"A very big thing," Nathaniel said, his eyes shining with the love he had for his wife. Another odd couple in his family. He wouldn't knock it. He was hardly one to talk when his only relationship in ten years had walked out on him after giving birth to his child.

A high-pitched scream rent the air, and the moms all jumped up to see who it was. Greg could tell it wasn't Ryan by the tone, but he still checked what was going on.

"Jillian." Ali raced over to the driveway where some of the kids were attempting to use Ryan's scooter. The little girl sat on the hot top, tears streaming down her face. Greg followed behind Ali to see if there was anything he could do.

Ali scooped her up and checked that nothing was broken, bones or skin, then cuddled her daughter to her shoulder. Jillian plunked her thumb in her mouth and curled up on her mother's shoulder.

"Is she okay, Dad?" Ryan ran over, his eyes filled with concern. "I didn't want the kids to use it, but they got mad when I wouldn't."

"She's fine, Ryan," Ali assured him. "I should have been watching her better. I'm sorry if she was pestering you."

Ryan's mouth tightened. "No, we were having fun, and I like hanging out with her. I think the scooter is too big for her to handle."

Greg walked over to the other children and picked up the toy. "I think Ryan's going to put this in the garage for now. How about if you all go play in the grass next to the back porch?"

That way the adults could keep a closer watch on them. It was getting later, and they might want to eat again soon. Ryan grabbed the scooter and wheeled it away. The other children scampered to where Greg had directed them.

Ali brought Jillian back to her previous seat and tucked the girl in her lap. Tanner climbed into Nathaniel's lap and mimicked Jillian's pose, except he used a small race car going up and down his father's arm to soothe himself.

Conversation started up again, but every time Ali tried to speak, Jillian would take her mother's face and turn it to her. Greg could see Ali's frustration, but she never got cross with her daughter. There must have been an entire class in college for teachers on patience, and Ali obviously had gotten top grades.

When Jillian whined again and started wiggling in her mother's lap, Ali stood and gave a tired smile. "I'm sorry. I think today has been a little overwhelming for her. She isn't used to so many kids for such a long period of time. She's accustomed to being the center of attention. She didn't have a nap today and must be exhausted. We should probably go."

Greg stood. He didn't want her to leave, but he certainly understood her concerns. "I'll take you home."

"Oh, no, it's fine. I'm only a few blocks away. You should stay with your family. We can walk."

Ali attempted to put Jillian down, but the little girl let out a whine and wrapped her arms around Ali's neck.

"Let Greg drive you," Nathaniel said. "She may be small, but after a while they get a little heavy." He indicated the boy in his lap who'd closed his eyes and was possibly sleeping.

"Let me tell Ryan where I'm going, and I'll give you a lift."

As Greg found his son and filled him in, Ali went around and thanked everyone for a good time. Ryan bounced over to her and hugged her best he could with a small child in her arms.

"I'm so glad you came, Mrs. C. Did you have a good time with my dad and my family?" Greg knew exactly why that question was so important to the boy, but luckily Ali didn't seem to know the deeper meaning.

"I enjoyed myself, Ryan. Thank you. I'm sure I'll see you soon."

Ryan shot Greg a look, and Greg chuckled at the overt hints his son was sending him. He wanted his father to ask her out again. He had the same idea, but he certainly wasn't planning on doing it in front of an audience.

"Whose SUV is this?" Ali asked after they'd secured Jillian in the car seat in the back.

Greg slowly drove down the road away from his house, and the party still going strong.

"It's TJ and Sara's. They give Hope and Zane a ride up from the Cape at times, thus the car seat."

"Darcy's brother and daughter, right? Doesn't Hope live with her mom?"

"Long story short. Darcy had Hope at seventeen and gave her up. Hope's adoptive mothers offered an open adoption, but only recently did Darcy tell Hope who she was."

"Oh, wow, I didn't realize. Hope looks like she belongs right in there with all the rest of the Storm kids."

Greg shrugged. "My family's like that. Hopefully, Jillian had a good time today."

"She did. Absolutely. But the no nap thing doesn't make for a happy camper later in the day."

They drove into Ali's driveway, and Greg helped get the little girl out of the car seat. But she was having none of it and wanted her mom. Ali sighed and lifted her daughter into her arms.

Greg accompanied them to the side door and took the key from Ali to help her unlock and open it. She pivoted to face him, a serene smile on her face.

"Thank you so much for everything today. It was marvelous. The food, the company, and especially inviting my grandfather to come. It meant so much to him. It meant so much to me."

"Mama," Jillian whined and wiggled in Ali's arms.

"I'm glad. I liked having you there today." Greg stepped closer and leaned in, but Jillian started to growl.

"Mama, go in. I want my snuggie."

Ali's eyes rose, then closed for a second. "I'm sorry. I've got to get her cleaned up and in bed."

"I understand. I know it's only two days' notice, and you might have plans already, but the Fourth of July is Monday, and Ryan and I were planning on going out on the boat. Do you think you and Jillian would want to come? It would only be a few hours in the late morning. We'd be back in time for a nap. For Jillian or you."

Ali smiled wide. "That sounds great. Text me the details."

"Will do."

Greg started to walk away, then turned back and planted a swift kiss on Ali's cheek. One of these days, he wanted to finally make it to her lips.

ALI PLANTED a kiss on her daughter's freshly scrubbed face. That was about all she'd been able to manage with the overly tired child after a day filled with too much sugar and an abundance of children. In the morning, she'd have to give the girl a full bath. Maybe let Jilly play in there for a while. Ali could sit on the floor next to the tub with a book, perhaps, and read.

Or she could moon over Greg Storm and the not quite kiss she'd gotten from him tonight. The feel of his lips on her cheek for the second time was delightful, but she had to wonder what they'd feel like on her lips.

The day had been much better than she'd originally anticipated. Not that she didn't think the Storms would be welcoming, but she'd thought she and her daughter would feel like outsiders. That couldn't have been further from the truth. She'd felt at ease with every one of them. Except maybe Greg. But that was a whole different kind of nervousness.

They hadn't spent the whole time glued to each other's side, and if anyone had been observing them who didn't know the situation, they might not have even figured out that it had been a date. Kind of. A date that included your kid and your elderly grandparent, who both needed to be watched all the time.

But the fact that Greg had suggested they pick up Tito and bring him along had melted her heart. She'd already been a bit giddy with the man ever since they'd been on the Crisis Team years ago. Then, she got Ryan in her class and her awareness of him had heightened even more whenever he was around.

After making sure the night light in Jilly's room was on, Ali tiptoed out, leaving the door open a crack. It was only eight-thirty. Hardly time for her to go to bed yet. The Storms were most likely still going strong. It would have been nice to stay and spend more time with them, with Greg, but her responsibility was always to her daughter first.

Her own family never quite lasted that long when they had a celebration. Valeria tended to shoo everyone out once her timeframe was through, and Mama got tired if she'd been up and about too long, especially if her grandchildren were too active. The few days a week she watched Jillian for her was plenty, according to Martina Cabrera.

Tomorrow was Sunday, and she and Jilly would meet Mama and go to church. Usually, they went to visit Tito after. Hopefully, today hadn't been too much for him.

Then Monday, she would see Greg again. He was taking them out on his boat. What did she need for this? Should she wear a bathing suit? Was there a place to change on the boat or go to the bathroom? Jillian was potty trained, but when she had to go, she had to go. So many questions. Should she text Greg with them or wait until he contacted her?

Slumping onto the living room couch, she pulled out her phone and tapped out the questions she needed to ask him. He might not see them right away, since he'd be busy with his family, but he'd hopefully see them first thing in the morning and answer her then.

She pressed send, then got up and put water on to make tea. She'd barely put the kettle on the stove when her phone vibrated on the table. Swiping the screen, she saw Greg had answered her questions.

—*I'll pick you and Jillian up around 9:30. Small bathroom onboard. I have life vests for all sizes. Bathing suits optional. But if you're taking requests, I'd love a teeny weeny bikini. We should be back shortly after noon. I'll have snacks and drinks for the kids.*—

Ali laughed and texted back. —*I'm not sure how you'd look*

in a teeny weeny bikini. I'm certainly not wearing one. We'll make brownies and be ready on time.—

The phone vibrated almost immediately. —*I'll try not to be so early this time.—* He finished with a winky emoji.

—*That would be great.—* She ended with her own winky emoji.

Her tea kettle whistled before she could think of anything else to say to him. Maybe best not to push it. Her mother always warned her about not being too forward with guys. That they got turned off by it.

She sat down with her teacup and blew on it to cool it. Her phone vibrated again, and she quickly checked the message.

—*I'm really looking forward to it, Ali. Night.—*

After responding with a sleep emoji, Ali knew he wasn't the only one looking forward to being together again.

CHAPTER SEVENTEEN

*G*reg couldn't take his eyes off Ali as she bent over and resecured her hair in a ponytail. The wind whipping off the ocean had pulled quite a few strands to blow around her face, and after too often pushing them back, she decided to fix it. Hopefully, it wasn't too much for her. Her enthusiastic face and laughter made him think she was enjoying it.

"This is such a great boat. How long have you had it?" Her gaze sought out the back bench where Ryan and Jillian sat. Both had on life vests, and Ryan had his arm around the little girl's shoulder as they watched the wake churning up behind the motor.

"It was a gift actually. From Wendy's dad after she died." Another secret he'd kept to himself. Most people thought Greg had been given the thirty-foot Bayliner because his father-in-law had moved to the Midwest and didn't need a boat any longer. Greg was well aware it was a bribe of sorts. Wendy had told her father what she was planning to do. Leave him and their child. Her dad hadn't wanted that information to become public knowledge.

"Oh." Ali's mouth formed a bow. "Does Ryan see him often?"

How did he tell a woman who was the epitome of love and motherhood that not everyone wanted to stay connected to their family?

"Wendy's mother died a few years before she did and her father lives in Kansas now. He sends cards and presents when he can." Usually, they included large amounts of money but rarely anything more than a signature. Never a phone call or visit. Ryan hadn't seen his maternal grandfather in over seven years. Luckily, the boy had Nick and Luci Storm. They made up for it in spades.

"But he's got your parents and sisters." Ali was on the same wavelength as him. "And all those cousins. You have such a great family."

"I won't argue with you there. They're the best anyone could ask for. They got me through a few times when I was pretty low."

Ali slipped off her captain's chair and stepped toward his, then put her hand on his arm. "I'm glad you had them to help you."

He was glad he had Ali right now so close. Peeking at the kids, he noted they were laughing and squealing at the water spraying up behind, getting them wet.

"I think you need a lesson on steering the boat." He sat back further on his chair and maneuvered her between him and the steering wheel.

"What?" she squeaked and shook her head, her hair bouncing around near his face.

"I'll teach you. No need to be worried. I'm right here behind you. Put your hands on the wheel." He placed his arms around her and put his hands over hers.

A tiny sigh escaped from her mouth, and Greg had to agree. It was heaven. He'd been wanting to see what it was like to hold her, and not just when he comforted her for something. Right now, it was only the two of them, and she was in his arms.

Giggles drifted behind them, and Greg peered over his shoulder again. Okay, they weren't quite alone, but the kids were happily bouncing on the back seat as they went over waves. He could pretend they were alone, to a degree.

As they sliced through the ocean, Greg nestled his nose in Ali's hair. The scent was fresh and alluring. Some light melon or berry fragrance.

"You smell good enough to eat."

Ali stiffened, and he cursed his stupid mouth blurting out whatever went through his mind.

"I mean your shampoo. It smells like some sort of fruit."

She relaxed against him and tipped her head so she could see him. "Yes, it's a berry blend. I usually get whatever's on sale. You know that huge teacher salary we make."

Greg chuckled and took another whiff. While they crashed through the waves, he pointed out some of the places on shore or the small islands they passed.

Ryan shouted over to him. "Dad, can me and Jillian have some of the snacks?"

"Go ahead. You know where they are."

Ryan dug in the cooler on the floor next to him. Often, he'd use the small fridge downstairs, but since they weren't staying on the boat for more than a few hours, he'd decided on a cooler today. Now, he was glad since it meant he didn't need to let Ali out of the circle of his arms.

"Are you hungry? Do you want a snack, too?" *Please, let her say no.*

That ponytail swung back and forth. "I'm fine right here as long as you are."

Yes! This was shaping up to be a great day. He kept his attention divided between the water in front of him, the kids behind him, and Ali wrapped in his arms. Maybe someday he'd have all his attention on her.

"We should probably turn around and head back. I know you said Jillian doesn't do well without a nap."

"Okay, but you need to do it. I have no idea how this thing works."

"We'll do it together." He loved pressing against her back as he slowed the boat down and steered so they were heading in the opposite direction. As much as he hated to go back, it would take as long to get there as it had to get where they were. He'd enjoy every second of holding her.

"Did you and Jillian have any plans later today?" He'd originally only asked her to come on the boat, but he'd been secretly hoping he could convince her to spend all day with them.

She pressed even closer to him and turned her head so he could hear. When she did, he skimmed his lips over her cheek. A soft moaning noise drifted his way. Shit, it was giving him thoughts he shouldn't be having in front of the kids.

"Jillian loves the fireworks, so I thought we'd go tonight to see them in the town common."

There was no mention of anyone else going with them. Had her ex seriously not even wanted to see his daughter over the long weekend? Or had they seen him yesterday? Greg didn't want to bring him up since Ali always got prickly mentioning the man.

"Could I possibly convince you and Jillian to come with us to the town fireworks tonight? Some years, I'm on fireworks duty but managed to get this year off. Alex is having a little get together at his house first, and we plan to all walk down together from there."

"Oh." Her lips pinched together. "That's a family thing. I don't want to butt in."

He tightened his arms around her and nuzzled into her hair again. "My family isn't like that. Ever. And I invited you, so you'll hardly be crashing the party. I'd like to spend some more time with you. And Jillian."

"It might be fun to be with a larger group. If you're sure you don't mind."

"I wouldn't have asked if I did." He pressed his lips to the side of her face again and grinned as Ali closed her eyes and relaxed against him. The sound of happy children's voices behind him kept him from doing much more.

It was almost an hour before they throttled down and cruised into Portsmouth Harbor, then down the Piscataqua River to the boat club where he rented a slip. As he drifted into his spot, Ali gathered their towels and bags. Ryan jumped out and grabbed the rope, then wrapped it around the hook to keep the boat from drifting farther. Now that he was older, he loved helping when they went out.

"Mama, I all wet." Jillian giggled, lifting her arms to her mother.

"You are, sweetie. From all the big waves. Did you have fun?" Ali swiped the towel around her daughter's face and arms, then tucked it in her bag.

"Yes!" Jillian shouted and bounced around the deck of the boat.

Greg shut everything down and jumped off the boat to make sure the ropes were tied tightly. When he knew it was all good, he put the life vests in the cabin and locked it up. Who knew when he'd be back next?

"Are you ladies all set to go?"

Ryan waited on the dock, holding his hand to help them up. Greg loved seeing his little boy growing into such a gentleman. After hefting the cooler onto the dock, he helped Ali and Jillian up, then followed them.

Ryan carried a few things as Greg slung his bag over his

shoulder and picked up the cooler. As they strolled down the dock to the marina, Jillian couldn't stop jumping and dancing as she held her mom's hand.

"I think you had fun, little Miss Jillian." The girl was adorable in her exuberance.

"I did. Can we do it again, Cap'in?"

"Jillian," her mother warned.

Bending to her level, he grinned at the child. "I'd love it if you came again. I need to give your mom more lessons on how to drive the boat."

"Can I drive it?" The child's face scrunched up in confusion.

"Not quite yet, sweetie." Ali's eyes opened wide.

Greg tousled the girl's hair. "Even Ryan isn't old enough to do it yet. But we'll get you there someday. Don't you worry."

Ali threw a sly look over her shoulder at him as they wended their way through the parking lot toward his truck. What was that for?

Because he'd told Jillian eventually she'd be able to drive the boat? Yeah, that wouldn't be for more than a few years. Would he and Ali still be together then? That was the question of the century.

ALI PEERED in the extended cab of Greg's truck as it pulled into her driveway. Jilly had nodded off in the few minutes from Greg's house, where he'd dropped Ryan off with his grandparents first, to her place.

"Why don't you let me carry her in? If you want to keep the car seat in there for later, it's fine."

Ali nodded and gathered their bag as Greg shifted her daughter into his arms. He managed to do it without Jilly waking up. Of course, he'd most likely done it with his son many times in the past. Quickly, she trotted up to the door and unlocked it, then led the way to Jilly's room.

Greg gently placed the sleeping child on the bed and backed out of the room. Ali fussed with removing her daughter's shoes, then made sure she had her snuggie blanket in case she woke up. As she passed by Jilly's mirror, she almost fell over. Her hair was a wild mess.

As she tiptoed down the hallway, she attempted to finger comb some of the snarls back into place. Greg stood in her kitchen, gazing out the window into her small backyard. It was nowhere near as nice as his, but it worked for her and Jillian.

"I'm sorry. You didn't have to wait for me if you have something else you needed to do. Thanks for bringing her in. And for taking us out on the boat. She had a blast. So did I."

She couldn't even put into words what she'd experienced when Greg had pulled her in front of him to steer the boat. With his arms wrapped around her. *Dios*, the warmth and emotions that had played through her while she'd stood there had been like nothing she'd felt before. And that included Jeff, the bastard. Looking back now, she should have seen what her ex was. A narcissistic, arrogant charmer who only wanted someone to wait on him hand and foot. But he'd given her Jillian and she'd never regret that.

"I'd love to take you out again. Anytime you want."

He was referring to going out on the boat, but she'd love to go out with him again anywhere. Any time. Especially if he'd hold her again like he did today.

"Thank you. I'm sure Jillian would love it."

Greg stepped closer and ran his hands up her arms. Chills exploded inside her. "How about Jillian's mom? Would she love it?"

Ali nodded, not sure what to say or do with him standing so close.

"Your daughter is precious, Ali, and I know Ryan has loved seeing her lately. Like I love seeing her mom. I was kind of hoping—" His lips tightened, and he glanced away for a second.

"You were hoping?" Her heart picked up the tempo.

His fingers pushed past her windblown hair and caressed her cheek. "I was hoping I'd get the chance to do this."

His face lowered toward her, and Ali forgot to breathe. His lips touched hers as he tugged on her neck to move her closer. The kiss was perfect. Soft, gentle, sweet. It got her insides fluttering like she'd swallowed a swarm of butterflies.

Reaching up, she slid her hands onto Greg's shoulders and felt the firm muscle under her fingertips. He eased away, but then his lips dipped back in for a second kiss. It made her dizzy with need and had her wanting more.

When he let her up for air, he kept his forehead pressed to hers. "I've been wanting to do that for a long time."

"Really?" As long as *she'd* wanted it?

"Yes, really." His breathing was as ragged as hers.

"Was it what you imagined?" *Please, let him say it was a good kiss.*

His head shook, and her stomach dropped. Had he not felt the same electric current that she had when their lips had touched?

"It was so much better." He dove in for another kiss, and relief had her looping her arms all the way around his neck, holding his firm chest against hers.

The sensations made her lightheaded, but she held on tight to the man stirring up all these feelings and emotions. It was like she'd never been kissed before. Certainly not like this.

When Greg's lips receded, the rest of him did not. She

was still snuggled close to his chest, his arms around her back.

"I'd love to continue, but your daughter is only a few feet away."

"Yeah," was all she managed to get out. What was wrong with her? Her mind had completely shut down to any sensible thoughts. Glancing up, she found his hazel eyes focused intently on her face.

"Do you think we could do this for another few minutes? How long does Jillian usually nap?" Greg's gaze wandered down the hallway.

"At least an hour, unless something wakes her." Why was her voice so breathy and raw?

"Then, we'll be very quiet." He kissed her again, and Ali gave herself up to the experience. Standing in her kitchen, kissing a gorgeous firefighter she'd been lusting after for years. His lips were like Heaven, and he'd opened the gate to let her in.

When they paused, she skimmed her hand along his neck to the back of his head and into his hair. It was thick but soft, and she relished being able to run her fingers through it.

"Mmm, that feels nice, Ali. I'm so glad I put my big boy pants on and asked you out."

"Am I that scary?"

"No, I just haven't done this since before Ryan was born, and I'm out of practice."

"Now that you've got it down pat, did you want to try it elsewhere?" Had she only been the guinea pig?

Greg pulled back and stared. "No, I wanted to spend time with you. Why—"

"I'm sorry." She patted his chest and tried to smile. "Jeff tossed me away easy enough when I wasn't the same woman he'd married. My self-esteem may have gotten a little dented, so there are times I'm a bit sensitive. You should know that. I can't always turn it off."

Greg stroked his fingers down the side of her face. *Dios*, that made her feel cherished and wanted.

"Your ex is an idiot. I asked you out, Ali, because over the last few years, every time I've seen you, there was something about you that pulled me in. When we first met, you may have still been married, I'm not sure. Then, later, I never said anything because you'd only recently been divorced, and I figured you might not be ready to move on yet. This year Ryan was in your class. But the more I got to know you, the more I realized what an amazing, loving, intelligent, fun, and genuinely nice person you are."

"Wow, you make me sound pretty good." In his words, she'd almost believe it.

He pushed a few strands of hair back. "Not just pretty. Beautiful. You truly are one of the loveliest women I've ever met."

"Oh, thank you." Her word turned into a yawn, and she tried to hide it. But too much fresh ocean air had made her tired.

"I'm sorry. You could probably use a nap like Jillian after being on the boat all morning. I forgot to warn you it can wear you out."

"I'll be fine. You've probably got stuff you need to do."

He shrugged and shook his head. "Not until later. What about you?"

She matched his shrug. "Can't go anywhere with Jillian napping."

His lips pinched together, and his head swiveled toward the living room. Then, he wrapped his arm around her shoulder and led her to the couch. "How about we both take it easy for a little while?"

He sat on the couch and tugged until she was next to him.

He placed his feet up on the hassock and lifted hers up there, too. With his arm still around her shoulder, he tugged until she rested against his chest.

"There, now we can both relax for a bit." Leaning his head back, he closed his eyes and began to breathe rhythmically. Maybe he could relax, but with half of her body pressed against him, it was far from relaxing for her. She was too aware of how close he was. And what his presence did to her.

"Stop thinking so hard." Greg chuckled and pressed a kiss to the top of her head. "We'll have to deal with energized kids later. Enjoy the quiet for a while."

What he said made sense, and he did feel so warm and safe. Maybe she could let go for a little while. Closing her eyes, she focused on how incredible this man was for knowing what she needed and not pushing anything more. Slowly, her body relaxed.

A grumpy whine had her popping her head up. The clock over her piano told her she'd fallen asleep for almost an hour. Greg stirred and yawned as she disentangled herself from his arms. Somehow, he'd ended up tucked in the corner of the couch, and she'd been draped over his chest.

"Oh, sorry, I, uh—"

"You rested, Ali. That's what you were supposed to do."

"Mama." The whine came again, and Ali popped off the couch as Jilly trudged out of her room.

"Hey, sweetie. Did you have a good rest?" After scooping her daughter into her arms, she carried her back to the couch. This time she didn't snuggle into the handsome man's arms, even though she'd love to do it again.

"Hey, Jillian," Greg said softly. "Thanks for coming on the boat with me this morning."

Jilly perked up and leaned toward Greg. Yup, he had something that attracted all ages of females. "I come on the boat again?"

"That's an excellent idea. But I think in a little while we're heading over to my neighborhood to hang out with some of my family."

"The other kids there?"

"Most of them will be." He glanced at Ali. "I didn't even ask if you wanted to spend some time at Alex's before we go to the fireworks. I can pick you both up later if you had other things to do."

As much as she'd love to hang out with the Storm family, she didn't want to push herself on them too much in the same weekend. But Greg wouldn't have asked if he didn't want to spend time with her, right? Heck, he'd just sat on her couch and held her while they'd napped. Had he slept or merely watched her while she'd slept? *Madre de Dios*, she needed to stop analyzing every little thing he did and why he was doing it.

"You don't mind if we come hang out?" Okay, maybe she was being ridiculous, but she didn't want to be where she wasn't welcome.

Greg inched closer and took her free hand. "I would very much like you to come hang out. If I've given you any other impression, then I need to step up my game. My parents were hoping to see you again."

She wanted to yell that they'd love to come, but she had someone else to consider. "Jilly, sweetie, do you want to go where we were at the party the other day for a little while before we see the fireworks? Or would you rather stay home and play here for a bit?"

"Mama, we go see the other kids? I like them."

Ali peeked up at Greg to see him grinning. Guess he did want her there. Both of them. And that was the best thing of all. Greg had never made it seem like Jillian was a burden.

"Okay, can you give me a few minutes to repack a bag for her and maybe see if I can get a comb through my hair?"

She glanced down at Jilly's snarled braids. "And maybe redo her hair, too. Sorry."

"It's not a problem. Can I help? I have two younger sisters, and my mom would pull me in for hair duty if we were running late."

Jillian bounced up and down. "Mama, he do my hair? Please?"

Ali rounded up a brush and handed it to Greg, then ducked into her room to do something with her own mess. The snarls weren't too bad, and she was able to get them out and twist her hair into a messy bun. Good thing it was in style right now.

Jillian's hair was back in neatly combed pigtails on either side of her round little face. Her dad had never attempted to do either her or Valeria's hair, and Jeff had deserted them long before Jilly had enough hair to do anything to.

Within the hour, the three of them were pulling up into Greg's driveway. Cars lined the street, and kids and adults dotted Alex's lawn like they'd done Greg's a few days ago. Leah dashed over to them and hugged Ali.

"I'm so glad you're here."

Greg scowled. "Has Ryan been a pest while I've been gone?"

Leah rolled her eyes at her brother. "He's been fine. Having the time of his life being admired and adored by all his younger cousins."

"Mama, I go play with Ryan?" Jillian tugged on her mother's hand.

"Sure. Give me a second, and we'll go over."

"Let's all go over now," Leah chirped and took Jillian's hand and led her away.

"My sister is so strange at times." Greg folded his arms over his chest and stared after her.

Ali tipped her head toward the party. "Shall we go?"

Greg touched her back and pressed his nose to her hair. "I guess. Of course, ideally, I'd love to spend a few more minutes kissing you."

Ali took in a deep shuddering breath. "Mm, that was nice."

As they walked across the street, Greg growled. "I'll need to do better if all I got was *nice*."

Ali laughed. "*Very* nice."

Once they got into Alex's yard, Ali was immediately pulled into greetings and conversations with all his family. Every one of the Storms and their spouses or significant others was extremely jovial and good natured. Sara's husband, TJ, stood back and observed more than participated, and Erik's wife, Tessa, spent most of her time fussing over the baby, who was attempting to walk. She never initiated a conversation but was happy to engage when asked a question. Ali had dealt with students who were introverted like that and was glad to see no one gave Tessa a hard time about not being as boisterous as them.

At one point, while Gina was talking about the wedding, she froze, spun, and pointed at Greg. "You need to bring Ali. You are, right?"

Greg's brows drew together. "I responded a month ago before we—"

"Doesn't matter." Gina waved him off. "Ali, you can come, can't you? Please say you can?"

"Next weekend?" What would she do with Jillian?

Alex frowned. "Twelve days, actually."

"But you must've had to give the reception hall a head count already." She couldn't just crash the party.

"It doesn't matter." Gina shrugged, her face beaming. "We can squeeze another one in."

Ali could see Alex working things out in his head. "Luke put down a plus one, and I'm sure he's broken up with whatever flavor of the week he's been seeing. It should be fine."

Gina squealed and clapped, then planted a kiss on her fiancé's cheek. "You're getting so good at this spontaneity stuff, Felix."

Ali laughed at the nickname Gina had for her very fussy other half. They certainly were an odd couple.

Greg took her hand and squeezed. "I'd love it if you could come, but I understand if you already have other plans."

"Any other plans were sitting at home with my daughter. I'll have to see about getting someone to watch Jillian. The girl down the street was hoping for more babysitting hours."

Pulling out her phone, she whipped off a text to the teenager, then stuffed it back in her pocket. More discussion started on wedding plans, and Ali only half listened. She'd had a big wedding with Jeff, and her marriage had been a disaster in a short amount of time. As she eyed Greg where he stood with his cousins, she wondered if he'd ever get married again. And why was she thinking of marriage now that he'd kissed her?

Greg sidled up to her. "Hey, the guys want to play a little b-ball. Do you mind? I don't have to."

All the other cousins were heading to the driveway where the hoop was located. A few pulled off their shirts. "That's fine. I've got company here. What team are you on?"

He twisted his head to see what she was staring at, then smirked. "What team do you want me on? Shirts or skins?"

She bit her lip and shrugged. "Doesn't matter."

Greg laughed and squeezed her elbow before he loped over to where the guys tossed a ball around. After a few seconds of chatter with them, Greg peeked over his shoulder and whipped his shirt off.

Madre de Dios. The snug t-shirt had not done him justice.

Quickly, she twisted away and found herself face to face with Leah. Her friend sported an amused expression.

"Something wrong?"

"No, no, it's kind of warm today." She lifted her shirt away from her skin and flapped it back and forth until some cooler air circulated around her overheated skin.

"Does something about my brother make you uncomfortable? Is he treating you okay?"

"No, he's great. Super nice guy. Considerate. I just...uh... don't tell anyone, please. He throws me a little off-kilter at times."

Leah laughed, her eyes glowing. "That's supposed to be a good thing."

Ali snuck another glance at the basketball players. One in particular. After throwing the ball and getting a basket, Greg glanced her way. Her phone vibrated, allowing her to look away.

Checking the screen, she saw Destiny could babysit a week from Saturday.

Okay, well it looked like she was going to a Storm wedding.

CHAPTER EIGHTEEN

The party started slowing down, and the adults gathered the kids to get them ready for the fireworks on the town common. Potty breaks, sturdy shoes for walking down there, sweatshirts in case the breeze from the river picked up.

Greg grabbed a large blanket and tucked it under his arm. Ali slid the strap of her bag over her head and around her torso, then called Jillian.

"You need to hold my hand when we walk to town, sweetie. There'll be lots of cars on the road, and we don't want you to get hurt."

"Does Ryan hold your hand?" The little girl peered up at him, her nose crinkled as she asked.

"Ryan's a little older, and he knows to stay on the side of the road. He'll probably hold one of his cousin's hands." Matty was already vying for Ryan's attention.

Jillian's little lip popped out. Poor thing.

Greg got down on one knee in front of her. "Would you like a ride instead, like that?" He pointed to Nathaniel, who had Tanner on his shoulders.

"I go up there?" Jillian whipped around to stare at Ali. "Mama, I ride up there on Cap'in?"

Ali chuckled. "You're going to spoil her, you know."

"She deserves a little spoiling. Like her mom."

Ali's eyes opened wide. "Do I get a ride up there, too?"

Greg bit his lip to keep the words that sprang to mind from pouring out. Instead, he said, "Not right now, but I'm sure we can work something out later."

"You ready, Jillian?" The child bobbed her head, so Greg handed the blanket to Ali for a second and swung her up. He kept one hand on her leg and reached for the blanket again.

"Oh, I can handle this if you can take care of her. That's my baby girl you've got up there. She's your first priority right now."

"Got it."

As he examined the area, all his cousins started moving down the street. His grandparents had been dropped off a few minutes earlier, but everyone else liked to walk since there wasn't much parking near the common.

Erik pushed the double baby stroller, while Tessa held Matty's hand, Ryan on the other side. Nathaniel, with Tanner riding on top, held Darcy's hand, who held Hope's, who held Zane's. TJ and Sara had their arms wrapped around each other and walked next to Gina and Alex. His sister, Sofie, chatted with Alex's friend, John, and Leah walked next to Amy. Kevin and Luke led the way while his parents and aunts and uncles strolled slower behind them.

"Do you do this every year?" Ali asked as they meandered toward Main Street.

"Since I was a kid. We're lucky that we live so close to the town."

"Yet your street is quite private, and the houses are gorgeous. It's like your own family estate."

Greg laughed. "We used to think of it like that at times when we were younger. Of course, Nathaniel, Kevin, and Amy didn't live on the same street, but they came over often enough."

The closer they got to the center of town, the more people they saw and the more crowded it got. Ali sidled up closer and grabbed hold of his elbow. Jillian sang a little song as they walked.

"Why don't we put the blanket over by that tree?" Greg suggested. "It's not usually as congested there, since most people sit on the other side of the common to be closer to the fireworks." The fire department worked with the fireworks committee to set off the explosives over the river. The best place to see them was still the town green.

While Ali set the blanket and her bag down, Greg finagled Jillian from his shoulders. "There you go, munchkin. One ride to town. You can pay me my fee now."

Jillian's eyebrows screwed up together and her nose wrinkled. "I don't have any money."

Greg held his hands up by his side. "Then, how are you going to pay me?"

Jillian copied his gesture. "I don't know. I can give you something maybe."

Tapping his chin, Greg tipped his head. "What do you think is a fair trade?"

The child's tongue hung out of her mouth as her eyes rose up. "Uh, a hug? I got lots of those."

"I think I could accept that in payment."

Jillian bolted toward him. He caught her up and swung her around, then held her close for a few moments. "That's one of the best hugs I've ever gotten."

As he put her down, she giggled. "Does Ryan give good hugs?"

"He does. But he's getting older, and he's a little more stingy with them now."

"What stingy mean?"

Ali crouched next to her daughter. "It means when you want to keep something for yourself instead of sharing it."

Jillian's mouthed puckered. "Like Manny when 'Lita gives him cookies. He don't want to let me have any."

"Kind of like that, yeah. I'm glad you weren't stingy with your hugs for Captain Storm."

Ryan darted toward them, huffing and puffing. "They haven't done the frog jumping contest yet, Dad. I'm gonna enter Jeremiah, okay? Can Jilly come watch?"

Jillian jumped up and down, but Ali frowned. "Where is this? I don't want her where I can't see her."

"I'll watch her, Mrs. C., and Auntie Sofie is putting a frog in, too, so she'll be there."

Greg pointed to a group of people not too far away. "The frog jumping contest is right there. We can see them from here."

Ali nodded and whispered in her daughter's ear, "Behave and make sure to stay near Ryan."

The two kids loped off, and Ali's shoulders rose and fell. "I'm not used to her going off without me. It makes me nervous."

"Ryan's pretty responsible. He'll watch her. But we can stay right here and see them, too."

An announcement was made over the speaker for the contest and more people congregated near the racecourse. Ali's eyes never left her daughter, but Greg examined the rest of the area for people he knew.

His family strolled around the grounds, connecting with friends or looking in the booths. Alex bought Gina some cotton candy, while Erik and his two oldest fished in a small pool for prizes. The games were great for the younger crowd, and a local band played oldies music for the more mature visitors. He was somewhere in the middle, but he still loved watching it all.

Luke wandered toward him, chatting with a young woman with long auburn hair. She looked familiar, but Greg couldn't place her. She didn't seem like his cousin's typical sort. There was a freshness about her, and her outfit was conservative, a simple sundress that stopped right at her knees. Luke's usual companions ordinarily wore either something that showed a lot more skin or so tight it looked spray painted on. Extremely attractive, very little substance.

Maybe his cousin was becoming more particular with the women he dated. When they'd played basketball earlier, Luke had confided in them that he was being deployed at the end of August. He'd known for a while but hadn't told anyone so no one would get all weird with him. After what had happened to Erik when he'd been overseas, the worry was always there.

Once the couple got closer, Luke touched the woman on the shoulders and nodded. She went in one direction. He straight-lined it toward them.

"Did Ryan's frog win?" Luke asked, glancing around.

Greg shrugged. "He's still over there. I'm sure we'll hear soon enough. Who's the gal you were talking to? She looks familiar."

Luke peered over his shoulder to where the woman had gone. "That's Ellie Russell. We were lab partners in every science class I had at Brookside Academy."

Brookside was the exclusive private high school Luke and Nathaniel had both been smart enough to get into with a scholarship.

"Wait, I remember her. Super smart and pushed ahead a few grades, right?"

Luke nodded. "Yeah, she graduated from high school at fourteen."

Luke had been in high school when everything had happened with Wendy. The pregnancy, marriage, baby, and then the car accident. The house had been Greg's home base, and he hadn't left it often other than to go to work and back.

Another memory surfaced. "Didn't you go to the prom with her?"

Luke's face twisted. "Someone had to. Most of the guys were total jerks back then."

Greg lifted his chin. "You got something going on with her?"

Luke eyed him strangely. "Ellie? Nah, she's a nice girl. I'd never fool around with her."

Ali, who had been standing quietly by during this conversation, suddenly piped in. "What? Nice girls aren't good enough for you?"

Luke smirked, his eyes gleaming. "I'm not good enough for them. Especially someone like Ellie. She's a class act. I just want to have fun."

Ali shook her head and laughed, then lifted her head. "Be right back." She scurried off to where Jillian waved at her.

Greg peered at his cousin and shook his head. "You and your bad boy rep."

Luke waved his hand in the air. "Hey, I heard you took Ali on your boat today. That's got a bed on it, right?" Luke's eyebrows waggled up and down.

Greg sighed. "Right? We left the kids to drive the boat while we went into the cabin and screwed each other." Thank God Ali wasn't here right now.

"Ryan's what? Ten? What age can you drive a boat?" Luke grinned.

Greg slapped his cousin on the shoulder. "Lord help you if you ever become a father."

Luke took a few steps back, hands up, head shaking side to side. "Whoa, whoa. Let's not go there any time soon."

As Luke trotted off, Greg wondered if maybe someday he'd grow up. He was worried Luke's time overseas would accomplish that all too soon.

Jillian and Ryan raced over a few minutes later, Ali lagging behind them. The large frog Ryan had plucked from the creek in the woods behind their house attempted to get free from the grip he had him in.

"Jeremiah won second place, Dad!"

"He jumped and jumped," Jillian cried, mimicking the frog's actions.

"That's awesome. I suggest you get him back in the bucket you brought him in, so he doesn't get stepped on by anyone here. Make sure to let him go once we get back home."

"Yeah, Dad. I will," Ryan grumbled. The boy hated to be reminded to do something. Of course, having his teacher present to hear his father's lecture might be slightly embarrassing.

"I know you will. I'm simply doing my Dad job and saying these things because it's in the Dad manual."

"It's true," Ali backed him up. "Like making sure Jillian cleans her hands after touching the frog is in the Mom manual." She dug in her bag and drew out some baby wipes and proceeded to clean up her daughter's hands. After Ryan had replaced the frog and put the bucket in a safe place, she held a wipe out to him.

"I'm not your mom, but can I suggest cleaning up your hands, too?"

Ryan's cheeks turned pink, but he took the wipe and scrubbed like he was going into surgery.

The night had turned dark, and the crowd started settling into spots on the grass. Greg picked up the blanket and shook it out. "Is here okay?"

Ali's head swiveled as she checked out where the other Storms were. Close by, but not on top of each other. "Looks good. Will we be able to see the fireworks with this tree here?"

Greg pointed to where the main street was along the river. "The fireworks go off there. Haven't you been here before?"

Resting on the blanket, she stretched out her legs. "We used to go to the ball field to watch them. Jeff never wanted to go once we moved closer to town. Last year, Jillian was kind of young and I wasn't sure if she'd like the noise. Plus—" Her lips tightened, and she looked away.

Greg sat next to her and placed his hand on her shoulder. "Plus…?"

She gazed back at him, frowning. "The divorce had just been finalized, and I wasn't in a good place. Not really in the mood for fireworks."

"I'm sorry, Ali. That's a tough situation to be in. Your ex is an idiot, but if that didn't happen, you wouldn't be here with me now."

Her shoulders rose and fell. "Thanks. It's so silly to complain. Especially to you, when the woman you loved was suddenly taken from you. And right after your baby was born. I don't know how you got through it."

Greg swallowed at the lies of omission about to come from his mouth. "I focused on Ryan. And I have the best family anywhere."

His fingers skimmed her cheek, and he shuffled closer.

"Mrs. C., hi!" Two young children barreled toward them.

Greg pushed back, while Ali twisted to face the newcomers. "Hi, there, Madison. Ethan. Are you having a good summer?"

Greg smiled politely as Ali spoke briefly to the two children. Then, a few more kids showed up to say hi to their former teacher. Some of them must have been from years ago, because they looked too old to have had her this past year.

Ryan sat on Erik and Tessa's blanket with Jillian, rolling a small ball around with his cousins, Matty and Kiki. Joey was in Erik's arms, asleep.

Nathaniel and Darcy had their blanket butted up against Erik's, so that Hope and Tanner could interact with the other children. He'd never felt so fortunate as when he was with his family like this. A few times today, he'd seen Ali stare at all of them with wistful eyes. She'd mentioned her sister a few times, but for some reason she never spoke of her with the warmth he felt for his family. Or maybe he was only imagining it.

The night grew darker, and the first test firework went up to get everyone's attention. Scurrying feet scampered past and settled into their watching spot for the next half hour.

With the darkness came some possible hopes to connect to Ali a bit more. He scooted over right next to her and draped his arm around her shoulder.

"Is this okay?"

She shivered. The cold or his touch? Sinking further into him, she said, "It's nice."

The fireworks started, and lots of "oohs" and "ahhs" floated around the common. Greg barely registered what was going on in the sky. He was too interested in watching Ali's expressive face as her eyes lit up and her mouth opened wide in awe at the display up above them. She was totally unaware that he couldn't take his eyes off her, and it made her expressions even more charming. A warmth he'd never felt before nestled inside him, making him want to prolong this small contact with her.

He desired her, too, no doubt, but simply sitting with her as they viewed the display was so comforting and felt so right. Like she had been created explicitly for him to hold.

About halfway through the show, Jillian toddled over and climbed into Ali's lap. Luckily, his hand didn't need to move to accommodate the child, so he kept it right where it was, his thumb rubbing back and forth on her shoulder.

A few times, he caught Ryan sneaking a peek over his shoulder to where they sat. The boy's wide eyes as he noticed where his father's hand was almost took up his whole face. He didn't need to ask if his son approved of them as a couple.

What did *he* think of them as a couple? It was too soon to even go there. They'd gone out a few times, and he'd certainly enjoyed his time with her, but there were so many other factors they needed to think about. Not to mention, he had no idea how Ali felt about all this. The kiss they'd shared earlier today had knocked his socks off. How had it affected her?

For now, he wasn't going to worry about any of it. He'd take it one day at a time, see what happened, and enjoy having a woman by his side again to do things with. Wendy hadn't been much in the companionship department. Mostly, they'd had sex. Until she'd found out she was pregnant. Then, it had all stopped, except for their honeymoon night, when she'd thrown him a bone. After that, she'd complained she wasn't feeling well.

Fireworks exploded through the sky, building to the grand finale. Cheers and claps rose as well until the last burst of color exploded, then fizzled to the ground. Greg's firefighter buddies would be running around at this moment, making sure none of the embers turned into anything dangerous.

The crowd surged to their feet and started the shuffle away from the town center. His cousins all still relaxed, waiting for the rush to pass.

Ali twisted to face him. "Should we head out?"

Pointing to his family still sitting, he said, "It's easier if we wait for a bit until the crowds clear out. That way, you don't have to fight your way through or worry as much about the cars in the street. Is that okay?"

She gazed down at the sleeping child in her arms. It had been a long day and Jillian obviously didn't stay up this late. "I don't have a problem with it. Jilly's not saying much at the moment."

As families strolled by, he and Ali nodded and waved at people they knew. He'd been in town his whole life, but Ali worked at the school where all the children went. Between the two of them, they knew lots of residents. Some of whom sent strange glances their way, as if trying to figure out why they were sitting together. Having his name hooked up with Ali's wasn't the worst thing to be gossiped about. He'd spent years being "that poor man who lost his wife tragically, leaving him with a newborn." Hopefully, most people would be happy to see him finally moving on.

Once the majority of the crowd had dissipated, Greg got to his feet and reached for Jillian. "Why don't you let me carry her? If you don't mind getting the blanket and bag."

She appeared about to object, then shifted her daughter in her arms. Yeah, the child wasn't super heavy, but carrying her a few streets over wouldn't be easy for someone smaller like Ali.

"Thanks." Once the exchange was done, Ali picked up their things. Ryan waved from where he stood with Matty's hand in his. The young cousin sure had some hero worship going on with Ryan. Greg nodded back, knowing Erik and Tessa would keep an eye out on all the kids. And probably appreciated Ryan helping out.

"Are you sure you're okay carrying her?" Ali asked as they started on the sidewalk. "I've done it plenty of times."

"She weighs a lot less than Ryan, and there are still times I carry him upstairs to bed when he falls asleep watching TV."

"Thank you for such a fabulous day. I'm sure Jilly and I will sleep for a week after this."

"I had a great time, too. I'm glad you came. Both of you."

The rest of the walk back consisted of casual chatter. His schedule for the week and what she and Jillian had planned for fun over the next few days and a few other things. When they got back, Sofie offered to stay with Ryan until he got back from dropping Ali off.

"Head to bed, pal, okay? Brush the teeth and wash those hands good. I'll be back shortly to say goodnight."

Ryan moved in close and softly said, "You don't have to rush back, Dad. I'll be okay with Auntie Sofie for a while."

Greg chuckled at the child matchmaker, then tucked Jillian into her car seat as best he could. The drive to Ali's place only took a few minutes, then he was scooping Jillian back out and bringing her to her room.

He stood in the child's doorway as Ali pulled off her shoes and shorts, leaving her in a t-shirt. After a kiss to the head, Ali draped the sheet over her and joined him. They moved down the hall together, and Ali walked him to the side door.

"Hmm, I guess this is goodbye for now." He cupped his hands around her face and caressed her cheeks with his thumbs.

"Yeah, but we'll see each other at the wedding on Saturday. If you still want me to come." That insecurity of hers peeked out again.

"I think Gina would hang me out to dry if I didn't bring you. Good thing I want to. The wedding's at one, so I'll pick you up by twelve-thirty, if that's all right."

"It's perfect."

He knew he couldn't linger, but he still took his time and placed his lips on hers. Absolutely perfect.

CHAPTER NINETEEN

"*I*'m not sure that's the right color for you, Alandra."

Ali stared at the red dress she held, clenching her teeth. Why did she think it was a good idea to have her sister come shopping for a new dress with her?

"Yeah, I don't think I'd want to wear a red dress to a wedding, anyway." Why did she always find excuses to agree with Valeria? The dress was adorable and had a cut that would most likely be flattering on her. That's what she wanted more than anything else. A dress that hid her less than favorable attributes.

Valeria snatched the hanger from her hand and shoved it back on the rack. "Some people could absolutely get away with wearing that dress to a wedding, but it's not for you. Let's find something else."

The aggravating thing was that her sister was actually great at finding clothes that looked good on a certain type of body. Unfortunately, Ali had to listen to her over and over when she lectured and pointed out exactly what she needed to do to make her body perfect.

"There's some incredible exercises for getting those hips

down a few sizes, Ali. I can introduce you to my trainer. He's marvelous at his job. And so freakin' hot."

"Thanks, Val. A personal trainer isn't really in my budget at the moment." Of course, neither was a new dress for this wedding. But the only other nice dress she had, aside from the one she'd worn on their first date, was for cooler weather. The last thing Ali needed was something to make her sweat even more than she usually did. Especially with the gorgeous Greg Storm by her side. The mere thought of him had her armpits getting damp, not to mention some other intimate places.

But that wasn't going to happen after the wedding. Even if Ali was ready to go there again. Which she wasn't. She only had Destiny for the afternoon and early evening, so unless she and Greg grabbed a quickie in the coat room at the Inn, it wasn't happening.

A quickie in the coat room? No, that wasn't what a well-respected teacher from the town did. Didn't sound comfortable either. The romance books might make it appear outrageous and decadent, but Ali doubted she'd ever be relaxed enough for that kind of stunt.

"How about this, sis? They have it in two different colors."

Turning, Ali examined what Val had chosen. It was pretty. Maybe a little sexier than she'd ever feel comfortable with, but it wouldn't make her look like a slut. That certainly wasn't the image she needed to project at a Storm wedding. The entire family had class galore.

"Try it on. Which color do you like best? The light blue or emerald green?"

Both colors were lovely, but the sensible side of Ali knew the green would hide any food if she dropped it on herself. The lighter blue would flash her clumsiness in neon.

"Let me try the green. It might bring out the little splashes of green in his hazel eyes."

Ali took the dress and entered the dressing room. She'd worn her nicest bra and panties today in case her sister pushed her way in to help her dress. Most likely, she'd put on a body shaper as well for the wedding. It was like wearing a boa constrictor, but it smoothed out some of the lumpier spots on her hips.

After slipping into the dress, she studied herself in the three-way mirror. The surplice top accented her chest but also had enough strength and elastic to lift and separate. The ruching at the waist made hers appear even smaller and flowed over her hips nicely. Loose cap sleeves added a nice touch and luckily Ali's arms got a workout between vacuuming, carrying Jilly around, and cutting the grass with their push mower, so they weren't a problem area.

"What does it look like?" Val shouted to her. "Let me see."

Taking a last peek in the mirror, Ali opened the door, stepped out, and waited. Her sister never gave up an opportunity to let the truth fly.

"Hmm." Val tipped her head, her lips twisted to the side. "You know, I think that looks good on you. It hides the heavy thighs and minimizes your butt. The dark green color was a good choice. The light blue would have made you look like a beluga whale."

If only she could buy her sister a filter to lessen the sting of her words. How did Max put up with it? Or did she think he was so perfect she didn't need to fix him? Doubtful. Valeria considered herself an all-in-one self-help guru and never missed an opportunity to fill another person in on how they could make personal improvements.

Spinning slowly, Ali checked out the dress from all sides. It definitely needed something dressier than her flat, slip-on shoes. The spike-heeled sandals she wore on her first date with Greg would go. Did it matter he already saw them? Did men even notice stuff like that?

After peeking at the price tag on the dress, she didn't even consider buying anything else to go with it. The dress alone would break her budget for the summer. Maybe if she cut out a few things, she could swing it.

"So are we getting this one?" Valeria cocked her hip, giving her another once-over.

One last glimpse in the three-way mirror convinced her. "Yeah. Thanks for helping me find something, Val."

As Ali ducked into the dressing room to change back into her clothes, Val waved it off. "Of course. What are sisters for?"

Valeria really didn't want Ali to answer that question. She carefully hung up the dress and put her shorts and top on. As they headed to the checkout, Val stopped and put her hand up.

"How about we go out to lunch? My treat?"

Whoa. Her sister was offering to pay? Nice. And her mom was feeding Jilly lunch. That was one meal she could put toward the price of her new dress.

"I'd love to, Val. Thanks."

"Great. I know this perfect little vegan cafe with excellent salads. You'll love it."

Ali doubted she would.

Heat poured off the ashes of the burned-out house as Greg did a final walk-through for any glowing embers. The Stratham FD had final clear out, but he never liked to leave a scene without at least knowing what the condition was.

Shuffling through the debris in what had been a bedroom, a flash of something pink caught his eye under remnants of the ceiling. Stalking closer, he lifted the debris with a crowbar. A half-melted child's kitchen set slumped against the wall.

Even knowing the house had been empty when it had gone up, his heart clenched in a knot. All he could think of was Jillian. What if it had been her in this house? And Ali?

God, no. He couldn't even go there. His feelings for those two had gone deeper than he'd ever been before, and the thought of them being hurt in a fire almost doubled him over.

Although he couldn't be sure, he had a feeling this fire was related to all the others they'd had in the area in the last few months. It wasn't his jurisdiction, so he wouldn't be involved in figuring it out.

After a last glance around, he headed back to his truck where his men were swigging bottles of water and pouring some over their sweaty, soot-stained heads. He'd take a shower once they got back.

"Load 'em up," he called out, and they all hopped in the trucks.

On the ride back, Greg checked his phone. Two messages from Ali. The first wishing him to be safe. The second asking him to text her when he was done. She was worried.

Tapping his fingers on the screen, he let her know he was fine and would see her soon. Unfortunately, not tonight. Luke had planned Alex's bachelor party at a club in Portsmouth, and he was expected to attend.

Glancing at the time, he knew he'd be late. He'd have some paperwork to finish before he could leave, then he'd need a long shower to rid himself of the soot and smoke scent that permeated every pore at the moment.

Sure enough, the party was swinging by the time he entered the bar. Luke had his arm around a scantily clad lady, and several more surrounded Kevin and some of Alex's friends. Alex leaned against a high stool, drinking what looked to be soda water. Erik's glass didn't appear to have alcohol in it either.

Chatting with Erik, Nathaniel had a full beer. Greg strolled over and greeted them.

"It's about time you showed up, cuz," Luke called out, waving him over. "I've got a few friends who came along. Thought you might be interested in getting to know them."

"Hi, ladies." No sense being rude, but this bachelor party would be different from some of his previous ones. In the past, he most likely would have joined in getting hammered and possibly hooking up with someone who was only looking for a good time. But with Ali in his life, there was no need.

Even though they hadn't taken any steps toward being intimate—not that they'd had an opportunity with both kids always around—he still wouldn't disrespect her by going behind her back with anyone else, and the thought of hooking up with a stranger held no appeal whatsoever.

"If you'll excuse me, I need to get myself a drink. Nice meeting you." Not that Luke had told him their names or vice versa. In Luke's world, names weren't important.

Greg ordered a beer on tap from the bartender, then slapped Alex on the shoulder. "Congratulations, cousin. A few nights from now it'll all be over."

Luke lifted his own beer. "You mean his life, right? Hooked to the old ball and chain."

Erik and Nathaniel snickered and shook their heads.

"Maybe someday Luke will understand," Alex said, holding his drink up to the others. Luke tugged one of the ladies closer.

As they tapped their drinks together, Erik muttered, "Not any time soon, though."

GREG GAVE a quick knock on Ali's kitchen door, then shouted, "Hey there," as he walked in. They'd gone out on a few dates now, but Greg still didn't feel like they'd reached the walking-into-each-other's-house-without-an-announcement stage yet.

Jillian skittered across the kitchen and hopped into his arms. "Hi. Mama getting ready. She smells really good."

"Ooh, I can't wait. What does she smell like?"

Jillian cocked her head, her brows drawn together. Then, she tossed her hands in the air and said, "I don't know, but it's good."

A teenage girl walked into the kitchen behind Jillian and gave a shy wave. "Hi, I'm Destiny."

"Hi, Destiny. I'm Greg. Thanks for hanging out with Miss Jillian today." He lowered the child to the floor and brushed his hands down his dark gray suit.

"I'll be right out," Ali called down the hall, her head poking out of the last room on the right.

"No rush. I'm a few minutes early."

Jillian held up a plastic teacup and waved it at him. "You want a cup of tea? I have sugar and milk for it like before."

Ali's heels clicked down the hall toward him, so he bent over and tapped Jillian's nose. "I don't have time right now, munchkin. We'll have to make it another time. Deal?"

"Maybe when Ryan comes for his next piano lesson," Ali suggested.

Greg stood and swiveled to greet Ali but stopped cold when he saw her. Wow. The dress she wore looked stunning on her. Add the heels, a few small pieces of jewelry, and her hair pinned slightly back from her face with the rest curling around her shoulders, and you had a woman who could stop traffic.

"You look incredible."

Ali's eyes lowered and pink tinged her cheeks. "Thanks. You clean up pretty nice yourself."

She took her phone from the charging station on the kitchen counter and tucked it into her small purse. Tapping on a pad of paper, she addressed Destiny.

"My cell number is here. We'll be at St. Michael's for the wedding, then The Inn at the Falls for the reception. That information along with my mother's number is all on here. Hopefully, you won't need any of it, but please don't hesitate to call if there's a problem or text if you have a question."

She stooped next to her daughter and kissed her cheek. "Be good for Destiny. You can take your nap on the couch with one show. Only one. No trying to get another one at naptime. Destiny can decide if you can watch another show later."

Ali rose, gave a few more instruction to the babysitter, then threw him a grateful look.

"Bye, munchkin." He tousled Jillian's hair as he walked past and out the door.

Ali chuckled when they walked outside. "Whose car is this?"

"This is Sofie's. She's the Maid of Honor, so she's going in the limo to the church."

He opened the passenger door for her and waited until she got her legs in, then closed it. Once in the driver's seat, he started the car and backed out of the driveway.

At the rear of the church, Greg placed his hand on Ali's back to guide her. TJ met them at the door.

"Go on down. I'm the only usher today. Family's at the front."

Ali sent him a questioning glance as she tucked her hand in his arm. "Who else is in the wedding party?"

"Erik is the Best Man, and Luke is giving Gina away. She

figured Luke would be happy to do it since he's had to put up with her and Alex being all romantic and stuff in the house."

They scooted into a pew half a dozen rows from the front and sat silently, watching the other guests come in and sit. Since Alex was active in the community, volunteering his time and skills, many people from town were here. Finally, Greg's parents and Leah entered, bringing Ryan with them. Ryan slid in next to Greg, while his parents and sister took the pew in front of them.

Peering past him, Ryan gave a tiny wave to Ali. She reached across Greg and patted Ryan's hand. When it reversed course, Greg snagged it and held tight, then winked at her as she glanced at him.

The soft music that had been playing changed tone, and Uncle Pete escorted Aunt Molly down the aisle. This was their third wedding in only a few years. Only Luke was left, but that would most likely be a while longer. Greg's mother was still chomping at the bit to get one of them married off. After ten years as a widower, he didn't count as being married anymore.

TJ escorted a woman with dark hair wearing a vibrant colored dress in some wispy, flowing design. Gina's mom. Greg remembered her from when they'd lived next door. It had been many years since he'd seen Nika Mazelli. She didn't look all that different from when they'd left almost twenty years ago. Gina had been worried she might not show up, so he was happy that she had.

TJ marched to the back of the church, and the music changed again. The congregation stood as Sara slowly sashayed with her husband past everyone. Next was his sister, Sofie, wearing the same teal dress as Sara.

Once they got to the front and stood off to the side, the bridal march came on. Alex couldn't take his eyes off his bride as she took small, graceful steps to meet him. Gina's dress was gorgeous. It had all her bohemian flare, while still making her look the beautiful bride.

Luke wore a smirk as he escorted Gina down. He gave her a kiss on the cheek, then handed her over to Alex, whose face beamed with pleasure.

The priest started talking, and Greg listened with half an ear. His own wedding ran through his mind. At least this couple standing at the altar loved each other and had chosen to spend the rest of their lives together. When Wendy had told him she was pregnant, he'd figured his life was over. He'd been a twenty-year-old college student with big plans to become a doctor. Those had been washed down the drain, but he couldn't regret any of it. He loved his job at the Fire Department, and Ryan was his pride and joy. All in all, things had turned out okay.

Now, he had this beautiful woman sitting next to him, holding his hand, and for the first time in ten years, he didn't hate the idea of getting married again. Which was ridiculous. They'd only been dating a few weeks.

He kept sneaking glances at Ali's expression as Alex and Gina spoke words of love. What had her wedding been like? Had her ex loved her when they'd gotten married or merely loved the idea of someone taking care of him?

Ryan fidgeted next to him as the wedding ceremony grew long. Greg tapped him on the knee and winked. Not exactly what a ten-year-old boy wanted to do on a Saturday.

When the vows were all said, they'd been declared husband and wife, and Alex had kissed the stuffing out of Gina—in a completely controlled way as only Alex could—the congregation applauded.

They all rose as Alex strode past, Gina clinging to his arm, both of their faces alight with pleasure. When it was finally their turn to leave the pew, Greg guided Ryan in front of him and took Ali's hand. Her glaze flitted around the inside of the church, landing on people, then darting away.

"Thanks for coming with me," he muttered as they exited through the back doors and descended the stairs. Alex, Gina, and the rest of the wedding party stood at the bottom greeting and chatting with everyone.

Leah caught up with them after they'd congratulated the happy couple and drew Ali in for a hug. Greg couldn't be sure, but it sounded like she said something about Ali's dress being a killer. If he eyed her gorgeous curves too much, it just might kill him. It had been a while since he'd been intimate with someone. Of course, with both of them having kids, it could be another long while. It wasn't something he'd bring up quite yet.

The reception was across the street at The Inn at the Falls. Sara and Nathaniel had both used it for their wedding receptions. The Inn was run by the Donahue family, and it had been owned by them for over a century.

Kristan Donahue greeted them at the door and pointed to where the table cards were. As they searched among the tiny, folded paper, Greg tapped on her elbow. "So Kristan and Alex used to be an item."

Ali tipped her head. "Really? You told me Alex and Gina have been in love with each other since they were kids."

Greg chuckled, then picked up the card telling them they were at table four. "I also said it took Alex a while to realize it."

"Poor Kristan."

They zigzagged through the tables and found their seats. Greg tilted his head toward the back door. "Actually, the relationship didn't work for a few reasons. The chef standing there? That's Kristan's fiancé, Mark. He joined the navy ten years ago and broke Kristan's heart."

Ali smiled. "Looks like he's back. So a happy ending for all?"

"For them, anyway. Maybe there'll be a few more here and there. We can't all get it right the first time."

Ali rolled her eyes. "Ain't that the truth."

"Mrs. C." Ryan's mouth dropped open. "You said, 'ain't'. That's incorrect."

Ali's laugh was sweet and pure. "That's excellent you picked up on it. You must have had a great fourth grade teacher."

Ryan snorted and settled in on Ali's other side. Hmm. Seemed his son was as taken with the beautiful teacher as he was. He couldn't blame the kid. Her looks were something else, but the sparkle in her eyes when she spoke and the warmth she exuded anytime she was near simply pulled you in and made you want to stay close.

"When are we gonna eat?" Ryan bobbed in his seat, his head twisting from side to side.

Ali placed her hand on his shoulder. "Usually, they'll spend some time taking pictures of the bride and groom and the wedding party. The family, too."

Ryan leaned past Ali. "Family? Is that us, Dad? Do we get a picture taken?"

"Probably not, pal. It's usually immediate family. Parents, brothers, and sisters. We're cousins. But I'm sure there'll be plenty of opportunity to take pictures of you with Matty and Kiki later. For now, if you want to find Tanner and Hope, they won't be in the pictures either."

Ryan's brows banged together as he searched the large room. Nathaniel was walking in with Darcy. Hope had Tanner's hand in hers. Greg nodded at the boy's questioning look, and Ryan shot across the room.

Ali smiled. "It's lovely to see all of these relatives happy to be around each other. Your family is so big, but you all get along. Do you know how rare that is?"

"Yeah, I do. You aren't the only one who's ever commented on that. My circumstances with Ryan's mother weren't ideal, yet I still consider myself fortunate for all I've been given."

As he gazed at Ali and she smiled back at him, he knew maybe there was something else to be thankful for.

CHAPTER TWENTY

*P*lacing the fork back on the table, Ali sighed and leaned back. "Oh, my gosh, that wedding cake was the best I've ever eaten. Did they get it at Sweet Dreams downtown? The cake they have there is scrumptious."

The grin on Greg's face showcased his adorable dimples, the ones that always got tingles crawling up her arms. "My mom made the wedding cake. She works at Sweet Dreams which is why you probably thought that."

"Right. I knew that. Too many details all floating around in my head. If they don't affect me, I sometimes don't keep them front and center in my brain." *Madre de Dios*, she sounded ridiculous. Too bad she didn't have any more cake. She could stick it in her mouth to keep herself from babbling.

Greg tipped his head in the direction of the dance floor. "Do you need to work that off with a little exercise?"

A fast song played, and everyone jumped around to the beat. "I'm not sure I should bounce around with all I ate. That meal was excellent."

"Mark Campbell, the chef here, was on the hockey team with me back in high school."

Ali peered toward the door leading into the kitchen, where the redheaded woman stood next to the dark-haired man Greg had pointed out earlier. "Didn't you say he's engaged to the manager? The one who used to date Alex?"

"Yeah, Mark and Kristan dated in high school before he left. I'm guessing the feelings never went away."

Greg got a faraway look in his eyes, and Ali had to wonder if his feelings for his wife had ever gone away. Losing someone the way he did was so sudden and didn't give you time to adapt. Not that Ali had ever expected Jeff to up and walk out on her and Jilly, but when she thought about it, her relationship with him had never been like a storybook.

Valeria had told her she'd be nuts not to go out with Jeff when he'd asked and insisted Ali would never be able to get another guy who looked like him to pay attention to her. Yup, her sister sure was good for the old ego. Jeff had been romantic at first, with flowers and candy. Too soon, however, they fell into a rut where she'd cook for him and clean up after, while he watched whatever sporting event was on. It hadn't changed after they'd gotten married, and Ali had been too stupid to see what her future would look like. She'd wanted a house and a family like her sister. Jeff had supplied her with it, then ran when she hadn't lived up to his expectations.

A slow song came on, and Ali gazed longingly at her date. Greg held out his hand. "Ready now?"

"Yes, this is more my speed for the moment."

After leading her to the middle of the floor, Greg stretched his hand over her left hip, took her right hand, and held it slightly down from his shoulder. As she glanced around, she saw all the Storm men in the more formal dance position. She liked that, although wouldn't mind wrapping her arms around Greg's neck either. She'd have to settle for one hand near his neck.

He started swaying to the music, and Ali was pleasantly surprised he did more than shuffle in the same place over and over.

"So piano lessons *and* dance lessons for all the Storm grandkids?"

His lips twisted to the side. "Piano lessons, yes. The dancing was more our grandfather and father making sure we knew the polite way to dance with a young lady. None of this *wrapped around each other crap*, as my Gramps would say."

She laughed. "I love that."

Greg eased in and whispered near her ear. "Personally, I'd love to be wrapped all around you right now."

His eyes suddenly popped wide, and he paused. "I'm sorry, that didn't come out the way I meant it to."

Ali pressed her lips together to keep from laughing again. "That's too bad, because I wouldn't mind having you wrapped all around me. Sounds cozy."

Greg's head dropped and his shoulders shook, then he straightened up. "Good to know for the future. When we aren't out in public, in the middle of my entire family."

Ali pressed in closer to Greg's body. The man sure filled out a suit. A little growl erupted from his throat, and his hand caressed her hip, dipping slightly over her backside, then back up to her hip.

"Have I told you how gorgeous you look tonight?"

Heat crawled up her neck at the compliment. "It's the dress. It has a flattering cut."

"Pretty sure you'd look terrific out of the dress, too." Again, Greg froze, and this time closed his eyes. "Oh, God, my mouth is not waiting for the brain to process things right now. Maybe it's best if I remain silent for the rest of the day."

Ali dropped her head on Greg's chest and laughed. "No,

this is perfect. It makes me feel better after having blabbered all over the place earlier."

"Is that what we do to each other? I don't know if it's a good thing that I get so nervous around you that I don't stop talking, or if you're going to dump me as soon as the evening's over."

"No dumping coming from this side. I like the fact I'm not the only one who gets flustered. Those Crisis Team meetings were a killer to sit through, trying to avoid staring at you while wanting desperately to stare at you. And, oh, *Dios*, now who's the one running off at the mouth?"

Greg pulled her snugly against him, then ran his hand slowly up and down her back. "You liked staring at me, Ali? Hmm, interesting."

"Oh, please." She rolled her eyes, attempting to downplay her recent confession. "You've got to know you're gorgeous. I'm sure women lose it over you all the time."

"Where are these women? I must be missing them somehow."

"How could you possibly miss Mindi Ferrera? The woman's interest in you is practically written in neon."

Greg nuzzled his nose in her hair. "Okay, I concede I may have been able to notice that woman's interest. As you said, it was hard to miss."

"And yet you never did anything about it. She's beautiful."

His lips pressed to her cheek. "Beauty is in the eye of the beholder."

The song finished up, and Ali felt as if she were floating on a cloud. She and Greg had somehow managed to segue into more of the wrapped-up kind of dancing than the original way they'd started. As they stepped apart, Ali caught Edele and Jay Farmer watching them from the corner of her eye.

"Darn."

Greg guided her off the dance floor with his hand on her back. "What's wrong?"

"Nothing. I just got a little carried away out there and forgot about some of the guests."

Greg's eyebrows inched toward each other. "Who are you worried about? And why?"

"The Farmers. I had AJ in my class this year and Ryan as well."

Greg's face hardened, but his hand remained soft on her back. "I don't think they're the type to make judgments on others. And you haven't done anything wrong. My own sister was encouraging me to ask you out long before the school year ended."

"Glad I had Leah in my corner cheering for me."

Greg tipped his head. "I think she was cheering more for me to get out there again. You were the unfortunate target of my lust. Uh…desire. No. Oh, God, you know what I mean. I had a thing for you."

The world seemed brighter listening to this man. "A thing? You do have a way with words, Captain Storm."

"And now I'm going to use them to excuse myself, if that's okay. I have to ask my grandmother to dance. And my mother and aunts and cousins. I hope you don't mind."

"I don't mind at all. I think it's sweet. I'm looking forward to seeing what you do out on the dance floor with Kevin and Luke."

"I'm not dancing with all of my cousins, smart aleck. I'll be back in between, so I don't desert you completely. Maybe I can get my tongue to stop tripping over itself if you're not pressed intimately against me."

Ali shrugged. "Guess I'll have to find some other handsome men to dance with. There certainly are plenty here today."

Greg pointed at the crowd. "Erik, TJ, Nathaniel, Alex, my

dad and his brothers, and even my grandfather. All great dancers."

Chuckling, Ali said, "All married, too. You didn't point out any available men."

A scowl crossed his handsome features. "Because you don't need to be dancing with any available men. You aren't available either."

"I'm not?" She pasted on a fake surprised expression, but secretly she loved that he'd said this. "Are you laying claim on me?"

"Yes." His eyes clouded over, and he glanced to the side. "I mean for today, at least. I know my sisters have said women don't like guys talking like they own them. And I don't. Own you. But you're here as my date. We can discuss the availability factor later. And my tongue is running away from me again."

He pressed a quick kiss to her lips and scurried off. *Dios*, he was so adorable when he was flustered. She kept her eyes on him as he approached his grandmother and took her hand. The song beginning was an old jazzy number, and Ali couldn't stop the grin that broke out as Ingrid Storm started two-stepping with her grandson. Greg wasn't too bad with the swing dance either. He wasn't the only one of the Storms out there swaying to the beat. Seems like most of them knew exactly how to move to this kind of music.

She got a kick out of Nathaniel trying to teach Darcy the steps. The woman was unique if nothing else and seemed to want to add her own personal flare to the dance moves. Her baby belly swaying back and forth as she flipped her hips from side to side was hysterical.

"I'm glad to see Greg finally interested in someone again."

Ali pivoted, her face like stone. Edele Farmer stood there, smiling.

"Hi, Edele. I didn't realize you'd be here today."

"Wouldn't miss it. Alex and I do a lot of work together for the Youth Center. I remember you helping out last year when they did that big renovation."

Oh, she remembered. Mostly that Greg had chatted with her for a while during the day. Her nerves had been frayed at having the handsome firefighter pay so much attention to her. Ryan hadn't even been in her class at the time. When she'd seen the boy's name on her roster for the next year, she'd almost done a little dance right there in her desk chair.

"It's nice to see you again. How's AJ's summer been so far?" Get her off the topic of Greg Storm and who he was dating.

"He's having fun." Edele shared some of the activities her son had participated in, then twisted her lips. "You look like you were having fun with Greg Storm, too. Are you two seeing each other?"

"Um, yes." Ali's lungs froze. "It's only been a few weeks. We didn't, um—"

Edele laughed and patted Ali's arm. "Please, don't worry. I think it's great. My brother, Mark, was on the hockey team with Greg in high school. He used to come over the house all the time."

"Your brother is the chef for the wedding?"

Nodding, Edele said, "He is." She waved to her brother and Mark moseyed over.

After introductions, Ali commented on the food. "It was excellent. Some of the best I've ever had."

"Thanks. I try. Now, I hope you'll try to keep my old buddy, Greg, from crawling back in his shell again."

Ali tilted her head. "His shell? He doesn't seem all that shy." Though he tended to get tongue tied around her. Which was so endearing.

"No, he's not. The thing is he used to be a super fun guy, but what happened to Wendy did a number on him. I haven't been around much in the past ten years, but I still keep in touch with the guys from our team. They've been worried about him."

"That's nice that you all still remain close. I think he's doing okay now. Plus, you can't have better than the Storm family as your support system."

Mark pointed at her and winked. "You're right there."

Over the next few hours, Ali danced with almost all of the Storm men, and in large groups with the women. Even Ryan had gotten up the nerve to ask her to dance. It was a fast song and they'd mostly been amongst other people, but she made sure to keep her focus on the boy, so he was aware she was dancing with him.

Greg had been true to his word and returned in between dancing with his family. He had great moves when it was an upbeat song, but she loved the slower ones where he slid his hands over her hips and back, and occasionally copped a feel of her ass.

She always sent him a chastising look, and he'd respond with, "Oops. My hand slipped."

Toward the end of the reception, the DJ, who'd apparently gone to school with some of the Storms, called everyone to the dance floor.

"I know all of you who've gone to Lincoln Elementary School know how to do this. So get your cowboy boots on and kick it up with Cotton Eye Joe."

The strains of the music began, and laughter drifted through the room. Sara dragged TJ to the dance floor, shaking her finger at him. Erik took the baby from Tessa and shooed her on the floor to teach their two little ones. Even the groom, who didn't like to stand out, allowed his new wife to pull him out there.

Ali's gaze zeroed in on Greg and managed to get near him

as the song picked up. It looked like he'd already been headed her way.

"Show 'em what you've got, schoolteacher." Normally, she didn't like doing anything that would draw attention to her, but just like she did during Field Day with her students, she got into the spirit and dug in her heels. Heel, heel, toe, toe, heel, kick. She made sure to give her hips a good swirl when the turn came.

Greg's deep laughter echoed along with all the other people's, and Ali couldn't remember when she'd had a better time. Looking at Darcy, Tessa, Gina, and even TJ who had all married into the family, she imagined what it would be like if she became a permanent member.

It was far too early to even think about anything on a long-term basis with Greg. They had only just started dating.

That didn't stop her from dreaming.

When the song ended, everyone wandered back to their tables to sit or get a drink. A slow romantic song came on, and Alex escorted his wife to the dance floor for their last dance. The rest of the guests circled them, linking arms and swaying back and forth. Ali had Greg holding her on one side and Ryan on the other.

As the tune played on, Alex and Gina strolled around saying goodbye and thank you to everyone. It was beautiful seeing a couple so in love. Ali wished them the best.

After the couple was finished and headed out the door, Leah ambled over and gave Ali a hug. "I'm so glad you came today. It was a blast having you here."

"It was."

"Why don't I take Ryan with me and stay with him while you drive Ali home?" The wink Leah gave her brother wasn't missed by either of them.

"Thanks," Ali said, eyeing her friend. "The babysitter's probably tired of playing tea party by now and will be thrilled to see me." A subtle hint to her friend that Greg certainly wouldn't be putting any moves on her today. Darn.

Ali gathered up her purse and said her goodbyes to the rest of the Storms. In the car on the way back, she thanked Greg for asking her to go.

"I'm glad you had a good time. It was a lot more fun with you there."

Those words felt so good and warmed her to the core.

Around the corner from her house, Greg pulled into the empty parking lot of the ball field.

"Why are we stopping here?"

After putting the car in park, he faced her. "Once I drop you off, Jillian will be right there, and you'll have to pay the babysitter and start giving attention to your daughter again. I didn't want to end the day without at least doing this."

Reaching over, he cradled her face with his hands and kissed her. So sweet. So gentle. He tasted of buttercream frosting and the mints that had been in the bowls on the table.

Curling her hands around his neck, she tugged and got as close as she could in the front seat of a car. Their lips touched again and again, his coaxing hers open, then sliding his tongue along her bottom lip, playful and sensuous all at once.

Time stood still as they kissed, and Greg caressed her neck with his hands, then skimmed down her dress, over her breasts.

"Damn, Ali, you are driving me crazy. I want to do so much more, but I know you've got to get home. Please, tell me we can go out another time. My crazy family hasn't turned you away from me."

"Not at all. I'd love to see you again."

"Tomorrow to visit Sebastien maybe?"

Ali sighed at Greg's suggestion. He'd come with her a few times lately and always got Tito into a great conversation.

"That's so sweet. He'd love to see you, I'm sure."

"Anything to make you smile at me." He kissed her one last time, then took her the rest of the way home. After walking her to the door and giving Jillian a quick hug, he said goodbye.

His words about his family couldn't have been further from the truth. Wouldn't he be surprised if she admitted how much she wanted to be a part of his family? Wanted to be permanently in his life.

CHAPTER TWENTY-ONE

*G*reg jumped off the boat and held out his hand to swing Jillian onto the dock. Ali came next, and he held her for a beat longer than necessary to get her safely there. Well, it was necessary for him, since he'd gotten to the point where he needed to touch her as often as possible.

Unfortunately, it wasn't as much as he wanted to touch her.

On Tuesday night, he'd invited Ali and Jillian over for dinner. Ryan had been great and taken Jillian out in the yard to run around and play once they'd eaten. Yet he and Ali hadn't done more than kiss a few times. With the constant yells and noises drifting in the window, they'd both been aware they couldn't go any further.

Thursday night, Ali had made dinner for him and Ryan. Again, the kids played together, which was so nice of Ryan considering he was seven years older than Jillian. He and Ali had been able to sit and chat and they might have snuck in a kiss or two, but more than that had been taboo.

This morning, they'd spent a few hours out on the

Piscataqua River, and he'd given Ali another lesson on driving the boat. Translate: He'd held her in his arms as close as was possible with the kids nearby. Maybe his hands had wandered over her luscious curves every now and then. She hadn't lodged any complaints.

"Is the nursing home going to have Sebastian ready when we get there?" He tossed the bags in the back of his truck, then helped Jillian into her car seat in the middle of the extended cab. Ryan's booster seat sat behind the driver's side.

Ali checked her watch. "They should. I said I'd call when we got closer to Squamscott Falls so they can bring him out front. You're sure you want to bring him to my sister's house? She's not that far from here. We'll have to go all the way back to town, then turn around to go to Valeria's."

He and Ali climbed in the front, and he started the truck. "Yes, I've enjoyed talking to your grandfather the last few times we've visited with you. He seems to perk up when we've taken him out for walks. I don't mind the extra ride if it makes him happy."

Ali bit her lip and stared out the window. "I don't know how he'll be at Valeria's. We need to make sure he doesn't fall in the pool. I need to make sure Jillian doesn't either. Manny gets her riled up at times. Hopefully, Ryan will get along with Manny. They're about the same age."

"I'll make sure we play with Jillian, too, Mrs. C. Don't worry," Ryan called from the back.

"Thank you, Ryan," she called to the back seat, then pivoted away. "I always worry." The soft words drifted toward the open window, but Greg still heard them.

He'd noticed Ali got caught up in trying to please others. She'd fussed quite a bit when she'd cooked dinner for them. The meal had been excellent, yet she'd apologized for every little thing. The house wasn't clean enough. The dinner wasn't ready on time. She didn't have any whipped cream for the brownies, and she hadn't frosted this batch. Jillian was tired and grumpy toward the end of the night. He wasn't sure where the lack of confidence came from. He'd seen her in the classroom, and she was an excellent teacher. When she was with her daughter, her parenting skills couldn't be called into question. She was so loving and patient with the girl. More so than he was when his son got on his last nerve.

Sebastien sat on a bench out front with one of the staff when they pulled up. He and Ali popped out and helped him into the front passenger seat.

"No, no, you sit with your young man up front. I'll take the back with these whippersnappers."

Jillian giggled. "Tito, I Jillian, not a whippasnap."

"I'll fit better with them," Ali replied. "We've got it all figured out. Besides, Greg wanted to hear more of those stories you had about his grandfather."

Greg helped Sebastien into the seat and made sure he buckled the belt.

"Grandfather? Who was that?" The old man's eyes grew cloudy.

"Hans Storm. You told me he liked to break the rules at times."

Ali climbed in the back, and Greg returned to his seat.

Sebastien stared at Greg for a few moments, then laughed. "Yes, Hans got into a bit of trouble at times. Not by himself, of course." Ali's grandfather launched into a tale of cutting down some trees to make more room for a baseball field. Without the owner's permission.

Ali's voice drifted from the back as she chatted with the kids. Greg was getting used to hearing it and had to admit he missed it when she wasn't around.

Following the GPS, Greg checked out the fancy neighborhood Ali's sister lived in. All the houses were enormous with manicured lawns. His Victorian was also large, but it was over a hundred years old with hundred-year-old-house issues. And he cut his own lawn.

"This white one right here," Ali pointed out. "Pull into the driveway. Val and Max have their cars in the garage."

The four-car garage. Wow. He parked the truck, turned it off, then hopped out. Ali was already helping Sebastien out, so he opened the back door to set Ryan and Jillian free.

"Greg," Ali called out. "Can you get the brownies, please?"

He rounded up the kids and held the plate of brownies, then in two strides caught up to Ali and Sebastien.

"You do like making these brownies. Do you ever get sick of bringing the same thing?"

Ali's head flew up, and her eyes were like a deer in the headlights. "You don't like the brownies? I thought—"

"The brownies are delicious, Ali. That isn't what I meant. I'm sorry. I know for a while everyone asked me to bring my famous chicken wings to every party, and I got to the point I couldn't stand making them anymore. Doesn't mean others didn't enjoy eating them."

Her gaze rounded back to her grandfather as he crept up the driveway. "It's the only thing Val lets me bring because Max likes them." Her voice held bitterness.

As they approached a gate into the backyard, a woman— Ali's sister, judging by the resemblance—trotted over and popped it open. When she saw Sebastien, her eyebrows touched.

"You...brought...Tito." A fake smile was plastered on the woman's face, but if she'd had laser beams in her eyes, Ali would have been dead right now.

"Hi, you must be Valeria. I'm Greg Storm. Thanks so much for inviting us today." He approached and handed her the plate of brownies. The ones she allowed Ali to bring.

The fake smile was replaced with bulging eyes and a big o-shaped mouth. "My, my, Alandra, you didn't tell me your fireman was so handsome. And in such great shape." Valeria's eyes skimmed his body, and Greg suddenly knew how women felt when guys catcalled them.

"Hi, Auntie Val," Jillian called out, dragging Ryan behind her. "This is my friend, Ryan. He plays with me all the time."

Valeria sent Ali a questioning look. "All the time?"

"We should probably get Sebastien into the backyard," Greg interrupted. "He's most likely getting tired. If that's okay?"

Suddenly, Valeria oozed charm. "Of course. Tito, it's so good to see you again." She kissed his cheeks, but Sebastien's eyes held no recognition of her. At a guess, Valeria didn't visit her grandfather often.

Jillian dragged Ryan along to a mature woman seated at a table under an awning. Ali looked exactly like her mom, twenty-five years younger. When the woman glanced up and saw Sebastien, her face tightened. Not in disapproval like Valeria, but in pain like she'd been hurt.

Greg rushed over to her location. "Hi, you must be Ali's mom. Your daughter obviously gets her beauty from you. I'm Greg Storm. I hope you don't mind, but we brought Sebastien along today. He seems to respond better when we get him away from the nursing home and walking a little."

Her face softened, and her eyes flicked to the old man. "Of course, it's fine." She still seemed uncomfortable but was pushing it aside.

Sebastien installed himself in a chair under the awning and smiled serenely at Ali's mom. "My, my, Martina. You are as beautiful as the day my Pablo first brought you to meet us."

Martina brightened up. From Sebastien's words or the kids gallivanting about, he wasn't sure. Maybe from Ali being here. She always made his day brighter.

"Hey, Mama. You've met Greg, I see. This is his son, Ryan."

"Hello, Ryan. It's lovely to meet you and your dad. I've heard from my daughter that you are an excellent student. Val, where's Manny? The kids can all play together."

Valeria pointed at the house and rolled her eyes. "He and Max are putting together some fancy toy Manny got. They'll be out soon. Can I get anyone a drink? Greg?"

Greg glanced at Ali. "What are you having?"

"I'll get us something. Val, are there juice boxes in the cooler for the kids?"

Her sister looked down her nose and pursed her lips. "Of course."

Greg shoved his hands into the pockets of his cargo shorts and rocked back on his heels as Ali trotted into the house. He wanted to go with her, but she'd made it clear she was nervous about Sebastien and her mother.

However, the two of them were engaging in a conversation about his son. Martina's deceased husband. From the way Sebastien spoke, he didn't seem aware his son had left this world. Kind of how he talked about his wife, Bonita.

Valeria toddled over on a pair of spiky heels, similar to the ones Ali had worn to the wedding and on their first date. Today, Ali wore a pair of canvas sneakers. Much better for the boat.

"Have a seat, Greg. Alandra will be out with drinks in a minute. I hear you met my sister when your son was in her class this year."

Greg lowered himself to a chair next to Sebastien, and Valeria perched on the one next to him. "Actually, Ali and I have known each other for a while. We've been on the Crisis Team together for years and worked on some projects for the Youth Center. Not to mention she works with my sister, Leah." Even though he'd been acquainted with Ali from those events, he'd gotten to know her better this year from class-room activities. But he'd let Valeria think they had more of a connection. No sense making anyone think Ali had been unprofessional with him.

A tall, dark-haired man opened the door from the house and held it for Ali as she carried out two glasses. A young boy, a smaller clone of the man, followed behind with juice boxes in his hands.

"Thanks, Manny, for bringing those out for me. Can you run them over to Jillian and Ryan, please?"

Greg jumped to his feet and reached for one of the glasses. "Let me help you."

Ali handed the drink to him. "It's iced tea. You got it when we were at the pizza place, so I figured it would be okay. Is it?"

"Iced tea is perfect." He would have said sludge was perfect if she'd offered it to him. He took a sip, then set the glass on the table.

"Max Delgado." The man stuck his hand out for Greg to shake. "Glad you could come today."

"Greg Storm. Nice to meet you and thanks for the invite."

Valeria wandered over and hooked her arm through her husband's. "We're so happy to finally meet you. How did you like the dress Alandra wore to the wedding? I helped her pick it out."

Greg caught Ali's expression as she rolled her eyes and sighed. "Loved the dress, but then, I think Ali would look amazing in a potato sack."

Valeria laughed and made some weird face he wasn't sure how to interpret.

"I'm going to start the grill," Max said, pointing to the large brick wall on the edge of the patio. That was indeed a grill. "Come give me a hand while Val gets the food out."

Greg followed Max, though he didn't need to help with anything.

"Ali hasn't told us much about you. What do you do?"

Was he getting tested to see if he was good enough for her? He already knew the answer was no, but he hoped it wouldn't matter.

"I'm a captain in the Squamscott Falls Fire Department. Paramedic, as well."

"Great. You involved in any of those nasty fires they think are being set in the area?"

"We've gotten called into most of them."

Max asked him more questions about his job, then shared his own career. While they chatted, Greg kept watch on the others.

Ali sat with her mom and grandfather, laughing at something Sebastien said. Her mom seemed to have relaxed from her previous anxious state. Good. He'd feel horrible if his suggestion to bring Sebastien caused any animosity between Ali and any of her family. It didn't seem like it would be hard to do with Valeria.

Across the lawn, Ryan and Jillian watched as Manny manipulated a remote-controlled hovercraft. After a while of watching, Jillian asked if she could play with it.

"No, you're still a baby and will break it."

Jillian's lip popped out, and she looked like she might cry. Manny held the remote out to Ryan saying, "You can use it since you're older."

Ryan glanced at the hover vehicle, and his desire to play with it was in his eyes. Instead, he shook his head. "No, thanks. I'll play with Jillian. Want to kick the ball around?" He pointed the little girl to a large ball, and she laughed and ran to get it.

Greg's heart swelled with pride at his son's actions. It was times like these he had to give himself a pat on the back. He'd have to reward Ryan with maybe an extra brownie later.

Valeria started lugging platters to the table, so Greg excused himself and offered to help. Ali also rose, and between the three of them, the table got set and loaded with side dishes and condiments.

"Oh, Greg," Valeria asked, "Can you put these covers back in the kitchen for me, please? Leave them in the sink. I'll get to them later."

"Of course." After taking the covers from her, he went inside and started rinsing them in the sink. No sense doing it later when he could help out now. When he heard his name, he shut the water off and peeked out. Ali and Valeria stood under the window, fiddling with the food.

"Don't lose this one, Alandra. He's a keeper."

"I'll do my best." Ali's mouth was tight as she responded.

"Make sure to keep your house clean. Get all of Jillian's toys off the floor and organized in her room. Especially that kitchen set. It takes up so much space and is always such a mess."

Greg frowned when he heard this. Jillian loved that kitchen set and used it all the time while Ali gave piano lessons or cooked. The little girl was too young to stay in her room for long without an adult watching her.

"Make sure to minimize all that other extra crap you have around the house, too. A man doesn't want to see scraps of your life littered all over the place."

Ali smiled at her sister, but it sure wasn't one of the beautiful ones she gave to him.

"Oh, and you might want to see if you can get Jillian to stop her naps. Manny stopped taking them at two. If Greg thinks he's still got a baby to take care of, he might bolt like Jeff did."

"We've only been dating a month, Val." Ali huffed. "I doubt he's thinking about marriage at this point."

Valeria's eyes narrowed. "You've got to think ahead and make sure to keep him interested. I told you my trainer can do a great job. And you might want to stop making those brownies. They go right to your hips."

What was the crazy woman talking about? He loved Ali's hips. Every luscious, rounded inch of them. His hands grew itchy every time he was close enough to touch. But as Valeria toddled off in her high heels, Ali deflated, and her mouth pinched tight.

Leaving the dishes in the sink for her Highness, Greg dried his hands and went back outside. Immediately, he sought out Ali and nuzzled his nose in her hair.

"Hey, beautiful. So glad to be with you today."

Her smile lit up her face, and he felt better knowing he was responsible. Had she been dealing with this crap from her sister her entire life? No wonder she doubted herself at times. Yet in the classroom, she was confident, probably because her sister had never entered that part of her world.

They all gathered and began eating, conversation flowing around the table. Max seemed like a good guy, but the more Greg listened to Valeria and the way she spoke to not only Ali but her mother and Jillian, as well, he wanted to shield Ali from the harm he knew it was causing.

The kids finished before the adults and asked to be excused. Making eye contact with Ryan, Greg nodded.

Ryan took Jillian's hand and led her to the yard to run around, and Manny grabbed his remote-controlled hover-craft again. So much for entertaining his guests.

"Are you getting tired, Tito?" Ali asked her grandfather once he'd finished eating.

Sebastien's eyes were filled with clarity today and he smiled. "Not really. The sun is getting hot, though."

Martina stood and cocked her head. "How about if I take you into the house? You can rest a bit in the lounge chair. I'll sit in there with you. It's a tad warm out here for me, too."

As Valeria and Ali carted dishes into the kitchen, Max and Greg assisted Sebastien in the house and into the chair in the family room. The A/C blasted, keeping the interior of the house a cool temperature.

Martina appeared in the doorway with a bag in her hand. "I'll sit in here with you and knit. I've got a few prayer shawls to make for the church."

When Greg got back outside, Ali took his hand and squeezed. "I can't believe Tito and my mom are like best of friends now. Thank you for suggesting this. I honestly wasn't sure how it would turn out."

He pressed a quick kiss to her lips and grinned. "It looks like he's forgotten anything negative he'd originally said to your mom. And she realizes it. But I've said it before, I like making you happy, Ali."

After another half hour of playing in the warm July sun, the kids got whiny, so Valeria suggested they go in the pool.

"Are you coming in, Dad?" Ryan's gaze ping ponged between him and Manny.

"Sounds like fun. Go grab the bag we left in the truck."

"Ryan, sweetie," Ali called out. "Can you get my bag, also?"

"Are you going in?" Greg asked as he sidled up close to her.

She nodded. "Jillian doesn't like going in without me. She barely touches the bottom, even in the shallow end, and doesn't trust the floaties by themselves yet."

"Dare I hope for that itty bitty bikini I requested a while back?"

Ali burst out laughing. "In your dreams, hose jockey."

Soon, the water in the pool splashed with people jumping in. Greg ducked under, then nearly went under again as he spotted Ali exiting the house holding Jillian's hand. She wore a scarf type thing around her that tied on one shoulder. Man, he'd never wanted to untie something so badly in his life.

Ryan jumped on his back and Greg submerged, then popped to the surface again needing to see Ali. She held Jillian's hand as the little girl stepped tentatively onto the first step into the pool. Ali followed, but when she got to where the scarf thing touched the water, she untied it and tossed it onto a nearby chair. Her navy bathing suit was conservative but clung to her curves deliciously. It was only held up by tiny straps and snugly pushed her breasts, so they were on show. The suit followed her trim waist, then floated in a skirt over those delectable hips he had a hard time keeping his hands off.

Whoa. Good thing he was in the water. His reaction was instant and almost painful.

"Let's make sure Jillian is comfortable in the water." Greg cocked his head toward Ali, and Ryan darted off in that direction, water flying everywhere. Maybe some swim lessons should be added to the list of summer activities for his son.

By the time he got there, Ali sat on the bottom step and Ryan had Jillian in his arms, swishing her through the water. The little girl was laughing, and her mother's face showed her happiness.

"Mrs. C., can Jilly get on the float with me? I'll be real careful she doesn't fall off."

"As long as you stay in the shallow end."

"Get on first, Ryan, and I'll put Jillian in front of you so you can hold her." Greg moved closer and scooped Jillian up. Once Ryan was settled on the round float with the sunken middle, he deposited the girl on the raft next to his son.

Both kids looked like they were having the time of their lives, and Greg's heart beat faster thinking about Ryan being a big brother someday. Would that ever come to fruition? Funny how only a few months ago, he never would have given that option a second thought.

Ryan floated in the shallow end, his foot swishing back and forth in the water moving them around. Greg settled himself next to Ali on the step, his lower half in the water.

"Ryan doesn't get to go in a pool often. My cousin, Nathaniel, lives on a lake, so sometimes we'll go swimming there, but until recently he worked so much he was never home."

"He's got Darcy and the kids now. Is he working less?"

"He's been working from home a bit more. It's nice to see him relaxed and more family-oriented than career-oriented."

As they chatted about the recent wedding and some of the locals they knew who were there, he placed his hand behind her on the step. Slowly, he inched it until it rested against her hip.

"I have to tell you this bathing suit is putting all sorts of ideas into my head."

She threw him a side eye. "What sort of ideas are you talking about, Captain Storm?"

He kept his eyes straight ahead and lowered his voice. "Ones that absolutely can't be discussed in front of small children, Ms. Cabrera."

A soft groan drifted from her mouth. "Mm, would I like these ideas?"

"Oh, I am hoping you do. But, for now, I might need to submerse myself in more cold water." He kissed her cheek and dove into the pool, her laugh growing softer as he sunk deeper.

Valeria sauntered into the pool area, her bathing suit showing a bit more skin than Ali's. He wouldn't call it risqué, but it was hardly conservative. She installed herself on a large raft shaped like a piece of pizza and floated around. When she floated his way, she lifted her glasses.

"So glad we finally got to meet you, Greg. I understand your cousin, Sara, is married to the son of Abe and Celia. What a rock star power couple. That's so exciting. Do they stop in often?"

Greg squinted at her. "Sara and TJ? They come up for Sunday dinner a few times a month."

Val twittered and slapped the water. "No, silly, Abe and Celia. Have you had them at family outings much?"

This woman was too much. Greg sighed. "I've only seen them a few times at some of the wedding events when Sara and TJ got married last year."

"Oh, that's too bad." She glanced around, then swished closer. "I'm wondering if now that you're around, maybe Ali will put some effort into losing weight and shaping up."

She ogled his chest and shoulders. "You look like you work out. Perhaps you could get her to go to the gym with you. Eat better. You know, improve her lifestyle."

"Ali has a great lifestyle, and she doesn't need to lose any weight. She's perfect the way she is."

Valeria made a face. "That's so sweet, but let's face it, she's a little heavy in the hips and buttocks. Slimming those down would make her appearance so much more appealing."

Greg faced her and folded his arms across his chest. Her eyes widened at the muscles he was purposely flexing. "I don't know where you get your information, Valeria, but most men like a woman with some curves. Gives them something to hold onto, if you know what I mean. I wouldn't change an inch on her."

He wiggled his eyebrows, took a glance at Ali, then dove under the water heading for those perfect curves he'd spoken about.

CHAPTER TWENTY-TWO

*A*li's phone pinged.

—I'm back from the Cape. Are you around?—

She glanced at the message from Greg and tapped back. *—Making supper. Nothing special. Spaghetti and meatballs. You're welcome to join us. It'll be ready in twenty.—*

The phone vibrated immediately. *—See you in ten.—*

Dios. She'd better do a ten-second tidy. "Jillian, sweetie, I need you to help Mama, please. Captain Storm is coming over."

"Yay!" Jilly jumped up and down and swung her lion in the air. "I like Cap'n coming over."

"I need you to put all your dishes back in your kitchen, okay?"

The little girl in her flouncy princess dress got started picking up the mess on the floor as Ali trotted into the living room and tried to declutter as quickly as she could. Jilly's coloring books, crayons, a half dozen dolls, and what seemed like a few hundred plastic animal figures. For now, they went in the large basket next to the door. They could be sorted later.

That would have to do. She needed work even more than the house. Greg had dropped Ryan off at baseball camp down the Cape earlier today, and she hadn't expected him to be back yet. Certainly not dropping in to visit.

The past few weeks, they'd been seeing quite a bit of each other. They had dinner three or four times a week, alternating houses depending on Greg's schedule. A few times, Ryan had stayed with her when Greg had worked. He hadn't wanted to take advantage of her, but Ryan seemed to like coming over, and he was such a help in keeping Jillian busy she'd been able to do other things. Like the summer curriculum work for the new math program the school had bought.

Scurrying down the hall, she thought about what she could change into. After pulling off her top and sliding down her shorts, she tugged on a sundress and slipped into a pair of cute sandals. A brush through her hair put that rat's nest in order. She squeezed some concealer on her finger, but the kitchen door sounded and her heart raced.

With the concealer rubbed in swiftly, she took one last glance in the mirror. It would have to do. Her sandals clicked down the hallway, and there sat Greg at Jilly's little kitchen set. *Dios*, the man melted her heart and got her ovaries throbbing every time he played tea party with her daughter.

"Hey, Greg. You got Ryan all settled at camp?"

"Yup. I think he was a little nervous at first, but once he started talking to the other kids, they all realized they had tons in common. Nathaniel and Darcy are going to bring him back for me next Saturday when they pick up Zane and Hope."

At the stove, she stirred the pot of sauce she'd made and threw the angel hair into the boiling water. She had to make sure Greg didn't distract her or the noodles would be overcooked.

"Thanks for the tea, munchkin." Greg rose and patted Jilly on the head, then ambled toward her, his eyes gleaming. "And thank you for inviting me over with last minute notice. I know you hadn't expected me tonight."

He wrapped his arms around her from behind and pressed his lips to her neck. The shivers were automatic. They always were when he touched her in any way.

"I'm glad you were able to get back early enough."

"I missed you." More kisses, and she leaned back against his solid chest.

"If you keep doing that, I'll overcook the pasta."

He nibbled on her ear, and she dropped the spoon in the sauce. "I love soggy pasta."

Ali gave a huge sigh, then took a deep breath. "Let me finish this, then I'll let you nibble."

"You promise?"

She canted her head toward Jillian. "To a degree."

"What time does she go to bed?" He made a comical face.

Ali laughed. "It's only five-thirty. Not to mention, I promised she could watch a movie tonight."

Greg kissed her cheek. "Fine. How about I set the table? That'll keep my hands busy."

"Good idea." She'd honestly love his hands to be busy with her.

In the six weeks they'd been seeing each other, they'd engaged in plenty of kissing and a little touching, but since they almost always had at least one of the kids nearby, nothing beyond that had happened. Honestly, the thought of having sex again scared the pants off Ali. Or maybe scared the pants back on her. The thought of Greg getting a look at her naked was something she tried not to think of.

Dinner was their typical casual affair. She and Greg had been taking turns cooking, and the kids had seemed to enjoy the routine. Jilly had gotten used to having Greg around and was never so happy as when Ryan played with her. Ali had to wonder if the boy was getting tired of it yet. He'd never said so, but she remembered plenty of times Valeria wanted nothing to do with her and she was only two years younger than her sister. Ryan was seven years older than Jilly.

"I think you're wearing more of that sauce than you got in your tummy, munchkin." Greg laughed, then got a washcloth and began the task of scrubbing the little girl clean.

As Ali picked up the plates and put the leftovers away, the deep emotions she'd been feeling for Greg grew and blossomed. He was such an excellent dad, and he'd stepped into Jillian's life and done more for her than Jeff ever had. The big question was if he would continue? Did he feel for her what she felt for him?

"What movie are we watching tonight?" Greg asked as he plopped Jillian onto the floor after scrubbing her down.

"If you and Jilly want to choose one while I finish the dishes, that would be great. But Jilly, you need jammies on before we watch it. Okay?"

"Mama, Cap'in help me in jammies?"

Ali peeked at Greg who shrugged. Her daughter had never allowed Greg to get her in pajamas before. This was a milestone.

"Sure, sweetie. Make sure to brush your teeth, too."

Jilly ran down the hallway, but Greg's hands snaked around her waist. "I hate to leave you with all the cleanup. Leave it, and I'll get it during the movie."

"No way. She's letting you do pajamas and teeth. Usually, she gives me fits when I want her to do that. I'm taking full advantage of it today."

He caressed her cheek, then gave her a quick kiss. "Okay, as long as I can take full advantage later." Winking, he strode down the hall. Jillian's giggles floated back toward her. What a beautiful sound.

Jillian and Greg ended up choosing a family movie that involved a lost dog who wanted to find his home. The little girl crawled up on the couch right between her and Greg and snuggled against them both. Greg still managed to creep his hand along the top of the couch and tuck it around Ali's shoulder.

When Jillian fell asleep in Greg's lap, he tugged on Ali to lean closer against him as well. There was no way she'd argue with that. The man smelled like a dream and kept her pulse kicked up to maximum speed. Yet she felt so relaxed and comfortable with him at the same time. How did he get all those reactions from her at once?

After the movie ended, Greg shifted Jilly in his arms. "If you pull down her covers, I can put her in bed."

Ali hated to leave the warmth of his arms, but she eased away and went to turn Jilly's covers down. Greg followed behind, her daughter held gently against his chest. Once he'd laid her on the bed, he pressed a soft kiss to her forehead, then let Ali move in for the same.

While they walked down the hallway, he slung his arm over her shoulder. "Jilly is so precious. I never knew how different a little girl could be. I miss that snuggly age. Ryan has definitely outgrown giving his old Dad hugs and kisses. I thought he was going to die of embarrassment when I dropped him off at camp and pulled him in for a hug. Until all the other parents did it, too."

"I'm sure Jilly will get to that age soon enough, but I hope I have a few more years of the sweet, little cuddly bunny."

Greg led her back to the couch in the living room and coaxed her to sit next to him. The lights were still dim from the movie, but the TV was now off.

"I'd be happy to be your cuddle bunny if you need one." Greg held her close and nuzzled his nose in her hair.

Ali laughed to avoid falling apart in his arms. He always

sent her to a place where her desire soared with every little kiss and nibble.

Greg cupped her face and began to kiss her. This part of their nights was beautiful. They'd sit on the couch and make out like teenagers. Unfortunately, they always had to be aware of little ones waking up.

"So you know Ryan's away at camp for a week."

Ali nodded as his lips found her neck. "Mmhmm."

"And you said your mom was taking Jillian for a couple days up to Storyland?"

"Yeah." What was he getting at? Oh. They wouldn't have kids. Was she ready for that?

"The last thing I'd ever want to do is push you, Ali. But I was wondering if you go to bed at night as frustrated as me."

"Maybe...sometimes...but I, uh..." How did she tell him what she was afraid of? Maybe they could do it if he kept the light off and didn't actually see her undressed.

"If you're not ready, it's okay. I have to tell you that every time I see you, I get so turned on. I want to touch you and kiss you and make you feel good."

She remained quiet and simply allowed him to keep kissing her neck, but he eased back and stared into her eyes. His hazel ones held desire but also tenderness.

"We don't need to do anything this week, or ever, if you don't want to. I just thought we'd been growing closer, and you seem to enjoy it when we're together."

"I do. It's just..." She pressed her lips together as she searched the room. For what, she didn't know.

"Tell me what's holding you back, Ali. I know up 'til now we've never been without one of the kids, but in two days, we'll have a couple nights to ourselves. If you have no desire to take that next step, tell me now."

"Then, it's over?" Why was her voice so wobbly?

"I don't want it to be. I've loved every minute of being

with you and Jillian. Ryan couldn't be more thrilled that we've been hanging out together. I kind of hoped that at some point—"

"Some point," she repeated.

"But…?"

She might as well tell him now. If he ended it, he ended it, and she'd know he wasn't what she needed anyway. "I, uh, still have lots of extra weight from having Jillian. I don't want you to see, uh…you know…me without clothes."

Greg's eyes grew intense, and he pressed a heated kiss to her already swollen lips. "Exactly how I've been dying to see you. But your idea of extra weight and mine are quite different. What I see and feel right now turn me on. I thought it affected you as well."

She licked her lips and froze when Greg's gaze blazed her way. "I do love when you touch me, but it's been a while. Most likely, I'm out of practice."

Greg stroked her cheek, then trailed his fingers down her throat. "I can't say I've been totally celibate since Wendy died, but it's only been a few hookups here and there at bachelor parties where I'd had too much to drink and got egged on by some buddies. Does that bother you?"

He looked so anxious, she couldn't stop from drawing him close. His arms looped around her and held her against him. "I want this to mean something, Ali. I don't want a quick hook-up or one-night stand with you. I want to take my time and get to know what you like and what you need."

"I want that, too, Greg. But if you don't like what you see, you might never want to do it again. I'm not sure I can handle you running off after that."

Easing away, he stared into her eyes, his brows drawn together. "Do you think so little of me that I'd do something like that? Or have you been listening to your sister's propaganda too much?"

"You really like the way I look." It wasn't a question. Just a confirmation. He'd been showing her for the past six weeks how much he liked being with her and how attractive he thought she was. She had to get past the opinion of others and focus on Greg.

The slow smile that spread across his face grew to a leering grin. "When Jillian goes with your mom, give me the opportunity to prove to you exactly how gorgeous I think you are."

She nodded, then tugged on his head to seal the deal.

GREG HELPED Ali onto the boat, then sat at the helm as she pushed against the dock. She was getting the hang of helping when they went on the boat. Usually, he allowed Ryan the chance when he was with them.

Today, they were kid free. Ryan had been at baseball camp for the past four days, and they'd dropped Jillian off at Martina's this morning. He'd instructed Ali to pack a few outfits in case the weather turned bad or they went out somewhere nice to eat. The rest of the day they'd enjoyed being on the boat and in the gorgeous summer weather. In another couple of weeks, Ali would be back in her classroom full time and the week after that Ryan was back in school.

"Are you sure it's safe to be on the boat after dark?" Ali settled into the captain's chair next to him and tugged her sweater tighter. The night was still warm, but the breeze on the river cooled the air.

"I don't like going on the ocean once the sun goes down, but the river is fine. Plus, it's only Wednesday and boat traffic is less during the week."

They'd taken a few hours to go into Portsmouth to grab dinner, and Ali had slipped into a cute sundress that showed off her figure and had little buttons all down the front. Greg had been having visions of what he could do to those buttons. But there was something he wanted Ali to see first.

A sigh drifted over from Ali's seat as she gazed at the multi-colored sky. "The sunset is so gorgeous tonight. Thanks for bringing me to see it."

He wished he could sit here all day and stare at her loveliness. The sunset had nothing on Alandra Cabrera.

"Give it another half hour and see what we have. There's a little cove not too far from here where, on clear nights like tonight, you can see every star in the sky."

They puttered along for a bit, both merely content to be in each other's company. It was nice how Ali never felt like she had to fill the air. He wasn't one for tons of idle chit chat either. Since they'd been hanging out together, he'd seen what a life with Ali and her daughter would be like. He didn't hate it.

While his routines with Ryan had grown familiar and comforting, he found Ali and Jillian fit right in. His place or hers, it was the people who felt comfortable together. What a change from months ago when he was averse to the idea of a permanent relationship with anyone.

The night grew darker, and soon stars twinkled into view one by one. By the time he reached the little cove he'd been aiming for, the sky was covered in white twinkling lights.

"We'll anchor here." He cut the engine and lowered the anchor, making sure his running lights were still on to alert anyone else of their presence. Doubtful they'd encounter another boat. He never had when he'd come here at this time.

"I think we're set. Come here." He held out his hand and led Ali to the back bench where he'd tucked a blanket for later use.

After settling on the corner seat, he drew Ali in front of

him and wrapped them both in the blanket. She toed off her sandals and tucked her legs up on the bench.

"Look at all those stars. And the moon is so big and bright." The awe in her voice seeped into his pores and filled him with the same wonder.

"The full moon isn't technically until tomorrow, but it is kind of impressive up there, isn't it?"

Her head bobbed up and down. No other words were needed.

This woman, here in his arms, brought him to a place he'd never been before. He wanted to do everything for her. Make everything in her life perfect. As perfect as she was.

"Being here with you, Ali, is a dream come true. Something I thought I'd lost years ago."

Leaning back, she tipped her face up. "Lost dreams? I have a few of those."

He pressed his lips to hers and surrendered to the desire she brought out in him. "Anything I can help you with?" He skimmed his hands across her stomach and paused below the generous curve of her breasts.

A soft moan drifted from her kiss swollen lips, and she shivered. "Those hands are doing a fine job."

"I'll have to try and do more than fine."

When he cupped her, the shivers grew, and tiny whimpers floated from her throat. He nibbled down her cheek until his mouth arrived at the spot on her neck that sent her spinning. He'd loved playing with it in recent weeks to see if he could make her lose control.

His hands squeezed and kneaded the generous curves, and Ali arched her back, thrusting them more fully into his grasp. But it wasn't enough. He needed to feel all of her. Skin to skin.

One by one, he slipped the buttons from their holes, exposing her lacy bra and the mounds trying to escape. The moonlight glimmered off her skin, allowing him a clear view of her incredible beauty.

She brought a hand to stay his. "Will people see us? On the land?" Her gaze traversed to the shore.

"There aren't any houses there. It's all marsh, so I doubt we have to worry about voyeurs."

Her shoulders relaxed, and she peeked up at him under hooded lashes. Shit, the desire in her eyes nearly knocked him over. He brought his nose to inhale her floral scent and nipped her earlobe. The tiny sounds she made were killing him.

"You are so beautiful, Alandra. I want to see more of you." He fiddled with the front clasp of her bra but waited for her permission. The rising and falling of her breasts had his erection pressing fully into her back. She had to know what the sight of her was doing to him.

At her slight nod, he flipped open the latch and spread the lacy fabric until her bountiful skin was exposed. Dusky pink tips poked up, calling to him to touch them. He was happy to oblige.

When he caressed the rounded skin and tight peeks, Ali wiggled in his lap. Her head fell back onto his shoulder, and he feasted on her neck once more while enjoying the sensation of holding her in his hands.

The expression on Ali's face pulled his glance from her breasts. Her eyes fluttered closed, her lips formed a large O, and her breathing grew uneven. As he assaulted her senses, she twisted on the bench between his legs, her knees close together.

As her knees rose, her skirt slid down around her hips exposing her gorgeous, tanned legs. Keeping one hand on her breast, he skimmed the other to her hip, then to her knee and back. This time on the inside up to the apex of her thighs. She clenched her knees tighter, but when he rubbed against her panties, they magically opened for him.

"I want to make you feel good, Ali." Mostly, sex for him had been quick and with the key goal of release. He didn't want that with this woman. Ali deserved for him to take his time and make sure she got as much pleasure out of the experience as he did. Maybe more.

It was that *more* he was thinking of when he continued stroking and pinching her nipple with one hand while lightly swirling between her legs with the other. As her movements grew in intensity, he slipped his fingers under the edge of the fabric and found her warm and wet. Shit. He hadn't been this turned on in…ever.

"You are unbelievable, Ali. You're driving me out of my mind."

Her mouth opened but no words came out, only moans and whimpers as he stroked her heated skin, licked and sucked on her neck, and flicked at the tender skin between her legs. His fingers surged into her, and she arched backward, her legs widening, inviting him to continue.

While he strummed his thumb over her nipple, he bit into her neck, and thrust his fingers in and out, playing with the tiny nub that seemed to make her undulate more. She grabbed his hand and held it where it was as she gyrated on his lap. He couldn't get enough of her. Her passion. Her energy. Her beautiful body as it hummed around his fingers. He wanted to do this for her. Make her feel all the emotions that were rippling through his body.

A gasp exploded from her lips as her core clenched around his fingers. Her body trembled, her eyes shut tight, her mouth whispering his name. "Greg. Oh, *Dios.*"

As she slumped back, still trembling, he drew the blanket around them both and hugged her tight.

"You okay?"

A laugh rang out, her head twisting to look at him. "I haven't been that okay in a long, long time. Maybe ever."

Had she felt it, too? That connection, that passion between them, the sparks that he'd never experienced before with anyone else. This had been mind-blowing for him, and he hadn't even finished.

Greg shifted so Ali faced him, still wrapped in his arms. He cupped her face and kissed her sweetly, but with a possession that took him in its grip and wouldn't let go. She snuggled closer, almost purring, her hands splayed on his chest.

"I'd love to show you even more how much you mean to me."

Her eyes darted around and darkened. Yeah, he hadn't planned to do anything more out in the open, even if there wasn't anyone around.

"There's a much more comfortable bed down below. It's slightly more private than out here."

He studied her face as she made the decision. He could tell immediately what her choice was. She slid off the bench, and without covering her exposed skin, began swaying toward the cabin. Peeking over her shoulder, she said, "Down below is good. We wouldn't want your goods to get blown away with the breeze."

CHAPTER TWENTY-THREE

*A*li sauntered down the stairs into the cabin, wondering what alien entity had inhabited her body. Aside from the explosive orgasm Greg had given her, something she'd rarely ever gotten from her ex, she now led him on for more of the same, with her top completely exposed no less. Where was the demure schoolteacher who acted conservatively and followed the rules? One did not have sex on board a boat with a sexy fire captain.

Footsteps sounded behind her. Well, maybe she did.

The moonlight slipped inside the boat through the few side windows and the one at the front. What did Greg call it? The bow? Basically, a big bed in a triangle shape like the boat.

Passing the small cooktop and fridge on the left and the bench and table on the right, she plowed forward until she dropped onto the mattress. Greg stood above her, watching, grinning.

"You are the sexiest woman I've ever seen. Please, tell me I can continue what I started up on deck."

Pushing herself back farther on the mattress, she pursed

her lips in a big pout. "I didn't come down here to take a nap."

"Thank God." He placed one knee on the bed and crawled toward her.

His lips touched hers, and she shivered with the anticipation of what was to come. He'd set her on fire with only his fingers. What could he do with the rest of his body?

Soon, he showed her. His mouth got busy as she slid his shirt off his beautifully muscled chest. Touching. She couldn't get enough of touching him. His firm shoulders attached to strong arms held him up as he hovered over her. His lips never stopped. They traveled everywhere. Her mouth, nose, cheeks, throat, down to the valley between her exposed breasts.

Her response was to touch him everywhere she could reach. The sensation of his skin on hers brought her to places she'd never been before. The world spiraled out of control around her, but she didn't want to stop. The dizzy feeling was addicting, and she wanted more. More of Greg Storm. In every way.

She found his belt and began to unbuckle it. Greg hadn't stopped running his lips over her body. As she lowered his zipper, a thought came to her.

"Um, do you have any protection?"

He eased back with a disappointed sigh. Because he didn't have anything?

"I do." He kissed her lips quickly. "I hate to stop touching you to get it."

As he reached above into an overhead compartment, she wiggled his shorts down.

"Eager, aren't you?" Those dimples would do her in. "I had to put them up here, so Ryan didn't accidentally stumble on them."

As he pulled down a few packets, she began to wonder.

"Ready at a moment's notice when you have a willing woman available."

His brows drew together, and he tossed the foil on the bed next to her, then kissed her again. "I put them there last week just in case. I was hopeful we'd eventually get this far in our relationship."

Relationship. She liked that word. Hadn't thought about it for a few years. Aside from the unsuccessful one she'd had with her ex.

The other word he said that she liked was hopeful. It described her, as well. Greg was eliciting more feelings in her than she'd ever felt before. Both emotional and physical.

He stared at her again, and she wanted to cover herself. But there was nothing in his gaze that said he was disgusted by what he saw. Maybe it was dark enough that all her flaws were hidden. The moonlight was the only illumination in here.

Greg cocked his head. "Now where was I? I think...right about here."

His mouth latched on to her nipple, and an electric shock ran from the point directly to her inner core. *Dios*, it was pleasure and pain at the same time.

Grabbing his head, she held it close and used her toes to push his shorts the rest of the way down his legs. His chuckle drifted up as he kicked the garment off his feet.

"That's a resourceful little trick. Makes me think I need to even things up a bit." Sitting back slightly, he unbuttoned the rest of her dress and spread the sides wide. Desire flared in his eyes, and Ali couldn't even conjure up any objections. The way he looked at her sent her the message she was beautiful. He made her feel it and believe it. No one else ever had.

Reaching down, Greg slid the dress off her shoulders, then removed the rest of the bra. Her panties were the only thing she wore. He only had his boxer briefs on. Dark gray and molded to his impressive arousal.

"I want to touch every inch of you, Ali. Show you how gorgeous you are in my eyes."

"You can touch as much as you want. As long as I get the same pleasure."

His grin grew wider. "If you touch me anywhere, the pleasure will be all mine."

She ran her hand down his chest, enjoying the sensation of the hair swirling on his pectorals and down to his navel. "Oh, I don't know. It feels awfully good on my end, too."

"Let's see if we can do even better."

Ali got lost in his touch and gave as much as she got. Their hands caressed and stroked wherever they could reach, removing the last barrier of fabric. Lips, tongues, even teeth nipped at exposed flesh. The flames between them grew higher, and she wondered if they'd incinerate. It had never been so hot and decadent and filled with passion before. Not for her, anyway.

Greg fulfilled his promise of touching every inch of her. With his hands and with his mouth. When he had his lips and tongue swirling between her legs, bringing her higher and higher, again and again, she cried out his name.

"Greg. *Dios*." A kaleidescope of colors burst across her vision, spinning her in its grip and spitting her out in his arms.

He moved away only briefly, then was back, his erection pushing between her legs. "Are you ready, Ali?"

His eyes spoke of his anxiety. That she would refuse him? Or that it wouldn't be good enough? Never.

She wrapped her legs around his waist and guided him home. Slowly, he buried himself deep inside her, holding himself up on his elbows. His hands played with her hair, and he pressed his lips to the tip of her nose.

"That feels...so...amazing." She licked her lips, and his eyes glowed.

"I don't want to hurt you. Let me know if I'm going too fast or rough for you."

"My whole body is shaking. Don't feel you have to wait for an invitation."

He rocked back, examined her face, then thrust back in. Her insides quivered with the excitement of what was happening. She lifted her hips, urging him to continue, to keep drilling into her, making her tremble, filling her with pleasure.

Ali twisted and shifted, grinding her hips into his. Greg's arms held firm as his hips rocketed, bringing her to the edge of that cliff he'd already tossed her off twice tonight. Third time's a charm. The first two had been pretty great, also.

She ran her nails across his back, then down to his taut butt and gripped what felt like steel. He slammed into her twice more, then stilled, goosebumps erupting on his legs. Had she done that? Wow. The feeling of elation that passed through her was new and exciting.

Slumping next to her, he rolled on his side, keeping them joined. His arms drew her in tight as he kissed her sweetly.

"That was unbelievable. You bring me places I've never been before, Ali."

"Really?" Her voice was soft. "That was kind of a different experience for me, too."

His eyes darkened. "Different good or different bad?"

She planted her lips on his, then grinned. "Definitely good. Better than good. Spectacular even."

Greg laughed, pressed another kiss to her lips, then eased away. "Let me get rid of this. Don't move."

She didn't, and within seconds he was back at her side nestling her head on his shoulder, his hand running up and down her back. She wasn't sure how long they rested against each other, but it was heavenly. Her eyes started to drift closed when Greg shifted and gazed down at her.

"I want to hold you all night long. Probably not on the boat. Is that okay? You know what I'm asking?"

She nodded and sat up, looking around for her dress. "I think it sounds wonderful."

He searched for his own clothes, and when they'd managed to get everything on and done up, he pulled her in for another kiss.

"My place or yours?"

Ali pointed to the foil packet on the bed. "You got more of those at your place?"

His grin grew bigger. "I do. Lots of wishful thinking."

As soon as Ali woke up, she knew something wasn't right. The sun was coming in from the wrong angle, and she was on the opposite side of the bed than usual.

She breathed in deeply and knew immediately what it was. She was with Greg. They'd had mind-blowing sex last night, a few times, and she'd spent the night. *Dios*, what did she look like now? Naked, for one. Her hair was also all over the place.

When she rolled over, hoping to escape before Greg woke up, she groaned. His admiring eyes were wide open, and his mouth twisted up in a smirk.

"Morning." Her voice squeaked. Embarrassing much?

"Mm, a very good morning. After the most incredible night."

Heat flared across her face and down her neck. Which he could see because she wasn't wearing anything. At all.

Tugging on the sheet so she could have a tiny bit of decorum, she smiled and trained her eyes on his chin. That was safe. The eyes knew too much and the chest, well, that chest had enticed her to do all sorts of stuff she'd never indulged in before.

"I've seen it all and touched it all last night, Alandra. Not that I wouldn't mind seeing it and touching it all again this morning in the full light of day."

"No, no full light of day." She bit her lip to keep her from searching his face for how he felt right now.

Shifting, he planted his elbows on either side of her head and ran his fingers through her hair and over her face. His hard torso pressed intimately against hers. She fought hard to keep her legs from hooking around his waist again and finding that perfect part of him that had made her head spin and her body sing Hallelujah.

"Alandra Cabrera. Have I not told you, and showed you, what I think of your most excellent body? You, my dear, are perfect and gorgeous, and I may have to have my wicked way with you again soon if I hold you in my arms any longer. That's the kind of effect you have on me."

She couldn't argue with that. Not when the evidence was poking her in the hip.

"You may have mentioned it a time or two. I'm sorry I don't always believe it. Habit, I guess."

He kissed her nose, then her forehead. "Your sister's lectures don't help. You need to stop listening to her."

"It isn't only Valeria."

His brows shot together. "Who else is feeding you such drivel? No normal man."

"My ex, though, he isn't normal. He's a rat."

Greg adjusted so he was on his side, one arm holding up his head, the other hand gliding across her ribs.

"Maybe you need to tell me a little about this ex. What happened, besides him being totally blind to your beauty?"

"You want to hear my divorce story? It's got a sad ending."

"Sad for a short while, but it got you here. I'm kind of looking forward to the sequel. They're always better, anyway."

She should get out of bed and get dressed before he saw her and all her glory. But his hand caressing her stomach felt sensuous, and she hadn't had that happen in a while, so she continued.

"Hmm, Jeff Cassidy. Where do I start?"

"Where'd you meet him?"

"In college. My senior year. He'd already graduated and was back visiting some friends. He was suave and confident and talking about his impressive job. He's a chemical engineer. For some reason, he started talking to me. He was interesting and asked what I'd planned to do once I graduated."

"Love at first sight?" Greg's eyebrows pushed toward each other, his mouth in a tight line.

"Not really. I actually told him I didn't want to go out. I think it made him push harder. My sister thought I was crazy not saying yes. Said I'd never get anyone as good looking or successful as him again."

His lips pressed together, his eyes intense. "I'm not going to say what I think about your sister and her opinions. How long did you two date?"

"Only about a year, then he asked me to marry him. Looking back, I think I convinced myself I was in love. I wanted a family, a house, the whole domestic scene, and Jeff was the way to get it. Now, I see that all he wanted was a slave. My mom and sister told me you needed to take care of your man, and so I did. Cooking, cleaning, laundry, anything he wanted."

"The perfect little wife." Greg's face hadn't softened.

"The perfect little doormat. It wasn't bad at first, because I had the time to do it all. He'd sit watching sports at night, and I'd catch up on schoolwork and chores. But when Jilly came along, everything changed."

A tiny smile lifted the corner of his mouth. "Babies will do that to you."

"Once we brought Jilly home, I was tired all the time. I could barely take care of her, never mind all the housework he wanted me to do. It didn't help that I had some postpartum depression. I tried to do it all. Wash and iron his clothes, keep the house immaculate, have dinner ready when he got home. Not to mention, take care of an infant. I was running myself ragged."

"The jerk never helped you with any of that?"

Ali snorted. "Jeff lift a finger to help? Hardly. When he left, he ran home to his mom who baked him brownies and did all his laundry for him."

"Does she still do that?"

Ali shook her head. "She moved to California about a year ago. I don't think Jeff was too happy about that, since it meant he had to get his own place and be a responsible adult."

"What was his reason for leaving you and your daughter?"

"He said I changed after the baby was born. I wasn't how I used to be."

"Of course, you changed, Ali. You became a mother, and your first priority was your child. I can't even wrap my head around any person not understanding that a baby's needs come first. A child is helpless and can't do for themselves. Your ex is a complete idiot if he doesn't get that."

"It wasn't only the clean house and laundry. I'd put on some weight during the pregnancy and had a hard time losing it. Mostly around my stomach, hips, and butt."

A grin grew on Greg's face as his eyes lit up. "I have to admit I like the weight there." He proved this by gliding his hand over her naked skin. A shiver rippled through her at his touch and the memory of what they'd done last night.

"Mm, Jeff didn't like it and didn't find me attractive anymore. He said I needed to stop wearing sweats and start dressing nicer. Except I didn't fit into any of my old clothes, and since I took half a year off work, I didn't have any extra money to buy new clothes."

"You can wear anything you like, and I'll still think you're the sexiest lady I've ever seen." Desire blazed from his eyes, and Ali wanted to believe him.

"That's because you're the nicest man I've ever met."

"Nothing nice about me if you knew what I was thinking."

She licked her lips and giggled when his arousal poked her again. "Would you care to share with the class?"

He lowered his head and nibbled on her neck. Arching her back, she made sure he had all the access he needed.

"I always loved Show and Tell."

And for the next hour, he made sure to show her in every way he could.

CHAPTER TWENTY-FOUR

"Thanks again for helping me rearrange the classroom. It was nice having hired muscle."

Greg stared at Ali's backside in the cute shorts she wore as she bent over to pick up her school bag. He'd lift the entire school if she asked.

"Happy to do it. Are we done for now or is there still more?" The desks and tables had been shifted around, and he'd helped put books in bins, but the room didn't look quite the way it had a few months ago when Ryan had been here.

Ali laughed. "There's always more. Bulletin boards. Name tags for desks and cubbies. I won't even mention all the supplies I need to label for my new students."

"You've still got a few weeks before the kids arrive. Will that be enough time?"

Propping her hands on her hips, she glanced around the room. "I hope so. Honestly, people have no idea how much time teachers put into their classrooms when the kids aren't here. Between packing everything up in June and taking it all out again in August, then the summer curriculum work we always get saddled with, it's not this great long summer vacation like everyone teases about."

Greg examined the room and what they'd done today. "I see that now."

Ali sighed as she gave the room one last look. "I guess that's it for today. I'd stay longer, except they like to close the building up at four on Fridays in the summer so the custodians can go home."

Greg picked up the now empty boxes and dumped them in the hall where many other boxes resided. They trotted down the back stairway and out to the parking lot.

"And what is my brother doing here on a gorgeous summer day?" Leah stood at her car having just shoved something inside.

"Helping a friend."

She crossed her arms over her chest and glared. "I could use help in my classroom, as well. Why does Ali get your strong muscles?"

Ali blushed and opened her car door. "Sorry, but I made him my frosted brownies. You've got to use bribery whenever you can."

Leah wasn't fooled. And brownies were the least of the things he'd been getting from Ali the past two days.

"I'd be happy to help you, Leah. All you have to do is ask."

His sister raised her eyebrow. "I have a feeling Ali asks much nicer than I do."

He laughed and slung his arms around Ali's shoulder, kissing her cheek. "You'd be right there. But if you do need anything, let me know. Hey, Ryan will be home tomorrow, and I'll bet he'd love to come in and give his Auntie Leah a hand with stuff."

Leah pointed her finger. "That's a good idea. I might take you up on that offer. Where are you both headed off to?"

Pink found its way to Ali's cheeks, and she shrugged. "I

was planning on making lasagna tonight. Greg said he loved lasagna."

Leah's eyes gleamed. "I love lasagna, too."

"Oh, um…Sure, you're welcome to come over for dinner if you'd like." Ali's gaze bounced back and forth between him and his sister.

Leah threw her head back and laughed. "Greg, you can stop shooting daggers my way. I don't plan on horning in on your romantic dinner."

He hadn't realized he'd been scowling. Good thing his sister could read him well.

They stopped at the grocery store and picked up the ingredients she'd need for dinner. A few people they both knew had given them strange looks, but he shrugged it off. If he had his way, he and Ali would be a thing for a long while.

"What can I do to help?" he asked once they brought the groceries into her kitchen.

"You've been helping me all day. It's time for me to do something for you."

He took her hands and kissed her knuckles. "I'm not looking for payback, and I don't ever want you to think you have to run around making everything perfect for me. I'm capable of taking care of myself. I've gotten pretty good at it, if I do say so myself."

"Thank you." She sighed and lifted on her toes to kiss him. "I guess I always feel like I have to take care of everyone else."

"Put me to work, woman. Otherwise, I'll sit here staring at this perfect ass and all the things I want to do to it. Then, the lasagna will never get made."

Her laughter rang out, and she threw her arms around his neck. That was a hint he certainly wouldn't miss. Drawing her closer, he held tight and simply felt. The emotions that raged through him were so deep. How had they gotten this strong when he'd only been dating her for two months? They'd only been intimate for two days, but she'd reached inside his soul and grabbed on for dear life.

Ali must have needed the embrace, also, because it was a few minutes before she released him. When she did, her cheeks were flushed.

"Can you fill my big pot with water for the noodles, please?"

"Of course." As he dug in her cabinets for the pot, she began opening cans of tomato sauce. They worked together for a while, moving about the kitchen with an easy rhythm. He'd come to enjoy these moments.

"What time does Ryan come back tomorrow?"

He stirred the noodles so they wouldn't stick together. "Nathaniel will drop him off noonish."

"That's nice of him. How's Darcy feeling?"

Greg chuckled, thinking of the unique woman his cousin had married. "She's still moving at full speed. Not much slows her down."

"Hopefully, she'll take a little time to recoup once the baby is born. It's difficult being a new mom."

"Yeah, that's what I've heard." Wendy had told him repeatedly and used it as an excuse to not do anything with Ryan.

Ali peeked at him sideways and pinched her lips together. "What?"

She shook her head and took a deep breath. "I was wondering about Ryan's mom. Did she have a difficult pregnancy and birth? Or was she able to handle it all?"

How much did he tell Ali? He hadn't even let his parents or sisters know the whole story. Yet Ali had confided in him all the crap her ex had put her through. He wouldn't even get into the way her sister made her feel.

"She was tired most of the time. Before and after Ryan was born."

Ali took the noodles off the stove and dumped them in a colander. After shutting the stove off, she faced him and touched his arms.

"I'm so sorry for all you went through. I can't even imagine losing someone you love that way. So quickly and after such a happy event."

The lie he'd been telling for ten years weighed heavy on him. Ali didn't deserve to be lied to, and he didn't want her thinking he was still pining for his dead wife. He'd allowed his family to believe it. He had an inkling most of them knew the truth of his marriage, though not of Wendy's deceit.

"The hardest part of the car accident was that Ryan grew up without a mother. But he would have anyway."

Ali tipped her head. "What do you mean?"

He glanced around the room before focusing on her again. "Wendy had packed her bags and was leaving when her car was rear-ended and pushed into oncoming traffic."

Ali's eyes grew wide, and her mouth popped open. "Leaving you? Was Ryan in the car?"

Shaking his head, Greg inhaled deeply, then let it out. "No, she'd left a note giving me full custody of the baby. She never wanted to be a mom and didn't think she'd be any good at it. I never had to use the letter."

"Oh, Greg. How awful. How could any mother abandon her child? I'd be lost without Jillian."

"Because you're a good, decent person, Alandra. Wendy wasn't."

The sauce bubbled, and Ali rushed to stir it. Greg rinsed the noodles and laid them out. As they worked to layer the pasta, sauce, and cheese, Greg decided to tell her the entire story. If she thought he was a fool for his actions, it was better to know now.

"I told you I met Wendy when I was in college. It was a big party, with lots of drinking and people hooking up. She came onto me, flirting, pressing against me, getting me excited. Granted, she did it because her boyfriend was on the other side of the room, making out with another girl."

"She was trying to get back at him?"

"Get back at him. Make him jealous. Who knows? I remember seeing him with the other girl and thinking he was a dick. Then, Wendy came onto me, and I figured they'd broken up and she didn't care. I was only thinking with my little head at the time. That's what twenty-year-olds do when they're drinking at parties."

"How long did you date her?"

"Date. Yeah, our relationship was mostly about sex. We used protection—well, most of the time—but at twenty, I was always willing to do it, and she was pretty hot. Obviously, at some point, we forgot."

Ali twisted away and picked up the bag of mozzarella. Was she that disgusted with him?

"Unfortunately, her outside beauty didn't match her inside. We'd only been together for a few months when she told me she was pregnant. I didn't really have a choice except to marry her."

Ali's brows knit together. "Many people don't get married when they're pregnant these days."

"Right, but those people haven't been raised by Nick Storm. Taking responsibility for your actions is right up at the top in the Storm rule book. Since Wendy's ex was still gadding about town with lots of other women, Wendy said yes."

"She did it to spite him?"

Greg nodded. "I actually saw her with him a month before Ryan was born. I was headed to work, and she was walking downtown with him. She was smiling and happier than I'd seen her since she told me she was pregnant. Now, I realize why."

"Did you ever ask her about that?"

"No. She was my wife, and I was supposed to trust her. Plus, I hadn't seen her so happy in forever and thought maybe she was coming out of her funk. Shortly after, she had Ryan. I'd hoped once she saw our son, she'd come around. Only she kept finding excuses not to hold him or take care of him."

"So the wine bottles you talked about having in the house were hers?"

He nodded. "I don't know if she'd been drinking when she left or not. The accident wasn't her fault, and since she'd been killed, I don't think anyone bothered to question it."

Ali placed the lasagna in the oven, set the timer, then stepped toward him, right into his arms.

"I'm so sorry. I know it wasn't a perfect relationship, but she was the mother of your child and that alone must have been difficult."

Holding her tight, he sighed, giving her the rest. "One of the worst parts was knowing I'd been used and played. I was so embarrassed, while everyone thought I was in mourning. I couldn't even grieve for her because I was so angry at what she'd done. I never even told anyone. Until now."

"But your family—"

"Doesn't know. I couldn't tell them. Couldn't even find the words to let them know that Ryan's mother didn't want anything to do with him. I went complete ostrich. I figured if I never said it, it hadn't happened. If my family didn't know, then they could never accidentally tell him. It isn't something I ever want my son to find out."

Ali lifted her head, her eyes soft and sincere. "Of course, you don't. I try and keep Jillian from realizing what a jerk her father is and that he isn't interested in her. She's still so young, but some day she'll understand, and it will break my heart. Thank you for sharing that with me. I know it's not easy admitting what happened. But as you've said to me about my ex, your wife was an idiot and didn't know what she was missing. You, Greg Storm, are one of the finest men I've ever met."

"Finest, huh? How long until that lasagna is ready?"

Ali's eyes narrowed, and she grinned. "Forty-five minutes."

"Think that's long enough for me to show you just how fine I can be?"

"You can certainly try."

～

ALI GLANCED out the window at the sound of a car and groaned. Seriously? Jeff chose today to finally show up to take his daughter. The man had a bad track record of not coming when he said he would. It had gotten to the point she never even told Jillian about the playdate. Why get the child's hopes up only to have her disappointed when he was a no-show?

Except the last few times when Jeff had managed to get her, Jillian hadn't wanted to go with him. Ali had coaxed her daughter into going and had instructed Jeff on places to take her she'd enjoy.

She wondered what it would be today. The playground? Always a good choice, and it was free. Unless Jilly wanted to go on the swings. God forbid Jeff push her, since she was too little to know how to pump yet. Or would he simply hang around her house as he often did/ He'd look around and chat but rarely interact with their child.

Jeff tapped lightly on the side door, then poked his head in. "Hey there. I'm here."

Trying to smile, Ali said, "Hey." He didn't deserve any more words from her.

Jeff's gaze swept down her body, and Ali wanted to scream. One of the reasons he'd left was because she wasn't as thin as she used to be, and now he had the audacity to gawk at her. It might be the sundress she wore. It accentuated her bust and minimized her hips. She'd worn it because Greg had offered to take them on the boat, but if Jilly went with her father, Ali couldn't go. Jeff tended to drop her off early if she got too whiny or annoying for him. Which she often did if she was tired. Ali didn't want to be unreachable on the boat if that happened.

"How's my little girl today?" Jeff leaned against the wall and glanced at Jilly. Their daughter peeked up quickly and said, "Hi," then went back to mixing her pretend brownies. So much for being excited to see her father.

"What have you been up to, Alandra? Your skin's even tanner than usual. Been hanging out in the sun?"

"Gardening, playing with Jilly." She sure as hell wouldn't tell him they'd been on Greg's boat a few times a week all summer. Jeff was all about the big boy's toys.

"Aren't you going to offer me a drink?"

How had she ever found him charming or attractive? Sure, he was good looking with his blond hair and boyish features, but he was so self-absorbed it detracted from his appearance.

Ali crossed her arms over her chest and stared. "Are you planning to take Jilly somewhere today?"

Jeff shrugged. "I thought I'd let her get used to me first. It's been a while since she's seen me."

"And whose fault is that?"

Jeff's eyes shifted to the side, and he waved. "Come on, Ali, you know I'm a busy man. I have to work extra hard to pay you that big child support payment every month."

"You mean the one you haven't given me yet this month? Or last month?"

His eyes narrowed. "I didn't? Gee, I could have sworn I mailed it. Must have gotten lost at the post office somehow. I'm sure it'll show up soon."

"Yeah, lost." She wished he'd get lost. There were times she wondered if Jillian wasn't better off without him in her life.

Her thoughts drifted to Ryan Storm and the fact he didn't have a mother. Greg's revelation had taken her by surprise, yet she was thrilled he'd confided in her. She was thrilled about many other things Greg had done with her. Unfortunately, not in the past week, since both the kids had been home. Being intimate wasn't something they wanted to do with the kids in the house. Not at this point in the relationship.

But she'd had three wonderful nights. Three nights where she'd had sex for the first time in years because Jeff didn't want her. She had to remember that when he stood here trying to charm her. It wouldn't work. She'd gotten immunity to that disease when he'd walked out on her.

"What 'cha got going on today? You're all dolled up. Got a hot date?"

"It's summer, and I'm wearing a sundress. What I have planned isn't anything you need to worry about. Are you taking Jilly or not?"

Jeff sauntered over and stood far too close. His cloying cologne overwhelmed her, and not in a good way.

Stroking his hands down her arms, he said, "Thought I'd hang out here for a bit and see how she does."

"As you can see, she's happily playing. She took a short nap and already had lunch. No better time to take her somewhere fun." She wanted to shove his hands away but hated to do something that negative in front of their daughter. She'd made the decision years ago that she'd never say anything bad about Jeff in front of their child. Jilly would learn soon enough what he was like. Potentially already had, if her not wanting to go with him the last few times was anything to go by.

"Happily playing. I see that. I wonder if we could do that, too."

What was he getting at? She tipped her head and raised her eyebrows.

Jeff stepped closer. Too close. "It's going to start getting cooler soon, Alandra. I thought maybe you and I could help keep each other warm on some of those cold nights."

"If you're suggesting what I think you're suggesting, then you've lost your mind."

He pushed her hair behind her ear, and Ali shifted away as far as she could. The counter behind her limited where she could go.

"Come on. We've done it before. What's a little fun between old friends? We both get something out of it. I warm you and you warm me."

Standing up straighter, she jutted out her chin. "Under no circumstance will I be warming anything of yours. Ever again."

His hands tightened on her elbows and drew her forward. "Let me show you what you've been missing."

His mouth met hers, and Ali wanted to gag. Like before, his kiss was wet and sloppy and churned her stomach until she wanted to throw up.

She shoved at his chest, but Jeff was a big man and didn't move easily. She could press harder, but she never wanted Jillian to see her get violent with him. Yet it sounded good right now.

Tearing her mouth from his, she attempted to step to the side to get away from him.

"I haven't missed that. Believe me. You're the one who walked away. Don't think you can waltz back in like nothing happened. If you aren't planning to take Jilly today, you should leave."

"Aww, come one. All I'm asking is we make a little heat."

Jeff must have struck out lately with his new ladies if he was willing to crawl back to her.

"I'm plenty warm. Thank you. I don't need you."

Jeff cocked his head and closed one eye. "Why are you playing hard to get, Ali? You got someone giving you a little something on the side."

"On the side? What side? We aren't married anymore, Jeff, in case you forgot."

He glanced down at their daughter. "Jilly, does your mom have a new boyfriend?"

The little girl's head shot up. "A boy? Ryan is a boy, but he's *my* friend. He plays with me."

Jeff's gaze pivoted back to her. "Who's this Ryan character?"

Ali crossed her arms again to keep distance between them. "He's ten, and I give him piano lessons." Should she mention she'd been dating someone else? Would it make Jeff back off or incite him to push forward?

"Ten, huh? No one else lusting after your very padded curves?" His gaze focused on her chest.

"We can't all be fashion models. Some guys like a little something to grab onto."

Jeff reached out and groped her breasts. "I will say I miss these."

Ali slapped his hands and shuffled away toward the table. "They aren't yours and never will be again. For the last time, if you aren't going to take Jillian, then you should leave. I have stuff to do, and I can't do it with you hanging around."

Jeff planted his hands on his hips and stared at their daughter. The one who'd barely acknowledged her father being here. "Yeah, maybe it'll be easier for her to come with me when she gets older. That way, I won't have to worry about her needing a nap or wetting her pants.

Ali ground her teeth together at the ridiculous words coming from him. Showed how much he didn't know his own daughter. She was almost four and hadn't wet her pants in a long time.

"Jillian, your father is leaving. Say goodbye to him." She wouldn't make her daughter hug him if she didn't want to.

Jilly tipped her chin and smiled. Her hand flew up and waved in the air. "Bye."

"Bye, kiddo. I'll see you soon, okay?" Jeff ruffled Jilly's hair, then left.

How could she have ever thought that man was attractive and worth marrying? His fancy car revved up and shot off down the street. Her short, quiet street with the twenty-five mile an hour speed limit and the "Watch for Children" signs.

Taking a few deep breaths, Ali calmed herself down and checked the time. Still early.

Jilly popped out of her seat and ran to hug her around the knees. Ali crouched down and returned the embrace.

"Mama, we go see Cap'in and Ryan today?"

Something beautiful expanded in her heart at the thought. "You know, sweetie, I think we can."

CHAPTER TWENTY-FIVE

*G*reg inspected all the people gathered in Alex's yard, then searched out Ryan and Jillian. They ran around with Erik and Nathaniel's kids, tossing a large beach ball in the air. Ali stood nearby chatting with Leah and Sofie. He loved how she'd blended in so easily with his family. Her sweet personality was a perfect fit, with him as well.

Over the last few months, he and Ali had gone from one side of the spectrum to the other. From barely touching to becoming intimate. From easy-going days to worry-filled nights. Today was supposed to be a celebration, yet Greg felt the anxiety in the air.

Uncle Pete sat in a chair on Alex's back deck with Dad, Uncle Kris, the aunts, and grandparents. Aunt Molly hovered around her husband, making sure he was okay. They'd had a scare a little over a week ago. Uncle Pete had collapsed and been rushed to the hospital. Luckily, the heart attack he'd suffered had been mild, but the rest of the family were all still concerned.

Today, they'd gathered at Alex and Gina's to celebrate

Alex and Nathaniel's birthdays since they both fell in late August. Two for one deal. They weren't milestone birthdays. Alex was twenty-nine and Nathaniel thirty-one. But it was a good excuse for the family to see for themselves that Uncle Pete was going to be okay.

And to say goodbye to Luke.

Greg took a deep breath in and held it before releasing it again. Luke was scheduled for deployment on Tuesday. No one knew exactly where, and if Luke did, he wasn't telling. They had a vague idea it was somewhere in central Asia. The fact Erik had been severely injured in a bombing there might have heightened the tension of Luke's journey.

Throughout Greg's worry, Ali had stayed by his side and provided comfort. A few nights a week, she and Jillian came over and she cooked dinner for all of them. Unfortunately, with Greg's schedule and the recent events, he hadn't been able to reciprocate this week.

They also hadn't found any time to repeat the events of when both kids had been away. They'd managed a few kisses, but beyond that was always stymied with the kids around. The few times Jillian had gone to her grandmother's, Ali had needed to work in her classroom to get ready for the start of school this coming week.

Gramps shuffled from the back porch and gave Greg a nod. "How's my friend, Sebastien doing lately? Have you been visiting him at all?"

"Yeah, Ryan and I have gone with Ali and Jillian almost every week. He loves watching the kids play outside in the nursing home's small garden."

"That's awfully kind of you, Greg. I can't tell you how it saddens me to see someone I once knew to be fit and full of mind, to lose so much of himself."

"I like to get him talking about his past. Seems he hasn't

lost most of those memories, and they're interesting to listen to."

Gramps patted him on the shoulder. "Your grandmother and I plan to go see him this week while the weather is still nice. We have a few other friends who live there as well. I'm so thankful we haven't gone down that path yet."

"I am, too, Gramps. But you're fit as a fiddle."

Gramps peeked over his shoulder at Uncle Pete and frowned. "It's hard to remember that when one of your children gets sick."

"Uncle Pete's going to be fine. Maybe this will get him to slow down at Storm Electric. You know how much overtime he puts in."

"Oh, no doubt he'll be putting in less hours. If Molly has anything to say about it, he'd retire right now. But my boys don't have anyone to take over the business since the grandkids all took different paths."

What could Greg say to this? He'd never had any desire to become an electrician and unfortunately neither had any of the other cousins.

"Sebastien's granddaughter is a pretty little thing. Sweet, too. Are you looking at getting serious with her?" Gramps put on his solemn face that he reserved for significant events. Like when Greg had gotten Wendy pregnant.

"We've only been dating for two months, but I really like her, and she's wonderful with Ryan."

"I can see that. With her daughter, as well. She isn't the type of lady you simply dally with, Greg. You know that, right?"

God, he felt like he was eighteen again, getting a lecture before a date. "I understand, and honestly, with the kids always around, there isn't really an opportunity for dallying."

Gramps laughed and slapped him on the back. "Well, I

like her if my vote counts for anything. See if you can keep her around. It's about time you found some happiness."

"Thanks, Gramps. Your opinion means a lot to me. I'll see what I can do."

"You're a good boy." Gramps wandered over to where the kids were playing.

Greg felt like a kid himself when his grandfather called him boy. But the man was right when he said Ali wasn't a lady you dallied with. Not without some serious future plans. How he'd gone from never wanting to get married again to wanting Ali in his life permanently was a mystery. Although if he was truthful, he knew it was her goodness, kind heart, warm personality, excellent cooking, and he sure couldn't leave out her stunning looks.

As Greg peered around the yard, Luke leaning against a tree looking at his phone caught his attention. The man shouldn't be by himself at this time. A distraction was what he needed to keep his mind off what would happen in three days.

"Are the kids too much for you?" Greg asked after making his way over to his cousin.

Luke peeked at the rowdy band of little ones, squealing and chasing each other all over the place. His contemplative expression held a bit of longing and maybe even remorse. That was new. Usually, commitment and having children were Luke's kryptonite.

"No, it's great seeing them having so much fun." His gaze wandered to where Uncle Pete sat on the back deck.

"Your dad's going to be fine."

Luke's eyebrows ground together as his mouth flatlined. "I hate that I'm leaving in a few days. I should be here to help him out. Help my mom."

Greg clamped his hand on Luke's shoulder, like Gramps

had done to him earlier. "There's lots of us nearby to keep an eye on him and make sure he has what he needs."

"Sure, but not his screw-up son who should have been here when he'd had the heart attack."

"Luke, you were at a wedding on Lake Winnipesaukee. You couldn't have known what was going to happen."

"I hate that half the family spent all night trying to reach me. I never even felt my phone go off. I forgot to turn the sound back up after the ceremony."

Luke glanced down at the device still in his hand, and a tiny smile appeared on his face. Curious, Greg peeked over at it. A young woman with long auburn hair sat on a bench swing by the water.

"Pictures of the wedding?"

"A few. I'm not one for that kind of sentimentality."

Greg pointed to the screen. "Isn't that Ellie Russell? The one you were chatting with at the fireworks?"

Luke's grin got bigger. "Yeah, it was her cousin's wedding. She was a bridesmaid."

Greg didn't want to pry, but his interest grew. "Still nothing between you?"

Luke swiped the phone off and shoved it in his pocket, then stared at the kids again. It was strange for Luke not to brag about a conquest, but he hadn't denied it either.

Ali strolled up behind them and rested her head on Greg's arm. He slung it over her shoulder, and she snuggled right in. Somehow, she knew he'd needed some comfort as he chatted with his soon-to-be-departing cousin. Displaying affection in public wasn't her usual style.

Luke clapped his hands and shouted to the kids, "I'm taking anyone who wants to come downtown to Sweet Dreams for cake or goodies. Who's coming?"

The kids all jumped up and down, screaming, "Me, me!"

All of Greg's cousins gathered around, making plans and

gesturing. Kids were sent in to use bathrooms and hopped off to find shoes.

"I guess we should get ready to go, huh?" He hated to release Ali for any length of time.

They strolled to where Luke stood with some of the others.

"This is a nice idea. We'll get—"

"Nope," Luke cut him off. "You don't have to come. Use the time for yourselves."

Greg scowled. "You can't take all the kids by yourself. There's too many of them."

Luke shook his head. "Nope. Me, Kev, your sisters, and Amy are coming along to help. All the married couples get some time to themselves to do whatever you want."

"We aren't married," Ali pointed out.

"You still have kids. Enjoy the time."

Ryan and Jillian dashed over, breathless. "We gettin' a cupcake, Mama. Okay?"

"Is it, Dad?" Ryan's eyes held hope.

"Yeah. Make sure to listen to Luke and the others. Keep Jillian's hand, especially when you're near the main road."

Greg dug in his pocket and pulled out some bills. Luke waved him off.

"I want to give the kids one last gift. Before I leave, I mean."

Luke glanced at his brother, Erik, who limped heavily holding onto his cane. The fear in his cousins' eyes couldn't be disguised. Luke was scared, but he was trying to hide it.

"It's at least twenty minutes to town, maybe longer with all these little feet. At least a half hour to order all the sweets and maybe eat them in the town common. The kids might need to run some of the energy off there as well. Then, another twenty or so minutes back. It could be an hour or more before we get back. Plenty of opportunity for a little Netflix and chill. It's the gift of time. Use it well."

Luke grinned and sprinted off.

As the entourage moseyed down the street, even baby Joey in his carriage pushed by Leah, Greg curled Ali into his shoulder. With a kiss to her hair, he whispered, "Netflix and chill sound good to you?"

Ali laughed and rolled her eyes. "You know what that's code for, right?"

Greg planted a quick kiss on her lips as he led her toward his house. "Oh, I absolutely do."

ALI SHOVED her lunch in the microwave and set it for three minutes. It was sad that anything that took longer than that couldn't be brought to school. With the short break they had at lunch, only two microwaves in the staff room, and at least twenty staff members eating at each lunch period, time was of the essence.

She ran to use the bathroom while her food was heating. Never waste a second. All good teachers knew that. She finished washing her hands as the timer dinged. Jamilla opened the microwave and handed Ali her container while placing hers inside. They were a well-oiled assembly line.

Settling into one of the chairs at the table the fourth-grade team typically sat at, Ali fished her phone from her pocket and swiped across the screen. There'd been another bad fire in the area, and Greg had been on duty today. Yes, there. Squamscott Falls FD had been called in to help. Damn.

"What's the frown for?" Steph asked, sitting next to her, sticking her knife into her avocado to peel.

"Another big fire. This one right on the outskirts of

Squamscott Falls. That's a dozen at least in the past five months." Ali kept skimming for information.

Phyllis forked salad into her mouth. "Do they have any clue what's causing them or who's doing this?"

Steph glanced at Ali with mischief in her eyes. "Ask Ms. Cabrera. She's got an in with the fire department."

Jamilla's gaze flipped back and forth between Ali and Steph. "What do you have going on with the fire department?"

"Nothing. I had Ryan Storm in my class last year, and his dad is a firefighter in town."

"And Ali's new man," Steph threw out.

Jamilla and Phyllis both twisted to stare at her. Steph smirked. How the woman knew she'd been dating Greg, Ali didn't know, but it was hardly a secret.

"You're seeing Greg Storm? For real?" Jamilla cocked her head.

Phyllis drew her brows together. "When did this start?" Yeah, Phyllis would be the one to go running to Reggie if anyone stepped out of line in the teacher code of ethics.

"Over the summer," Ali answered truthfully. "Ryan's piano teacher retired, and he began taking lessons from me."

Jamilla's finger pointed at her. "And that turned into you seeing each other, how? Details, girl. I'm married. I need to live vicariously through others, and Steph's been on a dry spell lately."

Steph rolled her eyes but laughed.

Ali shrugged. "After one of Ryan's piano lessons, Greg asked if I'd like to go to dinner with him." Okay, it had been the first lesson after school had ended. She didn't need to share that fact.

Jamilla spun her hand in a circle. "And…"

"And we went to dinner."

Jamilla flopped back in her seat, and Phyllis chuckled.

"We've gotten together a lot during the summer, though mostly it was all four of us. Ryan's mom is deceased and well...Jeff isn't exactly reliable for taking his daughter."

"Is that reprobate still shirking his fatherly duties?" Phyllis huffed and shook her head. "Has he paid you all the back child support he owes you?"

"He's paid me some. Greg's cousin, Nathaniel, is a lawyer and sent a letter meant to scare Jeff. It worked. I got two months back support right away. We'll see if it continues."

Jamilla winked at her. "Sounds like Captain Storm is good for something."

"Is he good for anything else, Ali?" Steph's eyes drilled into her.

Her cheeks heated, and she glanced back at the phone, so the others didn't notice as much. The phone vibrated in her hand and a text popped up. Greg. Like he knew they'd been discussing him.

—*If I know you, you've been checking the status of the fire all morning. I'm fine. Covered in soot, but relatively unharmed. Dinner tonight?*—

"Everything okay, Ali?" Jamilla touched her shoulder.

"Yeah. Greg letting me know he's back from the fire." She tapped out a return message.

—*Relatively unharmed? Do I need to do a complete physical when I see you tonight?*—

Dots popped up on her screen. —*I wish. It's been too long. Have we considered renting the kids out for a few weeks?*—

"What's that grin for, girl?" Jamilla crossed her arms over her chest. Steph gazed at her enviously.

—*Keep dreaming, hose jockey. I'll make dinner tonight at your place. I'll want a list of any injuries I need to tend to.*—

"Nothing. Making plans for dinner."

"Ooh, somewhere romantic, I hope." Steph sighed.

Ali took a bite of her now cold lunch. Leftovers from

dinner at Greg's a few nights ago. One good thing about seeing him was he always made a ton of food, and there was always a lot left over to take for lunches.

"His house. I'll cook. The kids'll be there. Hardly what you'd consider romantic."

Phyllis tipped her head. "I think it sounds like a perfectly wonderful night. You don't need to always go somewhere expensive or exciting in order to enjoy each other."

Her phone vibrated again. —*Injury list.*— After number one, he'd put a kiss emoji.

—*Stop distracting me. I need to get back to class soon and I haven't eaten yet.*—

—*C U 2 nite*— Another kiss emoji came in with it.

Ali stuffed her phone in her lunch bag, then dug into the rest of her food. Maybe with her mouth full, the other teachers wouldn't ask her anymore questions.

As she halfheartedly listened to the chatter of the other teachers, she thought about the time since she and Greg had been dating. Ryan and Jillian had loved being together, though lately they'd had some fights...just like real siblings. Would that ever happen? It was certainly too early to even be thinking about getting married. In another two weeks it would be Jillian's birthday and the three-month mark of being with Greg. Of course, they'd known each other for years. Did that count?

What did she know? She'd said yes to Jeff way too early, afraid no one else would ever ask her. If she'd dated the rat a little longer maybe she would have figured out he wanted a slave and not a wife. Or would she? Now she knew better, but it had taken getting crapped on to realize how she'd allowed herself to become a doormat.

Something Greg had never done. He treated her as an equal in all matters. They took turns cooking dinner if they were eating together. She might help him straighten up his house if the kids had gone wild, but he'd help out at her house as well. A few times she'd thrown some of his laundry in for him, but only because Jillian had soiled some outfit playing in the yard or spilling her drink. He'd transferred her laundry into the dryer a few times, as well, if he happened to be at her place.

Since school had started, they hadn't found as much time to be together. Ryan had lots of after school activities and playdates. Jillian got whiny if she wasn't in bed early enough, especially since she couldn't sleep late in the morning like over the summer. Add in all the planning and correcting Ali had to do for school, and the amount of time they had together had dwindled.

Greg and Ryan had come with her and Jillian to see Tito the last few weeks, but this weekend Greg was scheduled to work both Saturday and Sunday, so they wouldn't even get that. Unless she and Jillian stopped by after he got out of work. Yet she knew how tired he could be if they'd responded to an accident or fire.

Her mind roamed to what it would be like if they lived together. Jillian could go to bed at seven-thirty like always, and Ali wouldn't have to bring her home. They'd be home. Then, once Ryan had gone off to bed...those were the moments she dreamed of. She and Greg hadn't had any intimate times since Luke had taken all the kids to Sweet Dreams. Far too long ago. Okay, only three weeks, but she missed it. Hadn't realized how much she'd needed the physical connection to another person until she'd had it with Greg. And what a connection it was.

The other teachers rustling and grabbing bags caught her attention. Darn, time to get back already. Lunch break never seemed long enough. She scooped a last bite into her mouth, then closed her container and tossed it back in her lunch bag.

As she weaved her way through all the fifth graders

returning from lunch, she spotted Ryan getting a drink from the water bubbler. When he saw her, he wiped his face with his arm and rushed over.

"The kids said there was another fire this morning. Did you hear that, too?"

She squeezed his shoulder. "Your dad already texted me that he's back and fine. Jillian and I will be over tonight for dinner. I'll see you then."

Ryan dove in for a hug, and Ali embraced him tightly, giving him the reassurance he needed. She'd been freaked out, too, when she'd heard about the fire this morning, and Greg wasn't her father.

Pulling away, Ryan shook his hair out of his eyes. "I'll see you tonight."

A few more of her previous students waved or gave her a quick hug as she headed down the hall toward the fourth-grade wing. Ali loved that the town was small enough that all students from kindergarten to eighth grade attended the same school. She loved following them for several more years after they had her.

As Steph passed by her room, she bumped her shoulder. "Ryan looks pretty comfortable with you."

Yeah, she was getting comfortable with him, too. And Jilly loved being with Cap'in. Was that a good thing? What if it didn't work out between them? She and Greg wouldn't be the only ones to lose out.

CHAPTER TWENTY-SIX

"*D*ad, do you think Jilly will like the present we got her?" Ryan glanced at the gift he'd wrapped himself, with a little help from Greg, and frowned.

"She loves the walkie talkies you have, and her mom said she's wanted a phone for a while. This is close enough. Four is a little too young for a real phone."

Ryan snorted. "Yeah, I mean who would she even text?"

Greg threw his son a side eye. "The ones we got her have little games on them, so she can play with them by herself if you're not around."

"And they're purple which is her favorite color. I think she'll like them." His son's face grew more confident.

"She'll like them because they're from you. I appreciate all the times you've played with her when she and her mom come to visit. I know she follows you around like a puppy at times, and it can get annoying if you're not in the mood, but Ali is so appreciative of how you act with Jilly."

Ryan ducked his head and gazed at the window, his cheeks turning pink. Yup, that was exactly the right thing to say to make him feel good. The boy so wanted to be in Ali's good graces.

"Dad, do you like Mrs. C? Like really, really like her?" His eyes drilled into Greg at the question.

How could he tell his son that his feelings had gone way past like? He may not be ready to go shouting the other L word out in public quite yet, but he felt it was close.

"I don't think I'd be spending as much time with her if I didn't like her, pal. She's a special lady, and Jillian is precious, too. They're a matched set, like you and me. If you take one, you have to take the other."

Ryan bobbed his head. "Yep, a matched set. But I think she likes me, right? She'd want to take me, too? I mean, if we got to the point of taking each other."

As he pulled into Ali's driveway, he studied his son. Ryan was serious about this, and it obviously bothered him. More reason for Greg to take his time and ensure he and Ali would be able to make things work before talking permanence. He didn't want his son hurt.

"I think she likes you plenty. It's me we have to worry about. Now, let's get this birthday cake your grandmother made for Jilly into the house. That'll get us both some points."

While Ryan carried the present, Greg carefully manipulated the fancy cake through the door and into the kitchen. As he set it on the counter, Jilly galloped down the hallway, a huge grin on her face.

"It's my birthday party today."

Ryan bent down and picked the girl up and swung her around. This was her favorite thing from him. Pretty sure Ryan enjoyed it, as well.

"Hey, pal, maybe the swinging around can be done outside today. There's too much in here that can get knocked over." The counters were covered in platters and trays of sandwiches and appetizers. The kids ran out into the backyard.

Ali bustled into the kitchen, snapping some hair ornament onto her waves. "The cake? How did it come out?"

Greg drew her in for a swift kiss, then positioned her next to the box. When she lifted the cover, she gasped.

"*Dios*, it's wonderful." The crime-fighting puppies from Jillian's favorite cartoon pranced across the confection. "Are you sure I can't pay her for this? It must have taken her forever."

"Are you kidding? My mom can make a cake like this in her sleep. She was happy to do it. She's come to love Jilly just as I have."

Ali paused, and a funny expression crossed her face. Greg wasn't sure what it meant. Hopefully, something good. He understood that it was still early in this relationship, but he wanted Ali to be heading in the same direction he was.

"What can I help you with?"

Ali glanced around the room and shook her head. "I don't even know. I've probably made too much food, but I hate not having enough. It's my family, a few of Jillian's friends from preschool with their moms. I invited the teachers on my team, so they may stop in for a bit. Jamilla has two kids who are a bit older than Jilly, but they've played with her before."

Crossing her arms, she let out a big sigh. "We'll see if the deadbeat shows up."

"Did he say he would?" Greg wasn't sure if he wanted to meet this man or not. On one hand, he was interested to see the idiot who walked away from a woman like Ali. On the other hand, if the guy treated Ali poorly, he'd have a hard time not slamming his fist into the man's face.

"I texted him a few days ago as a reminder. He sent back some weird emoji. I have no idea what it means."

"As long as it wasn't an eggplant, it doesn't matter."

Ali cocked her head. "Eggplant?"

"Don't ask. Hopefully, the kids in your class are still too young for this. I just happen to work with a few ridiculously immature guys."

Ali laughed, then her eyes narrowed as a loud car revved in front of the house. "Oh, Lord, he's actually on time."

Greg exited the house next to Ali. A red sports car sat at the curb. Her sister's Audi pulled into the driveway right behind his truck. Greg elected to greet Val and Max first.

Martina sat in the back, so he opened the door for her and helped her out.

"Oh, you are the sweetest, Greg. I'm so happy Ali found a nice boy like you. Can you grab those packages in the seat there?"

"Absolutely." He reached inside and took out the boxes wrapped in fancy balloon paper. Valeria still sat in the front, tapping away busily on her phone.

As he escorted Martina into the house, Val finally exited the car and let out a yell. "Jeffrey. Look at you all decked out. Nice car? When did you get that?"

He didn't want to look, but he couldn't help himself. The man climbing from the Porsche looked like a million bucks. The outfit certainly didn't come off the rack at Wal-Mart. His dark blond hair was styled like something you'd see in a fashion magazine. Designer sunglasses got pushed to the top of his head as he puckered up and slapped a kiss on Val's cheek. Looked like they were old friends.

Ali stared at her sister with a look of disgust on her face. Or was that hurt and jealousy? No, Ali always spoke of this guy in derogatory terms. He had to stop seeing Wendy in every woman around.

A few more cars pulled up as Greg was bringing Martina's gifts into the living room. Ryan had placed theirs on the coffee table, so he deposited the ones he carried there, as well.

Over the next half hour, people poured into Ali's back yard. They'd set up some tables last night and now he helped her lug the food, drinks, and paper goods out there. Jillian scampered around, greeting all the guests like she was a royal princess. She dragged Ryan around introducing him as her friend to everyone. Poor Ryan, but he took it all in stride.

Ali instructed people to help themselves to food, and Greg took advantage of the time to sneak up behind her. She startled at his hands on her hips, then relaxed when she realized who it was.

"Who were you expecting me to be?"

She peeked over her shoulder, then shook her head. "No one. I just want to make sure everyone's got food. Did you need something?"

"To help you if I can."

Her face softened, and it filled his with warmth. "Thanks. I'm always a wreck when I'm the hostess."

"You've got the food on the table where the guests can get it themselves, the kids are all running around playing together, and even your sister seems content to chat away with your ex." Greg had overheard some of the conversation, and it seemed like Val was taking credit for organizing the party. As far as he knew, she'd only donated some leftover plates and plastic utensils from a summer get-together they'd had.

"Hm, yes, she always did love hanging with the popular kids."

Greg took another look at the man. Yeah, he could see how the good looks and air of confidence might attract some.

Ali sighed. "I wish Tito could have come today, but I know I wouldn't have been able to keep my eye on him and everything else at the same time. Not to mention, he has that cold right now. All these kids running around would have tired him out."

"You can see him tomorrow." He'd love to go with her, but he was scheduled to work.

"Yeah. Okay, now you go get some food. If you don't, I'll be worried and even crazier than I typically am."

Greg pressed a tiny kiss to her cheek. "I'll get food when you do."

They rounded up the kids and managed to get them sitting at the picnic table with plates in front of them. It might not last long, but at least they'd have something solid before devouring the cake inside.

Greg made the rounds, keeping his eye on Ryan and Jilly as he socialized with the others at the party. Max was easy to talk to and kept his eye on his son, Manny, though all too often the man would have to go over and discipline the boy for playing too rough with the little girls. Ryan was doing his best to protect the younger children but wasn't always successful.

As Max was off talking to Manny, Valeria sauntered over, dragging Ali's ex with her.

"Greg Storm meet Jeffrey Cassidy. He's Jillian's father."

The two men shook hands.

"Nice to meet you, Storm. Is one of these rug rats yours?"

The man's condescending tone didn't go unnoticed. "My son, Ryan, is the boy helping the kids on the slide."

Jeff gawked at the kids, then swiveled his head back. "He's a little old to be playing with Jillian, isn't he?"

Valeria waved her hand in the air. "Oh, Ryan was in Alandra's class last year. Doesn't he still take piano lessons from her, too?"

Was Val seriously going to ignore that he and Ali had been dating for months? "Yes, he's gotten much better since he's been with her." Mostly because he made it a point to practice any time she came over to their house. She'd sit with him and give him pointers, and he'd become quite good. Greg was a little jealous of the time they spent together.

"What do you do, Storm?" The guy wanted to make small talk.

"I'm a captain at the Squamscott Falls Fire Department."

Jeff laughed, but his face twisted weirdly when he did. "Ha. I wanted to be a fireman when I was a kid, too. Now, I'm a chemical engineer. I work at a company in Portsmouth where we..."

Greg tuned the guy out as he bragged on and on about his important job where he had to be super intelligent. All the old inadequacies stumbled back in as he thought about how he'd wanted to become a doctor.

Staring at the ground, Greg studied the expensive hiking shoes of Ali's ex. Probably cost more than his monthly mortgage with the fancy lacings and the interlocking circular tread that was supposed to help dig into the terrain as you walked. The man sure liked to show off his high-end gear.

"Great meeting you, but I'm going to check if Ali needs my help with anything. Excuse me."

With no destination in mind, Greg hastened away, his mind stewing over every mistake he'd ever made. Being manipulated by Wendy to make her ex jealous. Over and over again. To the point of getting her pregnant and marrying her. Losing out on his chance to finish college and go to med school. How stupid had he been? Not that he'd ever regret Ryan, but what a fool he'd made of himself so he could get a hot girl in bed.

Ali laughed across the yard at something her teacher friend, Steph, said. He loved the sound of her laugh. It was real and feminine. He'd gotten that hot girl in bed, too. Not as often lately as he'd like. But Ali was nothing like Wendy, and being with her wasn't only about sex.

Her ex watched her as she chatted away. Her dress swished around her hips, and Jeff's grin grew into a leer. What was he gawking at? He'd tossed Ali aside like a worn-out shoe, so he had no right enjoying her looks now. Greg's teeth clenched thinking of the man and the harm he'd done to Ali's self-esteem.

"He's a blowhard. Don't mind him." Max was back and observing as Valeria still chatted with the bastard.

"Your wife seems to enjoy his company."

"That's just Val's nature. She'd talk to a rock if it paid her any attention. She thinks Ali should take him back. I know Ali's talked about how she wants another baby, but Jeff's not the best dad material, so I doubt she'd ever want round two with him."

Not to mention the fact he'd abandoned her. "Does she talk about having another baby a lot?" She'd never mentioned it to him, but then the topic had never come up.

Max shrugged. "Nah, I overheard the ladies talking about it one day. Valeria is a one and done kind of mom, which is fine with me. Are you looking to have more kids?"

It was Greg's turn to shrug. "I hadn't given it much thought. I'm not opposed to it." Aside from using condoms to avoid another accident, the subject hadn't entered his head.

"Well, even if Ali doesn't have another kid, she sure could use a father for Jillian. Jeff doesn't come around often enough to deserve that title. I guess he's here today, so maybe he's turned over a new leaf."

Greg wasn't sure how to respond. He'd never want Jillian not to have one of her parents, but he didn't like Jeff Cassidy or the way he ogled the woman he'd walked out on.

Max yelled to his son and ran over to Manny again to

keep him from kicking the ball too hard. Ali headed toward Greg, and he sent her a warm smile.

"Have you relaxed yet? You finally seem to be having a good time." He gripped her elbow casually when what he wanted to do was hold her close and kiss the stuffing out of her.

"I'm sorry. I'm always like this when I have to plan something. I'll never be as easygoing as your family during parties."

"You don't need to be. You're perfect the way you are."

"She is perfectly perfect." Jeff swaggered near and cocked his head. "Perfect mom for the birthday girl."

"Thank you for making it here." Ali smiled tightly at her ex.

"What did you expect?" He flung his hand in the air dramatically. "I'd never forget my little pumpkin's birthday on September twenty-fifth."

Ali's brows shot together. "Her birthday was two days ago. We're having her party today because it's a Saturday."

"Of course. That's what I meant."

Ali touched Greg's arm. "Have you met Jillian's father yet?"

"Oh, we're old friends. Right, Storm?"

"Old friends." Greg didn't have the patience to say much more.

Ali's gaze bounced back and forth between them. "I need to get Jillian to blow out the candles on her cake, so I can serve it. Greg's mother made the cake for us."

As Ali strode to get her daughter, Greg found himself with her ex again. The last place he wanted to be. Before he could think of a topic he wanted to bring up, mostly because there wasn't one, Jeff smirked as his eyes followed his former wife.

"You know, she's not bad looking when she wears those dresses."

"What are you talking about?" Greg finally broke out. "Ali is absolutely gorgeous. Every single part of her. I can't believe you walked away from her."

Jeff still faced Ali and his daughter. "Hm, yeah she does warm up the cold parts when the temps get low. I'll need to make a point of visiting Jillian more often. Get me some more of that good lovin'."

The man's words swirled in Greg's head. Was he planning on taking up with Ali where he'd left off years ago? What woman was stupid enough to return to a man who'd left her? Wendy's face floated through his mind. The vision of her ex-boyfriend kissing another girl at that damned party drifted past, too.

Ali gathered Jillian and the other kids, then waved at him mouthing, "Cake."

Greg dashed into the house and brought it out, positioning it in the middle of the picnic table. While he'd been inside, the other guests had gathered around the birthday girl. Jeff had maneuvered himself behind Ali, his hand on her shoulder.

Why wasn't she pushing him away, or at least shrugging his hand off? His own lack of self-esteem was firmly rearing its head now. He wanted to be the only one touching Ali and keeping her warm at night. It wasn't something easy to do with kids in the house.

The thought of asking Ali and Jillian to move in with them had crossed his mind. That way they'd see each other every day, and no one would have to go home to put a kid to bed. But he couldn't do it with Ryan in the house, and he was pretty sure Ali wouldn't want Jillian exposed to it either.

More than that, his parents wouldn't be happy about it. Shades of when he'd told them Wendy was pregnant. He couldn't face that disappointment again. His dad had lectured him about taking responsibility for his actions and the consequences of those actions.

The bastard, Jeff, still hadn't moved away as the guests all sang Happy Birthday to Jilly. Greg sang along, his eyes focused on the man who kept encroaching on Greg's woman. Was she his woman? She'd been Jeff's woman first. Didn't make her still his. Unless his comments meant anything.

But then, what was all that shyness from Ali when they'd first had sex. She hadn't wanted him to see her because she was self-conscious of her body. Or had he warmed her up for her ex to waltz back in and take over? Had he just filled a gap for her, like he'd done when Wendy's ex had fooled around on her?

Maybe it had been karma for Wendy to get in the car accident. Not that he wanted anything bad to happen to Ali. He loved her. He did. She'd infiltrated his heart and claimed it as hers. So why was he having these doubts right now?

Stop. Ali isn't Wendy. He needed to put all the doubts behind him and move forward towards a permanent relationship with Ali.

Jillian blew out the candles, and everyone clapped. Ali's eyes shone with happiness as she pressed a kiss to her daughter's head.

She shifted the cake to cut it, and Jeff whispered something in her ear. Greg's heart skipped a beat when Ali grinned at her ex, and he drew her tight against him.

He couldn't watch anymore. He was blowing everything out of proportion. Enough was enough, and he had to stop.

Grabbing some of the cake plates, he began handing them out to the other guests. Once everyone was served, he took his own plate and settled beside Jillian to eat. Ali had run the leftover cake into the house, while Jeff chatted with Max.

"Are you having a good birthday party, munchkin?"

Jilly's head bobbed, frosting smeared across her face. "It's the best ever."

"I'm glad. You've got lots of friends and family here to help you celebrate. Plus, your dad is here." Now, why did he say that? Pumping a four-year-old for information wasn't cool. Was he that desperate?

Jilly quickly glanced at her father and shrugged as she shoveled another spoonful of cake in her mouth. "Yeah, he only comes because he wants to talk to Mama. And kiss her."

"Your dad kisses your mom? All the time?" Maybe she was remembering before he left. But no, Jilly had been a baby. No way she remembered that far back.

The little girl licked the spoon and tilted her head. "Just when he comes over. Yup, and sometimes he pats her on the bum." Jillian giggled and stuck her face in her cake again.

Had he heard correctly? From the mouth of babes.

"Did you get enough cake?" Ali scooted onto the seat next to him. "Your mom does such an amazing job. Make sure to thank her for us."

"Sure." He stared at Ali, attempting to understand what had just happened.

She peeked over her shoulder, eyeing her ex, then leaned in and gave him a tiny kiss.

"Hey, hot stuff. I've been watching you from across the room." Wendy peeked over her shoulder at her ex in a liplock with another girl. Her arms slid around Greg's neck, and she slithered her shapely body against his. "How'd you like to get lucky?"

Deja vu.

The contents of his stomach threatened to come back up.

CHAPTER TWENTY-SEVEN

*A*li kissed her daughter on the forehead and tucked the comforter over her shoulders.

"Sleep well, Jilly."

"Night, Mama. We see Ryan and Cap'in tomorrow?"

That was an excellent question. One she didn't know the answer to. "Well, it's a school day, so I have to go to work and they do, too. We'll see. I love you, sweetie."

Jillian hugged her lion tighter and closed her eyes.

As Ali slogged down the hallway, she tried to convince herself everything was fine. Greg was simply busy with work and other things and didn't have time for them this week. Or last week. It had been ten days since Jillian's party. Ten days since she'd spent any time with Greg.

He hadn't lingered after to help her clean up like she'd expected he would. He'd mumbled some excuse about cleaning out the garage while it was still light, then taken off. Ryan had looked as confused as she'd been.

He'd been scheduled to work the next day, so she and Jillian had visited Tito by themselves. Her grandfather had asked about Greg and Ryan which made her feel great. He didn't always remember new people in his life. Heck, he thought she was her grandmother at times.

Greg's next day off had been Wednesday, but he'd sent a text with some excuse about being busy and not being able to make it over. They'd had that happen often enough she hadn't thought anything of it. But when it happened each night since, she got worried.

Had she done something to upset him? If so, why hadn't he mentioned it? She'd seen Ryan most days at school, and he hadn't acted any different to her or said anything about his dad being upset. Not that Greg would involve his son in any of their problems.

That was the kicker. They hadn't had any problems since they'd started dating. Every couple had fights now and then. She and Jeff had fought constantly. Mostly him telling her she wasn't doing something good enough or often enough. That wasn't the case with Greg.

In the kitchen, Ali wiped down the counters and put away the last of the dinner stuff. Not that she'd eaten any of it. Couldn't even think about food at this time. Her pants had been thankful, and a little looser, but her mind was foggy with lack of nourishment. Add to that the lack of sleep, and she was one big walking mess.

After shutting off the kitchen lights, she entered the living room and plopped onto the couch. The remote sat by her hip, so she clicked the TV on and flipped until a sitcom came on. She couldn't handle anything heavier at the moment.

Her phone sat on the coffee table, taunting her. She hadn't heard the tone at all, but perhaps she'd missed it when she and Jillian had been singing their goodnight song.

Picking it up now, she swiped across the screen and sighed. No new messages. She scrolled through her old messages and reread the ones from Greg. Short and to the point. No kiss emojis or winkies or anything. Not even eggplants, and she'd looked that up.

Maybe she should send him an eggplant emoji. Or a taco. Or was it a peach? Who knew? Not her. Maybe that was why Greg was ghosting her now.

They'd had sex a handful of times, and in her opinion, it had been out of this world. But for Greg, it could have simply been average. Something Ali had been told she was all her life.

Did he finally get his mojo back after sleeping with her, and now he wanted to move on to someone thinner and more exciting? One of those ladies who wore a dress to go to the Granite Grill, even though it was a casual place? Was he already going there on the nights he'd normally be hanging with her? Was some woman even now enjoying the moon shining through the window over the bed in his boat's cabin? He'd never removed the condoms from the overhead compartment.

Should she ask Ryan what he'd been doing? The boy had showed up for his piano lessons on Saturday, but Greg hadn't come in with him. Some excuse from Ryan about errands. But after, Greg had honked the horn for Ryan to come out. His text had said something about the puppy. She'd been too upset to even question it.

Reading through the texts again, Ali tried to find answers in Greg's words. Maybe her brain had melted from lack of sustenance, but she couldn't find any. It was as if the last three months of dating, of spending time together like a family, hadn't existed.

She wanted to believe Greg had truly just been super busy, She'd been hammered with correcting and state testing, as well as planning for their first fall field trip to the State House in Concord. But thinking about field trips made her mind wander back to the fire house when Greg had hefted her over his shoulder and hauled her down from the fire engine. How could things have gone from there, to sleeping together, to...nothing?

If she were a stronger, more confident, person, she'd send him another text asking what the hell was going on. Or she'd drop by his house after school on a day she knew he wasn't scheduled to work. But her mother and sister had drilled into her not to be too pushy. Guys didn't like pushy women. Yeah, and look where that had gotten her with Jeff.

Too bad he didn't live on a main road because then she could cruise by his house to see if his truck was there. But there were three houses on his short street. All belonged to his family. She could hardly say she was stopping in to visit one of them if he saw her.

Her attention was caught by the ranting of two of the characters on the screen. They'd been having a fight and now held each other in an embrace, making up after the altercation. Could she and Greg figure things out and make them better?

She thought so, but first she had to find out what had gone wrong to begin with.

"HEY, DAD," Ryan called out as he passed by the bedroom door.

"Hey, pal. How was school today? Did you thank Mrs. Farmer for giving you a ride home after track practice?"

Not that his son ever gave him much information on the subject of school, but Greg felt like, as a parent, he was required to ask. That father's manual he'd spoken of before.

Ryan stopped in the doorway, and Greg swung his legs over the side of the bed. He'd been attempting to sleep since he had an overnight at the station tonight. He could bunk there, but if they had a few runs, it wouldn't be good to be tired.

"Yes, I thanked her. School was fine. We had gym today, and I got a couple goals in floor hockey."

"Excellent. So all those drills I ran over the summer paid off, huh?"

Ryan rolled his eyes. "I guess so." He twisted his lips to the side, and his brows pulled together. "Dad?"

"What's up, pal?"

Ryan's face was all scrunched up like when he wanted to ask something he knew Greg would say no to. What was it this time?

"I saw Mrs. C. today."

Greg froze, his nerves on high alert. "Did she say anything?" Stupid question. Of course, she said something to Ryan, even if it was only hello. Another reason he'd been attempting to sleep. He hadn't gotten as much as usual at night thinking about Ali.

"Just hi and gave me a big hug. You know she gives the best hugs, and they always make you feel better if you're kind of down."

"Good to know." He could use one. But not if her ex had been getting them, too. His jaw tightened thinking of the man with his hands on Ali's shoulders laughing in her ear. Or patting her on the bum.

"Dad?" Ryan's voice was stronger now. More determined.

He tipped his head and nodded.

"Why haven't we seen Mrs. C. and Jillian lately?"

This was the question he'd been hoping to avoid. Maybe why dating with kids was harder in so many ways. "You saw her Saturday at your piano lessons. I assume you saw Jillian then, as well."

Ryan sighed. "But you didn't even come in, and we haven't had dinner together in a few weeks. It's been since

Jilly's party that we've spent any time with them. But her party had lots of other people, so we didn't even get good family time together."

That was the crux of the matter. Ryan had begun to think of Ali and Jilly in terms of family. He had, too, and it's why it hurt so much not to see them. Maybe he'd gone about this situation all wrong. He'd be the first to admit ghosting Ali was more than childish, but he hadn't wanted to get into a huge fight. Or hear that she had been warming her ex up on chilly nights. It was one question he'd never asked Wendy. Maybe he should have.

"Dad?" Guess Ryan needed to talk about this, but Greg wasn't sure he had any answers for him.

"We've both been busy, pal. School takes up a lot of her time, and I've put in a few extra shifts lately."

"Your birthday is next week. Do you think we could do a little party to celebrate? It doesn't have to be anything big like we had for Uncle Alex and Uncle Nathaniel. Maybe we could just have Mrs. C. and Jilly over for dinner. Or we could get pizza, and you and Mrs. C. can share the gross peppers and mushroom again."

Greg laughed, mostly to cover up the emotion of the memory. "I'll think about it and check my schedule at work. Then, we can decide."

He already knew his schedule for the next three weeks, but it gave him some extra time to figure things out.

"Great. Can I take Guinness outside to run around? Honeysuckle is out there, too."

"That's a great idea. I'm going to jump in the shower before I have to leave at six. Auntie Sofe is staying overnight with you. She said she'd make tacos."

"Yes!" Ryan pumped his fist, then pounded down the stairs. The dog's excited barks could be heard all the way on the second floor.

Taking a deep breath in, Greg held it, then exhaled, hoping to calm his frayed nerves. He had to think about this. And talk to Ali.

After closing his bedroom door, he opened his bottom drawer and pulled out a small wooden chest. He slipped out the weathered envelope from inside and withdrew the paper from it. The sound of dog and boy beckoned him to the window. As he gazed out, that warm intense feeling hit him like it always did. God, he loved that kid.

Grinding his teeth together, he glanced down at the fancy sheet of stationery.

Dear Greg,

I'm so sorry that this didn't work out between us. For your sake. The truth is I'm still in love with Skip. I've never stopped loving him, even though he cheated on me. Which is why I came onto you at the party. I know it wasn't fair of me, but I was hurting and wanted to hurt him back. You were convenient. And the sex was great.

But I never wanted to be a mother. The pregnancy wasn't planned, but it did the job of bringing Skip to his senses and coming to realize he still loved me, too. I'm leaving with him to go cross country. Ryan is all yours. I'll file for divorce and even give you full custody of your son. You've been so happy with the baby, and I know you'll make a great father. You're a super guy and you'll be able to find him a new mom soon. Enclosed is a letter from me, certified, that gives my parental rights away. Find him a mom who can love him like a mother should. Unfortunately, it's not me.

Forgive me,

Wendy

Greg closed his eyes and crumpled the note. Why had he even kept it? He hadn't needed the certified letter since Wendy had died. He tossed it in the waste basket in his room, then headed into the connected bathroom.

In the shower, his thoughts turned to Ali. She wasn't

Wendy. He knew this. Of course, he did, so why did he allow what had happened with Wendy to keep coming back to haunt him?

Because it devastated you. Not because he'd lost her. He'd never loved her. But because he'd been so easily duped and his beloved son so easily cast aside.

As he scrubbed soap on his body and shampoo in his hair, he attempted to scrub away the pain and anger of the past. He needed to talk to Ali. Spell out his concerns and ask her truthfully if she'd been sleeping with Jeff.

What if she says she has? God, he didn't want to go there. But it's possible his knee jerk reaction was too hasty. He honestly couldn't imagine Ali having casual sex with the man who'd not only abandoned her but walked away from his own kid.

While he scrubbed a towel over his body to dry, memories of Ali drifted through his mind. It hurt not to have her around. Even if it was only sitting on the couch and falling asleep in front of the TV, he loved being with her.

The truth was he loved her and wanted to marry her. Yes, three months wasn't a huge amount of time, but they'd known each other for years, and he wasn't twenty years old anymore. He was a grown man with a ten-year-old son. It was about time he acted like the adult he was.

He glanced at the clock on the nightstand. Almost time to leave for work. Once he'd donned his uniform, he glanced at his phone. Should he text her now? Had she been as miserable as he'd been? Of course, she didn't even know the why of the problem. Shame on him.

His fingers flew over the screen.

—*Hey, I'm heading in for a 7 to 7 overnight, but was wondering if you'd be around tomorrow to talk. Maybe after I sleep?*—

He held the phone, waiting for a text back. Nothing. Like

how his insides felt without Ali around. He had to be positive. Maybe she didn't have her phone on her. Or her battery was dead. Or she didn't want to talk to someone who'd ignored her for almost two weeks.

He'd try again later. He wasn't giving up. There was one last thing he needed to do before he left. Something he should have done years ago.

Picking up the metal trash can, he pulled out a package of matches and lit one, holding the edge of the paper to the flame. Once it caught and was fully engulfed, he let it drift into the can.

Ryan didn't need to know this letter ever existed.

CHAPTER TWENTY-EIGHT

*A*li pulled into the driveway and sighed before she got out of the car. Jilly was staying with her Abuelita for both Friday and Saturday night. It had been Jeff's weekend to take her, but he'd texted a few days ago saying he had a business trip and would be away for a week. Her mom had volunteered to take Jilly, most likely thinking she was giving Ali and Greg some alone time without the little one. She hadn't told anyone yet that she hadn't seen Greg in almost two weeks. What would she even say?

Once in the house, tidying up the kitchen was quick since she hadn't eaten any supper tonight. Mama was making something special for Jilly, but Ali hadn't wanted to infringe on their time together. Jilly had started going four full days to school this fall, so her mom only got to see her granddaughter one day a week. She missed her. Next year, when Jilly was in kindergarten, she wouldn't see her at all unless they made arrangements to get together.

Which would be wonderful if Ali and Greg were still dating. Technically, they hadn't broken up, but something was wrong, and she didn't know what. Even Ryan had clung

317

to her a bit longer this morning in the hallway on his way to class. Like he knew there was a problem. At least one Storm male still liked her.

Now, what to do for the entire weekend on her own? She had her piano students tomorrow morning, including Ryan, though doubtful his father would be driving his son here. She knew his schedule had him working an overnight tonight, so he'd most likely be sleeping when Ryan's lesson time came.

After grabbing her school bag, she settled on the couch and plunked a packet of papers that needed correcting on the coffee table. Might as well get them done now. Wouldn't her students be surprised if she returned all their work on Monday?

Slogging through the pages was tedious, mind-numbing work, but once she got on a roll, it got easier. By the end of the second hour, she'd gotten through the whole lot and even entered the scores in her online grade book.

She stood up to stretch and headed to the kitchen to make a cup of tea. Once she'd put the water on to boil, she rested against the counter and scanned the room. The purple walkie talkies Ryan and Greg had gotten Jilly sat on the little girl's tiny table.

Suddenly, tears filled her eyes, and she couldn't stop the downpour cascading across her cheeks. Hugging her middle tight, she tried to stop herself from crying, but the more she glanced around the room, the more memories of Greg being here surfaced. Him sitting in one of the little chairs and playing tea party. Helping Jilly stir the bowl of pretend brownie mix. Wiping Jilly's hands and face clean of spaghetti sauce.

The whistle on the tea kettle blew. She filled her mug and turned the stove off, but overwhelming sadness still blanketed her, and she slid against the corner of the cabinets until she sat curled up on the floor, arms wrapped around her knees. She kept hoping it was all a mistake and that Greg had just been busy lately. But today at school, Leah had asked why she and Jilly hadn't been over for Sunday dinner last week.

Ali had made some excuse about Tito and her mom, but the truth was Greg hadn't invited them over and had texted some bullshit about working an extra shift. Obviously, he hadn't. It was like Jeff all over again. Only she loved Greg Storm so much more than she'd ever loved Jeff.

Yes, she was finally admitting to herself she had fallen deeply in love with the captain of the Squamscott Falls Fire Department. This weekend would have been great if they could have shared it together. But here she was, alone again. She didn't even have Jilly to keep her occupied, to take her mind off the loneliness.

Why did she continue to fall in love with men who didn't want her?

It had been forever since she'd had a good cry, and she was due. Her head fell on her knees, and she sobbed for the unfairness of it. To bring Greg into her life and show her what true happiness could be, and then rip that rug right out from underneath her, making her fall flat on her face yet again.

All this, and he didn't even have the decency to tell her in person that he didn't want to see her anymore. She hadn't thought he was that spineless, but then she'd had poor judgment with Jeff, too.

Finally, Ali hauled herself off the floor and mopped up her eyes and nose. Damn that man. She had a right to know if he wanted to call it quits. She deserved that much. Her gaze roamed the room until she spied her purse. Reaching inside, she grabbed her phone and swiped it on. Crap, the battery was dead. Not that she'd been expecting any calls, but it wasn't good to be on the road without a working cell. And now she'd have to wait until it recharged before she could shoot off a scathing text to Greg.

She stuck the dead phone in the charging port and sat at the table, resting her head on her arms. She was wiped out from her crying jag and felt like shit. Maybe she needed to eat something. The few bites of leftover mac and cheese from lunch today hadn't made it far. Especially since she'd barely eaten any of it.

She threw together a jelly sandwich, having run out of peanut butter yesterday. Going to the grocery store and getting food for the week would be helpful, but her finances were still trying to recover from not working over the summer. If it hadn't been for the two new dresses she'd bought to go out with Greg, maybe she would have been able to stretch her money a little more. What a waste.

As she sat down to eat her sandwich and drink her tea, her phone pinged with a few messages. She reached over, leaving it plugged in, and swiped across the screen. Jeff making sure Jilly had gotten to her mother's okay and she'd made it back from Portsmouth. That was strange. The man never worried about his daughter, and he certainly never worried about her. She shot him back a quick note, then swiped to see the other message.

Greg. Her stomach tightened and chills ran through her. Was it simply another excuse not to see her?

—*Hey, I'm heading in for a 7 to 7 overnight, but wondered if you'd be around tomorrow to talk. Maybe after I sleep?*—

Her hands shook as she held the phone. He'd texted a few hours ago before he'd left for work. What did she say to that? What did he want? Was the talk so he could dump her? Or explain what had happened? If she didn't ask, she'd never sleep tonight with the anxiety of not knowing.

—*What happened? What did I do wrong?*—

Okay, that text wasn't the badass, strong woman she needed to be, but it put the ball back in his court.

It was only a few seconds before her phone pinged again.

—*Probably nothing. I've got some ghosts I need to exorcise, and you got caught in the middle. Tomorrow? Please?*—

Ghosts? Well, he sure had been ghosting her. His words didn't sound like he was planning to dump her, but that could just be wishful thinking on her part. She'd at least let him explain.

—*I'll be home all day.*—

His volley.

—*Thanks. Oops, got a call, gotta run. See you.*—

He probably wouldn't see her return text, but she sent it anyway. —*Stay safe.*—

Placing her phone back down, she smiled. Maybe the first real smile she'd had in two weeks. She wouldn't get her hopes up, but perhaps whatever ghosts he'd been wrestling with would disappear. She'd fight for him if she had to. Fight to make the feelings they had for each other mean something. If he needed help, she'd stand beside him and battle them head on.

Now that she wasn't a hot mess and there was a light at the end of the tunnel, the heavy emotion of the last two weeks began to weigh on her. Maybe tonight she could actually get a good night's rest.

After finishing her sandwich, she tidied up the kitchen, spent a few minutes rearranging Jillian's toys, then locked up the house. Her bed was calling to her, and she might be able to use it for its true purpose tonight, knowing tomorrow she'd see Greg and make a stand for her happiness. And hopefully his.

Her eyes could barely stay open, so she slipped into pajamas, brushed her teeth, and burrowed between her sheets.

Within seconds, she was dreaming of tomorrow and holding Greg Storm in her arms once more.

"I'M GETTING tired of these big fires, Cap," Seamus said as he shifted the engine into gear and pulled away from the burnt wreckage they'd spent three hours trying to save. Not much left of the small warehouse. Greg wasn't sure what kind of inventory should have been there, but it had seemed empty when he'd gotten a look inside.

Had this been yet another of the possible arson cases they'd been fighting for half this year? They'd left the cleanup for the Portsmouth FD once the fire had been under control.

"Tired of fires? You might have picked the wrong career."

Seamus laughed. "Well, tired of these ones that are most likely being set. It takes us away from the town we're supposed to protect. What happens if we're all the way in Portsmouth and something happens—"

"Don't even think it. You'll jinx us."

Their tone sounded on the radio, and Greg glared at the engineer.

"Attention, Squamscott Falls Fire, we have report of a structure fire in progress at fifteen Holiday Lane. Neighbors reporting smoke and seeing flames inside the structure. Repeat: Squamscott Falls Fire, we have a report..."

Greg tuned out the repeat of the call. That was Ali's house. Shit. They were at least twenty minutes from Squamscott Falls and no other fire company was any closer. When had the fire started and how? It was almost one in the morning. Unlikely she'd still be awake at this hour.

Seamus flipped the sirens on and sped up.

Greg responded to the call, then said, "Step on it, Seamus. That's Ali's house."

"Oh, man, that sucks. I'll get us there fast as I can."

Greg grabbed his cell phone from the cup holder he typically stored it in and pressed Ali's contact. The phone rang and rang, then went to voicemail.

Maybe she'd gotten out but hadn't had time to take her phone. Of course, she wouldn't have taken her phone. She would have been more concerned for Jilly and getting her to safety. Oh, God, that little girl must be scared to death.

What if they hadn't gotten out? What if they were still trapped inside? He couldn't lose them. Both Ali and Jilly had come to mean something to him. Were important to his happiness.

He gripped the sides of the seat as the vehicle raced through the street, sirens screaming along the route. Greg had to breathe deeply, in and out, just to keep himself from falling apart. He was a trained firefighter and couldn't panic at a time like this.

As they made their way, finally, up Ali's street, Greg searched the roadway and yards for any sign of Ali and Jilly. A few dozen people in pajamas and bathrobes stood around outside, some scrolling on their phones, others holding each other.

No sign of either Ali or Jillian. Lord, please let them have stayed somewhere else tonight or be inside a neighbor's house.

The engine pulled up near the house, and BB jumped out to connect the hose to the nearby hydrant. Thank God there was one close by. They'd used most of the water on the truck for the previous fire.

Greg vaulted from the truck and raced over to the officer who was keeping the neighbors behind him.

"Is there anyone inside?" He said this automatically, but Ali's car was in the driveway. His heart raced and his lungs dried up, thinking she hadn't gotten out.

Flames shot from the roof on the entire left side of the house.

A woman wearing a fuzzy blue bathrobe and slippers broke into their conversation. "I saw her take the little girl somewhere earlier, but then Alandra came back without her. I think Ali's still in there."

Greg's hands shook as he started shouting orders. He couldn't fall apart now. His men grabbed the hose and focused the spray on the roof. Greg settled his helmet on his head, grabbed his flashlight from his pocket and trotted around the right side of the house. Where Ali's bedroom was.

The flames crackled loudly in the air, but Greg heard something else. Flashing the light toward the window, his heart stopped. Ali peeked out, attempting to lift the sash. Her face contorted in fear, before she bent over coughing. The smoke had to be debilitating in there by now.

"Ali!" he screamed, then raced back to pull a ladder off the truck. "Follow me with some tools," he ordered BB.

When he got back, he braced the ladder against the side of the house and started climbing. Where was Ali? She wasn't at the window any longer. Had she attempted to go through the house? No way she'd get through with the flames where they were. The house was almost fully engulfed.

"Ali!" Greg grabbed the crowbar BB handed him and wedged it in the window. It wouldn't budge. He didn't have time to figure out why the window wouldn't open, but he didn't want to break it if Ali was nearby. He'd have to risk it. The glass was less dangerous than the smoke and flames.

Turning his face, he smashed the windowpanes, then moved the crowbar along the edges to push any glass from the rim. BB tossed him the thick padded blanket so he could rest it on the broken windowpane, then Greg climbed in the window. Where...? There. Ali lay crumpled on the floor. No, she had to be all right. He hadn't told her how much he loved her yet.

"Come on, sweetheart. Let's get you out of here." He hefted her over his shoulder and moved to the window. The smoke was thick, and he hadn't bothered putting on his air tank and mask. He'd catch hell for it later, but he hadn't wanted to waste any time in getting Ali out.

Manipulating through the broken glass and getting back on the ladder was difficult, and all Greg could think about was how she'd be mad that he'd slung her over his shoulder again. God, he wished he'd get a chance for her to scold him about it again.

As he got near the bottom of the ladder, BB was there to take Ali from him and carry her to a clear spot on the neighbor's lawn. Fallon rushed over, her paramedic case in hand.

Greg gave a few more instructions for his crew, then darted back to her side.

"Is she going to be all right?"

Fallon had placed an oxygen mask on Ali's face and was doing a cursory check. "The ambulance is ready for her. She's got a good pulse, but her breath is reedy and she's unconscious. We need to get her to the hospital as soon as we can."

He could see how bad she was, and it scared the pants off him. He'd observed more than a few people die hours after they'd been rescued from a burning building even if they hadn't come in contact with the flames. The smoke was often more deadly.

As he helped Fallon lift Ali onto the gurney, he continued to talk to her.

"Come on, Ali, you can do this. Jillian needs you. I need you. Wake up and yell at me for slinging you over my shoulder. Anything. I'll let you yell at me for the rest of our lives if you just come out of this."

"I've got her, Cap. I'll keep you updated once we get to the hospital."

Greg didn't want to let her go, but he needed to take charge of this situation. He took one last look at the ambulance as it drove away, hoping it wouldn't be his last time with the woman he loved.

CHAPTER TWENTY-NINE

*T*he smell of smoke in Ali's hair was making her sick. The fact she was still coughing up black goo didn't help. She didn't have the energy to get up and take a shower, and the nurses all seemed super busy.

She was still foggy on exactly what happened. At some point in the night, she'd woken to find smoke surrounding her bed and flames crackling in the hallway. Her first thought had been Jilly, but slowly she'd remembered her daughter was at Mama's. Her sluggish responses must have been from the lack of oxygen.

The fear she'd felt when she'd realized she couldn't get out through the house rose up and threatened to choke her again. She'd been too weak to open the windows. Before she'd passed out, she'd prayed for Greg to come save her and had imagined him there.

"Hey. How you feeling, honey?" Leah popped her head in the doorway, a worried expression on her face.

"Tired, and my chest is sore. I'm so confused. I don't know how that fire could have started. I didn't leave anything burning or on the stove."

Leah scurried to sit next to her and took her hand. "I don't know for certain, but I don't think it was anything you did."

"How do you know?"

Leah peeked over her shoulder, then back. "I have connections with the police and fire departments. There's been lots of chatter between the two departments."

"How did I get here? Last I remember I was trying to open my bedroom window."

"A few of your neighbors called as soon as they smelled the smoke. Unfortunately, our fire department was still in Portsmouth on another big call, so it took a while to get to you. Greg had to break the window to get inside and get you out."

"Greg got me out. I thought I'd imagined him."

"Nope, and I can tell you he was pretty freaked. Since Sofie was doing Ryan duty for the night, he woke me up around two in the morning to come down here and make sure you were okay. He stopped in a few hours later, once he got a chance to get away."

"I don't remember."

Leah shrugged. "I'm not family so they wouldn't let me in to see you at first, but I've got connections. I stopped back home to grab a few more hours sleep, figuring I'd be able to visit now since you're in a regular ward."

"Where's Greg? Was he hurt at all?"

"The hardheaded brother? No. He was part of the crew that sifted through the house debris to look for clues." Leah glanced at the clock on the wall showing it was almost noon. "I'm guessing he's asleep now. It was a long night."

"Yeah." Ali didn't know what else to say. She wanted to ask if Greg had said anything about her or told his sister what had been eating at him lately. Would Leah be honest if

Greg wanted to break up? Would he have even told his sister?

Heavy footsteps in the hallway had her looking up, hoping it was Greg. Two handsome men stood in the doorway, but it wasn't the Storm she wanted. Kevin, and his partner, Mitch Wagner, nodded at her, looking very official.

"Ali, Leah, can we come in for a minute?" Kevin asked.

Leah stood and squeezed her hand. "I'm going to head out, but you call me if you need anything, okay?"

Ali nodded as Leah left, then faced the detectives from the Portsmouth Police Department. What were they doing here? Squamscott Falls wasn't their jurisdiction.

"Is this an official call? The two of you look serious."

Kevin frowned. "Yeah, it is. You know about all the fires that have been happening in the area in the past seven months, right?"

She nodded.

Mitch cleared his throat. "Your fire was related to those."

"My house? But none of the other fires had anyone home at the time. And some of them were businesses."

"Your fire was related but not set by the same people." Kevin's brows slid together.

"You know who's been setting the fires?"

"Yeah," Mitch said. "And who's been providing them with the chemicals to do it so there's little trace of it."

"Chemicals?" Her voice squeaked at the word. "Like a chemical engineer would have access to?" This couldn't be what she thought.

Kevin sat on the edge of her bed and took her hand. "Listen, we need to tell you something, and it might be difficult for you."

"My ex-husband is a chemical engineer. He works near the Portsmouth shipyards."

Kevin nodded, then took a deep breath. "When the arson

investigator was examining your house, the police took a look around the yard for clues. They found some shoe treads with a distinct pattern near both your bedroom windows. Captain Storm identified them as being from a pair of boots owned by Jeffrey Cassidy. As he's your ex-husband, it was enough for a judge to grant us a search warrant for his place. We went over first thing this morning."

"He's on a business trip this week." It couldn't be Jeff. He was a bastard but not an arsonist. What reason would he have to set fires?

"No, he's not," Mitch clarified. "He was sweaty and agitated when we asked to come in. We had a warrant, so he couldn't refuse."

"What did you find?"

"Your wallet and your laptop and enough accelerant to burn your entire house to the ground in short order. We took him in for questioning." Kevin gazed at the floor.

"What did he say? Why did he have my stuff?"

Mitch folded his arms over his chest. "Once we told him we'd charge him with all the recent fires, he folded like a house of cards. Broke down sobbing and told us everything."

Her heart pounded. "I don't understand. What in the world would Jeff be doing setting fires?"

Kevin stood and paced, then pivoted back to her. "Seems your ex-husband has a bit of a gambling problem. He owes some big money to a few nasty people. They blackmailed him to provide chemicals so they could rob some of these houses and buildings, then burn them down to get rid of any evidence."

"But why my house? My laptop is six years old, and I have about twenty dollars in my wallet."

Mitch glanced at his watch. "Apparently, you have an insurance policy at work that still names your ex as the beneficiary."

A cough wracked her body, and Kevin handed her some tissues. "I changed that right after we got divorced."

Kevin raised an eyebrow. "Except he still thinks he's on it."

"He told you he wanted to kill me?" Tears filled her eyes. How could she have been so stupid?

"I don't think he wanted to." Kevin sat next to her again and patted her hand. "But these guys he owes money to are bad news."

"He can't just sell his damn car?"

Mitch snickered. "Everything he has is mortgaged to the hilt. He tried to make it sound like it wasn't his fault. That he had to pay child support, and it took all his money."

"What? He still owes me at least four months of back support. How can he say that?"

"He was a mess when we questioned him. Crying about how he kept the key to your house. Your tox screen came back with a heavy sedative, and he confessed he'd put sleeping pills in your tea kettle earlier yesterday, since he knew your habit of having tea before bed. We found the windows in your bedroom were sealed shut, and when we mentioned that, he admitted he'd done it so you couldn't get out. He was desperate for the insurance money."

"I can't believe he wanted me dead. And that he confessed to all of this. What'll happen to him?" And what would happen to Jillian knowing that her father wanted her mother dead? The tears fell in earnest now.

"He's hoping to plea bargain a lighter sentence. He's given us information and evidence on the arson ring, as well as the crooks he owes money to."

"A lighter sentence. You mean he'll get out in a little while so he can try and kill me again?" Would she have to move and hide somewhere across the country?

Kevin grasped her shoulder. "A lighter sentence means

twenty years versus life. He's being charged with attempted murder, along with complicity in the arsons and a few other crimes. He won't be bothering you for a long while."

Mitch handed her a box of tissues, and she mopped up best she could. *Dios*, her life was one big mess.

"Do you want us to call someone to be here with you? This has to be devastating. If not your family, I've got lots of cousins who'd be willing and able to pop over within minutes."

The only Storm cousin she wanted didn't necessarily want her. Especially now with everything that had happened.

"No, thank you for coming to tell me everything. I appreciate it." Now what did she do? She didn't even know what was left of her house or her belongings. Thank God Jilly had stayed at her mother's last night. That's why Jeff had called to check. It was okay to end her life, but not his daughter's. The man had a fraction of decency.

Kevin stood. "Are you sure? After what we told you, I don't like leaving you alone."

"She won't be alone." Greg Storm stood in the doorway.

WHEN ALI GAZED up at him with tear-filled eyes, Greg was lost. How had he ever thought she'd cheat on him or have anything to do with that rat bastard? Especially after finding out what her ex had done. Thinking of how he could have lost the woman he loved, he wanted to find Jeff Cassidy and wring his neck. Maybe some of his new friends in the state penitentiary would do it for him.

His cousin stood and patted Ali on the shoulder, then nodded as he passed Greg. "I'm glad you're here." Greg also got a shoulder pat from Kevin before he and Mitch left.

Ali's gaze flew to the window and doubt suddenly

attacked him like murderous crows. He'd been a jerk to her for two weeks. Did he expect her to jump out of bed and declare her undying love for him?

No, but he should be doing something similar. Soon.

"How are you feeling?" First things first.

"I'll live." Her voice was rough but also pained. "Thanks to you, I hear."

He took a few steps closer. "It's my job. I had to sling you over my shoulder and carry you. Hope you don't mind."

A tiny laugh escaped. "I guess I can forgive you, again." She still wouldn't look at him.

"I've never been so scared doing it before." His own voice choked up, and her head swiveled toward him.

"Did you get any sleep?"

Just like Ali to be concerned about others even when she was pissed. "I grabbed an hour or so, but I wanted to come see you and talk about a few things."

Tears rolled down her cheeks, and she pulled a few tissues from a box in her lap to wipe them up. "Did you hear about…my ex?"

She couldn't say the bastard's name. He didn't blame her.

"Yeah, I've been talking to the arson investigator and the crime unit who've been working the case. I'm so sorry, sweetie."

She might not like it, but he needed to be closer. Balancing on the edge of the bed, he took her hand and stroked her soft skin.

Deep sobs shook her frame, so he drew her into his arms and held her. He wanted to be here for her for the rest of their lives. Would she let him after his blunder?

For a few minutes, he simply held her and ran his hand up and down her back, uttering soft words of assurance.

"Do I even want to know what my house looks like?" she said into his chest.

"You're alive and okay. Nothing else matters."

"I know, and Jilly wasn't there so she won't have those traumatic memories. But all our stuff…"

"Can be replaced. You can't. God, Ali, when I heard your address over the radio, I thought I'd die if something happened to you and Jillian. Then, I saw you in the window, petrified when you couldn't open it."

"I was so scared. I thought I'd dreamed that you came to save me."

"No dream, sweetheart. I'll always be here if you need me."

Her head whipped up, and her voice grew strong. "Will you?"

He swallowed hard. "I deserve that. I'm sorry about not calling you the last few weeks. We can talk about it later. Once you've been released from the hospital."

"They said I could leave maybe tonight or tomorrow morning."

"Yeah, smoke inhalation is no laughing matter. You'll need to be under observation for a little longer."

"My mom's going to come get me when I call her."

How would she react to what he planned to say? "I talked to her this morning and said I'd pick you up. It might be a good idea to keep Jillian with her for another day or so like planned. I'd like the two of you to come stay with us."

Her brows pushed together. "You want Jillian and me to move in with you? Why?"

"Ryan would be thrilled to have you there, and I've got five bedrooms. Your mom said she only has a pullout couch. You won't be comfortable there. I also talked to Reggie and let him know what happened. He wants you to take a few days off at least. He's already got a substitute lined up for your class."

"You've done an awful lot of planning for someone who

hasn't spoken to me in a couple weeks. Why would you want us to stay with you? You haven't called at all, haven't even come in when Ryan's at piano lessons."

This was going to be harder than he thought. But he deserved every roadblock she threw in front of him for being an idiot. He had to man up and tell her the truth, even if she hated him for the stupid thoughts he'd had.

"You know what happened with Wendy. It completely did a number on me, and trust was hard to come by after that. Several of the conversations I heard at Jillian's party shoved me back in time and threw me for a loop."

"What conversations?" Her soft voice clawed at his nerves, making him want to get back in her good graces.

"Someone mentioned you needing a second income."

She cocked her head. "Yeah, my piano lessons."

"And you wanting another baby."

"Sure, someday, if the right guy came along." Her face grew more rigid the more he talked. But he had to get it all out.

"It was too reminiscent of Wendy's pregnancy and how she used me. And then there was your ex hinting that the two of you got together and kept each other warm on cold nights. I didn't want to believe it, but Jilly made a comment about him coming over just so he could kiss you and that he patted you on the bum."

Ali's eyes flew open, and she glared at him. "Yeah, he suggested keeping each other warm, and I told him to go to hell. He cornered me against the counters and kissed me. I didn't want to make a scene in front of Jilly, so it took a few seconds until I could get him to back off. He got a little handsy before I could move away."

"I'm so sorry. Sorry about what I said and what I thought and for not trusting you when I know you never would have done anything like this. It's stupid, and I'm stupid."

She crossed her arms over her chest and stared at her lap. Would he ever be able to get back to where she cared for him again? He'd felt it when they'd been together. Doubtful she would have allowed him the intimacies they'd had if she didn't.

Blinking away the moisture that pooled in his eyes, he cautiously stroked her arm. "I'm sorry, Ali. I can't say that enough. But it helped me to see one thing…I love you."

Her gaze flew up at his words and her mouth quivered. "You do? That's why you ghosted me for two long weeks?"

"I knew my feelings for you were strong, and for the first time since Wendy left, I'd been thinking of adding someone permanent in my life. It scared me. With what your ex said, that fear doubled and tripled until I was choking on it. But I should have trusted my feelings for you. You're a remarkable woman, Ali, and I love every little thing about you. I had hoped you might return even a small amount of those feelings."

Her eyebrows tilted toward each other. "I do return the feelings, Greg. And I thought I'd felt yours as well. But your actions lately confused me."

His hopes rose. "But you return my feelings which means…?'

She rolled her eyes and grinned. "I love you, you idiot. Because most of the time you're also a remarkable person."

"I can live with that for now." He caressed her cheek and kissed her. When he pressed further, she eased back, her hands on his shoulders. Not exactly pushing him away but not drawing him closer.

"I still have too much gunk in my lungs. We'll need to take it slow."

"As long as you need, sweetheart."

She stared at the window for a minute, then looked him in the eye. "For your information, I need a man who'll stick by me. Me and Jilly. Forever. I don't want my daughter in a position to get hurt by someone again. And I don't mean physically. I don't want her coming to love someone and count on them, then have them leave again. Do you understand?"

"I do. Ryan and I had a discussion about anyone who takes me has to take him. Completely. We're a matched set. You and Jillian are the same. It's all or nothing."

Ali rested against the pillow and nodded. But he could tell she still had doubts.

"I love you, Alandra Cabrera. I know I have some work to do to win back your trust. I promise you I will. Even if it takes me forever."

CHAPTER THIRTY

*T*he bell above the door of Sweet Dreams jingled as Ali walked through. Greg held it for her and the kids. Ryan and Jillian had their noses pressed against the glass case before the door even closed.

"Guess this trip wasn't such a bad idea. Any idea what you want?"

"Anything your mother makes is incredible."

Greg waved his hand toward the goodies, then pointed to the other half of the bakery which was set up like an old-fashioned country store with penny candy and local products. "Order me a cinnamon roll. I'll be over there. Call me when they need payment."

As the kids picked out their cupcakes, Ali wanted to argue saying she could buy her own sweets. It wouldn't do any good. Over the last few weeks, everyone had been pampering her something fierce. She'd needed some fussing over with her house a total disaster and all of their possessions lost.

This town was amazing, though. People she'd never even met had popped by Greg's house with stuff they might need or dropped items off at the school for her and Jillian. Even some of her students had brought in toys they hadn't used in a while to donate to her daughter. Some of them had even used money from their piggy banks to buy them. She hadn't shed so many tears in forever.

Luckily, Jilly had taken her most snuggly blanket and her stuffed lion when she'd slept over her grandmother's. Ali wasn't sure anything could replace those. There hadn't been much salvageable. A few pots and pans, some dishes, and a picture or two. Her sister, with prompting from Max possibly, had dug through all her old digital files and created a photo album of pictures from when Jillian was born until her birthday a month ago. It had helped Ali feel like not everything had been taken from her.

This morning, there'd been a town-wide yard sale, and Ali had been invited to stop by and pick out anything she wanted for free. She'd tried to pay for some items, but it seemed all the sellers had agreed ahead of time. They argued it was all stuff they were trying to clean out of their houses, anyway. The biggest problem now was where to put it all.

She and Jillian had temporarily moved into Greg's house. They each had their own bedroom. Greg had done everything in his power to make them feel at home, even allowing her to continue piano lessons using the one he had in his living room. He'd even bought Jilly a new kitchen set filled with everything she needed, including a tea set.

Every day, sometimes a few times a day, he told her he loved her. Then, he'd ask if there was anything he could do for her or Jilly. He'd done so much already. Just giving them a home, even if it wasn't permanent, had lifted so many worries she'd had. She was still only minutes from work, compared to the thirty plus minutes if she'd stayed at her mom's. Not to mention, Jilly was loving being here with Cap'in and Ryan.

They'd taken turns cooking dinner, watched movies and

shows as a family, and each night he kissed her sweetly and left her by her bedroom door. Never once had he pushed or asked to join her. A few times after the kiss, she'd wanted to drag him into her room and continue what they'd started, but she never had. The doubts he'd had about her were still too fresh in her mind.

Having Jeff want to kill her had also played a huge part in her reluctance. She'd needed time to sift through all that had happened and all the stupid mistakes she'd made in her life. She didn't want Greg to be another one.

"Are we all ready?" Greg asked beside her, his hands full of little bags of penny candy.

"Oh, sorry, I wasn't paying attention." She smiled at Kelsey, the owner of Sweet Dreams and pointed to the case. "We'll have two cinnamon rolls to eat here."

Kelsey nodded and scooped out their desserts and placed them on plates. The kids already had their cupcakes half eaten. Greg paid for their sweets in addition to the candy, then followed her to one of the small tables near the window.

"Mama, when I get my costume?"

It was the weekend before Halloween, and Ali hadn't had much free time to do anything. Report cards came out soon as well as parent conferences, and she'd been trying to just get by one day at a time.

"I'm sorry, sweetie, I haven't—"

"I hope you don't mind, but my Aunt Molly offered to make one for her. She was making Ryan's anyway, and since these two are going as ally superheroes, I figured they should match. Is that okay?"

"Are you sure it's not too much for her? Darcy told me she's also making costumes for Hope and Tanner, as well as Erik's three kids."

"Darcy's about to pop with that kid, so Aunt Molly offered. She lives for this kind of stuff, and it gets her mind off the fact Luke is overseas. She said she can probably make Jilly's costume with the leftover fabric from Ryan's."

"That's nice of her." Fact was all the Storms were incredible people. They'd done so much to make her and Jilly feel at home and welcome any time they got together.

"Phew. Glad you said yes, because she said the costumes would be ready tomorrow."

Ali twisted her lips and dug into her cinnamon roll. When they all finished and the kids had the frosting wiped off, they drifted along Main Street until they came to the town common. The trees showed off their new fall colors, orange, red, yellow, and many of the leaves littered the ground.

"Cap'in," Jillian piped up. "We jump in the leaves at home after we get back?"

Greg and Ryan had done quite a bit of raking lately, and Jillian had been having a ball jumping in the leaves. Guinness had loved it, too.

Greg gazed at the sky. The sun had started ducking below the tree line. "Maybe if we have time. There's something really important we need to do first."

He steered them all toward the gazebo and climbed the stairs. Indicating Ali sit, he then placed Jillian next to her on the bench.

"This the 'portant thing we gotta do?" Jilly gazed up at him like he was an actual superhero. She'd never looked at her father that way. Now, she never would. They hadn't told her what had happened, and she didn't think she would for many years. The little girl rarely asked for him, anyway.

Greg knelt down in front of her daughter and took her hand. "Jillian, I wanted to let you know that I love you very much. I also love your mom very much. I want to spend every minute with both of you. I want us to all live together as a family."

Dios. Was he doing what she thought he was doing?

Jilly cocked her head. "We do live together, Cap'in."

"Yes, you both came to live with us because your house had a fire, but I was hoping I could convince your mom to marry me. That way we'd be a real family."

Jilly's lips puckered up. "Family. So that mean Ryan be my brother?"

Greg nodded, and Ryan mimicked his dad, his face anxious. Had the boy known what his father was planning?

"I want a brother. I can have Ryan. I like him."

Greg's shoulders lifted and lowered. "Thank you. Now, the hard part will be to convince your mom to take a chance on me. It has to be her decision, too."

Jilly leaned closer and whispered, "You needa ask her."

Greg pivoted on his knee and faced her. "Alandra, I hope you can forgive me for all the ridiculous things I thought and did. I've always admired who you are and how you're so well thought of in this community. When I got the opportunity to know you better, I had no choice but to fall in love with you. Your sweet nature, your patience with your students and daughter. How strong you are when dealing with any kind of adversity, especially these last two weeks. All the times the four of us have been together have been so comfortable and perfect. Topped only by the times we've been alone." The last words were a hushed breath.

He winked at her, and her heart fluttered. Then, he reached into the pocket of his jacket and pulled out a small box. "I love you, Alandra Cabrera, and I love your daughter as if she were my own. Would you please help us become a family, all four of us, together? Will you marry me?" He opened the box where a beautiful diamond ring sat on a velvet bed.

Tears welled up in her eyes, and she pressed her lips together to keep them from falling. Taking a deep breath, she faced Ryan, who'd been standing aside, his eyes wide.

"I guess if your dad asked Jillian for permission, I should probably make sure it's okay with you first. Ryan, would you allow me to marry your dad and be part of your family?"

Ryan stepped closer and his bottom lip trembled. "Can I call you Mom?" His voice broke and tears slid down his cheeks. "I've never called anyone Mom before."

Ali drew him onto the bench next to her and encircled him in her arms. Her own tears fell as rapidly as his. "Of course, you may. I would be so honored to be your mom."

Ryan gazed up at her, a smile lighting up his face. "And you'd be my real mom because we'd be married, right?"

"I would be. So I take it you're okay with me marrying your dad?"

Ryan nodded as he hugged her tight. "I wanted you to be my new mom since before I was in your class. That's why I asked Dad to put me in there."

Ali's gaze swiveled to Greg. "Did you pull strings?"

Grinning, Greg shrugged. "I might have dropped a word or two. I didn't realize it would send me to my knees by falling in love with the most incredible woman."

Greg scooped Jillian into his lap and slid next to her but glanced at Ryan. "I'm sorry it took me so long to find you a new mom, pal, but you deserve the best. I was waiting for the perfect one."

Ryan grabbed his hand. "You found her, Dad."

"I think *you* found her, pal. And led me to her. Thank you."

Ali rested against the man she loved, holding his son, loving him like her own. Next to her, Greg embraced her daughter and pressed a kiss to her head.

Ali could stay like this forever. All four of them happy and together. But the kids only had so much patience. Jilly wiggled.

"Can me and Ryan go run through the leaves?"

Ryan held her tight, but Greg lifted his chin at his son. "Why don't you give me and your new mom a few minutes alone?"

The kids flew down the stairs and Jilly yelled, "We gonna get married!"

Some of the people in the common laughed and looked their way, but Ali didn't care. The man she loved wanted to be with her, forever.

Greg held up the ring box and tipped his head. "You never said yes. I need the official word."

At times like this, when Greg gazed at her with all his love shining brightly, she wondered if she was dreaming. Being happily married with a family had been a lost dream once Jeff had walked out on them. But now she'd found it again, and she wanted to hold on tight to it and never let go. She had to trust that Greg would always be there for her and Jilly.

"Yes. I would love to marry you. I love you, Greg, and can't think of anything I'd rather do."

After placing the ring on her finger, he framed her face with his hands and kissed her. This kiss held all the emotions and longing he held for her. She could feel it.

"Since this isn't your first or my first wedding, can we forgo the big event and have a simple little ceremony? Or did you want to go all out again?"

"A simple ceremony sounds perfect with just our families. Of course, your family alone pushes it past the small category into the mid-sized one. But they've all been so fabulous, I can't imagine not having them all there."

Greg kissed her again, then eased back while keeping their foreheads touching. "Since it won't be a big event, can we do this soon? Like really soon? I hate having you in the room across the hall and not in my bed."

"Soon sounds perfect. And since these kids are incredible

sleepers, maybe we can find a way for a nocturnal visit a few times before the wedding."

The grin that broke out across Greg's face was the biggest she'd ever seen.

EPILOGUE

"*Y*ou may now kiss the bride."

Greg had been waiting for those words for what seemed like forever. Cupping Ali's beautiful face, he pressed his lips to hers. He wanted to do more, but it would have to wait.

"Are we married now?" Jillian cried out, breaking the kiss. Their families chuckled and Greg scooped her up.

"Yes, all married."

Jilly snuggled into his arms and whispered, "Do I call you Daddy now?"

His heart beat rapidly, the output of love for this child growing stronger every day.

"You can if you want to."

Jilly glanced down at Ryan clinging to Ali's side and nodded. "If Ryan have a new Mama, then I get a new Daddy. Okay?"

Perfect logic for a four-year-old. And if Nathaniel worked his magic, it would be coming true soon. With Jeff's crimes, it had been enough for Ali to push for her ex to give up his parental rights. He hadn't argued and signed the papers

346

immediately. Now, they just had to wait for the paperwork to go through for the adoptions. Ali adopting Ryan and him adopting Jillian. In a few months, they'd legally be a family. They already felt that way.

Looking around the room they'd booked at The Inn at the Falls for their wedding and reception, Greg couldn't think of a better Christmas present. It was still two days until the holiday, but they'd wanted to spend it together. As husband and wife. Tonight, they'd stay upstairs in one of the Inn's rooms while Ryan's new grandmother spoiled him and his new sister. The bedroom Ali had been using would once again become a guest room.

Greg held out his arm and escorted Ali down the aisle between the rows of chairs. Ryan held her hand on her other side while Jillian rode in his arms still. The photographer snapped pictures as they headed into the banquet room.

The night was a whirlwind for a while, then finally he found his wife in his arms on the dance floor.

"Can we pretend everyone else isn't here for a few minutes, Mrs. Storm?"

Ali kissed him sweetly and laughed. "Soon, Captain Storm. Soon."

"Have I told you how beautiful you look today, sweetheart?"

Ali glowed with acceptance and love. "You may have mentioned it when I met you at the end of the aisle, but it never hurts to repeat yourself. Just so your message is heard."

"You look absolutely exquisite today. The dress, the hair, all those little details I'm sure not to notice, but you can pretend I did."

He did notice many details. The dress was simple, off white and skimmed her delectable curves, making his mouth water thinking about what they could do tonight. Her hair was pulled back on the side, then left to caress her shoulders in waves. Already, he was imagining himself nuzzling into the gorgeous silky mane.

"Did I tell you how much I loved you today?"

Ali glanced sideways and grinned. "Pretty sure it was in the wedding vows."

"I do love you, Ali, and I want to make sure to let you know every single day. If I forget, make sure to remind me."

"I'll say how much I love you every day, and you can say it back."

He kissed her quickly as the music came to an end. "I hope I can do better than that."

"So far so good."

They meandered through the tables greeting all their guests. Joey had become quite adept at walking and was giving Tessa and Erik a literal run for their money. Matty and Kiki took turns rounding him up, but often they needed to be rounded up, too.

Sara, with TJ's arm around her, looked on at her niece and nephews, smiling secretly while holding her hand over her belly. She hadn't begun to show yet, but they'd announced last week they were expecting in June.

Nathaniel beamed as he held his two-month-old daughter, Faith, while Darcy boogied on the dance floor with Hope and Tanner. Kevin and Amy shimmied next to them.

His own sisters were taking turns making sure Ryan and Jillian were fine. They had told him he and Ali shouldn't have to worry about the kids during their wedding. Yeah, Leah and Sofie were great. He was so lucky to have them nearby.

Alex and Gina stood near the aunts and uncles, chatting. Uncle Pete had recovered nicely, though was nagged at quite often if he stayed too long at work.

Ali's family intermingled with his, making small talk and getting to know each other. Val, Leah, and Sofie had been wonderful in helping Ali plan a wedding on such short notice, though Val never missed an opportunity to mention it. Or sidle up to TJ hoping to be invited when his famous parents stopped in.

Tito Sebastien sat next to Gram and Gramps talking animatedly about something from the past. Their weekly trips to visit him always brought about new and interesting information from the past, and Greg loved hearing it.

The only one missing was Luke. They'd had word last week he was fine, and he'd sent Greg an email wishing him well. Unfortunately, he hadn't been able to make it back for the wedding. Hopefully, it wouldn't be too much longer before he could return.

Ali cozied up next to him and slid her arm around his waist. "What are you thinking about, dear husband? You had an interesting expression on your face."

"Thinking about how much I love my wife."

Ali laughed. "Right. That's it?"

"I was looking at everyone here, knowing how fortunate we are to have this family, especially the kids. Jilly is so special, and the way Ryan interacts with her touches my heart. But I was also thinking that between yours and mine, maybe sometime soon we can start working on ours."

A slow smile spread across his wife's face as she twined her arms around his neck. "I think you read my mind."

TAKE a sneak peek at book 6 in the Storms of New England series -*Faded Dreams*

FADED DREAMS

STORMS OF NEW ENGLAND, BOOK 6

CHAPTER ONE

"*A*bsolutely gorgeous."

The deep voice shattered the peace and quiet Murielle Russell had come to the lakeside for. When she turned, her heart picked up and her stomach dropped. Lukas Storm. What in the world was he doing down here? The party was up at the resort, not here by the lake where she'd come to escape the noisy revelers.

"It is pretty," she responded, gazing at the multi-colored sky over Lake Winnipesaukee in the White Mountains of New Hampshire.

"Wasn't talking about the sunset." His smirk highlighted the double dimples in his cheeks, the ones every girl swooned over. If girls actually swooned anymore. More likely, they simply draped themselves over him in invitation. Something he rarely turned down. They'd known each other for ten years, since they'd been lab partners in Biology. She hadn't seen much of him lately except for a quick chat at the Fourth of July fireworks in town this past summer, but she still heard gossip about his wild ways. Some things never changed.

"The view of the lake is great, too," she added. No way he was talking about her. The geeky little girl who'd bested him at every test. Though, in her bridesmaid dress with hair and makeup professionally done, maybe she wasn't ugly either. But he'd never seen her in that way.

Moving closer, he reached out and flipped her hair over her shoulder. "Don't underestimate yourself, Ellie. You're looking fine. Prettiest bridesmaid at the wedding."

"But not prettier than the bride. No one can outshine the bride on her wedding day." Not to mention her cousin, Nicole, had always been the one every guy had chased after. With her long blonde hair and bright blue eyes, they'd all swarmed over her while they'd been teenagers. Elle's hair could never decide if it was red or brown, though her eyes most definitely stayed in the dark brown category. Like mud.

"What are you doing down here? Don't you have bridesmaid duties and stuff?"

Glancing back up the hill to the fancy resort Nicole and her groom, Brad, had gotten married at, she shook her head. "No, all I had to do was show up and march down the aisle. My Aunt Sharon and cousin, Jenny, took care of everything else. That's what the Maid of Honor does. Bridesmaids are expendable." Pretty sure she was only asked to balance the wedding party numbers.

"Saw you dancing with one of the groomsmen. Is he your date for the night?"

"No, he was assigned to be my partner. I think he was on the prowl for something a little higher class than me."

Luke scowled. "Again with the put-downs. You look incredible. The guy's an idiot."

Shrugging, she said, "He knows I won't put out simply because we got partnered together."

"Because you have class." Luke's eyes narrowed and

skimmed the horizon, his mouth in a tight line. What was that serious look for?

"So, what are *you* doing down here? You're big into the parties. Got a lady friend meeting you here soon? There's a nice little cabana right there. Perfect for a secret tryst. I can get lost so you can have some privacy."

As she turned to go, he took her elbow and drew her closer. Man, he smelled good. Not a strong cologne scent but something woodsy and all Luke. His soap, maybe.

"I came down to do some thinking and can't really do it with all the noise of the reception."

"Won't your friends miss you?" Elle searched the hill up to the party, expecting to see a gang of Luke's friends converging on their location to find him.

"Brad's got enough to keep him occupied with Nicole dragging him around the tables to chat with the guests. The other guys have all scoped out booze and babes."

"Not you? Isn't that your typical MO?"

His eyes darkened, almost like she'd hurt his feelings. Since when did Lukas Storm, Casanova himself, ever care what people thought of his carousing?

"I've got a lot of other things on my mind right now. Brought a bottle down here to keep me company. Want some?" He pointed to the bottle of champagne sitting on the floor of the cabana.

"You said you wanted to be alone."

"Not alone. Just not in the partying mood. I'd love some company."

This was a different side to Luke than most people saw. She'd seen it a few times when he had something serious going on. A difficult test coming up or applications to colleges. Most people only saw the party guy who somehow managed to get straight As in all the advanced level classes. Or the talented jock who played three sports and excelled at all of them. Or the hot stud every girl wanted to be seen with. She'd been fortunate to see more.

"Sure. These shoes are killing me. I need to take them off or I might not be able to walk ever again."

Luke flinched at her words. What had she said? Then, he scooped her in his arms and carried her to sit on the large swinging bench in the half-enclosed building. Holy smokes, Luke Storm sweeping her off her feet. Literally. The cushions were soft and thick under her, and the swing started moving as soon as Luke sat next to her.

"Let's see about fixing these toes." He picked her feet up and swung them around until they lay on his lap, and she leaned against the padded side of the seat. What the heck? Wiggling, she tried to remove them, but he held on tight.

"Luke, what are you doing?"

"You said they were killing you. I can't have that."

Rolling her eyes, she said, "The shoes are too high and hurt my feet. They aren't actually going to cause me any permanent harm."

After slipping her shoes off, he massaged the instep on one foot, then moved to the other. Bliss. Nicole had insisted on the same shoes for all the bridesmaids since the dresses stopped at the knee. Surprisingly, she hadn't broken a leg trying to walk in them.

"That feels incredible. Thanks."

He picked up the bottle, pulled off the top, and took a healthy swig. After handing the bottle to her, he went back to massaging her feet. The cool liquid slid down her throat, warming her insides.

Luke's hands moved to her ankles, and Elle held her breath as they continued up to her calf. She stiffened, and he glanced up at her, but his hands didn't stop their movement.

"Making sure you don't cramp up."

The smile he gave her caused her heart to do cartwheels

and back flips. Those dimples were dangerous. She had them, too, but they never seemed to get the same reaction from guys. Maybe men were immune to their charms.

"It's pretty here. Peaceful. Gotta soak up as much as I can." His eyes had a faraway look as he gazed into the distance. Was he worried about something?

"Everything okay, Luke?"

Shaking her off, he smiled, those dimples blasting her way. "Yeah. So we didn't really get a chance to chat very long at the Fourth of July fireworks. What are you doing now? I know you went to college for engineering, like me." His hands squeezed her feet. He'd always said she had a great mind and would be an amazing engineer. She'd taken his words to heart.

"I work for Spectrum Engineering over at the Pease Industrial Park."

His eyes widened. "I work in Portsmouth, too. My firm has a lot of government contracts and does business with yours often. Have you been there long?"

"A few years," she answered. She'd seen him a time or two in her building. Of course, she'd never had the balls to approach him when he'd been there. "They've been paying for my Master's Degree. Two more classes this fall, and I'm done."

"Nice to get someone to pay for it. I finished mine last year courtesy of Uncle Sam."

"Do you still do weekends in the Guard?" He'd been in ROTC in high school, and she shivered remembering how incredible he looked in his uniform.

"Air National Guard, yeah."

Worry lines creased his forehead as his blue eyes grew unfocused. The dimming sky cast him in shadows. God, he was so good looking. His light blondish-brown hair was cut short but stylish. His strong jaw was covered in stubble, making her wonder what it would feel like against her skin. And those lean muscles that he'd honed to perfection called out for her to test drive. If only.

He'd removed his tie and opened the top few buttons of his shirt, so she got a peek of his chest hair. What she wouldn't give to run her fingers through it. *Don't even think along those lines. More champagne.* She tipped the bottle up for another swig.

A frog hopped across the floor of the cabana and onto her shoe.

Luke chuckled. "Remember in Bio freshman year, when we had to dissect that frog, and you made me do the whole thing." His eyes gleamed, and she scowled.

"I was only eleven. Asking me to cut up a cute little animal was cruel."

"I still can't believe you did high school in three years and graduated at fourteen. Little genius."

It hadn't really been her choice to move a few grades ahead. But once her aunt and uncle, who she lived with, got wind of the fact her IQ was off the charts, and that the private school was offering a full scholarship for her, they'd jumped at the chance. She still wasn't sure if it was to help her succeed or to get her into a different high school from their two girls. Her aunt loved her, but having your sister's kid thrust on you when you'd only been married a few years and already had two children of your own, wasn't easy.

"You weren't too shabby either, getting a full boat to Brookside Academy."

"Yeah, I was lucky." There were his dimples again.

"Not too lucky. You ended up with me as a lab partner in Bio, Chem, and Physics. I still don't know how that happened. In Bio, our names were next to each other in the alphabet, but not in the other two."

"Let me tell you a secret," Luke whispered, leaning in

closer, making her breath freeze. "I sweet-talked the teachers into assigning us together."

He had? "Why?"

"Because you were the best lab partner ever. You're the smartest person I know, and you didn't get all gooey-eyed when we worked together. I know I've got a reputation, even back then, but when I was in class, I was serious about my studies."

"I liked that about you." She'd liked a lot about him, but he'd never seen her as anything other than his super genius lab partner. The four-year age difference might have had something to do with it.

"And I liked that you spent so much time studying with me. Honestly, Ellie, you got me through a few of those classes."

"What are you talking about? You were certainly intelligent enough to handle them on your own."

"True, but I got distracted quite easily back then with… other more social endeavors."

Elle rolled her eyes. "Girls. You do have a weakness there. Yet you took me to the prom. Because you felt bad for me."

His hands stilled on her feet, and he took a swig from the bottle. "Actually, it was you who felt bad for me, and I'm glad. I was supposed to go with Taylor Markham, but she ditched me a week before to go with Graham Meisner. Guess captain of the football team beats track star any day."

"Taylor Markham's a bitch." At the mischief in Luke's eyes, she slapped her hand over her mouth. "Did I say that out loud?"

Luke nodded.

She glanced around nervously. Had she consumed too much champagne already? Alcohol wasn't something she drank on a regular basis. She should slow down.

"Don't worry. She's still up at the party trying to get her

hooks into Brad's older brother. She grew up next door to them. He's a doctor. He trumps even an engineer."

"What about a military man? Some women go crazy for a man in uniform. Is Taylor into that?"

Luke's eyes darkened, and he stared off past the lake again. "Doesn't matter if she is or isn't. I'm not into her."

"Not anymore."

Shaking his head, he said, "Not anymore. She might have been my first introduction into—" his eyebrows waggled up and down "—let's say certain grown-up activities. I'd like to think I've matured since then."

That wasn't exactly what she'd heard. Elle might have lived in Portsmouth for the past two years, but it was still next to Squamscott Falls. Her cousins, Nicole and Jenny, liked to keep her informed of all the small-town gossip. According to them, Luke still had his wandering ways. Never too long with any one woman.

"I'm not looking for anything right now." Luke's mouth pulled tight as he peered at his hands. "I won't be around for a while."

The way he said it got her pulse racing, and not in a good way. "Where are you going?"

He lifted his chin and glanced at her, then stared at the lake again. "My unit's getting deployed in a week."

MAKE sure to check out Luke and Ellie's story in Faded Dreams.

https://www.karilemor.com/faded-dreams

ABOUT THE AUTHOR

Find all Kari's books here:
   https://www.karilemor.com/books

Kari's mailing list - News and special deals, sometimes freebies!
   https://www.karilemor.com/

Join her Reader's Group -The Lit Lounge - for fun and first-hand friendship:
   https://www.facebook.com/groups/373521153021256/

Here's where you can connect with her on social media

- facebook.com/Karilemorauthor
- twitter.com/karilemor
- instagram.com/karilemorauthor
- pinterest.com/karilemor
- bookbub.com/authors/kari-lemor
- amazon.com/Kari-Lemor/e/B00ON2YDI6

Made in the USA
Middletown, DE
10 June 2022